HEARTS *at* DAWN

by

ALYSA SALZBERG

PROLOGUE: A MAGIC LANTERN SHOW

I *make myself watch it every night. His hands are suddenly covered by a shadow. Then, painfully, they begin to elongate. Claws emerge from their ends. He holds back cries of pain as the rest of him twists and changes. His body stretches, then falls back into place, another body, something monstrous and unnatural: hooves at his feet, dark fur everywhere, a muzzle overgrown with teeth.*

I watch it every night because this is what I have done.

I light a candle and place it inside what looks like an ordinary lantern. But its sides, you'll notice, are made of metal, keeping the light within.

This is a magic lantern, an old device that once brought wonder to mortals like yourself. It projected images from glass slides, making blank walls light up with stories. The effect is far from astonishing these days, but this human attempt to make magic has always moved me, and something about the simple drawings it projects brings me comfort.

Maybe if I show you the horrible thing I've done this way, you won't think so badly of me.

So, let's sit down together in the darkness for a while, just long enough for me to explain how a man became a monster, how he tried to change, and how he ended up crossing an ocean.

Then, we'll stop the show and follow him.

~~

In a nearly unnoticeable slot between the lantern and the neck of the lens, I place a glass slide divided into painted panels. The first image appears on the facing wall, many times larger than it really is.

We see a crowded ballroom. We are in Paris in the mid-1840's, the handwriting at the top of the slide tells us. The light of countless candles is reflected in mirrors. Gowns of all colors shine like jewels.

Two figures glow especially bright. The first is a tall, dark-haired man, the definition of "dashing." He cuts through the crowd like a ship's prow through churning water. The second is a stunning young woman, her raven-black hair arranged in the latest style, her gown elegant beyond measure and made of a fabric that seems otherworldly (it is). She is the definition of beauty. Of course they'll meet and fall in love.

But there, in the corner near the beautiful woman is a rather plain figure – can you make her out? Her hair is messy curls, her dress, while perfectly suited to the occasion, isn't the sort that would catch anyone's eye.

The most surprising thing, I realize now, is that she thinks this won't matter, that the dashing man, whose name is Charles Rush, will talk to her and laugh with her and be impressed by the flame of wit and goodness within her. But of course he chooses the beautiful girl to be fascinated by instead.

I gently move the glass panel to one side, so that the image changes. Now we see Charles Rush returning to New York City, back to his fine brownstone on the Fifth Avenue. The city is still young, but already full of energy and noise, never completely stopping. Carriages and carts force themselves along the street outside, their drivers yelling to one another or to any unlucky soul who thinks to pass in front of them. The ravishing woman from the ball is in Charles's drawing room, a faint, ghostly form. She followed him across the ocean, without needing a ship.

She's at once my friend and my rival. We'll call her Yselda. As you might have guessed, Yselda isn't exactly like you. Some would call her a fairy, others, a witch. Still others likely have other, better names.

Charles Rush is so taken with Yselda that they marry. On the same slide, just beyond the altar and further on in time is another scene: the couple is holding a baby.

You can see the plain girl with hair like a disaster at their wedding, in a dark corner again. She stares at the floor, where all her hopes have been dashed.

The girl with dashed hopes and a broken heart is me. Like Yselda, I'm what you might call a fairy or a witch, or some more accurate sort of non-mortal. In the next slide, my skin has dulled and taken on a bluish tinge. You can't see it, but the eager flame that was inside me has become a cool, angry fire. Here I am in a library in a place out of your world, searching through heavy books, some disintegrating from mold and decay.

I'm searching for something and the next slide shows the moment I find it: a simple curse, a surprise that I came upon, really – something scrawled in spidery writing in a margin, written down so long ago that the once-dark ink has become the light, unremarkable brown of my ringlets. The curse will be easy enough to cast, and so, I feel certain, it will be easy enough to break if it ever comes to that.

Now, I must change the glass panel and show you the next, terrible image, the first one I apologize for.

My hand is trembling, as though the slide could cut me.

But in the image that appears on the wall, I'm full of rage and confidence as I cast the curse. Not on Charles Rush. Not on Yselda. But on their baby, a boy called Orin.

If you want to know what I am, you could say I'm a monster.

That's what I made Orin – or what he would become. Starting in his twelfth year, every night he would transform into a horrible creature.

I was so angry, so heartbroken, it had driven me mad.

Even in the haze of my anger, I did try to be merciful. This was only something that would happen at night, I reasoned to myself; he could live perfectly normally when it was light.

The curse was my terrible message to Yselda. Had she known I loved Charles Rush? I don't think she ever stopped to wonder. She was more beautiful and powerful than me in every way. I hung about her like a baby sister, not an equal. In fact, if I cast the curse in the first place, it

3

was because she'd put a strong barrier of magic around her and the baby. None of our kind could come near them or even send them a parcel or letter. Perhaps if I could have done one of those things, perhaps if she'd made it easier – it wouldn't have come to this.

The next slide shows unkind times. Charles looks away, distracted, while Yselda and the baby reach for him.

He no longer loves her, and I no longer love him. I never really did, I know now; I just wanted him.

I become reasonable again. Now you can see me in a little, shadowy portion of the image, surrounded by musty tomes, searching desperately for a way to undo what I've done.

But I find nothing.

In the next slide, Yselda is gone. I can't tell you why. It wasn't mere flightiness. I've often wondered if there was a far more fearsome enemy that she wanted to keep far from her child. Or perhaps heartbreak had made her go mad, too.

Charles' face bears a distraught expression, and it is sincere. This will always surprise me. A cluster of policemen and detectives are lined up to hear his orders. In each corner of this new slide they're searching streets and cities, combing through letters and possessions she left behind. But no one will find her.

In the following slide, Orin is no longer a baby, but a toddling child. He stands beside his father at another wedding. The groom is Charles Rush again, now considered a widower, and the bride comes from an old, moneyed New York family. This is exactly the sort of wedding he should have had in the first place.

In the next image, Orin is a little older, and now there's a new baby – his half-brother Joseph.

We'll see them grow in the next series of slides, playing games, then jokes. Joseph is full of charm and has a quick, witty answer for everything. Orin is quieter, but laughs often. He's pale like his father, with Charles's dark hair and prominent nose. There's no sign of Yselda in him, except perhaps his eyes – green mixed with a sprinkling of gold.

He doesn't seem drawn to real magic, but he does become interested in sleight of hand. Here, he shows a card trick to his brother, who looks on a bit enviously; Joseph always wants to be the center of attention.

Now, now it's time to see what I've done. Here is the transformation. Orin's pale hands hold a splayed deck of playing cards. Suddenly, his palms are cast in shadow.

….I'm sorry. I'm sorry. The candle has gone out. I'll force myself to light the flame again….

Now his hands are covered in short, dark fur. His palms are like the pads of a dog's paws. His unnaturally long, fur-covered fingers end in sharp, curving talons.

I must show you what he sees when he looks up from his hands and into the mirror. The monster is his size, and covered in short, dark fur. Its feet are hooves. Its mouth is a muzzle, with white teeth protruding from it like thorns, nearly interlocking.

Orin has run into his father's office down the hall – away from the monster, he thinks, but he looks at his hands and realizes the truth.

You can't see his tears against the dark fur, and I don't deserve to show myself weeping.

The next slide shows Orin waking the following morning. He stares in wonder at his hands, which look as they always have. Joseph is sitting on his bed, joking about something. There's hope on Orin's poor face: maybe it was a nightmare.

Another slide – that night, he's a monster again.

The next slide is divided into two scenes: In daylight, Orin tells his father. Charles is skeptical at first, thinking it's one of his sons' pranks. It's not until Orin begins to sob (you can see the tears against his flesh, of course) that he realizes there might be something to it.

In the second scene, Charles has an arm around Orin, and offers him a handkerchief. There's writing at the top of the slide: "I have reason to believe that your mother bewitched me. I never thought anything was strange about our life together, until she left us. This, if it is real, may be some sort of enchantment."

In the following slide, Orin has opened his bedroom door and stands in his monstrous form, while his father looks on. More writing: "You must tell no one. It could bring trouble to our business and from decent people in society. We'll say you suffer from nightly headaches. And we will find a way to cure you."

A series of images shows Orin and his father visiting physicians and professors at first. Then, as they prove to be useless, mediums and mesmerists, magnetists and fortunetellers. Medical or metaphysical, all are paid handsomely for their services and their silence. Orin doesn't know it, but if Charles feels the slightest doubt, he sends rough men to remind them about the silence.

In a dreary building in the Five Points, they visit a woman said to be a witch. On Bleecker Street, another witch, from Haiti this time. In a dark room on Baxter Street, an old Chinese woman speaks to them through curls of smoke. These visits make Orin dream of the world beyond the city. But they don't cure him, and without a cure, where can he go?

A glass overlay makes the painted sparrows on the next slide flit back and forth. They come and go from birdhouses and the elaborate, miniature tiered pagodas and hotels on tall poles that have been built for them in Union Square Park. Orin sits on a bench, watching them, a book open on his lap. These are his summers. He won't venture to Newport with his family, or anywhere else beyond Manhattan. No matter what they tell him or how they reassure him, he worries what would happen if there were a delay or an accident and night fell when they were still on the road or the water, with people around to witness his transformation.

Another slide: Orin's bedroom has transformed into a library. His books bring him comfort when he has to leave school or the table or anywhere else as the sun begins to set. He sits on his bed, gazing off dreamily, a copy of Thoreau's *Walden* open beside him. Above him is a ghostly image of a deserted cabin where a little monstrous figure stands boldly outdoors, free, with no one around to see him.

On one side of the next slide, Joseph is curiously examining some white gloves that have been delivered to the house – not the first pair he's seen. They are larger than any man's hands, with long, tapering fingers. On the slide's other half, the brothers sit on Orin's bed, the gloves between them. Orin is telling him: "I never want you to see me when I'm like that."

"I think it's grand" are the first set of words above Joseph's head. And then, "Maybe one day you can perform at Barnum's Museum!"

The next slide is a small collection of images, touched with gold like fairy dust. We see some of the rooms and attractions of Barnum's American Museum, with the boys looking on at different ages. They've been regular visitors, even when Joseph was still wearing dresses. There's the Fiji Mermaid, General Tom Thumb standing proudly with his chest puffed up, the Siamese twins. Here are extraordinary animals, two white beluga whales floating in a tank like trapped clouds, tigers roaring in a cage behind them. There is the lecture room, three levels of balconies and elaborate decorations and trimmings. On the distant stage, some morality play is being performed. The boys sit in the back, planning and plotting how Orin could be a part of it all, while keeping his true nature – and his name – a secret. "I could wear a scarf around my mouth and nose, and then, after the change, remove it: the big reveal." For the first time in so many years, he's smiling broadly.

In the corner by the tigers' cage, you can see me, still desperately poring over books in a faraway place, still seeking a way to reverse what I've done.

And now, in the next slide, I've found it at last, in an old book reeking of mold and decay. There is the curse, printed this time. On the page facing it is its undoing: *Give your heart to another and have their heart. Love and be truly loved.*

It's so simple. I feel daft for not having thought of it. After all, love is a magic that exists in your world as well as mine.

Of course, it's not always easy to come by, I know. Still, at first it seemed to me that Orin had all the chances in the world. He was good-looking enough, with those arresting eyes. And kind and intelligent, with a sense of humor. Surely someone would fall in love with him with little trouble.

....Then again, in his privileged circle, betrothals and marriages were often simply ways to acquire prestige or a fortune. With his reputation as someone with an incurable malady to consider, Charles and perhaps Orin himself might think it best to choose strategy over love.

In the second part of the panel, you can see that my face has a panicked look to it. I must tell Orin – he mustn't choose practicality and tradition over real love.

Of course, Yselda's protections still stood. In the next slide, I'm trying to call out to Orin, but he hears nothing. The letters and telegrams I send go astray.

And so, I seek out a human mind. It's not a precise thing. The mind must be one open to my message. Here she is, in the slide that follows. She's just been let into the hallway of the Rush's home. She is, unfortunately, quite mad. Her hair sticks out wildly from her bonnet, her eyes are storm clouds, her clothing frayed, her cheeks ablaze.

Orin and his family have left the table and are standing in a stunned group in the dining room doorway. "You! Orin Rush!" we see the madwoman crying out. She points, singling him out. "A human heart is the cure!"

There is no omitted information between that slide and the next. Without anything further, she's left the house. Orin is running behind her. "Please!" he calls out, "Who gave you that message?"

8

"The ether," she replies to him over her shoulder.

"And is there anything more? Any explanation?"

"I thought it quite clear," she answers.

She's about to turn away again, and then – here's another slide I hate.

In desperation, I let the woman see me. I am standing behind Orin – you recognize me, my wild hair, my blue skin. My face is set in a terrible, stern glare. "Stop running," I say to her. "Explain it to him." This is the worst thing I could possibly have done. The madwoman stares at the horrible apparition, but to Orin, she is staring at him.

"Monster!" she screams. The word is so large on the slide, there in the middle of it, as if rending the image in two.

Oh, if only I could go back to that moment, if only I could have thought more clearly.

The madwoman has run away and disappeared into the stream of carriages and omnibuses, horses and whips, shouting coachmen and cab drivers.

There's no spell protecting *her* from me. I could make her stop in place. But it's no use.

Orin is standing beside the street's chaos, still with shock. He can't forget the terror on the madwoman's face.

There are many ways her words could have been interpreted. And many people would have simply discredited them altogether. But Orin can't deny that she knew his name and knew about the enchantment.

His thoughts float above him in red letters: *If I want to break the enchantment, I'll have to take the heart of someone else.* So, he truly is a monster, capable of something unspeakable.

He promises to keep himself carefully removed from everyone, to never risk hungering for a heart.

Instead of telling him how to break the enchantment, I've unwittingly let him create another curse.

I would like the next slide to be sparse and spare, to show how much I stole from Orin yet again. He hadn't worked up the courage to request to perform at Barnum's Museum, and now he won't risk it – what if he lost control of himself and put the spectators in danger? He can't bear to tell Joseph, and hopes that by not mentioning it and not suggesting they visit the place, he'll make his brother understand.

Orin loses out on the love I'd expected him to find, as well. Every time he feels the slightest interest in a young lady, he forces her quickly out of mind, and makes sometimes extraordinary efforts not to cross her path again. Luncheons are canceled, abrupt departures are common, many plays he'd looked forward to seeing see only his absence. After all, what if it turns out to be *that heart* that makes him give in to his beastly nature? It's so much easier to imagine things, anyway, so much safer to think of the plots of books – or better yet, to ignore romance and love entirely. That way, he'll never want them.

I will include a slide here that shows Orin deliberately turned away from another type of young lady, a type that fawns over him despite their not having exchanged a word. *They* are easier to ignore. Orin is no fool; they're interested in his money and family name.

An image, now, of Orin's bedroom door. The sun is about to set. A servant has locked the door from the outside. Others are pushing a steamer trunk filled with old pieces of metal in front of it, and a chest filled with old metal locks in front of that. All of this is at Orin's insistence. He's told the servants that he's started sleepwalking and fears he'll leave his room one night and fall down the staircase.

Charles doesn't argue with him, but he doesn't believe it's necessary. Lean in and look closely at Charles and his second wife in the parlor. He's whispering to her, "I saw him as a creature. His eyes don't change."

Down the corridor, we can see Joseph seated at the empty dining table, schoolbooks open before him. He stares up at the ceiling, in the direction of Orin's room, and mutters, "What nonsense."

Now, another slide. Large, bold letters proclaim WAR! Men in gray and blue uniforms rush over opposing grassy hills. Joseph and Orin are staring up at them from below; the soldiers and battles are only what they can imagine, since they're too young by a few years to take part. (Then again, even if they were of age, their parents would pay someone else to fight in their place, as is customary among most of the wealthy families of New York.)

Orin feels the same aversion to war as he does to any sort of carnage, but there are moments when he wonders what might happen if he could go to those battlefields, wait till nightfall, and attack just the right people. Could he make it stop? *No*, he always finishes by thinking. Even if it were possible for him to slay so many men singlehandedly, how could he bring himself to do so in the first place? How could you look into the eyes of another man and end his life?

Here's violence, now, in the next slide. The Draft Riots. The family hides behind closed shutters, listening, waiting. Outside their door, we follow the streets and find, not far away, mobs of men wreaking havoc, burning, lynching, roaring.

In the next slide, the War has ended, but there's more destruction still. Barnum's Museum is burning down. Wild animals leap through windows and are shot by firemen. Someone rescues the four-hundred-pound lady. Inside, the beluga whales' tanks are covered by a veil of smoke that hides their charred remains. Poor creatures. We don't see Joseph and Orin there, or poring over accounts of the fire, or visiting the Museum after its reopening. They can't bear to. Something in their hearts is left in ruins, as well.

In the next slide, Orin is a young man. He's fairly tall, with carefully combed dark hair. His green-gold eyes shine out from his pale face, though he wishes they wouldn't. He's quite handsome, and kinder in every way than his father. He's the age for university, but he won't let himself go and run new risks.

Here he is, instead, with Charles in his study, looking over land deeds, maps, and slightly blurred photographic prints of fields and forests. He's learning the family business, although they both know that he'll

11

never be able to conduct affairs the proper way; so much happens over cigars and brandy in the evenings.

On the same slide, we see another image of Orin. He's in his room with his books, and there are strange symbols all around him. No one has been able to cure him, so he'll try himself. He reads everything he can about magic and the occult – everything that's not a fairy tale, anyway. If only he *had* paid attention to some those, maybe he would have realized the simple solution.

Now and then, he comes upon the recipe for a potion that's said to break enchantments. If the ingredients aren't impossible, otherworldly things, he gathers them and secretly mixes it in his bedroom. See him here, lying pale beside a puddle of sick. None of the potions work. He never tells anyone.

Now we see Joseph, older as well. He looks a bit like his brother, but shorter and more wiry, with brown hair and eyes, and a perfectly clipped and waxed mustache. His manner is the most striking difference between him and Orin. He stands boldly facing the world, dressed in an impeccably fitted frock coat, with a peacock-blue cravat around his neck. His hands, encased in fashionable yellow kid gloves, set his top hat jauntily on his head.

In the next slide, he's in a gentleman's personal library, handing him a pile of books, and the gentleman is handing him a pile in exchange. Joseph has been gladly traveling up and down the East Coast, finding more books on magic for his brother, often making exchanges with others. We see in a small cloud that his thoughts, meanwhile, are on a table at a fine restaurant. A pretty girl sits on one side of him, whispering something in his ear; a handsome youth holds his hand and whispers in the other. There are oysters and champagne on the table, and Joseph's grin is nearly too big for his face.

In the next slide, Orin sits among his books with an expression that's quite the opposite. He reflects gravely on two facts that keep returning to him again and again. They're written on a sheet of paper in front of him:

1. *My mother once lived in Paris.* (Perhaps he might find her, or some trace of her, there, and that might lead to answers about what's happened to him, and how to fix it.)

2. *France has an inordinate number of reports of werewolves and attacks in its history.* (Strictly speaking, he isn't a werewolf, but there are similarities.)

Those two points led to a logical, but impossible, conclusion. After all, he won't even travel to Long Island.

I'll shift quickly through the other plates and slides: books, books, Joseph's adventures. Here's an attempt by the brothers to see if a medical student's dissection table might help. Orin somberly holds the cadaver's heart in his hands.

Not only is the spell not broken; holding that heart only makes Orin feel more lost. It's not the neat, orderly thing he naively expected from drawings and diagrams. He can only see the chambers when the student pushes aside tissue and sinew to reveal them.

In the following slide, Orin is back at home and in the bath. Sharply lettered words hover over him: *Is there a heart within my chest, or only a cavernous, empty chamber?*

More slides, more books, more life, New York summers and sparrows, laughing with Joseph, afternoon plays and staid society luncheons.

And now, the final image. It's edged in gold and glints against the candle flame's flickering. Orin has lived this way for so long, has searched for a cure or an answer without any kind of hope. At last, he's tired of it. He's twenty-four years old now, a monster for half his life. He thinks of how little he's seen and done, no matter how much he's read. He can't stay here, stagnating.

It isn't a simple decision. There are so many risks involved. But we see crumpled notes and confident lines in ledgers all around him.

In gilded letters arched triumphantly above him, we read "I'll go to Paris."

PART I
BLOSSOMS

I

At the Gare Saint-Lazare, the world seems to vanish and reappear between drifts of steam from the locomotives. Orin has arrived in the City of Light.

Behind him is an ocean crossing that would have been considered rather dull and uneventful by most. A great deal of time was spent in formal luncheons and obligatory polite conversations with fellow "invalids" coming to the Continent for their cure. But for Orin, fear had shadowed every moment. What if the ship started to sink and he was stuck in a lifeboat with the other passengers at nightfall?

Staring out at the boundless ocean was the single thing he would miss. He hadn't expected it to be like gazing into the flames of a hearth, full of calm and inspiration.

Behind him is also the two-hour's train ride from Le Havre, the first time he'd been on a train since my enchantment had begun. If he closed his eyes and concentrated only on the click-clack running up from the wheels to the floor and into his bones, he could imagine himself a child again, which was a handy technique whenever he thought too much about what might happen if they were derailed or delayed.

And yet, he had made it to Paris, and there was still light in the sky.

Beside him now is Joseph, which seems perfectly reasonable to me, though it wasn't part of Orin's original plan.

The day he told Charles about Paris, he'd left his father's office with a feeling of fear and satisfaction. He hadn't had time to dwell on that, though; Joseph had hurried over and pulled him down the corridor, into a niche where they vied for space with a large potted plant.

"So, when do we leave?"

For a moment, Orin was confused. But he knew his brother – of course he'd been listening at the door.

"This is something I need to do alone."

"Oh, I won't be a bother, Orry. We get on so well! And maybe I could be helpful. I am *now*, aren't I?"

"Yes, but this is no pleasure trip – I'm hoping to—"

"I know." Joseph gave a pointed glance at the door, and Orin rolled his eyes.

"You would've done the same, if you'd seen me march into Father's office as if someone had died."

"That's how I looked?"

Joseph brushed a piece of lint from his otherwise perfect sleeve. "More or less." After a moment, he looked up, his gaze full of desperation. "I've wanted to go to Paris for a long time."

"You have?"

"I have! Who wouldn't?"

Orin didn't reply.

"I'm exactly the sort of person who would want to go to Paris – and who will make the most of it."

"Fair enough."

This wasn't the reaction Joseph had been expecting. His brother's deliberately vague reply caught him somewhere between frustration and despair.

The expression on his face made Orin feel a small pang. "I'm going to Paris to look for answers, not to have a good time. I want to live simply. I want no one else involved."

"Not even me?"

"This would be simple," he said again, insistently. "Secret. No one would travel with me, or stay with me. Not even a valet.

"Anyway, why not go on your own? You probably know a great deal about Paris, and you speak French nearly as well as I do –"

"-*Nearly* as well?" Joseph couldn't help cutting in. "You know my accent is better."

"Maybe so. But I got better marks." Orin stopped and shook his head. "*Peu importe, mon frère.* I have no doubt you'd do just fine."

"Father and Mother won't let me go on my own. They worry I'll have too much fun. But you…are not particularly fun. If I tell them you want me to accompany you, they won't say no."

"I didn't think I was that serious."

Joseph raised an eyebrow. "You just…you're always so careful. Maybe Paris will change that. They say there are all sorts of incredible things that can happen there."

There was a long silence, which ended with Orin's resigned sigh. "All right, I'll ask if you can come."

~ ~

Joseph was the only family Orin expected to have in Paris. For years, he'd tried to find some mention of his mother in the books he read. He had only her first name, which he came (rightly) to suspect wasn't her real one. When he'd asked his father her last name, Charles was alarmed to realize that he couldn't recall it.

In the records of the church where they'd been married, his father's name was there, written by the attending priest and signed by Charles himself. But anywhere there should have been the name of his mother, there was only a blank space. Whoever she was, whatever she was, she didn't want to be found.

It took a long time to leave the train station. Their bags had to be meticulously searched for any item that could be taxed. They stood in

17

line with the other new arrivals as people rushed past them in all directions: men wearing sober suits and mustaches, women in full skirts adorned with tassels and trimmings in strangely jarring combinations of colors, children in pretty little clothes that I couldn't imagine would stay clean for long. Porters carried trunks, carts bore piles more of them, there were shouts and whistles, passengers-to-be talking and suddenly going silent as they turned to stare at the board that now revealed the location of their train.

In the midst of all of this, the brothers waited. The queue hardly moved, but both of their minds were in constant movement. Joseph felt at times that he had to hold himself back from running out to the longed-for city just beyond the doors.

Orin worried about the hour of sunset, though he'd already checked it in guides and almanacs countless times. But his anxiousness was soon dashed away by an unusual feeling of excitement. Here he was, in Paris.

Still, what might happen if the baggage inspection took a long time, or if they arrived too late at their hotel, or if, in the end, he found no answers at all?

Stop worrying, he told himself, thinking over what he knew already. There were bookshops here that had impressive occult collections, not to mention libraries and reading rooms, as well as the bouquinistes he'd heard about, with their crates of mysteriously acquired tomes. There were also a few physicians, perhaps a mesmerist or two to call on. And if nothing came of it, they would be able to travel to other parts of France or even Europe easily enough.

He took a breath and looked up at the station's high windows. Maybe he could pass the time by trying to count their countless panes of glass. But he was distracted by the fragments of Paris that he glimpsed on the other side. Tall buildings of yellow-white stone led up to blue-grey rooftops. Above them, he thought wryly, the clouds in the sky were moving more quickly than the line they were waiting in.

What seemed like hours later, they were free. They found a porter, who found them a cab. The driver gave a gruff nod, his horse a gave a knicker, and they rolled forward, swallowed by the traffic.

The feeling of movement all around them was like New York. But something here — maybe the architecture, maybe something in the air - exuded a rhythm, a call, that struck Orin's heart. He gazed at everything with his usual expression of caution and curiosity combined, but now, a light glowed inside him as well, like the buildings' bright stone in the rays of the afternoon sun.

~ ~

Soon they arrived at a tall Haussmannian building that stretched down two streets and met at the place de l'Opéra. Its rows upon rows of repeated windows were nearly dizzying, but the busy café on the ground floor fortunately interrupted the effect, like a smile spreading across a stern face

~ ~

This was the Grand Hôtel, where most of their New York friends and acquaintances had recommended they stay.

Orin had been happy to take their advice; a bustling hotel seemed the sort of place he'd most likely to go unnoticed. Joseph had gladly agreed for a different reason: the Grand Hôtel was modern and luxurious, with endless carpeted corridors lit and heated by gas, a high-ceilinged, breathtaking ballroom, and an elevator (among the first in all of France).

From the expressions on their faces as they stepped inside, I could tell that the place was everything their acquaintances and guidebooks had promised.

No one had mentioned, though, that gaslights weren't installed in the rooms, as they would dirty the elaborately decorated ceilings. Since they could afford it, Orin and Joseph agreed to pay for oil lamps by the day. If they hadn't been able to allow themselves this "luxury", they would have had to light their suite with candles instead.

This was a small detail, though. What struck Orin the most about the Grand Hôtel, and what would always immediately come to mind when he heard its name, were the columns everywhere on its ground floor, even in the café – an excessive amount, it seemed to me, not allowing a clear view in any direction. This was just what he wanted.

Still, when they arrived at their suite, he felt uneasy. At night, he and Joseph would only be separated from one another by a door — not stairs or long stretches of corridor, as he was used to.

Seeing his worried face, Joseph rolled his eyes. "Orry, you're the tamest person I've ever met, and, I'm sure, the tamest beast."

"Know a lot of beasts, do you?" Orin murmured. At least there was plenty to distract them. They stared up at the gilded details of the ceiling and the beautiful mural of a cherub-filled sky in its center.

The Grand Hôtel wasn't located in the most exclusive area of Paris, but one of the most exciting. Garnier's new, ornate, still unfinished opera house sat proudly diagonal to it, commanding the busy square. On the south side of the square, the Grands Boulevards passed by and continued in either direction, full of cafes, shops, brasseries, panoramas, and an almost perpetual, lively crowd, made up of members of every strata of Parisian life. The most fashionable people in the city strolled along the sidewalks, artists sang in café-concerts, and beggars sat in dirty heaps, hoping for a sou.

From the windows of their calm suite, the brothers could see the Opera House and the unrelenting traffic on the square in front of it. The omnibuses had seats even on their roofs, with perilous spiral staircases leading up to them. The cab drivers wove between other vehicles, heedless of any sort of order.

Joseph glanced up at the sky. "There's time for a walk," he said persuasively.

Orin shook his head. "Not for me, I think."

He could have gone out for a while, but if he did, he knew he'd want to stay on the boulevards forever.

2

They settled into their new life with ease. The streets of the City of Light were lit with gas lamps that seemed to glitter more brilliantly than those back home. Maybe it was because there were so many sparkling surfaces for them to shine on: the gilding on lampposts and buildings, jewelry in shop windows. This illumination was a part of everyone's life; even respectable Parisians – especially respectable Parisians – continued their revelry and visits and even meals long into the night.

Joseph often came home at dawn, exhausted but always happy. Occasionally he didn't come home at all.

And so, Orin had more time to himself than he'd expected. He spent his nights reading, as always, but now and then he'd gaze at the flickering light of the lamps that shimmered through the slits in the shutters. He'd listen to the rolling of carriage wheels and clops of horses' hooves echoing up from the Place de l'Opéra, or try to decipher the French of the passersby. Sometimes he'd fall asleep with the lamps still lit. He and Joseph were bathed in light.

Every morning, Orin left as soon as he could. Sometimes he headed to a library or bookshop. Other days, he'd rove small streets in the Latin Quarter, Saint-Germain, the Marais, searching for any shops that might sell curiosities, anything that might tell him more.

Despite his dedication, of course he stopped and looked at everything around him, at the old buildings whose dirty facades were imprinted with centuries of life, at new Haussmannian structures that gleamed with harmonious beauty. He spent a great deal of time indoors, too, gazing at the museums' treasures.

Orin was free, but there were some restrictions, in addition to the enchantment he was under. The mornings may have been his, but usually he had to be at the home of some wealthy family or another for lunch.

"This isn't why we're here," he often muttered to Joseph as they left and walked homeward.

"We have to take part, Orry. Otherwise, people will ask questions. Everyone knows we're here – it would be strange for us not to call on them."

"'Everyone'?"

Joseph rolled his eyes. "Everyone who counts in society."

"That's exactly why I wanted to travel in secret."

"Well, if you did, you'd risk missing out on something. After all, some of these people own books that might be helpful, and they're willing to lend them to you."

Joseph was right. But this wasn't what he wanted.

3

Late one afternoon, Orin closed his eyes and turned to face the sun, savoring its red glow against his eyelids. Dawn came earlier with spring, and twilight took a surprisingly long time to arrive. He was giddy with all of it.

Now, he and Joseph could leave even the latest luncheon engagement and go for walks around the city with little fear. Today, they were in the Parc Monceau.

Orin loved this place, with its follies lost among exotic foliage or cropping up unexpectedly on the edges of the lawns. It was at once ridiculous and convincing. You could almost imagine that the columns around the lake *were* the ruins of some classical temple, and that the little pyramid really had been seen by ancient eyes.

They strolled around, talking about this and that. From time to time, Joseph's eyes would follow a finely dressed gentleman and make notes for his new tailor.

They arrived at a white bridge that crossed a pond whose banks were studded with flowers. Orin had never liked this part of the park. If you didn't have someone you loved, its beauty made that absence feel even stronger and more hopeless. He turned back down the path, and Joseph shrugged and followed.

The sunlight's yellow was shifting into amber, but neither of them noticed. For a while, it hid behind some of those peculiar lavender clouds that often float in the Parisian sky.

Then, it emerged again, bathing the park in a washed-out orange. Orin turned to Joseph with a look of controlled panic.

"Let's find a cab," he said, quickly heading towards the park's main gate.

As they drove, the tumult on the streets was nothing compared to the agitated fear Orin felt inside. The ride was faster than they'd expected. Still, it was nearly too late.

When they arrived at the Grand Hôtel, Orin lifted his collar to cover his cheeks and kept his head bent into his coat, his hat pulled low over his eyes. They raced inside among those columns, every part of them thrown into relief in the brilliant mirrored light. Perhaps the Grand Hôtel wasn't a place for secrets, after all.

Suddenly, Orin felt the prickling. Like a reflex, he drew his hands from his pockets, and saw the shadow pass over them. He struggled to keep his footing as he hurtled up the grand staircase. At the second floor, he dove desperately down the corridor, relieved that Joseph had slipped him the key – his brother was, he realized, far behind him, still climbing the stairs. It wasn't that Joseph wasn't making an effort; he was still a man, while Orin had already begun to become an animal.

At their door, his hands were already monstrous things with talons, but still he managed to push the key into the lock and turn it.

Just as he was about to throw himself inside the suite, he noticed a flash of movement. One door down, a lady was staring at him. She'd given a start at the sight of him – that's what he had seen.

Orin had often told himself that the guests and staff at the Grand Hôtel had their own affairs to keep them busy. Who would notice any behavior from him that might seem strange?

But the woman had chanced to look over at what she thought was someone simply returning to their room, and she'd gotten a glimpse of him as he'd hoped no one ever would. Transfixed by fear, he stared back at her for a moment. In the woman's eyes, there wasn't fear at all, only perplexity and revulsion. Though, Orin thought later, that might have been her usual expression.

He turned away as quickly as he could, and launched himself through the door and shut it behind him. Breathing hard, he waited with his weight against it until he heard Joseph's light knock. "Orry?"

Orin turned the delicate knob carefully, trying not to look at his talons. When the door was open a millimeter, he said, "Count to ten before you come in." Then, he reached down to grab the shoes and socks he'd kicked off, and was inside his bedroom before Joseph had reached "Five."

He heard his brother shut and lock the door of the suite.

"Someone saw me," Orin declared flatly.

"What? Who?"

"Our 'neighbor' on the right. I'm not sure how much she saw."

Joseph sighed heavily.

~~

The next morning, Joseph was still asleep and Orin was preparing to leave for the day, when there was a tentative knock at the door.

A man who worked for the hotel presented himself and presented his excuses, but he'd been told by another guest that they were apparently keeping a large animal in the suite, "something against the rules, unfortunately."

"Animal?" Orin stalled for time.

Joseph strode calmly out of his bedroom, dressed in a dashing deep blue silk kimono and a lordly pair of slippers.

"I believe there's been a mistake," he said grandly. His American accent was slight, but what was most impressive about his French was the way he never faltered and always seemed to find the perfect words.

"Perhaps, monsieur," the man nodded.

Orin tried to imitate his brother's easy ways. "Ah, I believe the guest might have seen us coming back from a masquerade party yesterday evening."

The man nodded, seemingly grateful for an explanation that didn't involve wildlife. "Oh, of course, messieurs."

Joseph flashed him a kind smile in return. "You may check the suite, if you like."

"No, that will not be necessary. Good day, messieurs, and my apologies for having disturbed you."

"Well," Joseph said, shutting the door and waiting until the man was surely down the hall, "that's that, then."

But for Orin, the woman who'd seen him was everywhere now. She may have already moved on in her travels, but there would be someone to take her place. It's simply human nature. Maybe the woman's replacement would be nosy enough to peer into the keyhole, or press an ear against the wall between their rooms.

What would happen if he were found out? Orin wasn't certain, but it was easy to imagine at least some of the complications it might cause his family. Who would want to marry them, or who would trust them with business, if they might be something other than successful men, if they might carry something horrible in their blood?

The sense of being watched lingered. He wondered if there were a way for someone to see through the shutters' small slats into his room. Or what if there were some sort of hole in a wall, or someone made one?

Mad as these ideas might be, there was a truth to them: he couldn't hide here. It was time to leave the Grand Hôtel.

4

He knew what Joseph would suggest: a furnished *hôtel particulier*. His brother wouldn't think of the servants lurking around, possibly being paid to inform on them to someone or other. He and Joseph were too rich and there were too many American families here with eligible daughters for them to escape unnoticed.

So, then, *Why not live like a Parisian*, in an apartment in one of those buildings that surrounded him, towering six or seven storeys towards the cloudy sky? Perhaps his neighbors' routines would conceal him better than ornate columns.

He turned down a busy street off the Grands Boulevards. It was a new place, and like all new places in this city, he wanted to discover it. His gaze wandered here and there, up to the high slate roofs, down to the shops and brightly colored advertisements and the strange sculptures around some of the doorways.

Suddenly, something caught his eye.

Sunlight glinted on a small, brass-framed display case that was mounted on the wall beside a building's entryway. On either side of the entryway was a shop window. One shop sold umbrellas. A line of opened ones hung above the window like a garland. The shop on the other side sold lamps. Even unlit, the glass of their shades gleamed like colorful pearls. Some were suspended from the ceiling, strange and colorful clouds in their own sky.

The display case twinkled again. Orin walked over to look at it and broke into a smile.

Inside the case were photographs. Most were *cartes de visite* of theatre personalities, married couples, and children. All of them had engaging expressions, whether they seemed cheerful or serious. But there were more unexpected images scattered among them. For instance, a photograph of a smug-looking cat and a poodle posed on a chair. Or a woman turned almost fully away from the viewer, a fashionable hat perched on her head. She looked out over a painted backdrop of a seascape with a castle in the distance.

Beside the case was a white enamel plaque in the shape of a hand. "*Turin Photographe*" was engraved on it in black script letters. Orin's eyes followed the hand's pointing index finger upwards. There, higher on the wall, a notice was posted: *Chambre à louer, 6ème étage.*

He gave a start. One of the entryway's large doors was open. Hesitantly, he stepped inside.

He found himself in a stone-paved corridor that curved slightly and then split in two. To the left, it led to an outer courtyard. To the right, it was interrupted by a pair of casement doors whose windows were a grid of small panes.

Another enamel hand had been attached to the wall nearby. Its index finger pointed to the doors.

Orin crossed the short distance to them, turned the handle of one of the doors, and stepped inside.

He was in a smallish entrance hall, facing a sprawling wooden staircase that seemed to spill onto the tiled floor. Its rounded steps were covered in thick carpet held in place by shining brass stair rods. To the right, in the staircase's shadowy curve, was a brightly polished metal statue of a woman in a classical tunic. One of her arms reached sinuously ceilingward, bearing a flickering white gas flame encased in a flame-shaped smoked glass lamp. She looked up towards it, a slight smile on her lips.

In the shadows on the other side of the staircase, he could make out a small table with candlesticks on top of it and key hooks on the wall above. Beside that was a door with a sign: CONCIERGE.

He knocked, but no one answered.

There was another enamel hand on the wall by the staircase, pointing upwards. It seemed perfectly reasonable to follow its suggestion.

On the stairs, the carpet beneath Orin's feet was thick and red, scattered with a motif of white roses, their stems studded with thorns.

He stopped at the landing. Sunlight was beginning to creep across the carpet, but there was no other presence or sound. Another enamel hand pointed upwards. He went up the next flight of stairs.

The ceilings were higher on this floor, and the higher windows let in a little more light. But it was just as silent as the rest of the building.

On the wall near the staircase was another pointing hand.

When he reached the third floor, he could hear something at last: a violin was playing from behind one of the closed doors.

Another enamel hand pointed him towards another flight of stairs.

On the next floor, the carpet was thinner, with a slightly faded royal blue background. The roses were thornless and red. Down the corridor, he could hear a voice that seemed to be reading or giving some sort of speech. He followed an enamel hand upwards again.

Silence on the fifth floor, and no more staircases. Instead, there were three doors: one on the right, one on the left, and one at the far end of the corridor. An enamel hand pointed towards this door, so he walked to it and cautiously opened it.

Inside, a wrought iron staircase spiraled up from uncarpeted floorboards. He began to climb.

When he got to the fourth step, he noticed a photograph on the wall – the first of many, he realized, looking up. He examined each one as he passed. All of them were intriguing – lively portraits, artful still lifes, jolly images of babies, a man making a silly grimace and sticking out his tongue.

After a few turns of the staircase, he came upon his favorite: a little dog whose small, exposed teeth gave him a ridiculous air of trying to be ferocious, or maybe he was simply making a failed attempt at a smile.

A wind of the staircase later, there was a fellow he assumed was an actor, dressed like a character in an old play. His mouth was open, his expression lively. You could just imagine him uttering some famous lines of Molière, with the audience laughing in reply.

At the top of the staircase, two portraits faced each other on either side of an open doorway.

The one on the left showed a man and woman posed in front of a painted seascape. The man's extremely long, thin mustache stood out ramrod straight at either side of his laughing face. He wasn't actually laughing, Orin realized, but something about his expression told you he often did. The woman beside him was shorter by a head, and also had laughter in her eyes. There was a stuffed parrot perched on her shoulder. Between them was a heavy black object – a camera.

In the portrait on the right were a boy and girl, both probably around ten or eleven years old, with those same, dark, laughing eyes. The boy held a hoop in one hand, but instead of a stick, there was what looked like a lens in the other. The girl held a paintbrush in one hand, and what appeared to be a photograph in the other. It was the portrait that hung on the opposite wall.

A glint of white enamel drew his attention. On the wall beyond the doorway, yet another hand pointed. This one was a bit larger than the others. He stepped across the threshold and followed the pointing finger down the corridor.

On this floor, there was a slight, chemical smell in the air. The doorframes were painted a yellowing white, and the walls had been papered with a swirling purple and cream-colored floral pattern. There seemed to be flowers of some sort on the carpet here, as well, but the pattern was faded, and worn by many passing feet. Orin looked up and saw that there were several doors on the left wall, but only a single one on the right.

This one bore a large, rectangular enamel plaque, painted with that black flourish of a signature: *Turin*, and the word *Photographe* in bold letters beneath. Circling it, like stars, were small, round symbols. Leaning in, Orin saw that they represented award seals from photography competitions.

Just then, the door began to open. He staggered back in surprise and watched as bright sunlight poured into the dim corridor. A woman with a messy chignon came into the doorframe. She was short in stature, with a pleasantly proportioned, somewhat generous figure. A tall, thin woman came and stood beside her.

"They did turn out well, didn't they?" the smaller woman was saying. Though the bright light made her nearly a shadow, Orin could see that her merry eyes were the color and shape of almonds. He thought that they shone in a different way than the sunlight around her, one that seemed to make it dim a little.

The thin woman said something, and the shorter woman laughed. Orin thought it was an extraordinary laugh, a perfect kind of joyful music. He was looking at her as I've never seen him look at anyone before.

Suddenly, she noticed him and gave a start.

It brought him back to himself.

"Oh! Are you here for a sitting, monsieur?"

"No I-I'm terribly sorry. I'm in the wrong place." He gave a curt nod and turned back towards the stairwell.

He descended the staircases rapidly: twisting metal, then the roses, blurs of red, then white.

Suddenly, just a few steps from the ground floor, his hand ran into a pile of soft fur.

He missed a step and nearly fell forwards.

On the banister, a black cat lifted its head from the tight curl of its body. Its yellow eyes fixed Orin's. Orin held his breath, bracing himself for the cat to yowl or attack the instant it sensed the monster he was. But it only yawned, uncurled itself, and jumped down from its perch, stretching its back legs languorously as it wandered towards the concierge's lodge.

It's frightened of me, Orin thought – the same thing he thought about any animal who came close to him. But he couldn't be certain, seeing how slowly the cat sauntered away.

"Excuse me, monsieur, may I help you?"

There was the concierge. She was a pale, tall woman whose dark reddish hair was streaked slightly with gray. Her face was serious and suspicious, and why shouldn't it be? She'd had no idea he was in the building. *Good thing I'm not carrying a satchel*, he thought, as her gray eyes stared hard at him. *She might suspect I was a burglar.*

"Bonjour, madame. I'm sorry – I've come to enquire about the room."

"I don't imagine you would be interested. It's only a small garret room." She'd taken in his costly clothing and, after hearing the few words he'd spoken to her, had made note of his accent – one that usually belonged to wealthy tourists.

"I understand," Orin told her, speaking slowly to lessen his accent. "I'm quite interested."

The concierge considered for a moment, then shrugged. "All right. I can show it to you now."

He followed her back upstairs, over the soft carpet with the white roses, over the thin carpet with the red, up the wrought iron staircase, surrounded by those wondrous photographs at every turn. When they reached the landing, she noticed him glancing again at the two portraits.

"Those are the Turins," the concierge told him.

Where was she? Of course – the girl with the dreamy expression.

"They seem like a lovely family." It was truth, not pleasantry. The photographs said as much.

To his surprise, tears sprang to the concierge's eyes. "Madame and Monsieur Turin are gone now, two years. And Monsieur Paul has gone away, married and living in Normandy. Only Mademoiselle Turin is left."

She took a breath and discreetly wiped her eyes. "She's a skilled colorist. Quite creative, and works especially well with animals. That photograph of the dog is one of hers. I told her she ought to display it."

"You were right to say so. That's my favorite one."

The concierge gave him a different look from those she'd bestowed on him before. This time, it was a look of approval.

They walked together down the dim corridor.

"Will it be quiet?" Orin suddenly thought to ask.

The concierge shrugged. "Quiet is for the countryside."

"Would I have many neighbors, I mean?"

"Only during daylight."

When he said nothing, she added, "The studio closes around sundown. Some days, when there's little light, it may not even be open at all."

He glanced pointedly at the row of doors on the wall beside them.

"Those were for servants, but now the residents use them for storage, or let them out to others to store their affairs. Monsieur Duchesne's valet was in the room you're interested in, but he recently married and naturally wants to have a home of his own. Monsieur will keep the man on, but he'll be living somewhere else. So I suggested they let the room.

"So, really, monsieur," she said in a tone he sometimes heard the French use: flat, almost annoyed that she had to justify her claim at all, "you won't have to worry about neighbors."

She took a key ring from her reticule and opened the last door in the row. Then she moved away and let him step inside.

The room was larger than he'd expected, though its ceiling was low.

Orin stood in the middle of it and looked around. There was a small, simple fireplace, a set of sagging wooden shelves that looked like they might topple at any moment, a narrow bed, an armoire, a washstand, and a window.

He walked towards it, transfixed. Outside was the sky, nearly covered with the usual gray-lavender clouds. If you watched closely, you could see they were turning with the turning of the earth. Just below eye level was a patchwork of slate rooftops, spotted with terra cotta chimneys. A few pigeons sat near them, their feathers puffed against the wind.

It was beautiful. The sky, the world, Paris – and best of all, no one to see him. "I've never lived this close to the heavens," he remarked.

The simple explanation is that this was a typical modern apartment building that one would find in Paris in 1870. The owners of the shops lived in low-ceilinged rooms on the first floor. The second floor, with its large windows, balconies, and short distance from the street, was for the richest residents: the Duchesnes and another family belonging to the haute-bourgeoisie. The wealth diminished with each subsequent floor, although there were no desperately poor residents on the sixth floor.

Instead, there was a photography studio.

Such a thing wasn't entirely unique, especially here, near the Grands Boulevards. But what was strange were the empty rooms across from it and the perpetually locked door to the service staircase. I couldn't say how many Parisian buildings had no servants left in their servants' quarters then. It seemed strange that not a single one remained here, or, at the very least, that the rooms hadn't been rented to poor tenants.

The situation was ideal for Orin, and apparently suited Monsieur Duchesne well enough. A few days later, he received a letter informing him that the man had accepted his offer. He would never meet Monsieur Duchesne, who felt that anyone renting a lowly room wasn't worth dealing with outside of correspondence. That was the final detail that convinced Orin he'd made the perfect choice of new residence.

When he told Joseph the news, his brother sighed. "You don't need to leave, Orry." And then, before Orin could say anything else, he sighed again, a sadness in his voice. "But I understand."

They walked to the building together and climbed the stairs.

The room wasn't charming to Joseph in the slightest. "This sort of place will get frightfully cold in winter," he warned.

"That doesn't matter to me," Orin replied, with a pointed look. After all, on those cold winter nights, he would be covered in fur.

5

One afternoon, Mademoiselle Turin stepped through the doorway of her building and nearly fell over a steamer trunk.

Outside her lodge, the concierge was surveying something. Her cat was at her feet, cleaning his whiskers. Both turned their heads at the commotion.

"You've been to a museum. You couldn't see for the stars in your eyes."

Mademoiselle Turin shook off her dreaminess like snow from a cloak and came to stand companionably beside the concierge.

I peered into Mademoiselle Turin's thoughts and helpfully discovered the woman's name: Madame Marcel. Mademoiselle Turin had known her most of her life.

There was a sense of loss — Madame Marcel had lost her husband when Mademoiselle Turin was a child. I caught a memory of the concierge weeping, the building's residents coming by with condolences, Madame Marcel sobbing in the arms of Mademoiselle Turin's mother. It seemed the Turins had liked the Marcels from the moment they'd arrived at the building, when Mademoiselle Turin was very young.

And...I delved a little deeper...it seems the Marcels had always kept cats. They told the residents it was to rid the building of rats and mice, but Mademoiselle Turin was convinced it was mostly because they liked them. She did, too.

"Your new neighbor's arrived." Madame Marcel nodded towards two men who were standing near the statue that held the gas flame. One was dressed in an impeccably cut frock coat of sapphire blue. The other wore a simple black coat and stood a bit in the shadows. Mademoiselle Turin got the impression that he preferred it this way. He was taller than the man in the blue coat, but seemed to make himself small.

"Ah! So Monsieur Duchesne accepted the strange American's offer."

Madame Marcel nodded, smiling over at them. "He did," she said quietly, "though I advised against it. It's odd that someone who seems to have money would want that room."

"Well, it does have a beautiful view."

"That's the same thing he said!"

Mademoiselle Turin didn't know what to say to that.

"Well," Madame Marcel went on, "that's something he *said*. But we all know the kinds of people who have money and rent rooms like that. He seems too wealthy to use it for trysts with a mistress; surely he'd take her somewhere nicer. He doesn't seem to be an artist, either. I think he must have lost a good deal of his fortune. Maybe he's a gambler."

"A mysterious American gambler…." Mademoiselle Turin's voice was serious but I saw a smile playing at her lips.

"But then," the concierge conceded, "he did say something else: No neighbors. He seems to be seeking solitude."

There was a flash in Mademoiselle Turin's mind. Her apartment, her childhood home, had always been full of people. But these days, she was its only occupant. It was lonely, and yet those words made her think of the things she hadn't been able to do before. Nowadays, she filled up the space with things that interested her, slept and rose without worrying about disturbing anyone, and took her meals when and where she pleased.

~ ~

As they waited for the last trunk to be carried up the stairs by the boys they'd hired, Joseph and Orin went over certain particulars. "You'll have to find a *porteur d'eau* to bring buckets of hot water all the way up there every time you want a bath. And every time you want a shave, you'll have to fetch the water yourself, I suppose, from the pump in the courtyard." Joseph shook his head.

"It's fine. And anyway," Orin glanced at him slyly, "I can always come visit you at the Grand Hôtel and have a bath there."

"That's much more reasonable.".

"As for keeping the room clean," Orin continued, "The concierge told me about a girl she knows, called Sidonie, who'll do that as well as take care of my laundry."

"Excellent. And the lock on your door…."

"The lock is fine," Orin's voice was calm. "And remember, no one else lives on the sixth floor, and the servants' staircase is locked – there's no danger anyone would accidentally open my door at night."

And there will be no one to block me inside my room at night, either. The unwelcome thought had visited him occasionally over the past few days. What might happen if he ever truly became monstrous and sought out a heart? A feeling of panic began to creep through him.

Suddenly, he felt something by his legs. There was the black cat he'd seen the other day.

Orin stiffened, and then, a strange thing happened. *If the cat's doing this, he isn't afraid of me,* he thought. He looked down and said, "Hello there."

Joseph stared at him in surprise.

BANG!

The cat raced away and disappeared in the space of time it took the rest of us to jump a mile.

"Sorry, sorry monsieur." A pair of boys had dropped one of the chests.

"It's all right."

He'd always had servants, of course, but never thin urchins carrying heavy loads up six staircases. Orin leaned over and opened the clasps of the trunk. "Here." He took out several heavy books and placed them in

Joseph's arms, then reached in and took out more for himself to carry. "We'll follow you up."

"*Merci, monsieur*," one of the boys said, and they took up the trunk again.

"*Merci*, Orry." Joseph shifted the books in his arms and rolled his eyes.

Madame Marcel approached him. "You are very kind, monsieur."

"No," Orin said, a stronger sense of protestation in his voice than anyone normally would have made at such a statement. "I'm cruel to have packed so many books."

Still standing near the lodge, Mademoiselle Turin raised her eyebrows and thought, *He's kinder than I would have expected for a profligate American gambler.*

And how to explain all of those trunks of books? she wondered. *Could they have been someone's wager?*

As he started up the carpeted stairs, Orin felt someone's gaze. There – near the concierge's lodge was a short, shapely person with a messy chignon. *Mademoiselle Turin.* He turned away and continued to climb.

6

The view from his window often took him away from the world. This was a new place, where clouds greeted him and pigeons came to rest and the wind howled or whistled, ruffling the birds' feathers on its way. The rain landed like footfalls or hammers on the roof just above, not far at all.

It was easy to forget that there could be people just outside his door.

But the mornings usually reminded him. The sound of footsteps on the stairs often woke him or accompanied him while he got dressed or sat with a book for a while before going out. First, there were two people – the photographers, no doubt, opening their studio. Sitters would arrive sooner or later, their footfalls usually accompanied by conversation.

At first, Orin waited until the photographers had gone into their studio, but then, he thought, why should he waste even a moment of light? And so , one morning, he stepped out of his room when he was ready, only to find a man with wild hair sitting on a bench beside the studio's door. The man looked up from the book on his knees and give him a strange, close-mouthed grin.

"*Bonjour, monsieur.*" The words had just left Orin's lips when a noise made him turn towards the stairwell.

There was Mademoiselle Turin, walking towards them.

He found himself thinking that the dark brown of her dress was like so many of his books' covers. He imagined their smooth softness, which he could feel even with his transformed hands and talons. Her eyes seemed to shine in the shadows, and her mouth had a slight upturn to it as she prepared to speak to the wild-haired man – and then she noticed the shadowy figure standing near him.

"Monsieur Rush." Her voice was serious and polite, but she kept her usual expression: a slight smile, eyes subtly twinkling, as if finding everything a bit wondrous or amusing – perhaps both.

Orin steeled himself, without understanding why he would need to steel himself at all. "Mademoiselle Turin," he replied, just as graciously. "I apologize for disturbing you the other day."

"Oh, it's no trouble. I'm sure you were just excited at the prospect of living in such a lovely room."

Orin was surprised, even a bit frustrated; she'd made exactly the excuse *he* should have. "You seem to understand me quite well."

"I have the same view from my studio." After a moment, she added, "We're neighbors, after all." Was that a twitch of laughter at the corner of her mouth?

Suddenly, he remembered what he'd said to Madame Marcel about neighbors. She must have mentioned it to Mademoiselle Turin. He felt sick with embarrassment, but squared his shoulders and rejoined, "Well, I couldn't have asked for a better one. I rarely see you!"

The photographer gave a surprised laugh. Then, she turned to the man on the bench, whose frizzy hair puffed around his head like a brown-grey cloud. There was an energy that radiated from him even though he was still, which made the cloud seem full of lightning bolts. The remarkable glint of his small blue eyes drew attention from his slightly puckered mouth, which seemed to be lacking a number of teeth.

"This is Monsieur Émile Rouline, a dear friend and my assistant."

He stood up from the bench and turned to Orin with a slight bow. "I help bring the images to the world."

"A pleasure to meet you." Orin bowed, following suit.

"Well, we should be going," Mademoiselle Turin said. "We work when the sun allows."

"Of course. Enjoy the sunlight."

She smiled and drew a key from her dress pocket. "You, too, Monsieur Rush."

She opened the studio door, and for a moment, bright light shone into the hallway. Then, she and Monsieur Rouline crossed the threshold and closed themselves inside, and everything returned to how it had been.

7

Paris was full of bookshops and reading rooms, and Orin visited them often. One was a small, dark shop on the rue Monsieur-le-Prince that was filled with that heavy, dusty air that's intoxicating to anyone who loves old books. But Orin was there for research, not for pleasure. The shop specialized in volumes on the occult and magic. Between old books that seemed permanent as bricks and new acquisitions in precariously balanced piles, each time he came with the idea of a long search ahead of him.

He rarely found anything that seemed promising, but today, he approached the counter with a slim volume in his hand. A small hope burned inside of him, like a fragile flame hovering on a candle's wick.

I knew nothing would come of what he read, but I felt happy for him. There's something wonderful about hope.

Beside the counter was a wooden board covered in advertisements posted by charlatans. For example: *Mademoiselle Aubépine, Chiromancie.*

Or *Philtres d'amour. Monsieur N., rue de la Parcheminerie.*

As he waited for the bookseller, Orin read them with amusement and just a bit of outrage. He wondered how many naïve people might have sought out these tricksters.

At the bottom of the board, he noticed a black card. In spidery white writing he read: *Magic investigated. Curses broken. Le Cercle des Thaumaturges.*

It was followed by an address.

His sure smile wavered. Something about the advertisement unnerved him. He couldn't say why – maybe, he tried to reassure himself, it was simply the unusual effect of the white writing against black paper.

The bookseller's polite cough broke Orin's reverie.

"Do you know anything about Le Cercle des Thaumaturges?" he asked.

The man stared down at the counter for a moment, then hesitantly back at Orin. "They are only to be contacted for serious matters, monsieur. And it can be…dangerous." After a moment, in a lighter tone of voice, he added, "They are so curious," as if that would clarify things.

Orin began to wonder if this advertisement was no lie. Still, no matter his curiosity, his need, he kept in mind what the bookseller had said. How, precisely, was the group dangerous?

Unfortunately, he could tell from the bookseller's closed expression that the conversation was finished. He paid for his book and left the shop.

He resolved to keep poring over the books he bought and borrowed. He'd visit the private libraries and collections of curiosities of the connexions Joseph was helping him make until he was certain there were no answers there. He sighed. Already several months in Paris, and nothing. If he didn't love the city so much, he would have been even more disappointed.

8

After their meeting in the corridor, Orin had changed his ways again, waiting until he heard Mademoiselle Turin and Monsieur Rouline go into the studio for the day, much to my frustration. Why should he waste his time in his room?

The answer was, the way he felt when Mademoiselle Turin was near unsettled him.

As the days went by, he decided on another strategy. He'd leave his room early enough to be gone before Mademoiselle Turin or Monsieur Rouline had arrived.

This didn't always work. And so, on days when he did see them as he left or returned home, he hurried down the corridor, giving them only a polite "*Bonjour*" or "*Bonsoir*" in passing.

They didn't see Orin for quite a while – or what they did see was mostly a flash of coattails.

They'd think of his name and what English they knew, and exchange a joking glance: Mr. Rush was always rushing.

They wondered where to.

~ ~

Monsieur H., a mesmerist, worked in a shabby apartment near the Palais Royal.

Orin wasn't entirely convinced of his skills, but of all the gurus and charlatans, doctors and witches he'd seen over the years, he'd never consulted a French *imaginationniste* before, which meant it was exactly the sort of thing he'd come to Paris to try.

"Everyone considers mesmerists charlatans, and worse: utterly unfashionable," He'd told Joseph at lunch the day before. "If he were to let out something I revealed about my...condition, it would only sound like quackery – even madness."

Still, some part of him was ill at ease. If this mesmerist really did have some sort of gift, what could he make a man do when his mind was caught between waking and dreams?

That was why he'd asked Joseph to come along.

Now, they waited, sitting on cane chairs with worn cushions in a dusty, blue-painted parlor. When Monsieur H. finally opened the door to his consulting room, he was exactly as Orin had expected: Wild white hair, cobalt blue eyes a bit wild, themselves, and a frayed frock coat that looked like something that would have been worn by fashionable Parisians a hundred years ago. But he welcomed the brothers with a businesslike handshake. His attitude was more that of a doctor than of a madman.

After Orin and Joseph had settled into another pair of decrepit chairs, Monsieur H. installed himself behind a desk more elegant than anything else in the room and asked them why they'd come.

"A cure for my headaches," Orin said simply.

The mesmerist fixed him with those powerful eyes. "You must be willing – wholly willing," he insisted, "in order for this to be a success."

Orin nodded, wondering if Monsieur H. could feel his doubt.

After a few moments of silence, he stood and walked to Orin's chair. Towering over him, the mesmerist fixed him again with his ice-blue eyes.

"Sleep!" he called out in a commanding voice.

Orin gave a start at the sudden bark, but didn't sleep.

Monsieur H. shook his head.

"Sleep," he said softly, "sleep." Now his persuasive tone was like a lullaby.

Orin didn't feel tired at all, but he didn't want to disappoint the man or give up on what might be a cure or some sort of insight towards one. So, he shut his eyes.

Monsieur H. asked him to perform a few small, easy tasks, like lifting his left hand and putting it down in his lap. Orin complied.

After a while, the mesmerist's voice softened again. "Tell me what is troubling you. Where is the pain?"

Orin could have come up with an answer for the first inquiry. But as for where the pain came from — he found himself without words. *Maybe*, he thought, *this is a way to discover something.* He thought about what happened every night when the change came.

"The pain is everywhere," he finally said, trying to make his voice sound like a half-asleep murmur.

Monsieur H. seemed surprised by this. "Hmmm… It's not only your head?"

"No," Orin's voice still sounded ghostly, floating.

There was a long silence. Finally, the mesmerist spoke. "Your pain is one of the spirit, not of your physical being."

Orin nodded respectfully.

Monsieur H. continued, "Your spirit has spoken. In a few moments, I will command you to wake. You will rise from this chair a healed man. Take the sorrow and push it from you."

Orin felt that he was waiting for something.

"I will try," Orin finally said.

"No!" the mesmerist demanded. "You will push it away!"

Orin hesitated a moment, then made a gesture of shoving something away.

"Now, wake!"

He opened his eyes and blinked at the sunlight shining brightly on the dingy walls. Across the room, Joseph was staring at him curiously. Orin stood up from the chair.

"I have done my best to heal you," the mesmerist proclaimed.

"Thank you," Orin said, then added a slight bow. He paid the man generously and they took their leave.

As they walked down the busy street, he realized Joseph was still staring at him. "That wasn't real, was it?"

"Unfortunately, not at all." They headed to a restaurant for lunch.

"Do you" – Joseph carefully sipped a spoonful of soup "- remember anything that happened?"

"I remember all of it." Orin paused. "I think. He didn't have me do anything strange or —"

"No," Joseph shook his head. "It was rather boring, actually. Just lifting your hands and asking what was the matter. It was like a physician consulting with a somnambulist."

Orin snickered. "I wasn't asleep."

"Not at all?"

"I only acted that way to see what would happen. Maybe he could do something. And to be polite."

Joseph gave a laugh. "Well, dammit, you had me convinced! Orry," he looked a bit melancholy, "it's a shame you never performed at Barnum's."

"I have to disagree."

Joseph didn't argue, but stared sadly at his soup.

"Wake!" Orin hissed at him, and he looked up with a grin.

9

I n the darkness, Orin could hear something rustling. Mice, or maybe a rat?

He lay still under his coverlet, listening carefully.

The sound grew faster, frantic, and then louder until it was a series of thuds. Now there was a muffled cry, another thud. Thud, then cry, thud, then cry.

It was coming from the armoire.

He fumbled to light his lamp, then stood carefully, still half asleep, and walked toward it. Part of him wondered if he were dreaming as he slowly opened the armoire's door.

The moment the opening was wide enough, something leapt out and flew across the room, over the bed, landing on the other side.

An instant later, Hippolyte sauntered around the bed and came towards him.

~~

The scene wasn't as unexpected as you might imagine.

Sometimes, Orin would hurry into his room and find Hippolyte sleeping on the bed. The cat must have found a way to slip in when he left in the morning.

He'd pick up the little black figure and remove him from the room, locking his door again to be sure it couldn't be pushed open. He was always afraid as he put the cat into the corridor. What a risk to open the door when the change was about to come. But when he'd think about it later, it was funny, too. What a persistent, annoying, puzzling little character Hippolyte was.

Now, he started to laugh - but the sound stopped in his throat. Hippolyte had never seen him at night. What would he do when he realized he was trapped inside a room with a monster?

It was difficult to tell what worried Orin more: the possibility that the cat would yowl and attract someone's attention, or the thought that Hippolyte would at last know what he really was.

He leaned against the closest wall, hoping - foolishly, he knew - to be mistaken for a shadow. But even if that might have been possible, his stifled laugh had given him away. Hippolyte glanced up at him. Orin flinched. Then, the cat turned around and leapt onto the bed, where he began giving himself a bath.

For a long while, they stayed that way, Hippolyte making himself comfortable and Orin standing uncertainly a few feet away.

Then, the cat jumped down from the bed and came towards him. Orin braced himself for a hiss or a bite. Instead, Hippolyte gave his usual curl around Orin's legs. Wondering again if he were dreaming, Orin bent down as he would in his other form and hesitantly, carefully gave a few chin scratches with his talons.

Hippolyte leaned in appreciatively for a moment, then sauntered over to the door and lifted a commanding paw. Orin would never open the door when he was in this form, but he worried that Hippolyte still might panic. So, he did it quickly. Hippolyte took his time leaving the room and padded leisurely down the corridor.

Orin closed and locked himself inside again and sat down, his heart beating fast. Was it because he'd opened the door? Or was it because this was the first time that anyone had seen him as he was in those nighttime hours and not been bothered at all?

As he came down the stairs that morning, he started to wonder if Hippolyte would act differently towards him, even so. But everything was as it always was. Madame Marcel wished him good morning from her lodge. Hippolyte was sleeping in the curl of the bannister.

The cat continued his nighttime visits now and then. Orin realized that he looked forward to them, no matter that they meant he'd have to open the door at some point. Those nights, he didn't only have books for company.

IO

Mademoiselle Turin was leaving the studio later than usual. She'd lingered behind, working and straightening and going through the ledger. She was in the corridor, locking up, when Orin flew by her, all coattails, as usual.

Only, this time, as he passed, she heard a thud. There, on the carpet between them was a book he must have dropped. Without thinking, she went to pick it up for him.

"Monsieur Rush! Wait!"

Already at his door, Orin turned.

"You dropped your book," she explained, walking briskly to him.

"Thank you, Mademoiselle Turin." He seemed to want to say more, but stopped. It was no use making conversation right now, when he desperately needed to be on the other side of his door.

"It's no trouble. It gave me some sport."

"I'm terribly sorry."

"What is there to be sorry for?"

She looked down at the book that still hadn't left her hands. On the spine, in gilded letters were an English title and a French name: *Walden or Life in the Woods*/Thoreau. The spine's fabric was slightly frayed and there was a smooth, worn spot on the front cover. "You've read it quite a lot."

She wondered why she'd bothered saying something so obvious, or even talking to him at all. If he really was a gambler, from the hurry he was in, he might have debt collectors at his heels. Maybe Madame Marcel would keep them at bay.

"Yes I-I often have it with me," he answered, and there was something in his voice that she hadn't heard before, a softness. "And do you—" he continued, and then, he seemed to stiffen.

It looked as though he was making some effort to stand upright. She wanted to ask if he needed help.

"Thank you again." Orin quickly turned his key in the lock and opened his door.

Wordlessly, she held the book out to him. He reached for it, and without his meaning to, his fingers brushed hers.

It felt like the world was reeling.

Mademoiselle Turin drew back with a soft gasp and Orin shut the door.

On the other side, he sat down on his bed and closed his eyes, trying to settle his racing heart.

The reeling passed quickly and both put it deliberately out of mind. Orin thought that it was simply the rare sensation of ungloved fingers on his. Mademoiselle Turin laughingly told herself that perhaps Monsieur Rush's rushing had been contagious.

~~

The next morning, he heard Mademoiselle Turin and Monsieur Rouline in the corridor and came out of his room. Best to get this done quickly.

"Bonjour, Mademoiselle Turin," he said with deliberate nonchalance. "I'm sorry for taking my leave so abruptly yesterday evening – or rather, not taking any kind of leave at all."

She shook her head. "There's no need to apologize. You were…"

Monsieur Rouline fixed them both curiously.

Orin pressed on. "Every night, I suffer from horrendous headaches. They begin around sundown, and once they set in, I can only lie down and wait for them to end. The headache was starting when we spoke."

Now, compassion took over Mademoiselle Turin's face (as he'd expected). "Oh — I didn't think you were impolite. I could see that you were…in distress."

Orin nodded. Like everyone else, they believed his story. "I'm glad you didn't take offense."

"*I'm* glad there was nothing I could have done. How awful to have had someone just outside the door who was of no help whatsoever."

He was surprised to find himself making a joke: "That would have made me dislike having neighbors even more."

Mademoiselle Turin laughed, then stopped. She hoped he didn't think she was mocking him. "I'm truly sorry to hear about your condition. I suppose you've already seen many doctors?"

"Yes, I have. In America, and now here. I plan to continue, though."

The photographers nodded sympathetically. Perfect, he thought.

"And what brings you to this building- to such a small room?" Monsieur Rouline inquired.

Orin's voice was deliberately light. "Oh, the view, as you know. I've never lived so close to the sky, and I've certainly never woken up every morning to the sight of Parisian rooftops."

"Then you don't live on a high floor where you come from? And where exactly is that, if I may ask?" Émile was grinning, happy to be having this conversation at last.

There was a very short silence before Orin answered, "There are no residences in New York as high as this."

He might have explained that he lived in a brownstone on the Fifth Avenue, but, I realized, he didn't want them to know who he really was. They didn't seem to have recognized his name, so there would be no need to present himself a certain way, or explain any of his actions.

And now, he thought, *I can take my leave properly and be done with all of this.*

Only…. "And – Do you much care for books, as well?" he found himself asking Mademoiselle Turin.

A little flame lit in each of her eyes. "Monsieur Rouline and I are both readers, which helps to fill the time on slow days."

"I know exactly what you mean! Only, for me, it's the nights that are slow —" Orin stopped, noticing her puzzled expression. "That is, when there are lulls in the pain. When I can manage it, reading helps make the time pass more quickly."

He tried to divert their attention from his misstep. "What do you like to read especially?"

"History books. But then, I also love good fiction – or poetry."

"She reads everything!" Monsieur Rouline laughed. "But not enough philosophy."

An hour later, with their *Bonne journées* echoing in his ears, Orin began to descend the staircases. His thoughts veered between two things. The first was a new author called Zola, whose books Mademoiselle Turin called beautiful but without pity. The second was how on earth he'd ended up talking with them – with her, mostly – for so long? That hadn't been his plan at all

II

And he hadn't planned that such a thing would continue. But it did. Every time they crossed paths in the corridor, there was some conversation: books, the city, the weather, the places they'd gone or wished they could go.

~~

I decided to leave Orin for a while and watch Mademoiselle Turin more closely.

She wasn't in the studio when I sought her out the next morning. Instead, I found her in an apartment just below it.

There was a large parlor, with massive bookcases rising from the floor to the ceiling along one wall. I moved towards them to look at the books and objects scattered on their shelves, and then I noticed the floor.

It was almost entirely covered by small buildings and streets – the streets of Paris, I realized, but long ago. The girl lay asleep on a divan above them, like some sort of celestial giant on a green brocade cloud.

Sunlight shone through the slits in the shutters and danced on her face till she woke. I was surprised that her expression was sad, instead of the way she usually looked. But the smile that always played about her lips appeared soon enough. It was as if she were laughing that the sadness still it hadn't gone away.

She stood, stretched, and went to open the shutters, then stared up at the clouds for a while. There wouldn't be light for long enough to open the studio today.

She moved down a long corridor on stockinged feet. Her destination, the kitchen, was a narrow, cluttered place, with long stone countertops on either wall. There was a basin with a pitcher by the window, and a stove beside it. A small object caught my eye. A finely sculpted marble hand that an ancient Roman woman had once used to apply creams and powder to her face now sat on a small shelf, gesturing towards the sugar.

Mademoiselle Turin – whose name I knew at last: Claire - took half a baguette and some cheese from where they lay on one of the somewhat neglected countertops, and walked back up the shadowy corridor to a small dining table in the parlor.

When she'd finished her breakfast, she got dressed. Her dresses were usually simpler than all the frills and fringes and clashing patterns that were in fashion, and yet I'd noticed that she always added some unusual touch to whatever she wore. Today, she put on a dress of deep green that suited her nicely enough. The overskirt was a golden yellow embroidered with red Ottoman roses.

As she stepped out into the corridor and locked her door behind her, something echoed through her: *Now I'm the only one with a key, besides Madame Marcel.* I could tell that thoughts like this came to her often, and when they did, she felt as though she were falling.

"Mrow?"

"Bonjour, Hippolyte." She bent down and extended her hand, and the cat pushed his muzzle into her palm.

After a long petting session, she stood again. *"On y va?"*

Down the stairways they went, a girl with sparkling eyes, a black cat beside her like a shadow.

~~

When they arrived at the ground floor, Hippolyte jumped up to his spot on the bannister for a doze. Claire hung her key on its hook by the concierge's lodge, then passed through the casement doors and followed the stone path to the entryway.

The busy, narrow street meandered for a while and then opened like a breath onto the wide boulevard. Claire wove through the crowds that were beginning to form on the sidewalks, then stepped down and crossed expertly through the morning traffic. She followed a small street southward, then another and another.

The city was fully starting to wake, like turning on a gas light, the hiss a thousandfold louder: shopkeepers unlocking doors, merchants and organ grinders tentatively beginning their songs, the clop of hooves followed by the heavy roll of the omnibus wheels, or the lighter swoosh of the fiacres.

I could feel that Paris invigorated her. Her feet were never painful in her boots, no matter how long she walked.

The Seine was brown under the cloudy sky. Crossing it, Claire thought of the sea, so many windings and waves of the river away. She imagined the smaller river her brother lived by now, with Le Mont-Saint-Michel rising in the distance like some sort of enchantment.

Her thoughts shifted as she reached the Latin Quarter. There, visions of a distant past washed over her, ghosts of the old streets that had disappeared. She strolled along the new ones for a while, and then spent the afternoon browsing through books in the crates the bouquinistes set out every day on the stone walls overlooking the Seine.

~~

Back home, after a short, pleasant chat with Madame Marcel, Claire spent the rest of the evening in her apartment. I discovered that she was the one who had made those extraordinarily detailed miniature streets. They followed a map of the city that was old even before I had first come there. Working on them, constructing little buildings and architectural elements, adding details with a fine brush, brought her a sense of escape and joy.

Eating the mediocre supper she'd cooked, however, did not. But a pastry she'd kept for dessert cheered her a little.

Long after nightfall, she lay down on the sofa and struggled to fall asleep. I noticed that she never seemed to go into the bedroom.

Reading thoughts is not always an easy task. And it's even more difficult to fall into someone's memories. They have to be unguarded, and so do I. In a moment just before sleep, Claire Turin was lost in a memory, and so, I let myself in.

We were in a bright place – the studio. Windows of slightly blue-tinted glass made up the better part of one wall and the ceiling. But the brightness didn't come solely from the sunlight shining through them. The people who were there also illuminated the room. I recognized them from the photographs at the top of the stairs: Her mother and father, still alive, her brother Paul, still in Paris.

Her father and his assistant, the wild-haired Émile Rouline, were discussing the preparation of the plates. Her mother was putting away some costumes they'd used for the last sitting. Paul went to fetch the morning journals. Claire sat dreamily near the doorway, imagining what she might set up for the next sitter. Her father had begun to let her collaborate with him….

….And now her memories dissolved into dreams, and she slept.

I stayed with her. She needed company, even though she certainly didn't know I was there.

The next morning, the sun woke her from behind the shutters again. She looked out the window and gave a nod, then dressed and hurried to the boulangerie for some bread and three small brioches, stopping by the butcher's as well before returning home.

After putting all but two of the brioches in the kitchen, she left again, this time climbing the stairs to the sixth floor, mindful of her bustle as she took the turns.

Émile was waiting on the little bench outside the studio. She handed him a brioche and he greeted her the way I knew he did nearly every morning, "You shouldn't have, woman!"

Émile was her father's dearest friend. "We were young men in Paris together," he'd often told Claire and her brother. This alone, they should understand, was enough. He'd employed Émile in his studio ever since he'd started his business, nearly two decades before. But it wasn't solely friendship that made him keep his friend there. Émile manipulated the plates with the grace of a waltz.

Claire had grown up in the studio. She, too, had never seen such deft movements. Émile's hands never faltered. Any blurs or imperfections were the fault of Claire or her father, or the sitter not keeping still.

~~

I don't believe I had ever seen a photograph's creation – at least, not this new sort. It began with taking a polished pane of glass through many steps of smoothing, chemical coatings, cleaning, dipping, then setting it into a special frame. All of that was what Émile did.

Meanwhile, Claire did the work that the rest of her family used to do. She greeted sitters, as her mother had. This wasn't as unusual as watching a photograph be developed, but it was important to me in its own way.

Everyone seemed warmed by Claire's warmth. After a pleasant conversation, she'd give clients a few albums to look through for inspiration, and when they'd chosen a pose they liked, she brought them over to the backdrops. There were so many; the Turins, I could tell, had always been a bit theatrical. After the sitter made their choice, she'd secure the backdrop and then motion them to sit or stand in front of it, helping them find the right position, as her father used to.

That done, she turned to the camera.

Once she'd adjusted the lenses to the right focus, Émile brought out the plate in its holder, protected from the light. Claire inserted it into a slot near the back of the camera, then, in a single, smooth movement, she lifted the front of the frame. The glass pane would be exposed to the light as soon as she removed the cover from one of four small lenses at the camera's other end.

Before doing so, "*Ne bougez plus*," she'd warn the sitter in a soft breath.

After a wait that most mortals found interminable, but was only a question of seconds, Claire covered that lens and let the sitter relax for a moment. Then, she'd uncover another of the lenses and they'd start again: "*Ne bougez plus!*".

It went on for a time, Claire shifting and adjusting the plate and covering and uncovering lenses. When she finished, Émile would come to take the plate in its holder back to the darkroom, where he performed many more ministrations. At last, an image would begin to form, the dark parts light, the light parts dark, like some otherworldly reflection.

After this, the plate was moved to another frame, where it was pressed tight against special paper. Émile then brought it to sit on a table beneath the windows, and the sunlight would do its part.

In the end, there would be one sheet, or more, if the sitter requested, of a grid of small images that would be cut and mounted and end up as cartes de visite – those photographic calling cards that were popular at the time.

Later, if the sitter (who'd gone by now) had requested it, Claire would take out her set of paintbrushes and add color to cheeks, a pupil onto an accidentally closed eye, perhaps some gilding onto a military decoration. Her father had often told her that her coloring work was excellent, but she preferred the way the images first appeared, rather than covered with something false.

Their work was long and meticulous, but like Claire and Émile, I never found it dull, no matter how many sittings I watched. There was something magical about an image suddenly appearing on a clear pane of glass, even when you knew why.

~~

As she'd told Orin, when they waited for sitters to arrive, Claire and Émile mostly spent their time reading. Her books of choice were usually about the history of Paris, although she also read novels and poetry. Émile mostly read newspapers and philosophy. Often, he'd voice his thoughts on some complicated philosophical concept or another – or at least, Claire thought, they were certainly worded to seem complicated. Sometimes she understood him, but other times what he said just seemed like a flood.

Some days, she could tell that it was difficult for Émile to be there. This was part of him, something that others might call madness, something he had once or twice told her was a curse. His energy waxed and waned like tides, but without any kind of predictability. When the tide was high, she got many lessons in philosophy.

Their workday ended when the daylight faded. They tidied up and then Émile gave her an affectionate kiss on the cheek and walked homeward to his apartment in the Latin Quarter.

Claire went down the stairs to her apartment, where she spent some time on her models. Finally, her growling belly reminded her she should have supper. She went to the kitchen and tried to make something of the meat she'd bought at the butcher's that morning.

After supper, she read until she couldn't keep her eyes open. Then, she changed into a nightgown, washed her face, and went to sleep – or tried.

She lay on the sofa, trying to conjure a thought to calm her. She liked to imagine the places her parents had traveled to. When they'd met, they'd liked to say, their hearts were so wild that they couldn't stay in one place. They'd decided to see as much of the world as they could, using money her father had inherited from his family (I had a brief glimpse of her imagery of a dull bourgeois upbringing in the countryside). There was a whirl of countries and landscapes that stopped at Constantinople, the city where they decided to come back and make a life in Paris, since Paul was well on the way.

Sleep didn't come, so she tried to think of something else. The story of the apartment, for instance. It had been made from one large apartment and a smaller one. I delved into her memories now.

As a girl, she would sleep on a divan in the corner of the parlor. There was a fine fireplace with a mirror over it that her mother had been surprisingly proud of. The usual trappings of bourgeois life had never seemed to interest her, except for that mirror with its gilded frame. Growing up, Claire would often see her glance over at it with a look of satisfaction. Or maybe it was what was reflected in it that made her feel content – those massive shelves stuffed with books, papers, and photographic paraphernalia, as well as the odd sculpture or exotic object she and Claire's father had come upon in their travels.

As a family, they'd never traveled much, besides trips to the country and the occasional one to the seaside. They were too occupied with the demands of their studio. These were the years when cartes de visite were novelties and all the rage.

Work wasn't always as regular as they would have liked, but at least they never had to worry about being hungry or without a home. The fortune her father had inherited had allowed him to purchase their apartment, as well as the studio, and ensured they'd never want for anything.

Now her thoughts drifted again to the old days in the studio. Those memories carried her to sleep.

~~

When she was still, I leaned close and listened to her heart.

Claire might have been lonely, but she knew she lived a remarkably free life. Any man she fell in love with might steal that away from her. Maybe it would simply be opinions on how to run the studio. Or maybe he'd insist she stop working altogether, or dress a certain way, or behave in some fashion that restricted her but earned his approval.

She was determined not to bother with anyone unless they were intriguing and loved her as she was. I saw many flirting customers gracefully deterred; handsome actors from the theaters on the boulevards subtly encouraged to see her as a sister.

None of this had been difficult. She'd never been in love and didn't plan on that changing.

It had been a long time since I'd seen Orin. I flew upwards and rested by his bedside.

12

That afternoon, Orin and Joseph sat at a café table on the boulevard. It was the sort of day that calls you to do nothing but have a glass of lemonade. Their serious conversation was as incongruous as a winter greatcoat in the warm weather.

"How goes your research?" Joseph asked, sipping from his glass.

"Not terribly well, as my nights show. But there may be something."

"Oh?"

In the back of Orin's mind, the thought of that card at the bookshop prickled. Still, he didn't much believe it. "Maybe a secret society – only, not really terribly secret, since they've posted an advertisement at a bookshop I go to."

"So, then," Joseph forged onward. "Are we planning to stay for a while yet? *I'd* like to."

"So would I."

"We'll have to write Father. Of course, it will be easy, as you have that bookshop lead to go on."

"Yes. Although, we should probably be taking a train to small villages where there were werewolf sightings, or…but then, those happened so long ago. And anyway," He looked around, "it would be hard to leave just now, wouldn't it?"

They sat quietly for a while, relishing the late afternoon sunlight, pale gold glowing down from the powder blue sky.

At last, Joseph yawned languidly and said, "I've been meaning to get some cartes de visite made. How's that photographer in your building?"

"Mademoiselle Turin? Her photographs are extraordinary. You've seen a few in by the door, and in the stairwell."

"*Mademoiselle* Turin?" Joseph smiled broadly. "I had no idea you'd met the photographer, let alone that she's a woman and—"

Orin ignored him. "It's probably too late now. The daylight's already fading. You might as well go to Nadar's – he's close and his *atelier* has electric lighting."

He remembered Claire telling him this during one of their frequent morning talks. They didn't always have time to stop for long, but often there were at least a few words exchanged – a remark on the weather, a book one or the other had liked, Claire's insistence that he try a pastry at a particular boulangerie (she was shocked when he confessed he didn't much care for pastries).

"And it's supposed to be quite elegant," he went on. "Mademoiselle Turin's studio is small and —"

"- But you said her photographs are extraordinary."

"Of course," Orin agreed. He wasn't sure what to say next, but then the perfect, distracting dig came to him: "She has a way of really showing a sitter's personality. She's especially good with dogs."

"Well, if she can do that with a dog, I'd think she could with me," Joseph agreed amicably. "If you don't mind, I'll come by tomorrow morning, if there's sunshine."

"Of course," Orin said again.

They were silent a while more, watching the crowds on the boulevard pass by, women in skirts with those elaborate, garishly colored layers and trimmings, children whining and tired at the end of the day, beggars staggering along with hands outstretched. And beyond, the traffic, omnibuses fighting with cabs and fiacres, carts with heavy, lumbering horses carrying loads to other parts of the city, and everyone calling out: street merchants vaunting their wares, gentlemen at the tables in political arguments, a singer in a distant café, the drivers yelling to each other in accents so broad and words so vulgar that the brothers sometimes had no idea what exactly was being said.

Orin shifted and gave a sigh. "Well, I should be getting back."

Joseph watched as he picked up something that was resting beside his chair. His brother often had a book with him, but this was a large, flat, parcel wrapped in colorfully printed paper.

"What's *that*?"

I could feel a twinge of frustration from Orin. But then, it quickly faded to acceptance. After all, anyone would have noticed such a parcel. "There's a shop called À La Porte Chinoise – it's quite extraordinary. They sell things from all over the Orient. These are some prints I found by a Japanese artist called Hiroshige. He's —"

"You must be eager to have a look at them, to be leaving so soon. Or perhaps Mademoiselle Turin is also interested in prints by an artist called Hiroshige?"

Joseph knew him too well, only, not at all. He had no romantic intentions, Orin thought with annoyance. He only wanted to show them to her, after she'd shown him the photographs her family had taken of the Japanese Pavilion at the Exposition Universelle that had been in Paris just a few years before. Unlike pastries, it turned out they both liked Japan.

"I can't imagine why you think there's some romance between me and a neighbor I barely know."

"I'm sorry, Orry. It just – you spoke of her with so much admiration, and you know, it's entirely reasonable to fall in love now and then."

"You know that's the farthest thing from my mind."

"Farther than Japan," Joseph muttered.

"Exactly."

"It's all right, Orry, I was only teasing. You know that's what happens when I'm idle for too long."

"Have a nice evening," Orin said. "I'll expect you around ten tomorrow?"

Joseph groaned. "I'll try to manage it"

~~

Crossing the threshold of the studio was like swallowing a horrid drink in one gulp. Ever since the enchantment, Orin had hated cameras. He couldn't be sure what a photograph might reveal. He deliberately avoided looking at the dreaded device a few feet away, and gave a single, wary glance to another one lurking in a far corner. Then, he tried to forget them.

"I wanted to show you something I found today," he said to Mademoiselle Turin, "- if you have some time."

She nodded, intrigued, and he followed her to a low table and unwrapped the parcel, opening the cardboard cover of a dossier.

At the sight of the bright, acid colors of the first print, Claire's eyes grew wide. She drew it out and stared, then handed it to Orin, distractedly, taking in the next one.

She examined each of the prints so meticulously. Her eyes shone even more brightly than usual. "The colors," she murmured, "they're like fruit…"

"Yes! They are, come to think of it!" Orin exclaimed.

They continued to gaze at these impressions of daily life so far away from theirs.

"Look at this one!" Claire held up a print of a turtle that hung from a string attached to a window frame. A trick of perspective made it appear as though it loomed over the faraway Mount Fuji.

"That one is my favorite," Orin remarked when she came to a street scene under a full moon. "Change their clothing and the style of architecture, and they could be strolling down one of the boulevards here."

"I wonder what this is?" She reached towards what looked like some sort of stall, while he moved to point to the balconies on the rooftops. Their hands were so close — the world reeled.

They drew back, looking away from each other and that image where their fingers had nearly met. After a moment, Claire laid the print aside and held up the next one, without a word.

They stared at landscapes, at a solitary cat admiring the view of that same mountain from a large window, "with his feet tucked under him like Hippolyte when it's cold," Claire murmured.

A few sheets further on, she gasped. In the starry sky above a distant mountain, a hawk hovered, its form surprisingly curled as it fixed something on the ground. "This is magnificent."

Then, she felt something change. Orin had that same stiff posture he'd had the day of the dropped book.

"Oh – the headache's coming." There was disappointment in her voice, he noticed. Of course; she hadn't finished looking at the prints.

"Keep them with you tonight."

"I couldn't —"

But he was already leaving the studio.

13

Around ten o'clock the next morning, Claire was surprised to see Monsieur Rush and another man standing on the other side of the door.

"Bonjour," Orin nodded, lowering his eyes from the studio's blinding light. "This is my brother, Joseph."

Now she noticed the finely cut frock coat. This was the man who'd been with Monsieur Rush on the day he'd moved his trunks up the stairs.

Orin wanted to apologize for forgetting to tell her about this yesterday evening, but more than that he didn't want to put any ideas into Joseph's head, so he stayed silent.

"It's a pleasure to make your acquaintance," she said, her warm smile giving truth to her words.

Joseph concealed his curiosity about this woman behind a great deal of charm. "The pleasure is mine, Mademoiselle Turin. I hear you take extraordinary photographs. And since I consider myself extraordinary, I thought I'd see if I might arrange for a sitting?"

Claire grinned. "I'd be glad to take your photograph. You'll make fine subjects."

"Oh," Joseph said breezily, "I'll be the only sitter today."

"Oh?"

"My brother hasn't told you? He hates having his picture taken." He turned to look at Orin, who glared at him, then turned back to her. "It's nothing against you, Mademoiselle Turin."

Claire was surprised by how disappointed she felt. "No harm done," she said to Orin. "You're far from the only person who doesn't like being photographed. I've heard that some people, like Balzac – and even Nadar himself – think the camera takes away a little layer of the soul each time it captures your image."

Joseph laughed. "Should I be worried, mademoiselle?"

"Oh no," she smiled. "I don't believe that. But I do believe that it's a photographer's job to *reveal* something of your soul." Orin watched her eyes sparkle as she said this. Then, her voice became businesslike. "That's what we'll try to do now. Extraordinary…cartes de visite?"

Joseph nodded.

"…for an extraordinary gentleman. Let's choose a background." They walked together to the far end of the studio.

Orin hoped she would be too distracted by his brother's careful inspection of the backdrops to notice that he hadn't moved very far from the doorway.

After a long while, Joseph decided on a backdrop depicting a parlor with a large window looking onto a forest of tall pine trees. "It's as if I'm at once in civilized Europe and the wilderness of the American frontier!" he exclaimed delightedly.

Orin rolled his eyes. "Not that we've ever been to the frontier."

"True. But many of the French people I've met believe the contrary."

"I'm sure there's a bit of wildness in you," Mademoiselle Turin assured him.

"I'm sure there's a wilderness," Orin added absently, and she stopped for a moment, thinking, *That's what there is in me.* Thickets of loneliness, brambles of fear, laughter shining down like sunlight through leaves….

Claire shook the distracting thoughts away and moved towards the camera, while Émile set the prepared plate into place. "But you're also quite civilized, monsieur," she remarked, "to know that black is a better color to be photographed in than blue – at least, if you want your coat to look dark in the carte de visite."

Joseph looked very satisfied with himself. "Yes, I've read a bit on the subject, not on photography as such, but on how to be photographed."

Claire shot a laughing look to Orin, who gave her the same.

And then, before Joseph could ask how she'd known about his blue coat — and be flattered that she remembered it - the first image of the set was taken. Claire covered the first lens and stood ready to uncover another.

"You think that will make a good carte de visite?" Joseph asked doubtfully, placing himself in a more elegant posture.

The moment he'd finished, with a somewhat defiant look on his face, Mademoiselle Turin uttered her near-whispered command: "*Ne bougez plus!*"

As uneasy as Orin was to be there, he knew he would have regretted missing this. Her whispered voice had something of magic in it.

She uncovered the second lens.

"Shall we try one with you wearing your hat?" she asked when that pose was finished. Joseph obliged.

For the fourth, they discussed things for a time, how Joseph liked Paris, what he did in his free time, what he wanted his carte de visite to convey to those he'd give or send it to — and as he described this — "*Ne bougez plus*," she said softly, like a breath, and took the final photo.

The darkroom was too small a space for them to follow Émile inside, which was a pity. Only he and I saw the grid of negative images appear on the glass pane, row after row of Joseph. It didn't matter that the images were upside-down, that his dark clothes were white, his face and hands coal black. I could already see that Mademoiselle Turin had captured him perfectly.

~~

Joseph liked every pose and decided to have cards made with each. Four different cartes de visite — "So that people will invite me to call more often, in order to have the complete set," he told them, with a wry smile. Orin suspected he was only half joking.

"I think we should celebrate Mademoiselle Turin's fine work!" Joseph went on. "And Monsieur Rouline's as well, of course. I'd like to invite you both to lunch, along with my brother."

"Oh no, monsieur," Claire protested, out of pride and perhaps a sort of protection. Rich men who took women out for meals often wanted other things. But then, she reminded herself, why would they be interested in her, when all the women of Paris were in their reach? And anyway, they'd asked Émile to come, too.

"Oh that's very kind, but certainly not necessary," Émile demurred. Was this a ruse by the apparently wealthy American to get out of paying?

"Joseph, perhaps they have other plans," Orin said softly, caught between a surprising happiness at the idea, and a worry that crept over him – what would they talk about? How could they fill the time?

Joseph nodded. "If that's the case, I hope you'll forgive me. I presumed that as it's nearing lunch hour, you might be free...."

But with his remorseful expression, Émile's feeling of reassurance once he'd seen him draw out a large bundle of francs to pay what was owed, and the temptation of not having to cook, Joseph had them.

~~

So they all went down the stairs together, Joseph and Claire leading the way, chatting merrily, and Émile joining in now and then. Orin came up behind, the worry and excitement still vying in him.

The street outside hummed with the low roar of a living city. The sun shone down, blindly bright. The air was nearly too hot. For a giddy moment, Orin thought of bringing them to Tortoni's for an ice cream.

But he and Joseph were the type of wealthy people who are rarely ostentatious when it's not called for. Joseph led them to a far more ordinary brasserie.

The place was full of talk and laughter, and so crowded they were lucky to find a table. Orin was surprised to realize at some point that he hadn't noticed the time passing, and that their table was contributing its share to the noise around them.

Even after their many conversations in the sixth-floor corridor, he and Mademoiselle Turin still had so much to say to each other, he discovered. And whenever she answered a question he might have, or made an observation of her own, there was so much to it. She was like a book you could never reach the end of. There would always be some detail to ponder, some hidden or omitted story to imagine or wonder about, and, sometimes, wondrous revelations.

Joseph and Émile took part in the conversation as well, of course. But I noticed that often they let the two others talk, and only looked on with a sort of knowing expression.

Finally, the photographers had to take their leave.

"Thank you for a lovely lunch," Claire gave Joseph a smile and then quickly nodded to Orin.

"What a pity it's not a cloudy afternoon," Joseph replied. She and Émile nodded in agreement, then made their way through the tables back onto the boulevard.

~~

Orin had already reached his door by the time Mademoiselle Turin, who'd been listening, managed to open hers. "Monsieur Rush!" she called out.

He turned, almost in spite of himself. "Good evening, Mademoiselle Turin."

"Sorry to disturb you, but I forgot to return these to you today." She was holding the folder of Hiroshige prints.

"Oh – well," he grinned, "a visit from Joseph would distract anyone." But his put-on carelessness didn't work. "You could have kept them longer," he added, his voice softer now.

I could feel her guilt at being tempted. Monsieur Rush suffered all night and these sublime images might transport him for a while, she reminded herself. She had enough in her apartment to take her away. "It's all right. I assure you, I've kept them in my mind's eye. Thank you again for lending them to me."

She held out the long folder and he took the other end. There was no way for their fingers to meet.

Orin tucked the folder beneath his arm and moved to put the key in the lock. "Have a nice evening," he told her.

"You, too." She paled. "That is - I hope the prints will bring you some distraction."

To my surprise, Orin gave a genuine laugh. "I understood what you meant!"

Inside his room, he sat on the floor and opened the folder. Maybe the change wouldn't be so bad if he could lose himself in those beautiful images. But all he could think of were her hands touching each sheet.

14

Was this the start of something?

Maybe Orin's story was changing.

But then another change came that threatened everything.

One day, the Emperor finally gave in to those around him who'd been begging for a war.

It was a rather stupid matter that caused it. A French ambassador had been sent to bother Kaiser Wilhelm in the spa town of Ems, insisting he swear that no Hohenzollern would ever accept the Spanish throne. An annoying request, not to mention beyond the Kaiser's powers and lifespan. The Kaiser refused and the matter was ended, or it would have been if not for a telegram.

One of his staff had sent word to Bismarck, who published his own deliberately insulting account of what had happened in the press. This set the French into a rage.

That, of all things, is what forced the Emperor to declare their wished-for war.

"They'll surely lose." Joseph's words were muffled by the noise that roared in from behind the shutters of the suite at the Grand Hôtel. They were used to the noise by now; there had been rioting on the boulevards just a few days before.

"I've heard rumors that the telegram wasn't that bad, really. Bismarck exaggerated, hoping it would lead to war. Clever bastard."

Orin grinned, but it quickly faded. "If that's the case, what he's done is truly horrible, whether it unites the Germans or not. How many soldiers will die? And civilians?"

The civilians in question didn't seem concerned with that, though. It was as if all of Paris had turned out onto the streets, fervently patriotic, singing the long-banished *Marseillaise*, waving and draping the *tricolore* everywhere.

What fools to celebrate war and butchery, what fools not to realize what was to come.

It's true that things weren't perfect before. The poor had been pushed out of the newly beautiful city center. The press was censored. A man named Victor Noir had been shot point-blank by Pierre Bonaparte, who faced no repercussions. And it *was* the 19th century, an age of revolutions, after all. Things would have changed one way or another.

But maybe not in this way.

The brothers had no personal ties to anyone who'd be called onto the battlefield, and no obligation to fight. They knew that what was going to happen would be terrible. They could leave, as many of their rich friends were doing.

But this was Paris, and they were in love with it, and not finished.

"So then," Joseph said, raising his voice above the din, "are we staying? *I'd* like to."

Orin nodded. "So would I."

15

The roaring didn't die down as the day did.

"Perhaps you should stay here for the night," Joseph suggested.

Orin shook his head. "I'll be fine. I can hum the song, anyway." Another round of the *Marseillaise* had started up outside.

"Fine." Joseph stood up from his chair and walked over to one of his trunks. "Take this," he instructed.

"You know I won't fire a gun."

"Come to think of it, your aversion to firearms may be an advantage at the moment. You don't want to draw any attention or get caught by the police."

"I'll be fine — and if I'm not, I expect you'll hear about it."

The Place de l'Opéra was chaotic, but large enough that Orin was able to make his way towards the eastern stretches of the boulevards. But once he reached the Boulevard Haussmann, the crowd was tightly packed and relentlessly flowing in both directions.

Though he was concentrated only on getting back home, certain sights stayed with him: a group burning a crude effigy of the Kaiser; tired children waving little flags as they trailed alongside parents whose faces were alight with zealotry; a man and a woman kissing passionately, her chignon all but undone. Masses of people undulated like flags at the café terraces, singing patriotic songs or listening to speeches and proclamations shouted over the rest of the noise.

At last Orin reached his street. It was quieter here. When he came to his building, he saw that the shops on the ground floor were shut, their wooden curtains down. The entry doors were closed, as well, as they never were in daytime.

He stared and prepared to knock. Then he remembered something that Joseph had explained to him. *"Cordon, s'il vous plaît!"* he ventured. Nothing happened. "It's Monsieur Rush," he called out.

One of the massive doors opened.

Orin stepped through it and shut himself firmly inside. When he passed through the casement doors, Madame Marcel was standing outside of her lodge. "I'm sorry, Monsieur Rush. I thought it might be best to shut the doors in case …."

"Of course."

"What a turn everything has taken," the concierge muttered. "I wonder what will happen now?"

"I wish I could say," Orin told her earnestly, and yet, there was something distracted about him. He took his leave and started up the stairs.

As he climbed, I noticed something very strange. The soft buds and thorny stems of the roses seemed to rise ever so slightly from the carpet.

I thought it was some sort of trick of the light. But then I saw Hippolyte picking his way awkwardly over them until he gave up and moved to the uncarpeted sides of the stairs. Further up, I heard a muffled curse as, I imagine, one of the building's other residents caught his foot in the stems and nearly fell.

Orin didn't seem to notice. He moved steadily up the staircases, looking ahead. When he reached the sixth floor, instead of going to his room, he knocked on the studio door. Émile opened it, grinning.

"What a din! Have you ever seen anything like it?"

Orin thought for a moment. He'd watched parades and protests, patriotic celebrations and fervor during the War of the Rebellion, had experienced his own small portion of the chaos and terror of the Draft Riots. And yet, none of it had been like this, not exactly. There was a wild abandon to the people here that wasn't quite the same in New York – perhaps because, at the heart of things, those in New York longed for a prosperous life, while those here longed for ideals.

"No," he said simply. He was too tired to elaborate – and, I suddenly understood, too preoccupied.

"Monsieur Rush!" Claire walked towards them from the back of the studio, where she'd been tidying the props in an armoire. "We went outside for a short time, to see what all the fuss was about. What madness, don't you think?"

Orin nodded. "And are you – Now that there's a war, perhaps you and Émile will go to stay with your families?"

"Haw!" came Émile's guffaw. "My family fears me more than any war!"

He saw Claire stifle a laugh. Then, she looked at him, suddenly serious. "I'm staying, too. I'm sorry for this war – you-you could have had more time to search for a proper doctor." She turned away and looked fixedly through the windows on the ceiling, intent on the clouds drifting across the sky.

"I might find one still." Orin was surprised at how easily the words came to him. "I'm staying, as well."

Claire closed her eyes against the sun. "Well then, we'll face the war together."

Now Orin, too, seemed to find the clouds fascinating. "It seems we will."

76

16

Little more than two weeks later, the Parisians got news of the Battle of Wissembourg. A defeat, a disaster.

That afternoon, Orin entered the suite at the Grand Hôtel and gave a start.

Heavy wooden trunks lined the walls. "Are we leaving after all?"

Joseph shook his head. "These, in fact, are to help us stay."

Orin walked to the nearest trunk and lifted its lid. Inside were carefully stacked tins. He took one out. "Peaches?"

"And ham and beans and just about anything you can get in a tin in Paris. The French are losing the war already, Orry. They're saying at the Embassy that it won't be long before we're besieged. And tins are the answer – the French don't buy them much and would never think to make a reserve of them."

Orin didn't answer right away. What was happening and what could happen seemed more real now that his usually unflappable brother was frightened. "Brilliant," he said at last. "You've found the only way I might ever have considered eating tinned ham."

I saw Joseph's unusually worried face relax into a smile. "Yes, that might be one of the few things I'm looking forward to."

17

The sandy pathways are lined with incongruous lampposts and trees whose branches are hung with lights. If you follow one of these paths, you'll end up in a large clearing where dancers are leaping, kicking, caterwauling.

Claire plays the game she always plays when they come here, to the Bal Mabille. From her bench at the edge of the clearing, she tries to spot her friend Anne in the crowd of wildly moving limbs and skirts and coattails.

I use her thoughts to learn who this thin, tallish young woman with pretty, pert features, fashionable dress, and dernier cri hat might be. They grew up, I discover, in the same Parisian neighborhood, attended the same school. Anne is a milliner, which explains her striking headwear: a small emerald satin hat worn high on her hair, tipped with three curling black feathers that glisten green whenever they catch the light.

The air is heavy and everyone shines with perspiration. But the thick crowd of musicians in the pavilion at the center of the clearing are far from sluggish – they play loudly and incessantly. Carried by their energy, the notes rush between the trees and lampposts.

Claire idly watches the people around her. Those who aren't dancing are strolling and talking together. Some exchange glances and steal away from the clearing, into the leafy shadows. Men nervously offer drinks to the lady they think is the most beautiful there – or the most available. Other ladies sit on benches, fanning themselves, waiting.

It seems like the perfect place to fall in love, or at least to have a romantic adventure. But Claire never feels like the others here, no matter how much she likes to watch them dance, no matter the occasional time she's joined in, herself. There have been times, too, when a man has bought her a drink and sat with her for a while. There have been a few furtive kisses.

But there was always a distance between them. Most of the men were kind, many handsome. A few had made her laugh. But it was as if each of them were humming a tune the other couldn't hear.

Here in this enchanted garden, Claire has spent many evenings considering what she's usually able to ignore: she's never been in love.

Why had she never met a man with the same song inside of him?

The noise of the music dulls conversations, but you can hear by the cadences of voices that the Bal Mabille hasn't lost its reputation as a must-visit place for tourists, or at least for the foreigners who are cautiously staying in the city, whatever their reasons. Italians, Portuguese, Dutch, Americans….

"Why," Anne laughed, coming back to their bench, breathless, "you're *smiling*! You were supposed to tell me it was time to leave by now! What's got into you?"

"Nothing. It's nice to be out."

Her friend sat beside her, an eyebrow raised. "Who is this new man in your life?"

Claire gave a start. "Now *you're* the one acting strange!"

Anne nodded, playing along. "Well, be careful."

"No need," Claire retorted.

~~

"It's his birthday tomorrow," she giddily confided sometime later, after she'd had a few drinks.

She thought of the letter she and Émile had received that morning:

> *Mes chers amis, I hope you will do me the honor of attending a surprise performance I have organized for my brother's birthday, tomorrow at 4 o'clock, at the address below. Cordially, Joseph Rush*

"Then you must give him a present!" Anne laughed, when she told her.

They left the glowing, roaring clearing, the couples coming together just beyond the lights, the dancers still yelling and leaping, the women kicking up their legs, the men howling like dogs.

"My feet are tired," Anne said, "let's take a cab."

Claire gave her a surprised look.

"It's been a profitable summer, and a long time since I've been out. It's my treat."

In the cab, they sat close together and looked up, trying to make out stars beyond the gaslights all the way home.

"Good night," Anne said when they reached her building. "And good luck with this fellow. Tell me more about him someday." She kissed her softly on the cheeks, and then gave the driver Claire's address, slipping him a few more sous.

Normally, Claire would have protested – she could have easily walked from there, after all – but she was lost in thought.

It was rare for her to see her building's doors shut. They seemed like giants.

"*Cordon, s'il vous plaît!*" she called out, pulling the rope that would ring the bell in Madame Marcel's lodge. Madame Marcel obliged and pulled the cord that opened the door.

She'd been asleep, Claire thought guiltily: the lodge was quiet and closed, and no light shone from under the door. She fumbled for her key on the hook and then for her candlestick on the table, and headed a bit unsteadily upstairs. The carpet felt strange around her heels, like walking through weedy grass.

~~

Thanks to windows she'd left open, her cavernous apartment was cool. She lit a lamp and went to the kitchen where, mercifully, there was a pitcher of water. After downing a glass, she put some more on a cloth and dabbed herself.

Back in the parlor, she gazed at her models lined up along the floor. Maybe she'd work a little.

But she stopped and turned to the tall bookshelves instead.

Standing on the tips of her stockinged toes, she reached for an album of photographs – one of many on that same shelf. This album had a cover of olive-green leather, embossed with the year 1867. Not so long ago at all, and yet, she thought, feeling an emptiness in the pit of her stomach, it seemed as though a lifetime had passed.

Lifetimes had ended.

She leafed quickly through the thick cardboard pages. In their cut-out frames were photographs, some slightly blurred, of pagodas and women in Japanese dress, and images of her and Paul smilingly holding a placard marked 'Exposition Universelle'. She flinched and turned to the next page. There it was.

When she'd finished, she sat still for a while. Then, taking a deep breath, she left her apartment and went up the staircase to the sixth floor.

She wouldn't knock and risk waking him. Sleep must be precious to someone who suffered so much. So, at the top of the stairs, she took her boots off and crept along in her stockings. She was certain Monsieur Rush wouldn't hear her. It had been a family joke that Claire was excellent at moving through the apartment without making a sound when she wanted to.

Her reputation was well-founded. Despite his acute senses, Orin never heard a thing. It may have been, simply, that he'd unexpectedly fallen into a deep sleep, his lamp still lit. Just that night, he'd found a new solution to his room's stifling heat: in addition to keeping the window open behind the curtains (held in place at the bottom with heavy books), he'd placed a block of ice in a raised dish at each end of the bed.

As I observed this, I also spotted something else. There was no key in the keyhole. I ached to wake him, to warn him....

On the other side of the door, Claire knelt down to place the now-framed photograph on the floor beside it. She set a note on top:

> *Dear Monsieur Rush,*
>
> *This is a photograph my father took at the Japanese pavilion of the Exposition Universelle. Doesn't it look a bit like the Hiroshige print you like, with the crowds milling around? I hope it brings you joy and that you will look at it whenever you want to take an imaginary voyage. And I hope that one day, you'll take a real one to Japan.*
>
> *Happy birthday,*
>
> *Claire Turin*

The thought of him finding it the next morning made her smile.

Still, lost in thought as she was, she couldn't help noticing something. There was a smell, strong and strange, but somehow familiar. It was the smell of wild animals, a smell like the zoo.

She stood up and sniffed the air. It didn't seem to be coming from the hallway in either direction, or from the studio. It seemed to be coming from behind Monsieur Rush's door.

No, no, no! I screamed soundlessly.

Confusion and curiosity overcame any reserve she normally would have had. She quietly lowered herself to the level of the keyhole – where that blasted key should have been – and placed her eye against it.

The light didn't surprise her –it had helped her find the keyhole in the first place. Inside, though, she was intrigued by a pile of black fur on what must have been the bed.

It was impossible to tell what exactly it was, and where Monsieur Rush was in all of it. She stared for a while longer, and then, realizing it was useless, finally drew herself up and crept back down the hall.

As she put on her boots, the giddiness of the evening disappeared. Maybe she'd been too forward in leaving her present there. Monsieur Rush didn't like having neighbors, and now he'd wake and find something one of them had left at his very door, reminding him how little privacy he had.

She'd give her gift to Monsieur Rush when she and Émile joined him the following afternoon. She crept down the hallway again and took back the photograph and her note, and still Orin slept, the fool

18

C laire woke feeling the way you might expect after a long night of dancing and indulging. I was grateful: maybe she'd forgotten about the smell and what she'd seen. Maybe we had nothing to fear.

Then, she turned with a groan and spotted the framed photograph and her note on the low table beside her.

It came back to her, of course, and she wondered about it as she slowly, stiffly got dressed. She'd probably just seen a coat or coverlet on Monsieur Rush's bed. But then, what was the smell? Maybe she'd gotten close to the cab's horse and the smell of him had lingered in her nose?

Unlikely, she thought as she went to the kitchen to see if there was anything for breakfast. She ground up some coffee beans, regretting it as she tried.

19

L e Théâtre Robert-Houdin." Joseph came to a stop. "Did you know it was here?"

"I must have, before." There was a sad and distant expression on Orin's face.

How thrilled his old self would have been. The legendary magician no longer performed here, but the illusions and automatons he'd created would still be in the show, surely. But, Orin reminded himself, he was no longer the boy perfecting card tricks, dreaming of dazzling spectators at a performance.

"All right, let's keep going."

"This is our destination."

"There aren't any shows in the afternoon."

Orin didn't need to look at the plaque near the doorway that informed potential spectators that the performances took place at 8 o'clock; he still remembered it from Robert-Houdin's autobiography, which he'd read many times as a boy.

But he *didn't* know that one night about a week ago, Joseph had made the acquaintance of a certain Monsieur François Eugène Lahire. They got along famously – or Joseph made sure that they did, once he discovered that Monsieur Lahire was none other than Cleverman, the magician who currently ran and performed at the Théâtre Robert-Houdin. After some discussion, some laughter, some wine, Joseph offered a formidable price for a private afternoon performance.

For some reason, I could never read very deeply into Joseph's thoughts, and there was much I didn't know about him. But this I did know: Joseph was a good brother.

Another thing that I knew about Joseph was that he didn't really follow rules – or, I should say, not the ones he didn't care for. He fit perfectly into New York society, as well as all of the desirable expatriate and local circles in Paris. He attended the obligatory events and suppers, outings and evenings at the theater or the opera, and seemed quite content.

He could have insisted on introducing Orin to some of the wealthy, well-born young ladies he knew, hoping that some sort of love or affection – or at the very least, a credible illusion of those things– would blossom, and his brother could experience life, perhaps even make a favorable marriage (complicated as that would be).

But that wasn't what he'd chosen to do.

Joseph was one of those people who love *love*, and hold it sacred. When Orin was around Mademoiselle Turin, he was happy and seemed like himself. No feigned interest, no closing himself away…well, significantly less than usual.

This wasn't what their family would have wanted: a woman photographer with no connexions and no particular allure. This last part, though, Joseph found himself reconsidering. When Mademoiselle Turin smiled or laughed, something happened and you couldn't look away – and she smiled and laughed so often. And she made *Orin* smile and laugh.

And that's why, now, Mademoiselle Turin and Monsieur Rouline were crossing the boulevard to meet them.

~~

"Well, it seems this won't be a surprise for *you*!" Émile laughed.

Claire, I discovered, went to see the illusions at the Théâtre Robert-Houdin several times a year. She'd gone regularly for most of her life, sometimes with her parents, or just with her brother Paul, and these past few years on her own entirely.

These days, having no one to go with didn't deter her. Instead, she found that being by herself in the audience made it even easier to disappear into what was happening on stage and to imagine for a while that perhaps magic did exist. What if a suddenly budding orange tree and the butterflies that appeared to float around it were real, not mechanical tricks? What if a sleeping boy really could float as though he were lighter than air?

"Happy birthday!" she greeted Orin, and then, turning with a smile to Joseph, "Thank you for inviting us."

"Mademoiselle Turin, Monsieur Rouline - *bonjour*! What a surprise!" There was gladness in Orin's voice, but I could also feel a frustration with Joseph tugging at him. Why had his brother done this?

"I hope not an unpleasant one," Émile gave him a grin like a jack-o'-lantern.

"Far from it." Orin admitted to himself that it was true, and his voice was warmer.

Joseph led them to their places inside the empty theater— "The best and *only* seats!" he said grandly.

They settled in: Émile, then Claire, then Orin, and Joseph.

"So you like magic, Monsieur Rush?" Claire asked, intrigued that they had something else in common.

"I...don't know that I do. But it seems to be present whether one wants it or not."

She looked so disappointed that Orin wondered if he'd offended her. But then: "Does it? I wish it were more present for me."

"But it is!" The insistence in his voice surprised them both. "Your photographs are astonishing —they show the magic that's in our world."

"That's very kind of you to say."

"It's true."

"I suppose I wish I were on the other side of the lens, then."

No, you don't, he wanted to tell her. But he only smiled back.

Just then, the magician called Cleverman stepped onto the stage and greeted them. The show began.

They spent a suspended time watching marvels: lectures about scientific subjects illustrated by floating phantasmagoria, Robert-Houdin's little automaton Antonio Diavolo performing his trapeze routine and nodding his responses to questions just as a real person would, caged doves and other improbable objects drawn out of a large folio.

Orin felt joy and enchantment gently flow into him. He marveled at what he saw, and sometimes he tried to understand just how Cleverman had done it. Memories of the card tricks, of practicing and longing to perfect sleight of hand, came back to him and were useful; at times, he believed he caught some misdirection, some slipping of an object subtly down a sleeve or out from behind a mirror, and when he did, he only appreciated the illusion more.

Sometimes – often – he thought of Mademoiselle Turin. He could feel her presence and see her eyes shining with delight, even without turning his head, which he wouldn't dare to do, now, with enchantment all around them.

The performance ended with the orange tree, a magnificent automaton whose beauty and refinement even impressed *me*, a little. It starts as a pot of soil, then as if by magic, a tree grows so quickly from the pot. Blossoms appear among its leaves, and these become oranges, surrounded by fluttering butterflies. At last, one of the oranges is plucked from the tree and sliced open to reveal a ring that had gone missing earlier in the act.

As the little orange blossoms started to appear, I longed for Orin to turn and see the joy on Claire's face. If only real magic were always like this.

The illusion ended the show. They clapped and clapped heartily, gleefully tasting the orange slices Cleverman offered them in farewell.

"Thank you again," Claire said when they were outside.

"It was lovely." Émile eagerly echoed her.

And now, another surprise: "If you aren't busy," Orin said, "I'd like to treat all of you to an ice cream at Tortoni's."

Joseph raised an astonished eyebrow.

The café was grand and loud, but they hardly noticed. They sat at the terrace, enjoying the cool sweetness of the ice cream and marveling at the illusions they'd just seen.

After a while, Orin reluctantly stole a look at the sky.

Joseph noticed and said, "I suppose I should be heading back."

"So should I," Orin told them. "Thank you, Joseph."

"It's nothing. Happy birthday."

Émile guffawed. "A fine birthday – we got a treat, too. I thank you, sir, and many happy returns." He stood with a bow, leaned down to kiss Claire on the cheek, and took his leave a bit more quickly than I would have expected.

"Well," Claire laughed, her cheeks red from the sunlight or perhaps simply from the situation, "We must decide if we'll walk together or each choose a side of the street."

Orin suddenly found it difficult to meet her eyes. "I'd be glad to walk with you, if you like."

"I would like that," Claire said, trying to keep her voice merely cheerful. "And don't worry," she grinned, though I know she was worried about the setting sun. "I can keep pace with you."

As she'd promised, she hurried her small steps to match his. He couldn't find words as they walked. He decided it was because he was worried about the hour, after all. Not that she was close to him again. Not that they were walking together as they might have if they were courting, or -

89

When they arrived at their building, she gave a start of recollection. Checking the sky, she reached into her reticule. "I nearly forgot – this is a present for you.

"Please don't open it now," she asked, as much, she realized, for him, as for herself; it seemed strange for him to read the note in front of her.

"Thank you," he said simply.

She nodded and stood aside to let him go up the stairs.

"Good evening, Mademoiselle Turin," he called softly back to her, and though he moved swiftly away, his ears pricked for her reply:

"Good evening, Monsieur Rush."

She let herself linger on the staircases, still dreamy from the afternoon. The carpet was its strange new texture, like walking on a tangled forest floor, yet Claire calmly let the stems and petals cling to her bootheels.

~~

Orin locked his door and laid the key on the side table again, to my dismay. Then, he sat down on the bed and looked at the parcel she'd given him. First, he read and reread the note she'd tucked into a fold in the paper. He started to read it a third time, but stopped and set it aside.

Now he opened the plain brown wrapping.

She was right. The photograph was perfect. I could see the wonder on his face. Orin hesitated, then placed it on the small table beside his bed. He read the note once more, then stood up and walked to the rickety shelf on the far wall and gently slid the paper between two books, as though covering Claire's eyes.

He sat on the bed and waited for the first pricklings of the change.

20

After supper and some work on her models, Claire still wasn't ready to sleep. Her thoughts wandered to Monsieur Rush and then, when they had stayed there for a while, they took flight...and circled back, but not quite to the same place. Now she found herself wondering what had happened outside Monsieur Rush's room the night before.

Some people might have dismissed it. But something drew her to the sixth floor on stockinged feet and made her lower herself to peer into the keyhole again.

There was the smell, and there was the fur. And this time – She gave a start. It was hard to make out much, but she could see that it seemed to be moving.

Something - a large claw or talon - nearly brushed the door.

Holding a gasp in her throat, Claire crawled to the stairwell.

What she had she seen? What was Monsieur Rush hiding – and why?

PART 2
THE BROKEN BRANCH

21

There was still a small chance that Claire could have put the whole thing out of mind, if it weren't for what she noticed the following afternoon.

As she left the studio to bring up lunch for herself and Émile, she realized that there was no animal smell – there never was, at this hour. So, the animal it seemed Monsieur Rush was keeping in his apartment must not be there now.

But if he'd taken it out with him, surely she or Émile or Madame Marcel or someone else in the building would have seen or heard it.

Cautiously, she moved towards Orin's door. Although she was almost certain he wasn't there, she gave a tentative knock. After several long, silent seconds, she lowered herself and looked through the keyhole. She couldn't make out much, but there was still no trace of an animal smell, and no sight of fur or talons.

~~

After the madwoman's visit had destroyed Orin's life, I'd vowed that I'd no longer interfere with anyone around him. But now....

Everything was going perfectly. His and Claire's hearts were like bare branches in spring. Their love, I knew, would blossom. They were perfectly matched. The curse would be broken. His story, my mistake, would have a happy ending.

So that was why I had to break my vow. I would make Claire forget what she'd seen through the keyhole.

I watched her and waited for the right moment. That evening, she leaned out of the kitchen window as she often did, ignoring the noise from the other kitchens below and gazing skywards. Her thoughts were dreamlike and open. I cast my spell.

But nothing happened.

I tried another incantation.

Nothing changed.

Panic held my throat in its hands. I shook them off and flew down to Madame Marcel's lodge and tried to make her forget where she had put her sewing needles. That didn't work, either.

I rushed outside to the courtyard and tried to make Hippolyte forget about the rat he was hunting. He didn't even turn to sniff the air.

Forget forgetting spells, then, I thought, desperately. No one was looking – I tried to make him fly. His paws stayed on the cobbles. *Or turn orange, then!* He stayed black.

I screamed and hurtled through the air, seeking Émile's presence until I found him in his modest apartment. He was describing the magic show to a cheerful-looking woman with an ample bosom and blond hair. His Marguerite. I would make him sing a song to her. But he only went on speaking.

Marguerite didn't sing, either, when I tried the spell on her.

Desperately, I flung myself out of their window and raced to the Grand Hôtel.

I had never been able to influence or understand Joseph, and that was the case now, as he sat reading a letter and sipping brandy. But I was desperate. I tried to make him drop the letter. I tried to make it shiver in a draught. I tried to make his glass slip from his hand, or the shutters fly open, or an already precariously perched book fall off a table. Nothing happened.

I realized what I should have long before, when the roses started rising from the carpets on the stairs. The magic here was different. There was little that I could influence in Orin's life before. Now, I could do nothing at all.

22

L ate that night, Claire crept upstairs and put an eye to the keyless keyhole, and that inexplicable other magic gave us another trick. The keyhole had become a sort of enchanted loupe. She could see the whole room clearly.

She drew back and stared. The keyhole was the same size as always. *So how...?* But she was too curious to waste time. Instead, she peered into it again.

There, on the bed, was something —

Short black fur, hooves for feet, a snout rendered nearly unidentifiable by the blade-like teeth that jutted from the mouth below it. Long, white appendages in the place of hands or paws – no, they were covered in white gloves, she realized curiously.

Her mind flew to illustrations of demons in illuminated manuscripts.

She searched the room for Orin, wondering if he was hurt, wondering if he were a prisoner of this beast.

Suddenly, it stood and calmly walked to the wall opposite the door, where there was a bookshelf that looked stuffed to bursting. The creature selected a thick book, then, holding it in the crook of its elbow, quite like a man would, took another one and moved towards the bed again. Where was Monsieur Rush? Perhaps he no longer slept there and only let this...thing inhabit the space?

The creature placed one of the books on the bed with a surprising gentleness. Then, it opened the other and appeared to read.

Claire gazed through the keyhole for a long while, trying to understand. The creature's long, glove-encased claws occasionally turned a page.

At last, her eyes were tired, and her mind was like a racing horse, frothing, needing rest. She returned downstairs, where she opened her door, closed it behind her and locked it, then lay down on the sofa and immediately fell asleep.

In her dreams, the creature was dressed in a man's suit. He looked at her with something like supplication. And then she noticed Monsieur Rush, standing, ghostlike, just beside it, the same expression in his eyes.

23

The next morning, it wasn't surprising that she gave a start when she came upstairs and saw him, without the creature of course, walking down the corridor.

"Bonjour, Mademoiselle Turin," he said to her, as he always did.

"Bonjour, Monsieur Rush." Then, "Are you feeling well today?" she added quickly.

Something in her regard troubled him. Concern – but this he got from nearly everyone once they knew about his "condition." No, it was curiosity. Strange and unsettling. He attempted a reassuring smile. "I am. And you?"

Orin's deliberately easy manner made her give up. It had only been a dream, then, and perhaps even what she'd seen through the keyhole was something she'd imagined. "Maybe I ought to try my hand at spirit photography today," she remarked, half to herself.

"I've been saying we should try it!" Émile hollered from the bench by the studio door.

"Does it work?" Orin was both intrigued and wary.

"No. It's a way for charlatans to make money."

"Yes, lots of money," Émile retorted. "Money could be a useful thing to have if the world – well, our part of it - changes forever." He looked at Orin. "I've heard something….Your birthday present may have been the end of the Empire!

24

C laire didn't want to go upstairs and see the creature again. But the dream had stayed with her all day. She was certain Orin was in trouble.

That night, as she climbed the winding metal staircase, she suddenly wondered if the monster could get out of the room. What if it was waiting for her up there in the corridor?

No, she told herself firmly. *It's never left the room before, and who knows how long it's been there?* She tried to think of something else. The troubled look on Monsieur Rush's face in the dream came to her again. How long had this been going on? She felt a flash of anger. How could he have brought this creature to them? How could he put everyone in the building in danger? But then something made her think he couldn't help it. Maybe the creature was invisible to him.

By now she'd reached the top of the staircase. She crossed the threshold, holding her breath. But even in the dim light offered by the candle, she could tell that the creature hadn't gotten out. She breathed deeply now, and continued slowly and quietly down the corridor.

At Orin's door, light emanated from the keyhole. She put her eye to it and drew back for a moment as the enchanted view came to her again.

There was the creature, sitting on the floor with a book. No – she realized, it was the portfolio of Hiroshige prints. She marveled in spite of herself at how carefully it handled each sheet. Its long appendages, covered in those strange white gloves, were like instruments created just to hold them.

She took a breath and looked at the creature's terrible face. The curling teeth gleamed cruelly against the wiry dark fur around them.

And yet, the creature's expression was far from ferocious. It didn't look hungry or enraged. It looked as if it were thinking of something far away. She knew this because of its eyes. Green-gold ....

She searched the room again for Monsieur Rush. Was he on the other side of the bed, asleep or unconscious on the floor? But then, why wouldn't the creature be near him, trying to harm him?

Instead, here it was, calmly, almost dreamily - *longingly*, even - looking at those brilliant, beautiful prints, savoring the views of that distant world just as she and Monsieur Rush had — She gasped.

The creature looked up from the prints.

If Orin had tried to appreciate and develop his beastly senses, he would easily have known she was there. He would have smelled her, and recognized the sound of her gasp instantly. Instead, he waited, listening, finally calling on that special hearing, but hearing nothing.

Outside the door, Claire had turned away from the keyhole, so that not even the glimmer of her eye could warn him.

At last, I could feel them both tire of being on guard. Orin went back to looking at the prints, longing to be a normal man who could travel wherever he liked, not just in pages.

Claire put her eye back to the keyhole and watched.

She had begun to understand, but there was still hope. Such a thing was so unbelievable that most mortals would simply explain it away, no matter how convoluted the explanation. Claire might have done that, too, if it hadn't been for what she saw the creature do next.

Orin's heart could no longer bear the sense of loss and frustration. He set aside the prints and went to the bedside table, so near the door. Claire forced herself not to turn away.

He tried not to look at the photograph on the table, but reached for the book beside it.

Claire recognized its well-worn cover. She saw the creature open it to a page somewhere in the middle and begin to read without surprise or curiosity, as anyone would who was perusing something they read regularly.

It was *Walden* and the creature, she knew now for certain, was Monsieur Rush.

Shakily, she made her way down the stairs, gripping the railing so tightly her hand would ache afterwards. As she descended, she stared at the faces in the photographs, illuminated by the candle flame that danced with her trembling. It was as though she were beseeching them for some sort of comfort.

Inside her apartment, Claire sat on the sofa for a long time, still shaking. The candle flame flickered, throwing shadows over the walls. At times she willfully shook her head, denying everything.

At last, she stood up, lit a lamp, and began pacing. She was still trying to find an explanation, but she knew the truth already. Her tears fell onto the miniature streets below, like monstrous drops from the sky.

They landed with dull, regular thuds that grew louder and louder and louder. No – she realized – the noise wasn't here, but outside the windows — a constant sound punctuated by the shouting of a single word. She listened: *Déchéance! Déchéance!*

Decay! Decline! Fall! Forfeiture!

Claire ran to the nearest window and flung it open. Leaning outside, she made out a shadowy mass of people marching down the boulevard in the gaslight.

It took her a frustrated minute to find her boots. As soon as she'd hastily put them on, she snatched up her key and candle and left, making her way quickly down the stairs, her hand still trembling, but shielding the flame.

There were no flowers rising from the carpets now, but she didn't notice. At the ground floor, she knocked at Madame Marcel's lodge.

"What's going on?"

"I don't know," the concierge whispered. She held Hippolyte in her arms.

"I'll go outside and see."

Their own street was fairly quiet, with a few solitary souls walking or stumbling slowly along. But as Claire approached the boulevard, she was hit with the heat and noise of an endless river of Parisians. Their shadowy faces were enraged. *"Déchéance! Déchéance!"*

It took an unbearably long time to move through the bystanders and get to a café. She wove around the people and tables on the terrace and scanned the patrons inside, trying to find someone who wasn't shouting.

An old man sat with a journal rolled like a baton, occasionally calling out, but still he seemed like he might be calm enough to talk with her. She moved towards him.

"Please, monsieur," she asked between the shouts of the people around them, "What's happened?"

"The rumors are true -we've been betrayed! The Emperor capitulated at Sedan days ago and the press said nothing. It was kept secret from us! *Déchéance! Déchéance!* "

The old man stopped after a moment and turned to her again. "But no longer!" Claire nimbly stepped back as he spat on the floor. *"Déchéance! Déchéance!* He's no longer our Emperor! *Déchéance! Déchéance!* Strip him of his title, of his power – let's start anew, the right way – a true Republic!"

Suddenly, he stood up: *"Dé-ché-ance! Dé-ché-ance!"* He jabbed his newspaper baton into the air in front of him to punctuate every syllable of the crowd's outraged cry.

Claire didn't wait to take her leave. Outside the café, she stood for a moment, surrounded by every type of humanity – rich, poor, children, men, women, shouting where they stood, or moving down the street in a blur. Others looked out from windows and balconies, crying out *"Déchéance! Déchéance!"* like an echo of the crowd below.

She made her way back to her street and took a breath, savoring the uncrowded air there, before continuing towards her building.

"It's me," she called out at the closed doors. *"Cordon, s'il vous plaît!"* One of the doors opened and she stepped inside and went to Madame Marcel's lodge to tell her what she'd found out. The concierge gave a resigned sigh. "I suppose it was time for another change."

Claire nodded and Madame Marcel's face creased in concern. "My dear, you look terribly shaken. I shouldn't have let you go out into that crowd!"

"Oh! No, I'm glad I got to see it – it's history, after all." *And anyway,* she thought, *I was shaken well before all of this.*

Madame Marcel nodded, her eyes glinting in the lamplight that escaped through her door. "Would you like to come sit for a while?"

Claire chose a chair at the table while Madame Marcel poured them each a glass of wine.

"An old man I spoke to said that there will be a Republic – or should be. Do you think that's what we'll have?"

The concierge laughed and shook her head. "It's difficult to keep track. I've lived through so many changes! Even a young lady like you has known a few. Born in…"   "1849."

"Born in a Republic that turned to an Empire, and now, well, we shall see."

They were quiet for a while.

"Do you think the change will be easy?" Claire asked.

"That depends," Madame Marcel mused, slowly twirling the wine in her glass. "Of course, even if the Empire falls without a fight, change is rarely easy."

Claire stared at the deep red liquid in her own glass. It glittered and darkened by turns in the flicker of the hearth flames. She thought of the streets that had changed so much since the days she and Paul had rambled through them as children. She thought of her parents' deaths and Paul's new life. She thought of Monsieur Rush and what she now knew. "No, it rarely is."

25

Orin rarely dreamed, but tonight, he was dreaming of Mademoiselle Turin.

She had fallen into the Seine and was being swept along by the current. She cried out and water filled her mouth. She was going to drown, but something kept him from reaching out to her. It was as though his arms were lead — and then he remembered they weren't his arms, but the arms of an animal. There were stars in the sky, though the water reflected daylight. Mademoiselle Turin was silently swimming away. She let the current give her speed.

~~

Despite her exhaustion, Claire awoke a few hours later.

The sun hadn't been up long. She could tell by the weakness of its light. She got dressed quickly. She couldn't bear to see him.

Holding her boots in her hand, she crept up the spiral staircase, just as she'd done the night before. That thought sent a spear of sorrow into her chest. She tried to think of something else: the coloring work to be done, the cold of the metal beneath her feet.

When she arrived at the studio, she quickly unlocked the door and slipped inside. Émile wouldn't arrive for a while yet. She'd listen for his footsteps and beckon him in. And if Monsieur Rush heard them then, she'd make some excuse, say something had just fallen and she had to tend to it — and not look at him, not speak to him, and hope Émile would hurry inside after her.

26

A dream?" Joseph laughed in disbelief that afternoon at lunch. *"That's* what's got you so quiet?"

Instead of laughing in turn or making some sort of retort, Orin only nodded.

"But Orry, you've always told me you don't put any faith in dreams!"

"I've never had one like this. It felt so real that I still half believe Mademoiselle Turin is in the Seine, swimming away."

"Swimming away? What- "

Suddenly, he stopped talking. A large group of national guardsmen filed past the window.

"They're heading for the Palais Bourbon!" someone shouted. "If the Assemblée isn't planning to proclaim the Republic, they'll make them."

Worried murmurs rose up around the room. A crowd on the Pont de la Concorde. The troops might fire on them.

I could detect only one thought in Orin's mind: Was this what the dream had meant? Was Mademoiselle Turin in her studio, or was she in that crowd on the bridge?

"I forgot something. I have to go back home to fetch it."

Joseph turned to him in surprise. "It must be important. I'll come with you."

Of course he would, Orin thought with an inward groan. But then, what kind of brother would let him fight through the rushing crowds alone?

~~

The flowers on the carpets were still flat. That let Orin run more quickly up the staircases, Joseph panting behind.

As they approached the sixth floor, he began to wonder what exactly he was going to do. If the dream were any guide, she wouldn't want to see him. *I'll just have to wait in my room for a while and listen.* Hopefully, somehow, there would be sitters, despite what was happening outside.

He unlocked his door.

"Leave it open," he told his brother when they were inside, trying to seem nonchalant. "We shouldn't be here long."

"What did you forget that's so important?" Joseph asked, sitting down on the bed and trying to catch his breath.

"Oh, I.. ." Orin looked around slowly, trying to find some reasonable excuse.

And then, he heard a knock on the studio door. "Be quiet for a moment and maybe I'll remember."

~ ~

Anne's cheeks were flushed with excitement. "My dear," she told Claire, "I'm sure you've been locked away all day. Do you know what's happening?"

Claire shook her head. "Do you want to come in?"

Her friend shook *her* head in return. "No time. I came to tell you – some friends and I are going to the Assemblée Nationale. Isn't it exciting?"

Émile emerged from the darkroom. "Exciting indeed. Everyone was talking about it on my way here this morning."

"Come with us, both of you!"

Claire gave her friend a regretful look. "We have to stay. We've got appointments. Maybe some will cancel, but one's for a wedding photograph, and those sort never do. But as soon as the good light's gone, I'll come out."

I could sense that Émile was secretly relieved.

"Please be careful," Claire told her friend.

"We will," Anne gave a breathy smile and kissed her on the cheek, then hurried downstairs.

"I found it," Orin said, seizing a book by chance from the shelf. He couldn't believe his luck, knowing she'd be safe…at least until it would be too late for him to go out. He tried not to think about that.

"Let's get back outside." He pulled Joseph down the hall, past the studio door, which Claire had already shut behind her friend.

~~

All that afternoon, Claire and Émile got news from sitters — those who had made appointments, and those who came by thinking they'd take advantage of everyone else being occupied. The crowd had managed to get inside the Palais Bourbon, the people and the assembly members were moving to the Hôtel de Ville. There was no shooting. Everyone was peaceful, but feverish with excitement.

~~

The large square in front of the Hôtel de Ville seemed small now, with so many bodies pressed close into it. They came apart to let the deputies pass. The dynamic Gambetta drew the most cheers.

It didn't matter how Orin felt to be witnessing history. Even at their place on the edge of the crowd, he was nervous about the hour. The sunlight had gone from yellow-white to orange. It was early still, but how would he get past them all and back home in time?

Suddenly, a single window on the Hôtel de Ville's many-windowed façade opened and Gambetta stood and shouted a proclamation over the crowd. The Third Republic was born.

The crowd cheered and roared and chanted *"Vive la République,"* and sang a few rounds of the *Marseillaise*.

The sunlight was verging on copper now. Orin gently tapped his brother's shoulder. "You stay here. No reason to miss this."

Joseph nodded, sad gratitude on his face.

Orin slid quickly past him, working his way along the outer edge of the square, towards the rue de Rivoli.

106

"I prefer to hear about history from the comfort of my home. And anyway, Marguerite will be worried," Émile said, as they closed the studio.

"Well, we can walk to the Hôtel de Ville together, anyway," Claire pointed out, and so, they did.

It would be impossible to find Anne in that dense crowd, Claire thought. *But at least I know she's safe.*

She hoped they weren't too late to hear Gambetta speak. Later, she and Émile would laugh that they did *see* him, but they were so far from the packed square that all they could hear were the cheers of the crowd. Still, it was something, the start of a new era.

They embraced and went their separate ways.

By the time Claire had returned to the boulevards, the exuberant spirit of the crowd had arrived there, too. "Come have a drink, mademoiselle!" a happy group of young men called out to her. She smiled, but shook her head and hurried home. She called out to Madame Marcel and the doors swung open, and soon she was inside, telling the concierge everything she'd seen.

When Claire went upstairs at last, the quiet in her apartment was at such odds with the clamor outside and the clamor inside her. In warm lamplight, she pulled together some sort of supper. The silence made it easy to forget the fall of the Second Empire. There was nothing to distract her now, and so her thoughts returned to him.

It was difficult to accept what Monsieur Rush really was, and impossible to explain. But there was no way she could see the truth being otherwise.

And because there was nothing to understand or explain away, there was nothing more to let herself hope for. He was a monster.

My heart stopped and my blood turned to ice. It was over.

27

When Orin came out of his room the next morning, Mademoiselle Turin and Monsieur Rouline were in the corridor. He squared his shoulders. *It was just a dream.*

"What a mad day yesterday was!" Monsieur Rouline guffawed in lieu of an ordinary greeting.

Claire couldn't bring herself to meet his eyes. But she also had to force herself not to stare at him. Was his human form some sort of trick or disguise? She glanced at his hands. They were long, but reasonably so, and pale, with clean, perfect fingernails. How could they conceal the enormous – what she felt were claws – that he hid beneath the gloves?

Poor Orin. She didn't think to wonder *why* he wore the gloves at night.

She felt his eyes on her and looked away, feigning interest in the stairwell.

Luckily, Émile had plenty to discuss this morning. "What do the Americans think of all this? Do you know what the press is calling our new government? The government of 'Jules,' since that's the name of so many of the ministers!

"Look!" He held up the newspaper he'd been reading.

There they were, in individual circle-shaped portraits.

Orin grinned. "The proportion of 'Jules' does seem high, but the Americans won't fault you for that."

Claire urged herself to say something. Her silence would have to end at one time or another, or else he might realize what she knew. "Getting into this war so unprepared is fault enough."

"Yes." Orin's frankness made them all laugh, even her a little, though they all knew there wasn't much to laugh about.

Usually on mornings when none of them were in a hurry, they'd linger and talk for a while. Claire wondered how she could bear that today. All she seemed capable of was avoiding his eyes and thinking how convincingly like a man he looked in the light.

Orin was unnerved by her silence. "Well, if the streets are safe —"

"They are, sir," Émile confirmed.

"Then I'll be on my way."

28

The population of Paris had changed in recent weeks. Vagrants and prostitutes had been shipped out in anticipation of a siege; this would mean fewer mouths to feed. Then, refugees from the suburbs and countryside were welcomed within the city walls. This, no one seemed to realize, would mean *more* mouths to feed.

In their own building, people came and went. The umbrella shop remained open, but the owners of the lamp shop boarded up their windows and left for the countryside (sometimes Claire would think of all of the lamps, waiting in the darkness).

Her neighbors across the corridor left, and she wasn't sad to see them go. In all the years they'd lived there, they'd never exchanged more than a sour *Bonjour* with her and her family.

Refugees arrived to occupy their empty apartment. A family of farmers, their skin and hair were dirty, their expressions rough. They carried their things in several trunks, and brought cage after cage of chickens with them, as well.

Claire greeted them and they nodded at her coldly. It was funny, she thought: These new neighbors were nothing like the old ones in appearance, but they shared the same unfriendliness.

~~

In those early days of the new Republic, Orin and Joseph had their now-familiar discussion once more:

"Do we stay?"

"*I'd* like to."

Orin closed his eyes. He felt tired. He also felt Joseph waiting. "Let's send Father and Mother a telegram."

Joseph gave a delighted chuckle. "I hope they won't be utterly furious."

29

Now, Paul's letters ended with the same question: Why would she not come out to them, to safety?

Claire worried that the studio and their home would be requisitioned and ruined. There was more, of course, and both of them knew it: She loved Paris too much to part from it. The city held her close.

And there was another reason, something her brother couldn't have guessed, something she would never have admitted. Deep inside her tangled thoughts, a flame burned in a clearing.

One of the things I liked most about Claire Turin was her eccentricity. I admired her for capturing images of people, animals, and objects in her own way. She never looked to what Nadar or Disdéri and their equals were doing with their portraits, except with a sort of professional curiosity. I liked that she was a bit wild, having never been taught to do much she didn't care for.

That's why I was so disappointed in her now. I'd expected her to come to her senses. *What did this creature do at night?* she might logically ask herself, and the answer would be: *Read books.*

But she didn't think of any of that. She'd seen Orin in his monstrous – his *untrue* – form, and she'd closed her heart to him.

To her credit, Claire was disappointed in herself. She considered herself tolerant and accepting. She'd longed for the magical and the bizarre to enter her life. And here it was, and she only felt afraid.

It was a primitive reaction, she thought disdainfully, a sort of old superstition. But no matter how much she tried to be reasonable, it was difficult to imagine that this creature that looked so much like a demon, wasn't one.

If he'd looked like a cat, or an elephant, she wondered, would she have thought the same thing? What if he became a deer or a horse? Or perhaps if he'd transformed into a phoenix?

Then again, whatever form he had, she knew that things would be different. She would never love a beast.

But that didn't mean she wouldn't try to understand him. And – the flame in the clearing inside her flickered and stretched towards the brambles – maybe she could find a cure.

She had no particular knowledge of magic, and she had no idea what Monsieur Rush knew or might have already attempted.

Still, she could try.

~~

On the first cloudy day, she headed to the Seine.

The simplest place to start was the bouquinistes' crates. Spread on top of the low stone wall that stood between the street and the riverbanks below, they were tightly packed with used books and an occasional engraving or trinket.

The first crate she came to belonged to a bouquiniste with a wrinkled red face and uncombed gray hair. She told him what she was searching for, a bit lost for words, which never happened when she was talking about books – but this wasn't the sort of book she ever read.

The man gruffly shook his head and she moved on to the next crate.

Slowly she went from crate to crate, frustration her companion, like a little, nipping dog. After an hour or so, she finally found a book that looked promising. It might explain what she had seen, what Monsieur Rush really was.

If he was dangerous, I heard after that, like an echo, *and how to stop him.*

I read the title. That book wouldn't tell her anything.

But then, there was a small section, a remark, really, about how love could often break enchantments. If she read this – if she paid attention…. Maybe she would. She had started to love him already. Maybe those words would convince her not to stop.

I shook with excitement so much that, for a moment, Claire felt the wind around her rise up.

And then – "Mademoiselle Turin?"

She turned around. "Monsieur Rush! I- Good afternoon! What a surprise!"

It wasn't unusual for Orin to browse through the bouquinistes' crates, of course. But how had he happened to pass by just now? I could sense he hadn't followed her; this was a coincidence. But I wondered if it were the sort of coincidence that the magic happening here, the magic that had blocked my own, might have aided.

I was enraged. I knew already that the book Claire had found may not ever make it home with her.

Claire was also thinking of the book. Surely he'd ask her about it. She had to hide it, but how could she? She had no satchel with her, no parcel paper, and it would be impossible to stuff such a thick volume inside the folds of her skirt.

And so, she made a hasty decision that would be as foolish as most hasty decisions are. Leaning with seeming carelessness towards the stone wall that overlooked the Seine, she slid the book up from her side, under her arm, under her palm, and, barely suppressing a flinch, let it fall to the riverbank below. She prayed it had landed close to the wall and was somehow unnoticeable, so that she could return later to try to find it.

Concealing and dropping the book had happened in a few seconds' time, and the shawl she wore had helped to hide her desperate act. Still, while Orin hadn't been able to see exactly what she was doing, he did notice that she seemed ill at ease, as she had for days now. For days, he'd been trying to understand what had happened, and how to fix it.

"I'm sorry if I startled you. I didn't expect to see you here."

"Oh! Yes, well, it's a cloudy day so I came to find something to read."

"Did you find anything?"

She kept her expression neutral. "Not yet."

"I'll let you get back to looking, then."

A few days before, she might have dared to say "Let's look together," and her heart would have raced. At least now, she told herself wryly, she could concentrate on the books. Orin had gone to have a look at another crate.

For a time, there was the rushing noise of carriages and omnibuses, and conversations passing like scents in the air. And then, as sometimes happened, there was a lull, and they could hear the cries of the gulls that traveled so far inland from the sea.

They'd gotten closer to each other without realizing it. "It's a nice day," Claire remarked, because it felt strange to let only the birds speak. "The sun's good for business, but it gets so warm inside the studio."

Orin looked up from the books, uncertain of her sudden attention. "I can imagine. And anyway, I've never understood why people consider cloudy days to be unpleasant. Especially here. I don't believe I've ever seen an ugly day in Paris. There's always some beauty."

They looked away from each other, out over the Seine, whose little waves moved swiftly, pushed by a light wind. To their right was the Pont d'Arcole, and beyond it they could see the river widen until it was cut in two by the Île Saint-Louis. They gazed at the buildings' beige stones and blue-grey rooftops, at the sky whose clouds were never simply one color. At the moment, some were white, and others nearly the same shade as the rooftops. The dry leaves of the trees along the quais scintillated dully with the breeze, making a slight music.

Orin had something to tell her.

"Mademoiselle Turin, excuse me, but you seem – troubled lately."

Claire paled.

114

"I-I was wondering if it might have to do with your brother. If you'll permit — is he all right? Has he joined the army?"

She was so surprised that she turned to face him. "I should hope not!"

Seeing his own surprise, she explained, "My brother fell in love and went away, about a year ago now, to a village near Le Mont-Saint-Michel. He's a happily married pacifist. We love our country and will defend it if it comes to that, but we've never loved war."

Orin nodded. "My…condition meant that I couldn't fight in my country's recent war. At times I've been ashamed about that, but more and more I think I feel the same as you and your brother do."

I knew that he'd just told her something profound, something he'd never even said to Joseph. Still, he reminded himself, that wasn't his purpose. He pressed on. "If you're worried about him — and his family — I-I thought perhaps I could offer my services. Joseph and I know many people at the American Embassy, and they often help those who need to leave the country. I'm not certain they would help French citizens, but we could try."

He'd surprised her yet again. "That is — That is very kind," she murmured. It was more than simple politeness. Her voice was full of revelation, of wonder. Suddenly, for the first time in days, she looked at him openly, meeting his eyes. "*You* are kind."

Those words were kind, but something about what she said wounded him. He forced himself to give a small laugh, to keep his voice light. "You didn't think me kind before?"

"No" She spoke like someone recalling a dream. "You've always been kind."

What had hurt him, he realized, was that she had become such a part of his life, and he thought he had become a part of hers. But she was looking at him as if she didn't know him at all.

Something had changed in the past few days, and it wasn't worry over her brother. What could he have done?

It never occurred to him that maybe he'd been seen, maybe she'd learned his secret. Being the sole occupant of the sixth floor seemed like a guarantee of privacy. And then there was the way his new life had lulled him into a sense of happiness.

Orin took a breath. "I nearly forgot, I have an errand this afternoon. Please excuse me."

Before Claire could say anything, he was walking away, with those familiar fast steps.

Claire forgot about the book she'd let fall onto the riverbank below. She hurried home. She didn't look at the shop windows, or at the world around her. She didn't stop to call on Anne, or pause for a moment as she often did before returning to the boulevards. Everything was drowned out by the beating of her heart in her ears.

Back in her studio, she spent the afternoon doing coloring work. She hoped she could lose herself in it for a long while.

A few hours later, she went back to search for the book she'd dropped. But it had disappeared by now, picked up by a curious passerby or lapped up by the river.

~~

After leaving Mademoiselle Turin, Orin turned southward. There was nothing in his mind, only anger that he couldn't set on any one person or thing. He moved without thinking.

He crossed the Seine and wove through the streets of the Latin Quarter until he arrived at the bookshop on the rue Monsieur-le-Prince. It was boarded shut, but this wasn't surprising. The shopkeeper had left the city, like so many others.

On the ground, something stirred and caught his eye. A black piece of paper. He picked it up and saw the white letters. *Le Cercle des Thaumaturges.* He folded it carefully and put it into his pocket.

30

C laire went back to the bouquinistes' crates in the days that followed, and then to reading rooms. Still, she only found two other books that might yield the answer. At night, she'd pore over their fantastical illustrations and stories, searching.

It quickly became clear that the authors weren't claiming these creatures actually existed. And anyway, nothing that they wrote about resembled Monsieur Rush. Still, she thought she might learn something useful. She paid careful attention to the drawings and descriptions of *loups-garous*, especially. But Monsieur Rush didn't transform only on nights lit by a full moon. He didn't look much like a wolf and, she had to concede, his eyes didn't take on a murderous glare.

When she closed the second book, she had no answers. She thought of all the books Monsieur Rush had brought with him. Were any of them full of information like this? Was any of it at all useful to him? The fact that his condition persisted made her think it was exactly like what she'd just experienced, only over years, not nights. Searching for truth while watching an illusionist's spectacle, imagining you were living, when you were really only turning pages.

~~

Anyone who had thought that the War would end quickly or that Paris would be spared from siege now knew better. Before the Prussians could cut the city off, soldiers came from all of the regions of France to try to beat them back. They wore their strange traditional clothes and spoke their sometimes indecipherable dialects. There were military demonstrations on the streets and the greatest destiny a man could have was to die for his country.

Large indoor spaces were used to store up food. Most of the museums were sending their treasures to safer places. Sandbags were piled against their windows.

One cloudy afternoon, Claire saw Anne walking along the boulevard. Anne's usual expression was something between snobbish, challenging, and flirtatious. But today, her friend only stared dully ahead. Beside her was an old, pinched-faced woman whose bearing and clothes were the very epitome of bourgeois. She was followed by a slightly huddled, round-faced woman of nearly the same age.

When they greeted each other, Claire was relieved to see a little light come back into Anne's eyes. "This is my Aunt Honorine, and her maid Euphraisine." Her introduction was more akin to explanation than pleasure or even politeness. The pair had fled their comfortable home in the suburbs and were now staying with her in the city.

For all her stylishness, I was surprised to sense that Anne had only recently come out of mourning for her parents, who'd died within days of each other, taken by cholera. Their deaths were like a cavern inside of her. Like a Haussmann of her own small world, she'd redecorated the family apartment. She could breathe better this way, she thought. She didn't think of what lay below the new fabrics and furnishings, of what was lost.

Her aunt was shocked by her modern taste, or rather, Anne muttered to Claire while Honorine and her maid were discussing some trifle, "It doesn't matter what it looks like. She's just upset that I've changed it."

Claire felt terrible for her, and also guiltily grateful she had no relatives like that to shelter. As much as she longed for company, it had to be company she'd enjoy. Sometimes she found herself wishing that her brother and his wife had never left, that they, along with her little niece, all shared the apartment. They could have found a way to manage it, or perhaps she would have rented the room Monsieur Rush now occupied.

How strange to think that if that had happened, she would have never met him.

Anne was sharing an optimistic opinion that many Parisians had at the time: the inevitable siege couldn't last more than a month or two. "And during that time," she brightened, "ladies might grow bored and decide to commission hats that are more interesting than the patriotic or black ones everyone's wearing now."

Claire shot a look at Aunt Honorine and Euphraisine, dressed in expensive mourning.

"Look at how dirty the streets are," Aunt Honorine suddenly remarked.

Claire smiled at her. "Thank goodness Anne is here to help make Paris a little more beautiful."

The old woman graced her with an annoyed glare, then turned back to her maid and resumed her complaining.

Claire leaned in close to Anne's ear. "Call on me whenever you need to. We'll try to do something amusing, even if the Prussians have us pinned on all sides."

31

I never thought the first danger would come from another sort of enemy.

Claire was putting her boots on one morning when she heard heavy footfalls in the stairwell. Then, Madame Marcel's voice: "You're making a mistake."

"We've had a complaint," a man replied, his tone flat and a bit exasperated. "This is the person in question. Just take us to his residence."

They continued down the corridor...towards the staircase to the sixth floor.

Claire didn't know what she felt about Monsieur Rush. He was still her neighbor – more - her friend. But that didn't change his strange double nature. She pictured his tooth-prickled muzzle.

Then, she opened her door, raced to the spiral staircase, and began to climb.

It's daylight, she found herself thinking as she ran up its twisting steps, *there's nothing for him to fear for now.*

She crossed the threshold before they'd reached Monsieur Rush's room.

Madame Marcel was surrounded by three men wearing what she recognized as municipal police uniforms. "Good morning," she said, careful to sound merely curious (and also not out of breath). "Madame Marcel, is something wrong?"

"Who is this?" one of the officers asked.

"This is Mademoiselle Turin," Madame Marcel answered promptly. "She has a photography studio on this floor and perhaps was concerned that —"

"What do you know about your neighbor – a..." The man looked at the others.

"-Rush."

"Monsieur Rush?" So they *were* looking for him. Claire kept her voice steady: "He's a good neighbor. Quite civil and respectable."

"They think he's a spy!" the concierge exclaimed, outraged.

This was something none of us could have imagined. What could possibly have happened, who could possibly have said—

One of the policemen looked a little sheepish. "A woman across the street says that he keeps a lamp lit at all hours...."

Claire's shock turned to anger. "What business is that of hers?"

"She says that the light flashes at precise times, as though the curtains are being moved to make a signal of some sort to someone in another building."

She stared at him incredulously. "What nonsense!"

The first policeman spoke now. "These are dangerous times, mademoiselle. The enemy is approaching the capital and they must get their information from somewhere."

"But Monsieur Rush isn't giving them information. He has no connection to Prussia – he's American."

The sheepish one shrugged. "Who knows what a man will do for money or perhaps so that his own secrets will be kept?"

The first officer gave a determined nod and pounded his fist on Monsieur Rush's door. "Monsieur Orin Rush? This is the police."

"What will you do to him?" The loudness of her voice surprised her.

"Don't worry, mademoiselle." The sheepish one looked at her pityingly. "We're only taking him to the Commissariat for questioning."

A cold hand clenched her heart. Orin wasn't the first suspected spy. Sometimes, a crowd would drag a passerby to the nearest police station if they seemed to have a Prussian accent, or the wrong sort of shoes or mustache. With all of this added to the usual load of crimes and complaints, the Commissariat would be crowded. How long would it be before Orin had a chance to defend himself or speak with someone? Sunset might come well before then.

I half expected her to stop fighting. I waited for her thoughts: *Let someone else see what he was. They'd probably imprison him, and then everyone would be safe.*

Instead, "You can't take him there!" she blurted out. "He's ill! He won't... have his...medicine, he won't be able to rest or—"

At that moment, Orin opened his door. "Good morning, officer. Has something happened?"

He'd been absorbed in a book and had only vaguely paid attention to the voices in the corridor, thinking they were sitters who'd arrived early. Even now, he didn't worry for himself — his thoughts went to Joseph. Had there been an accident? Or maybe all Americans were being evacuated from the city, regardless of their choice?

The officer who seemed to be the leader answered with a rehearsed-sounding speech:

"Monsieur Orin Rush, you are accused of espionage. You must come with us at once to the Commissariat of the 9th Arrondissement."

I saw tears in Madame Marcel's eyes. Her fragile belief in the new Republic was fracturing. "I'm so sorry," she told Orin. "We know you haven't done anything wrong. I fear my country has gone mad."

Inside, Orin was frantic. How had this happened? What was he going to do? If he was at the Commissariat at sunset, that would be the end of this life, and most likely some sort of imprisonment as a public danger. And the news would get out, and get back to the other

Americans, travel back to New York, ruining his family. He was a fool for leaving his safe life, for changing anything, for hoping anything would change.

Outwardly, he never looked anything but calm. He took a breath and drew himself up. "These are disturbing allegations. I would like to be taken to the American Embassy, which your government knows to be a trusted ally."

The sheepish officer exchanged a look with the others, but their leader stayed firm, his gaze never leaving Orin's eyes. Perhaps he felt he could peer inside them and discover the truth. Under other circumstances, I would have laughed.

"You may request the presence of a representative from the Embassy at your interrogation, monsieur."

Orin kept his face as expressionless as possible, but there was the smallest flicker, the smallest flinch.

Suddenly, footsteps echoed from the stairwell. It was Émile.

"What's all this?" he whispered, coming to stand beside Claire.

"Someone has accused Monsieur Rush of espionage."

"Espionage? Haw!" The guffaw broke out like a trumpet sounding. Émile slapped a hand to his mouth.

The sheepish officer strode down the hallway towards them.

"You!" he barked at Émile, all sheepishness gone. "What are you doing here?"

Émile grinned at him mockingly.

This appeared to enrage the officer. "State your business here, sir!"

"He's my assistant!" Claire interjected.

"Not caught up in any of this, then?"

"How dare you!" Madame Marcel gasped. "He is as French as you are!"

"I'm sure he is. But that doesn't mean he stays on the right side of the law."

Claire gave Émile a puzzled look.

"I arrested him last week for public drunkenness."

"No!" Émile corrected, "public disturbance. I was not drunk, as you found out." He met Claire's eyes, with an expression caught between anger and reassurance. "Our friend doesn't know anything about our line of work."

"I thought he smelled of drink," the officer conceded. "But I apologized for the mistake when he told me about the chemicals you work with."

"What luck that you are here this morning, sir," Émile cut in. "Now you can see for yourself that I was telling the truth."

Before the officer could reply, his leader called from down the corridor, "We're not concerned with you, monsieur. This is more important business than your nonsense." And with that, he grabbed Orin's shoulder. "Come on. We're wasting time."

"But I beg you," Madame Marcel said again, "this man is innocent! He has been nothing but kind! He is here to find a cure for his condition, he spends his nights suffering —" (Claire must have told her this; Orin never had.)

"Hearsay," the officer retorted, and gave Orin a push to start him walking.

Orin's mind was racing, his heart —A terrible thought came to him. Was Mademoiselle Turin the one who'd made the report to the police? Was that why she'd been acting so strangely?

But as the officers marched him past her, she leaned towards him. "Where is Monsieur Joseph? Where does he live?"

The look on his face made her feel how cruel she had been before. He was so afraid and so glad – like a beaten dog being offered a scrap. It made her want to weep. "I'll find him and he'll go to the Embassy for you."

The officer pushed him forward. "At the Grand Hôtel," he said just loudly enough for her to hear.

Claire took a breath. "Please," she told Émile, "go with him."

He nodded and moved so close as to be on top of the officers' heels.

Claire followed behind.

~~

She didn't look as they marched him down the street. And she didn't wait for the omnibus or even a cab – she simply, swiftly walked the distance to the Grand Hôtel, though her mind was at the Commissariat, imagining the crowded halls full of misery and noise, families clinging to accused fathers, officers bustling about with paperwork and orders. She wondered if Orin would be put into his own cell or grouped with other men. She wondered how long they had until sunset. Still some time, so much time, but she knew how quickly time could pass.

The Grand Hôtel loomed ahead now. Heedless of the traffic, she crossed the Place de l'Opéra and walked through its doors for the first time in her life.

It was like a palace, full of columns and light. If she had been there under different circumstances, she would have stopped to admire the sumptuous surroundings. Instead, she sought out someone, spotted a man behind a desk and walked swiftly to him.

"Please, I must speak with one of your guests – Monsieur Joseph Rush."

The man took her measure in a single, rapid glance and finished with a subtle sneer. She realized she must look flushed and dusty after racing over the unwashed streets. Disheveled, as well. Her chignon was coming undone. She would never be allowed up to Joseph's quarters.

She even doubted the man would let her leave him a message. But she had no choice.

"Please," she said again. Fear rang out in her voice, enough to make the man pay attention. "It's about Monsieur Rush's brother. I'm his neighbor."

That seemed to have some effect. "Wait here, mademoiselle," the man said stiffly. He leaned over to a uniformed boy who stood near the desk. "Please go up to Monsieur Rush's room and tell him there is someone here who must speak with him urgently."

"About his brother," Claire found herself interjecting.

It was difficult to wait. She shifted from foot to foot. The Grand Hôtel had maintained its grandeur for the time being, but it was no longer the busy place it had been just a few months before. No other guests came to the counter. Instead, there was only the soft rush of the traffic beyond the door, which had been left open to let in the air from outside. Claire tried to distract herself by watching the horses and people go by. How many hats could she see that looked like one of Anne's creations? How many brightly colored dresses (a rarity in these sober days)?... Still, her heart was beating hard in her chest.

Luckily, Joseph wasn't long. Always impeccable, he arrived a bit disheveled now. His hair was barely combed, his mustache hastily waxed.

"What's happened?" he asked as soon as he was close enough to her to be discreet, bypassing any courtesies.

"Just now-Some policemen came and arrested your brother – he's been accused of espionage. A woman in another building says his curtains move at night – it's that easy -" she stopped to catch her breath "- it's that easy now, to be brought in for questioning."

Joseph's face, already pale from waking so early, now went white.

"They're taking him to the Commissariat of the 9th Arrondissement," she went on. "They're only going to question him, but it could take a very long time. You must tell someone at the American Embassy. They're our allies, they can help him."

For a moment, Joseph was silent. When he spoke, his usually bright, confident voice was stained with doubt. "I don't know if they'll be able to get him released as simply as that."

"So there's no hope?"

They exchanged a look, like two children terrified of a coming punishment.

Then, Joseph straightened his shoulders, as Orin had when he'd faced the officers earlier that morning. "Quite the contrary. You're right....I'll-I'll go to the Embassy."

"Bring the most important person you can," she instructed, uselessly, she knew, since that was certainly what he would do. "What can I do in the meantime?"

"Stay with him," he told her. And then, he left, without taking leave.

32

C laire passed through the doorway of the Commissariat and emerged into a bleak waiting room. Émile was there, leaning against a far wall. Orin had already been led away somewhere.

Perhaps I should have gone with him, you might be thinking. But I knew that there was nothing I could do to help. I had never before been in a situation with so many men whose minds I could not influence, so many bars I could not break, so many doors I could not open. I couldn't even comfort him.

I think I stayed with Claire and Émile because I was so afraid.

How long were we in that crowded room? Civilians and officers constantly came and went. At times, the sound of footsteps and conversations were drowned out by the chattering or wailing of children and babies.

After a while, some families took out food they had packed with them, some mothers tried to rock little ones to sleep. From far away, the orders of officers echoed now and then, and the sounds of doors opening and shutting, as if to keep anyone from even a moment of calm.

Émile watched everything. Claire paced and paced until her feet ached, and then finally sat down on the floor like everyone else.

She turned to Émile.

"Was that true, about you being arrested?"

He gave her a small, slightly rueful grin. "It is, though it's not a matter of national security."

"But you -" She hesitated. She'd felt strange calling Émile her assistant earlier that day. He was her family.

"Did they hurt you? Is Marguerite all right?"

He shrugged. "She wasn't there when it happened. I was walking home when I ran into an old acquaintance. We started talking about this and that, and he got a bit animated. I might not have, but he misquoted Blake. I couldn't stand for that and he wouldn't let me correct him. So we were yelling on the street corner when that policeman came to stop us. He smelled the chemicals on me and thought I'd been drinking, and I told him I hadn't – maybe a bit more adamantly than I should have. So they brought me to the jail for a while."

"Were you frightened? How did you get out?"

He shrugged. "I wasn't really frightened. After all, what had I done but yell? There's a war on. But I worried for Marguerite, as she'd wonder why I wasn't home. Finally, someone saw reason and they let me go with a warning and, I suppose, a black mark against my name."

"Why didn't you tell me?"

He shrugged again. "What would have been the point?"

Claire understood, but there were tears in her eyes, all the same. "Well if something like this happens again, get word to me and I'll come and defend you."

"I don't doubt it. And if I did," he gestured around the bleak room, "this is proof. You take care of people you care about."

She shook her head. "Monsieur Rush is just someone who deserves our help."

Émile was about to say something when an officer came through the door, yelling out over the din, "Mademoiselle Claire Turin!" They stood and followed him.

Joseph and a small crowd of neatly dressed, bemused gentlemen were waiting in a long corridor.

She and Joseph nodded at one another, and then he greeted Émile. *"Bonjour, Monsieur Rouline. J'ignorais que vous étiez là aussi. Je vous remercie."*

Before he could make any introductions, the officer led them down the corridor.

As they walked, she saw Joseph discreetly take his fine gold watch from his vest pocket. Two o'clock. It seemed some sort of magical trickery that had made the hours go by so quickly. There was still a good amount of time before sunset. But how much time would they need? And of course, was time all they *would* need for Orin to be released?

The officer took them to a heavy door, unlocked it, and stepped aside for them to enter. The room was nearly bare, with walls of water-stained white plaster and a small, high window whose dusty glass was barely visible behind heavy black bars. Orin was sitting at a battered-looking table. His expression was somewhere between fear and exhausted resignation.

"Orin!" Joseph called out, hurrying to him. "This is a fine mess, isn't it? I've got our friends here from the Embassy. They'll make it right."

I didn't feel much hope in Orin's heart. But he smiled weakly, mostly to reassure his brother and to show his gratitude to the men and – was that Mademoiselle Turin and Monsieur Rouline?

Several officers came in now, with what I suppose was a sergeant in the lead. They faced the Americans, and Joseph introduced each man by name – secretaries, adjutants and the like, and there was also a doctor.

"All of these gentlemen," Joseph added, "can attest to the good character and innocence of my brother."

One of the Americans nodded and began, "I am a personal friend of the Rushes, one of New York's wealthiest and most prestigious families."

Émile and Claire exchanged a surprised glance.

"I can assure you they have no interest in the Prussian cause," a second man put in.

"We have an attestation of Mr. Rush's innocence, signed by Monsieur Elihu Washburne, Ambassador of the United States and great friend to your country and its new government."

The sergeant took the paper. "This is all very well, gentlemen, and I appreciate your words for your friend. But he is just that, a friend. What is this story of the curtains, of the lit lamp?"

"He suffers from an illness, monsieur," Joseph replied. "Severe headaches that begin at nightfall and often keep him awake."

"Would light not exacerbate his condition?"

"No, monsieur," Orin said quietly. They all gave a start, having seemingly forgotten he was there, he had been so quiet and so small. "The pain keeps me from sleeping, but at times there are breaks. When they occur, I pass the time by reading until I fall asleep. Sometimes I forget to put out the light."

It sounded like an intonation more than anything else. Orin, usually so good at playacting, had completely fallen apart. I could see the alarm on Joseph's face.

"And why, then, have you not tried to find a cure for your ailment?"

"He has!" Joseph insisted. "That's why we came to Paris in the first place."

"To Paris? Why not take the waters somewhere?"

One of the men from the Embassy took over. "They *have* tried many cures, have you not?" he looked at Orin, who nodded. "They believe they might obtain some sort of information about this condition here. Is that not so?"

"It is," Joseph affirmed.

"And have you visited any doctors while you have been in Paris?"

"Oh, a good deal of doctors, but none have been able to help."

The sergeant didn't look convinced.

"We've also consulted a mesmerist," Joseph added softly.

"A mesmerist?" Several of the officers laughed.

And then, *"Pardon, messieurs."* It was Claire. The Americans turned to stare at her. She walked past them and approached the table.

Orin had stopped listening the moment Joseph mentioned the mesmerist. He stared down at the table's wood, worn and scratched by years of worried hands.

"What is it, mademoiselle?" The sergeant asked impatiently. His courtesy didn't extend to those who weren't Embassy staff, it seemed.

"I know why the lamp is lit in Monsieur Rush's room, and-and why the curtain moves." Her voice sounded strangely innocent – no, coy.

"Why is that, mademoiselle?" The sergeant's voice was slightly less exasperated. *At last,* he was thinking, *confirmation of espionage.* His first spy!

"I…When Monsieur Rush is suffering from his headaches, I bring him some broth. My skirts often catch on the curtains, and I suppose that must be what shifts them." She spoke quickly, then stared at the floor.

There was a murmur from the Americans, except for Joseph, who stared at her in utter astonishment. Mademoiselle Turin was a liar – and a rather good one.

There were also murmurs from the officers, even a few low, lewd laughs. "What is your name, mademoiselle?" the sergeant asked.

She looked up from the scratched floorboards. "Claire Turin, monsieur. I am Monsieur Rush's neighbor and…friend. My photography studio is on the same floor as his room."

"And do you swear that what you have told us about your nightly visits to Monsieur Rush is the truth?"

"I do."

More murmurs from the men.

"There you are," Joseph said with a sigh.

The sergeant shook his head. "I don't know if I can accept this testimonial without a witness —"

"It's true!" Émile called out from the back of the crowd. "I'm her assistant. When we close the studio, she hurries to warm the broth. She tells me how ill Monsieur Rush was the next day. I think she might even fancy him —"

The officers were laughing now, and the Americans' faces were very red. "Enough!" the sergeant said sternly.

"I just bring him broth, monsieur," Claire said, quite unconvincingly.

"Clear the room for a moment, gentlemen," he turned a stern look to Claire, "and mademoiselle."

This time, I stayed.

The sergeant came and stood before Orin. "Monsieur Rush!"

Orin looked up.

"Is this true?"

Orin hesitated for a moment, then nodded.

"Why did you say nothing before?"

Now, Orin met his eye. "The arrest happened very quickly. I had no time to explain myself. And I…was concerned about the lady's reputation."

The sergeant gestured to the other officers to follow him from the room.

Orin sat alone now, nearly imperceptibly trembling.

Outside, the officers followed their sergeant down the hall like a cloud of insects.

A few minutes later, the sergeant and a single officer returned, holding a sheet of paper.

"This document exonerates Monsieur Orin Rush. The République dismisses the charge of espionage. I will not apologize, as I hope you gentlemen understand the circumstances. We cannot be too careful." He gave a stiff nod and returned up the corridor without another word.

The officer unlocked the door and approached Orin. "Monsieur, you may go. We have dismissed the charges."

Orin's accusation would thereafter remain a story that was told within the walls of the Commissariat and – with the names forgotten – outside it. It would take its place among other, equally absurd accounts, like the one about the green signals in a window that turned out to be a pet parrot's wings.

Claire and Émile wanted to cheer at the officer's words. But seeing the faces around them, they knew it was best to keep quiet. They waited as Orin weakly rose up from his chair, and then they all filed out in silence.

After they were a fair distance from the Commissariat, Orin said in as strong a voice as he could manage, "Thank you, gentlemen. I cannot express my gratitude for your presence and your support."

The men nodded. "Of course we could not let such a ludicrous accusation stand." Then, they got into the carriages that had brought them and rode away, not wanting to dwell on what had really proven the heir to the Rush fortune's innocence.

Now only Joseph, Claire, and Émile remained.

Orin turned to his brother. "I know I don't have to thank *you* for coming and speaking for me, but good show on getting the men from the Embassy."

Joseph shrugged. "Would you have expected anything less?"

"I confess I would have been greatly disappointed if there hadn't been at least two of them here."

Now he turned to Émile and Claire. "But you two, I owe the sincerest thanks of all."

Émile laughed, "Thanks, but no praise for our performance?"

Orin chuckled, but I could feel it wasn't wholehearted. "Was that something you practiced beforehand?"

Émile shook his head. "I'm as surprised as you."

"We were getting nowhere," Claire cut in. "Despite the Embassy staff and the letter."

"Washburne stopped everything to write that letter," Joseph remarked wistfully.

"And it was completely useless," Claire finished his thought. They all laughed, giddy with relief.

Somewhere, a bell chimed. "Shall we head for home?" Joseph asked.

Orin could only nod.

Joseph hailed two cabs. "I'd gladly travel with you, but I need to speak with my brother." He handed their driver a sum large enough to make his eyebrows raise.

Émile and Claire told him it wasn't necessary; they weren't far from the studio. But Joseph insisted. "We've all had a shock and that weakens one's legs."

33

In the brothers' cab, Joseph said, "I haven't eaten anything today. And you haven't either, I'm guessing…"

"I just want to go home."

"I know, but what good will that do? You won't be able to go out if you get hungry tonight-"

Orin shot him a look.

"Who knows if there will be some sort of military curfew imposed on the restaurants?" Joseph asked, all innocence, and they both shared another one of those giddy laughs.

Not long after, at a restaurant that was far less bustling than it would have been just a few weeks before, Joseph carefully cut into his steak and broke the silence. "She *was* lying, of course?"

"If she saw me at night, she wouldn't have come today."

"You underestimate her."

"You underestimate what I look like."

Joseph shook his head, annoyed. "So, what she said —"

"—is another dark part of today. The whole thing was horrible – terrifying – for me, for our family – but what has she done?"

Now it was Joseph who was silent.

At the end of the meal, he did, of course, order champagne. "Let's drink to this day being over."

"And-And to friendship," Orin added quickly, as they clinked their glasses. He downed his rather fast for a man who rarely drank. Joseph poured him another.

They walked back to Orin's building together. Hearing them in the entryway, Madame Marcel opened the door of her lodge. "Thank you," Orin told her, "for telling them I was innocent."

"I don't like living in a country of fools. I'm glad to see you've returned, Monsieur Rush."

At the bottom of the stairs, Orin patted his brother's shoulder. "Job well done. Thank you again."

"Ah, we know who all the thanks really belong to."

"Good night, Joseph."

Joseph turned, gave a gracious nod to Madame Marcel, and stepped outside. His footsteps were light but not quite sure, an effect of everything that had happened, not to mention the champagne.

As he walked, I was surprised to see a troubled look on his face. And then, about halfway down the street, he stopped, hesitated a moment, and turned around.

~~

Back in his room, Orin examined the curtain. It was a thick red velvet, and fell nearly to the ground. But that hadn't been enough. The following day, he decided, he'd start searching fabric shops for something stiff to reinforce it with, and have a seamstress do the work as quickly as possible. Perhaps weights could be added to the bottom. In the meantime, he put piles of books there, to hold it tightly against the window. Then he lay down on the bed and fell quickly and immediately to sleep, even while there was still light in the sky.

~~

In their cab, Claire had told Émile, "Thank you for your help."

"No need. There's good in that man, and no good in authority putting good men in cages."

She nodded. "Yes, but if you hadn't said what you did at the end—"

"I'm sorry for that. I think I might have taken things too far."

"You had to. There was no other way they would have let Monsieur Rush go so quickly."

He nodded neatly. "And that is that."

"It's too late to work today, and the driver certainly has enough fare. Why don't you go home and we'll start fresh tomorrow?"

"You'll be all right alone, after such a shock?"

Her laugh was nearly as loud as one of his guffaws. "I won't be alone — can you imagine how long I'll have to spend telling Madame Marcel every detail?"

~~

As she'd expected, there was the concierge, waiting outside her lodge. "So, what happened?" Madame Marcel nearly pulled her arm from the rest of her as she tugged her inside.

When she'd finished her story, the concierge sighed with relief and gave a smile. "So, you saved him! You and Monsieur Rouline are fine friends."

"I don't know that 'friends' is the right word. ....I just think he didn't deserve to go to prison."

"Well, of course not," Madame Marcel's voice was soothing. "You did the right thing, you and Monsieur Rouline." Suddenly, she noticed how tired Claire looked. "Do you have anything for supper?"

Claire nodded. There was always something in the cupboards.

"Then why not go upstairs and rest?"

But that wasn't what she did.

Instead, she took the winding staircase up to the sixth floor.

There were many things that calmed her. Often, it was making her models of the old streets of the city. But this afternoon, coloring work was what she wanted. She sat down at her table.

And then – there was a very quiet, but distinct, knock. Was it him? She felt her heart jump.

Slowly, she approached the door, slowly opened it.

"Mademoiselle Turin?"

It was Joseph. His voice was low, and he looked carefully down the corridor towards his brother's room. "May I speak with you a moment?" She nodded and he stepped inside, nearly shutting the door behind him.

"Is everything all right? Is Monsieur Rush–How is he?"

"Much better than he would have been without your help. I don't think he quite has his wits about him yet, of course.

"And," Joseph went on after a moment, "I don't know that even on his sharpest day, when his mind is in perfect order, he will quite know how to thank you. I know that I won't."

"What else could I have done? He was innocent."

"Yes, but you didn't simply say that – you sacrificed your honor."

I wondered if this made her worry a bit – it was already the second time someone had brought it up. "I-I hadn't planned to. It was the only thing that could be done."

"I agree. But now…" he cleared his throat. "I don't know what this means for you now. But if it will limit you or hurt you in any way – your prospects, or your business – we're not the kind to turn our backs on our friends, either.

"What I mean to say…" Joseph stared down at his hands holding the brim of his hat, and then took a breath and uttered lightly enough, "Well, if you need him to, I'm sure my brother would marry you."

Claire's mouth dropped open, and so did mine, unseen.

And yet, shocked as I was, I admit that I leaned in hopefully. Would Claire accept? And if she did, would it break the curse?

A laugh nearly escaped from her. It came from deep inside her chest. Not long ago, she might have considered this proposal. It was the first one she might have accepted – perhaps the only one. But now... Her suppressed laughter changed to something like acid, burning near her heart... If she'd agreed, when would she have found out? And how? What would Monsieur Rush have done to her the first time they were together after sunset?

She didn't want him removed entirely from her life, that she knew. But he could only be a friend, nothing more. She could not marry a monster.

"That is very kind," she managed. She made her own voice light, "but not necessary. We've had enough talk of the future for today – let's ..."

"...savor the present," Joseph hastily agreed. "Of course."

After a moment, he added, "My brother is free. Thank you."

She could only nod. She was exhausted and everyone had gone mad.

Joseph stood and searched for his gloves, then remembered that he hadn't taken them with him that morning. With a slight bow, he was gone.

Claire put away her supplies and left the studio for her apartment, just as everyone had (wisely) told her to do. Soon she, too, was asleep.

34

As soon as he heard Claire's footsteps in the corridor the next day, Orin came out of his room.

"Good morning," he greeted her and Émile. "Thanks to you two, I'm here to say that."

Claire shook her head. "No," she said firmly, "thanks to justice." She was surprised to find that it wasn't as hard to look at him now. Maybe, I thought, it was because she'd nearly lost him.

Émile grinned. "Those officers had no business with you. We couldn't let them think otherwise."

Orin laughed and leaned down to shake his hand. "Thank you all the same. I'm glad we were able to show them."

And now, he took a breath and subtly squared his shoulders. "May I speak with you for a moment, Mademoiselle Turin?"

Claire's stomach lurched. "There's no need to – "

Émile shrugged. "Go ahead. I've got the paper to keep me busy."

She followed Orin halfway down the corridor. As soon as they'd stopped, she blurted out, "You needn't – that is, your brother came to see me yesterday – and I-I gave him my answer."

"Your answer? About what?"

He has no idea what happened, Claire realized. Relief nearly made her knees buckle.

Orin continued, embarrassed, "I'm sorry if Joseph bothered you. It was such a difficult day. I'm sorry if he said anything that offended you, or —"

"It wasn't important. I-I didn't want you to tire yourself asking again."

"Well, I do have a question that I don't think he asked."

He noticed her uneasy expression and all grace parted from him. "Why did you help me?"

Claire was silent for a time, thinking of how to answer the exact question she'd been asking herself. "We're neighbors," she said finally. I flinched at the word. Not friends. "And I hope I'd help anyone who was wrongly accused."

Orin didn't seem to notice the slight. "I *was* right about you being a good neighbor, then."

"And-And you offered to help my brother. And besides," she finished boldly, "you already have so many difficulties in your life, why add another?"

"Hm. But, what I mean is- you made everyone doubt your honor."

"Don't worry about me. Justice has been done, and that's all that matters."

Then, she grinned, in spite of herself. I could see that sleep had done her good. "Anyway, I'm a woman who lives alone and works on her own account, with only a man in my company all day as I take the photographs of complete strangers. Do you think anyone there thought much of my honor to begin with?"

Orin tried not to laugh. "I —" He sighed. "Imagine if one day, I don't know, a-a prince wanted you to take his official portrait? Could he be seen here if you have a questionable reputation?"

"I hardly think that would matter to a prince! And anyway, do you think someone like that would seek out my small studio?"

"I don't know. I'm not a prince."

The corner of her mouth twitched. She hesitated, but she couldn't help it: "From what I heard yesterday, you come from one of the finest, wealthiest families in New York City. For an American, I'd say you *are* a prince."

Orin's cheeks went as red as if she'd painted them (poorly). He spoke in a low, careful voice, fixing the worn carpet. "I... fell ill when I was twelve years old. I've never really participated in society. I don't really feel a part of it."

Claire's smile disappeared. She'd insulted him again. "I'm sorry."

He gave her a reassuring smile. "No need to apologize. It's not your fault. And anyway I've never cared much for long, dull suppers and only paying attention to the audience at an opera."

Despite her regret, something in her was like a coiled spring. She knew this candor might not come again. "Are you....the only one who has this sickness, or do others in your family suffer from it as well?"

"It's only me, fortunately. I can't imagine Joseph being confined to a room for the night."

At Claire's silence, he asked, "I hope you won't think of me any differently, now that you know my reputation among the Americans?"

"Of course not. That doesn't matter." She thought, sadly, that other things do.

35

Orin walked around Paris that morning, relishing his freedom. But his mind kept returning to the conversation he'd had with Mademoiselle Turin. It had been difficult to admit certain things to her, and he still worried about what she'd done, and yet she'd actually spoken more than a few words, and laughed - and looked at him.

All of this kept him so distracted as he crossed streets and boulevards and made his way towards the Seine, that he didn't notice the conversations around him, or the newspaper headlines, or anything much, really.

When he reached the river, he stopped to look out at the water rolling quietly by, sparkling here and there with reflected light. He gazed up to watch the gulls in the sky, then down at the pigeons pecking at the pavement. He even savored the traffic. He let the sounds of the city rush through him, and sighed in happiness.

~~

That afternoon, Joseph was just knotting his cravat when Orin knocked on the door. "Come in, Orry. I'm so glad to see you."

He seemed about to say something else, but Orin had something to say, as well, something Mademoiselle Turin had mentioned that stuck to his other thoughts like a burr.

Still, there were other matters to discuss first. "It's good to see you, too, and all of Paris. I'm sorry that I nearly ruined us all."

Joseph winced. "Nothing happened. It's fine and it always will be. We've never been caught, and we never will, trust me on that."

"What makes you so certain?"

"Well, for one thing, we're excellent liars. And now it seems we've got some friends who fit that description as well."

Well, he thought, *Joseph brought her up, not me.* "Speaking of that, Mademoiselle Turin mentioned that you asked her something yesterday. What was it?"

Only someone who knew him well would have noticed that Joseph seemed the slightest bit worried. "What?"

"She said you asked her something and she gave you an answer. What was it?"

Orin hoped that she'd simply refused a typical courtesy. Perhaps, for instance, Joseph had offered her money for her kindness. But he could tell from the way his brother's posture changed, the way he made his voice and gestures light and dismissive, that it was something much worse.

"Well, Orry, you know, with the shock of it all and the champagne – I got a bit dramatic, perhaps, a bit romantic –"

"What did you ask her?" Orin demanded flatly.

"You told me that Mademoiselle Turin's compromising her honor was a dark shadow on the day. And I was worried for her, too, and I thought I might have a solution, and – again, you know what a day it had been, and then we'd had a bit to drink —"

"And?"

Joseph took a breath and tried not to cringe. "I-I told her that if she needed to save her reputation, you would probably be willing to marry her."

"What!" Now Orin grew pale. "Why would you do that?"

"I'm sorry, Orry." His voice was barely a whisper.

Orin sank into a chair and stared at the floor. Joseph busied himself straightening already straight picture frames on the walls.

Finally, in a voice so low Joseph almost didn't hear, he asked, "What did she say?"

"She-she took it all quite lightly, and said it wasn't necessary. But," he added, "she did seem to appreciate the gesture."

Orin inhaled sharply. "All right."

"All right?" Joseph's face perked up almost into its usual cheerful expression.

"I have to leave."

"All right, I'll meet up with you later if you like."

"The city," Orin clarified. "I can never come back here." He thought of how he'd spoken to her that morning, utterly oblivious. He was mortified.

He thought of what might have happened if she'd said yes, if he'd had to refuse her — or worse, if he hadn't been able to and then –

"I have to leave today. Now."

Joseph stared at him. "But we said we'd stay. We—"

"That was before. I'm going to – no – I have my papers already. I'm going to take the next train leaving a station. I don't care where to." He strode to the door.

"Orry!" Joseph laughed in spite of himself. "Do you not realize what's going on? We're officially in a state of siege since this morning! What train are you going to take? The last ones have already left!"

Orin sneered at him. "And what about the Embassy? They failed yesterday, so now I'll arrange safe passage with them."

Joseph caught him by the sleeve, and Orin spun around to face him with such a look of ferocity that both Joseph and I recoiled.

"I-" Joseph let go and stepped back. "I don't think that right now is the right time. If you don't want to go back, you can stay here – not even with me; I know there must be plenty of other empty rooms. And we can see in a few days what your -"

Orin went back to the chair he'd been in before and put his head in his hands.

Joseph sat down in a chair farther off.

The only sound was a clock ticking somewhere, and the world moving and calling out from behind the still-closed shutters.

At last, Orin looked up.

"I'm so sorry, Orry," Joseph told him softly.

"It's all right."

Joseph nodded, then, after a moment, ventured, "So, you'll find a way to leave…?"

Orin shook his head. "You're right – it's not the time. And we did say we would stay. But I'm going to spend today alone."

"I understand," Joseph told him.

But he didn't, not entirely.

36

I followed Orin closely out of the room and outside onto the boulevards. He was both dazed and determined. Back at his building, he went up the stairs slowly, listening for any sound of Mademoiselle Turin. He couldn't bear to see her now.

At least, he thought, she didn't know that he knew about Joseph's proposal. But there was another problem, something he'd indulged for far too long.

Hours went by as he searched through his books. All of his energy was there, and yet, from time to time, thoughts whirled in to distract him. How close they'd come to disaster. What if Mademoiselle Turin had accepted the proposal?

Other times, he wondered why she'd said no. Did he seem too sickly? Was there something unappealing about him? Had he done or said something that could have offended her or changed her opinion of him? And then, he'd brush all of that away. It didn't matter. She had said no, and he should be glad. He could bear no more of it.

Shortly before sunset, he shut his books.

I've often thought about what he did next. Orin had studied magic for many years, and, what's more, it was certainly in his blood. He'd read and learned from books and grimoires from some of the most prestigious magic collections in the mortal world. In that very room in Paris, he had with him several tomes that held a solution. And yet, he chose to do something else entirely.

From the drawer of the bedside table, he drew out a sheet of paper and a pen and inkpot. With a breath, he began hesitantly to write something. Soon, his pen moved more surely. I read over his shoulder:

Every time I see Claire Turin, the world reels. It trembles if our fingers meet.

She is not a particularly stunning woman. Her hair is dull-colored and flies from any hairstyle she tries. No feature is enough to make her the sort who would cause you to stop and stare at her in a crowd.

Still, I confess that whenever she's close by, I have trouble seeing anything or anyone else.

She is at once a stranger, and someone I have always known.

She is charming, intelligent, talented, enchanting, unique in the world.

I confess, I've lied about her not being beautiful. Perhaps a worldly Parisian wouldn't notice her in a crowd — but I believe an artist would. Her features are delicate but her face nearly always bears an indelicate expression; she often looks as though she's about to laugh (and I believe that she is). I imagine any man who looks at her is caught off guard — is she mocking him? Her eyes always twinkle — I've never seen them dull, even when she's worried, they sparkle.

There is a small crease at the left side of her mouth. Perhaps it might be seen as an imperfection, but I cannot help wanting to run a finger over it— or to kiss it. As I wish I could kiss the beauty mark on the right side of her neck, often covered by her cascading, messy hair.

We always have so much to say to each other. I dream of talking to her every day for the rest of my life.

Let it be finished. Love crossed out, flame extinguished.

His heart poured out, now, he stood up and squared his shoulders. From a box on the bursting bookshelf, he took out half a white candle.

It was an ordinary object. He reached into the box again and searched for something else – an ordinary box of matches.

This wasn't anything from a spell book. But there was power here. Instinct told him certain gestures and symbols might work, might awaken the old magic that has always existed by the side of ritual.

Orin's whole being was the lit match. His soul was the flame carried to the candle's wick.

He lifted the paper and let one pointed edge meet the hungry fire.

In moments, the paper had been completely consumed. He'd gladly burnt his fingertips to be sure it was all ash.

Had it worked? Full of dread, I left the room to see.

I noticed that the colors of the flowers on the carpets had dulled. The blossoms appeared flat and fragile as burnt paper. Cold cut through the air.

I flew downwards. At the ground floor, the gas flame in the statue's lamp dimmed, then disappeared.

Hippolyte had been sleeping in the curled crook of the bannister. Suddenly, his head shot up and he made a strange sound. He ran to the door of Madame Marcel's lodge and scratched. Puzzled, she opened it, then gave a shiver.

But this wasn't a proper spell. Perhaps Orin was afraid of the real magic he knew, because of what it had done to him.

Or maybe with the way my curse had strangely warped, nothing he could have done would have worked. Perhaps that sort of spell was impossible in this city whose shape, delineated by the walls that surrounded it, bore a bit of a resemblance to a human heart.

Or perhaps it was that, within his own heart, Orin didn't really want to stop loving Mademoiselle Turin.

In less than a minute, everything had returned to its prior state. The flowers looked as they always did, the temperature rose to what it had been before. The gas flame appeared once more in the statue's globe. Hippolyte returned to his place on the bannister, and Madame Marcel stood at her lodge's open door, wondering why she had felt that strange sense of cold emptiness, and very, very glad that it was over.

~~

The next morning, Orin didn't care if he crossed paths with Mademoiselle Turin in the corridor.

He went to the washbasin and began his morning ritual: a splash of water and some soap, a meticulous shave. He took out a newly laundered shirt from the teetering wardrobe, buttoned it steadily. He searched for a moment for the rest of his clothes and found them, as usual, on the floor by the foot of the bed, where he must have kicked them off as he slept – as man or beast, he couldn't be certain. The spell had exhausted him and he'd fallen asleep almost immediately after he'd cast it.

He returned to the small square of mirror, the smallest that he'd been able to find, and neatly tied his cravat. His hat was on the bedside table, by *Walden*. He took it up swiftly, leaving a few fingers to pinch around the candlestick holder, which he would bring back to Madame Marcel along with his key on the way out – to where? He had no particular plans for the day. He was a man entirely at ease, light…

…but deliberately so.

Monsieur Rouline was sitting on the bench in the corridor. They nodded to each other amicably and Orin continued on his way.

And then, Mademoiselle Turin came up the stairs.

I held my breath.

Orin didn't hesitate. Instead, he walked surefootedly in her direction.

"Good morning, Monsieur Rush," she said as they crossed paths.

He nodded, quickly returned her greeting, and continued on.

Halfway down the spiral staircase, he stopped and clenched the railing until his knuckles were white.

The world was reeling.

He took a breath, furious, and resigned himself to navigating the flowers that seemed to rise higher than ever before from the carpets on the stairs below.

Orin decided, then, that the simplest solution was to make sure he didn't see her. This would be easier on cloudy days when the studio was closed. But when the weather was fine, he'd stay in his room until he heard her and Monsieur Rouline shut the studio door behind them.

37

A day after the Siege started, the French had a chance at ending things. But when Jules Favre, one of the governing Jules, met with Kaiser Bismarck, he declared that the French wouldn't cede an inch of their territory. So, the Prussians wouldn't get the coveted Alsace-Lorraine, and the Parisians would stay trapped within the city walls.

Well, most of them would.

Early one morning, I went with Joseph and Orin to La Villette. I've seen many mortal inventions, but I'd never been close to what we stared at now.

Two enormous balls of cloth encased flammable gas that would make them fly when a flame was (carefully) lit below them. They were bound with netting and attached to one another by a bar. This hot air balloon was named, fittingly enough, Les États-Unis, a fact that made the brothers exchange a laughing look. But they quickly turned back to the sight in front of them. They were as fascinated by it as I was.

Men were tending to the balloons, running here and there and verifying everything, loading bags of mail, carefully attaching cages of pigeons to the basket. The cloth globes blew slightly in the wind, seeming at once nervous and impatient to fly.

At last, the pilot was ready. He stepped steadfastly into the basket and pulled a cord that sent a column of flame into each balloon. Like the rest of the small crowd on the ground, we cheered as the contraption lifted from the earth and the crew around it hurried to untie the tethering ropes.

"*Lâchez tout!*" Finally free, the balloon rose rapidly. This was the only way out of Paris, this ungainly vehicle that floated like a dream away from us.

38

Nowadays, Claire awoke long before sunlight. She layered shawl after shawl around herself, put her mantle on over them, and headed determinedly downstairs by candlelight.

At the door to her lodge, Madame Marcel nodded gratefully and handed her a small card. "Thank you," she whispered.

Every morning Claire gamely replied, "It's no trouble; I'm going anyway."

There were always other cloaked and shadowy forms moving down the dark street. They all fought the same fatigue. They were all headed to the municipal butcher's or boulangerie, where they'd wait in line for hours until it opened and they could get their rations of meat or bread.

There was food for everyone in Paris, but getting certain essentials had begun to involve suffering.

The crowd of mostly women was quiet. They stayed bent in towards themselves; otherwise the cold wind would creep down their necks and up their sleeves.

It had all seemed easy at first, with predictions that the Siege wouldn't last long, and the comforting sight of countless sheep and cattle grazing in the parks. Rationing was a precaution then, but they all knew that by now it was a necessity.

The lines at any municipal butcher's or baker's were such miseries that some people simply gave up. Claire often thought that it helped that she wasn't only going for herself, but also for Madame Marcel, who couldn't leave her post. If she gave up, it would mean two people and one cat wouldn't have enough to eat for the day. She got into the line outside the butcher's and tried to turn away from the wind.

Suddenly, voices rang out. "How dare she show her face here again. *Mère Michel.*"

A *Mère Michel* was a woman who gave her rations (or at least part of them) to her cat. Claire knew the term well; she was a *Mère Michel's* accomplice, after all. But she didn't think she was the one they were yelling at. *How could any of these strangers know about Madame Marcel?* she reasoned to herself. She stared down at the wet stones beneath her.

Most of the other people in line were as quiet as she was, though probably not because they were hiding their guilt. They were just tired and miserable. Still, arguments were becoming more common, especially whenever the butcher or baker told people who'd waited for hours that there wasn't enough.

But the angry women today didn't lapse back into silence. "How dare you take meat from children's mouths? I'll find out where you live and steal your cat to feed my sick father!" She heard one of them spit.

There was the sound of a struggle, followed by cries of pain. Now Claire, like everyone else, couldn't help but look. The angry women were trying to push the *Mère Michel* out of line, but she fought back, pushing and scratching at them in turn.

"Mesdames!" an old man admonished, "Remember that we are all fighting for the same side! This is our effort for France!"

"She'd give meat to a cat instead of the children of France!" the angriest, loudest voice retorted.

The man said nothing more. He probably hated *Mères Michel* just as much as they did, and if he didn't, he was too cold and tired to do anything about it. The agitated pushing started again, along with yelling, curses, and now the sound of slaps. A little girl a few places ahead of Claire started to cry.

Finally, the old woman was pushed out of line, holding her hat, her chignon undone, scratches on her face.

"Don't come back unless it's to offer your cat up to the butcher's!" one of the women laughed.

Claire understood their anger, but how could anyone who loved a pet simply let it starve? Madame Marcel thought there was no harm in a person doing whatever she pleased with the rations she had a right to.

To pass the time, she decided to make a game of what her friends would think of all this. Anne would shrug and say why not eat the cat and use its fur for something, if its coat was nice? Émile would laugh and suggest something like letting the cats eat any pigeons who didn't return to Paris with secret messages in their feathers, or quote a philosopher in some roundabout way.

Paul would – that was hard to think about. She'd sent a few letters by balloon, but there was no ordinary post, and no telegraph, so no way to receive a reply. She had never gone so long without hearing from him. Every day, Émile perused the journals nervously; the Prussians were moving towards the coast. She could only take the news in small doses, and from him, not in decisive newsprint.

Added to this worry was simply his absence. The absence of his humorous stories, his letters about his life and their work – it felt like a hollow echo inside of her.

If she let herself listen for it. She wiped the tears that had sprung to her eyes and continued her game.

What would Monsieur Rush think? As a rich American who got his food from restaurants and had never been in a breadline, he might be objective. She'd ask him the next time she saw him. Only, these days, he was like a ghost, or sometimes in the evenings, like the old Mr. Rush, true to his name, only coattails and a hurried "*Bonne soirée*".

She wondered if something had happened. But how could she ask or infer anything? They never spoke.

Anyway, she thought, didn't that make her life easier?

A gust of wind rose up and sliced through the crowd like a blade. Claire drew her mantle close.

39

Orin's plan wasn't infallible. One morning, he came out of his room just as the studio door opened and a sitter came out, followed by Mademoiselle Turin, wishing her a nice day.

It would have been absurd to go back into his room. So, he walked towards her.

"Bonjour, Mademoiselle Turin."

"Bonjour, Monsieur Rush."

She was paler than usual, with shadows under her eyes. The sight shocked him.

"It must be awful," he couldn't keep himself from saying.

"What must?"

"The breadlines. At least," he went on hastily, "I imagine you must wait on them."

She nodded.

More often than he liked to admit, he'd thought of her shivering outside in those cold, miserable hours.

Claire was about to ask him the question she'd thought of the other day, when he said something that made her forget it entirely: "I wish I could – that is, I'd offer to go in your place sometimes, but…"

She pictured him out there before sunrise, terrifying the miserable masses. Or would they even notice? "No, of course you couldn't. And anyway, it's not—"

Before she could say more, a group of sitters arrived at the landing and scattered their conversation away like startled birds.

40

That afternoon, Claire and Émile closed the studio early. Both headed down the stairs and outside together, then Émile turned southward towards home, and Claire stood where she was, waiting. A few minutes later, Anne appeared, hurrying towards her.

They walked northward for a long time. From the look on her face, Anne was clearly glad to be away from her aunt. There was a chill in the air, but being out and free for a while did her enormous good.

Not so for Claire, I could feel. Something held her, weighing her down from the pit of her stomach.

Still, she walked in time with her friend, and at last, feet aching, they arrived at their destination: a station of the Petite Ceinture, the railway that circled Paris, its tracks very near the city walls.

Its sooty, sturdy black trains held no particular luxury or appeal, and the route offered few striking views. Mostly, there were the courtyards of country houses to the west, and facades of cracking plaster to the east. In between these views were dark tunnels, mosaic tile walls, and deep, stone-paved hollows.

Still, it was one of the most alluring attractions for trapped Parisians.

And there were some sights worth seeing, a few stops that could leave passengers breathless. Even if that hadn't been the case, at least it was a change of scenery from the dense heart of Paris. The city's outskirts felt like the countryside at times. There were few buildings and the sky seemed big.

The air was clearer, except when the train arrived, surrounded by its sooty cloud.

Instead of going inside the wagon in front of them, they climbed a small staircase to the *impériale* - an open second floor whose roof was a once-white canvas that weather and smoke had turned yellow-gray. Somehow, they managed to find seats, even though it was already very crowded. There were soldiers, bored passengers who looked as though this ride were a part of their daily comings and goings, and excited tourists (of a sort) like them, staring eagerly outwards at everything.

The train gave a jarring whistle and rolled forwards.

The nearest impressive sight was Montmartre, with its old brown church crouched on top. The riders craned their necks. Just weeks before, Gambetta himself had left in a balloon from the Place Saint-Pierre, at the base of the hill, on a mission to rally troops in the rest of the country to come liberate Paris.

The train turned a bend and for a while, the view was mostly residential buildings and houses. Claire wondered what it must be like to live so close to the tracks.

Soon enough, things changed again. The train passed over the tall, elegant arched stone viaduct that stood atop the Pont du Jour. This was the most important part of the journey for nearly everyone aboard. From this height, they could see most of Paris sprawled out on one side, and on the other side, the fortifications that were now installed along the city walls.

National Guardsmen surveyed the peaceful-looking river and hills beyond. Then, a loud, booming echo shook the stones beneath them.

"They're firing!"

Claire had brought a spyglass with her, something her parents had purchased on one of their own, much farther journeys. She took it out and fixed the landscape, searching clearings and the windows of factories beyond the city wall. But there was no sign of the Prussians.

"Oh – can I have a look?!" Anne begged, practically tugging at her sleeve. Claire laughed and handed her the spyglass.

Another blast of canon fire. Anne gave a start as if the spyglass had a small recoil.

The train had stopped in the middle of the viaduct. After a few moments, the passengers started to wonder if on this day, for the first time, the Prussians might decide to make it their target.

The war had felt at once distant and immediate to them, its effects on their everyday lives more about deprivation than fear. Now, for a moment, they felt death very near.

They had mostly gone quiet, except for a little boy who kept asking his mother questions. "Would you like to see?" Claire offered, grateful for the distraction. The boy grinned and she helped him, hoping he actually did see something through the spyglass, even though he didn't understand that he had to close his other eye.

The train lurched and moved on.

They were closer now to the city's sea of gray rooftops. On the other side of the *impériale* they could see the landscape south of Paris — scattered villages, fields, lakes, the Bièvre. Farther out was the Fort du Bicêtre, a stack of severe lines near the horizon. Claire knew that if you could fly over it, it would look like a star.

Soon, the views were intercut with tunnels, which disappointed the riders so much that some groaned. Think of what they might be missing! Still, Claire found the variety of it thrilling: below Paris, then above it. Darkness, light.

They crossed the Cours de Vincennes, with the two columns of the Place du Trône not far off, standing sentinel. The passengers grew a little quieter; dead and wounded soldiers were often brought back into the city from the nearby gate.

Then the series of tunnels between Charonne and La Villette, broken up by glimpses of the buildings and wilderness. Ivy leaves tumbled down the walls from the Parc des Buttes Chaumont.

Claire noticed that Anne was looking at her, instead of the sights around them.

"What is it?"

"You seem sad."

"Who isn't sad these days?"

"The people getting married." They both giggled.

Anne went on, "Is it because of your gentleman? What's become of him?"

I thought, *How skilled she is at reading hearts!*

Claire chose her words carefully. "He's…not what I thought."

"Has he done something unforgivable?"

She gave a bitter laugh. "He hasn't done anything. But everything's changed."

41

So, this isn't love, only circling.

I tried to calm my anger. At least it was a start. At least it was proof that Orin *could* give his heart to someone. Now, I'd try to find the right person.

But who in Paris could that possibly be? Orin wasn't interested in the society ladies who spent their days organizing benefits and volunteering and let their servants wait in the cold for the food that would be on their fine tables.

Women in Mademoiselle Turin's social class were far too occupied, it seemed to me, to become enthralled by an odd foreigner who kept mostly to himself and was more interested in books than war, and never went out of his way to find any sort of amusement. That last was particularly unappealing to the average Parisian.

Searching for prospects, I came upon such misery – hunger, and worse than that, constant, biting worry for husbands or lovers or sons on the battlefields. And then there were those who had already lost everything. At least for now, their hearts were buried with their fallen loves.

42

A little more than a month after the start of the Siege, Paris was a city in decline.

Parks were pastures and abattoirs. The trees that once made the boulevards and avenues so lovely were slowly being cut down for firewood. The forests just outside the city had been cut down, too; they provided too much coverage for enemy soldiers.

During certain hours, people could pass through the city gates to tend to fields or search for provisions in the deserted land between Paris and the string of forts that were like a second wall. This land in between was full of devastated forests, abandoned towns and villages. It had seen battles and would become the site of many more.

Even deep within Paris, you could hear canon fire from the forts. It had become just another sound of everyday life.

Amusements, on the other hand, had nearly left it. Joseph no longer spent time in plush seats and gilded balconies, and anyway, nowadays the theaters usually only featured readings of *Les Châtiments*, patriotic songs, and recitations and the like. All other art had more or less vanished.

The upstanding members of society that he called on were utterly absorbed in the latest fashionable hobby: helping at, or, even running, an *ambulance* – that is, a makeshift hospital for wounded soldiers. *Ambulances* were set up everywhere, including wings of wealthy homes, and even in a theater or two. The *ambulance* at the Comédie Française had the reputation as the best one. Soldiers there were well-fed, and doted upon by beautiful actresses.

Anne's shop window seemed to hold the charred remains of her colorful, extraordinary creations. At first, everyone had wanted hats with patriotic colors, no matter how extravagant. Now, color of any kind was out of fashion. Even Worth himself had closed up shop, and no wonder – the most fashionable ladies in the city only promenaded around in bleak black.

And yet, despite everything, the Parisians laughed. There were jokes and cartoons in the news journals — not just political satire, but drawings of things that happened in this strange new everyday life.

Gavroches on the boulevards spun bold lies about items they claimed they'd stolen from battlefields: Prussian helmets, buttons, bullets, now for sale to passersby. Men and women of all sorts, anyone who was becoming hungrier and wanted money, would spread a blanket down on the sidewalk and try to sell what they could, in the most humorous way that they could – and sometimes shockingly so. Claire once saw someone peddling a drawing of the former Empress naked, kissing her son as the Emperor looked on like a doddering old man.

It was a lawless time, and those who were inside the walls of Paris were like children left alone at home. Marriages abounded, which wasn't such a bad thing for a photographer, she and Émile jokingly admitted.

Laughter was what helped them to go on, but it wasn't always easy to laugh. The days were growing colder. Bellies were emptier. Wounded soldiers and the bodies of the dead were carried through the city gates.

43

I still visited Claire from time to time. She may not have been the one who would break Orin's curse, but I liked her anyway.

One night, I was sitting in her parlor as she worked on her models of old Paris. Suddenly, there was noise in the stairwell – a frantic sound, a panic that you could understand without hearing any distinct words.

Claire stood up quickly and opened her door. The voices belonged to some of her neighbors. She went down the staircases until she reached them.

"...fire," one was saying.

"Or they're firing," another retorted.

She followed them to the ground floor.

Most of the building's inhabitants, including Madame Marcel herself, were standing just inside the massive doorway, staring upwards.

The night sky was overlaid with strange reddish waves. "Do you think the Prussians are bombarding us?" a woman from the fourth floor asked.

"Let's go out onto the boulevard," Claire suggested.

They wove through clusters of curious souls, some getting lost or delayed along the way.

Once Claire and Madame Marcel arrived on the boulevard, they could see more of the sky. They realized that the light didn't seem to come from any earthly direction.

A murmur went through the crowd. "It's the aurora borealis."

Claire watched the red glow undulate across the darkness. She found herself thinking of a trip to the sea when she was young. She and Paul had let the cold water rush over their bare feet, laughing as the waves came and went.

She was like a cloud, adrift in her heart, joining the sky. She thought of her mother and father. Perhaps this was what they saw, always, now. She thought of her brother and his wife, and her little niece.

She thought of Monsieur Rush. He was so close to the sky, but he wouldn't see this, not after what had happened – his curtain would be drawn.

"I'll be right back," she told Madame Marcel, and raced down the street without waiting for a reply.

She hurried through the open door, across the ground floor. For the first time in weeks, the carpet on the stairs clung to her bootheels, but she hardly noticed.

At last she reached the sixth floor. She stopped to catch her breath for a moment, then walked to his door. "Monsieur Rush? I'm sorry to disturb you – but if you can, you must look out of your window."

Would he say something? *Could* he say something? "It's the aurora borealis. It's magnificent. I thought you might want to see it.

"I'm going back outside now," she added. "Good night."

I wondered why she didn't think to watch it from her studio. Perhaps it was the tinted windows, or maybe it was just the sort of situation where it's hard to think practically at all.

Instead she raced back to the boulevard. It was easy to find Madame Marcel; like everyone else who was watching, she hadn't moved.

~~

Orin listened to her carefully, afraid at first that something had happened, that he would have to leave the building, that she would try the door. But his fear faded and turned to surprise and then to gratitude.

He said nothing. He couldn't bear to speak to her this way. He couldn't allow this part of his life to touch her.

When she was gone, he dimmed his lamp and drew the curtains slightly to the side. Then, he gasped.

The entire sky was illuminated with a strange, undulating light, red and then flashed through with yellow. It waved above the chimneys. The stars stood steady behind.

The colors rose and fell like something breathing, as though the whole soul of the earth were there. He felt as though he were witnessing something greater than himself, than anything. The red wave rippled among the stars, at once something unknown and the blood of his heart.

He felt gratitude again. He felt an ache.

All other feelings flowed away from him, and he was filled with sorrow at the thought of Mademoiselle Turin missing even a moment of this because she had come to tell him. And then there was a red flash of anger: *I could say nothing to her. I could never invite her in.*

And then, another undulation. That sense of immensity returned, furling through him like the magical, indescribable scarlet light, a flag across the sky, a banner.

It was nothing he could understand, but everything: the shout, the energy, the whole essence of himself that he wished he could cry out.

~~

Claire's heart felt whole and immense.

"It's magnificent, isn't it?" Madame Marcel whispered softly.

All too soon, the lights began to fade, then disappeared. Orin carefully closed the curtain again.

~~

The boulevard came back to life, and Claire and Madame Marcel returned to theirs.

When they arrived at their building, she noticed the concierge brushing away tears. "I was thinking of my husband," she said. "He and I saw the aurora borealis here, years ago."

Claire gently touched her shoulder.

"Good night," they said to one another, and upstairs she went again, slowly, giving halfhearted kicks to whatever was pulling at her boots.

She returned to her small streets and towers for a little while longer, then went to bed. I don't imagine that she dreamt of anything; her dreams that night had been in the sky.

~~

Orin had fallen asleep easily, his memories of those red celestial waves illuminating the darkness of his room.

He woke and looked at his watch. Mademoiselle Turin would already be in her studio.

He prepared himself slowly. Perhaps he might leave her a note? The thought of her holding the paper he'd written on, her fingers running over his words, flew into his mind like a bothersome fly. He squared his shoulders and took a sheet of paper and his pen and inkwell from the drawer of his bedside table.

No spell this time, I was relieved to see. Instead, he took his time writing what should have been a simple message:

Mademoiselle Turin,

Thank you. I have never seen anything like it. I hope you didn't miss too much in coming to tell me.

Yours Sincerely,

Orin Rush

He didn't want to knock on the studio door, but he realized that he couldn't leave the note where she lived, since he wasn't sure which of the apartments on the fifth floor was hers.

So he made the difficult choice to ask Madame Marcel to deliver it. When he handed it to her, the concierge stared at him in pointed puzzlement. He avoided her questions by giving Hippolyte a quick scratch behind the ears, and then hurried outside.

44

That afternoon, there was a luncheon hosted by some wealthy Parisians who wanted to raise funds for their *ambulance.* Conversation consisted of the price of bandages, the sacrifices of the soldiers, the difficulty of obtaining nourishing food.

After all of that had been discussed, someone mentioned the aurora borealis.

"It's a portent," an older gentleman declared knowingly. "Whenever there's such an event, it signifies that the tides will turn."

"It was an apparition of the blood shed on the battlefields," a woman insisted.

Their hostess, Madame Lamber, looked wistful. "I was too busy at the *ambulance* to see it. I heard it was magnificent."

Joseph stirred in his chair. "Well *I* experienced quite the opposite."

He told them about a group of friends he'd been out with (out carousing, they all understood). One of them happened to know someone at the Palais de Justice, who agreed to let them into the building's courtyard, where the Sainte-Chapelle was located. Orin and I glanced at Madame Lamber, whose husband, I sensed, was the chief of police. What would she think of all this? But her expression was neutral as she listened.

"There was some scaffolding on one side, I think from the Sainte-Chapelle's restoration. So, we just climbed up that and onto the roof."

"Weren't you afraid?" someone asked.

Joseph chuckled. "I confess that we didn't exactly walk like acrobats; instead, we climbed desperately, and then straddled and shimmied along the ridgepole. It helped that it was dark," he added gamely, amid the laughter, "so that we didn't entirely realize the distance to the ground.

"Finally, we arrived at the spire. There's space to stand and look out at the base, a bit like a gazebo, actually – quite convenient. And that's where we stood, watching until the aurora disappeared. It was magnificent." There was no humor in his voice now; this last statement was nakedly sincere.

Madame Lamber sighed longingly. "Oh, to be so close to the heavens while those lights were dancing across it."

Joseph nodded. "It was one of the best moments of my life."

Then he added, "Getting back down to the scaffolding, however, was not."

~~

Walking home, Orin turned to his brother. "You took a risk last night."

Joseph shrugged a bit theatrically. "Yes. But I'll never forget what I saw."

"But what if you'd fallen?"

His brother looked thoughtful, although not at all afraid. "I think that sometimes when you want something badly enough, the risks don't seem so great."

Then he added, "I'm sorry you didn't get to see it, Orry."

Orin decided to tell a partial truth. "I'm happy to say that I did."

"Don't tell me you're not closing your curtains?"

"Oh no, the curtains are always drawn. But I heard a commotion in the corridor and then, luckily, I could hear Mademoiselle Turin and Madame Marcel. They were saying that they'd have the perfect view of the aurora borealis from Mademoiselle Turin's studio, so I took a peek and I also don't regret the risk."

Joseph grinned broadly. "Well, I'm thrilled that it worked out! What a sight, wasn't it?"

45

I t wasn't easy to find sleep tonight. Claire lay on the sofa, waiting for a soothing thought. She found herself wondering what might have happened if she had watched the aurora borealis from her studio. And what if she could have invited Monsieur Rush into the studio, whatever his form, and they'd stood there together beneath the glass?

~~

"Monsieur Rush asked me to give you this the next time I saw you." Madame Marcel said when she came to get the concierge's ration card early the next morning.

"Thank you." Claire opened the envelope and quickly read the lines, then put the note into her pocket. "All right, I'll see you in a while." The concierge looked disappointed that her curiosity hadn't been answered, and who could blame her?

Claire went out into the darkness, into the cold that was getting colder by the day, and walked determinedly to the bakery and took her place in line.

Just as Orin had imagined, her fingers ran over his words many times in the ensuing hours. But maybe it meant nothing. She kept her hands inside her skirt pockets for warmth against the cold, after all. Or maybe it meant everything.

When she returned home, she did as Orin had months ago with *her* note, and folded it between two books on her shelf. *A curiosity*, she told herself, and turned to her models. But the thought of it floated over those streets like strange lights in the sky.

~~

It's not impossible for the aurora borealis to appear in the sky above Paris. But it is strange. It is unusual, just like the turn all of this had suddenly taken. Perhaps, I thought, a train might derail no matter how firmly its tracks have been set, no matter if it's bound on both sides by walls and stone.

PART 3

THE ADVENTURER
AND THE VALKYRIE

46

She was walking with Paul through the old streets of Paris. They passed wood-beamed medieval facades and tavern signs that had disappeared centuries ago.

But the buildings weren't made of stone or timber. They were plaster.

Suddenly, a tower above them began to fall.

An enormous, shadowy hand reached towards her. She reached for it desperately in turn and discovered that her small hand fit neatly into its palm. Now, she was flying above the streets of Paris. She stared down, marveling, and awoke.

~~

It was much later than usual. The sun hadn't woken her. By the time Claire had gotten ready and opened her door, Monsieur Rush was walking past, headed out for the day.

"Bonjour, Monsieur Rush."

"Bonjour, Mademoiselle Turin." *So that was where she lived.* He was about to thank her again for telling him about the aurora, when he gave a start.

"There seems to be a...tower on your skirt."

Claire's eyes went wide. She looked down and saw it, herself: a little white turret from one of her models. The glue must not have been dry when she'd hurried past it just now.

As calmly as she could manage, she bent to retrieve it.

"Where did it come from?"

Gingerly, she pulled it from the fabric, then took a breath. "I made it."

It was sculpted out of plaster that looked old yet new, a fissure there, an exposed stone here. Orin was impressed by the details she'd thought of. "It's rather good."

"Oh – thank you."

It wasn't his fault what happened then — only that he was taller than her. He saw past her into the parlor.

Nothing was immediately remarkable, although his eyes lingered for a moment on the bookshelves. And then, he noticed the floor, nearly covered with small buildings and streets.

Claire knew from his face that he'd seen her great secret. Those models were her past, her dreams, her memories, her comfort, and even her ambition. She couldn't tell him this. "They're models of the old streets of Paris. I-I make them."

To her relief, he didn't mock her. "That's a wonderful way to pass the time! I wish I could do the same at night."

Her instinct was to assure him that he could, maybe give him a bit of advice about getting started — and then she remembered what she'd seen through the keyhole. For the first time, the contrast between those talons and his beautiful hands in daylight made her pity him.

She had to fill the silence, since whatever she felt couldn't be as much sorrow as he felt, himself. So, she went on, "They're making a museum dedicated to the history of the city. And I-my dream is to donate my models."

She laughed at the strange expression on Orin's face. "I said it was a dream! I doubt the museum's future directors would be interested in the creations of some unknown woman with no high social standing or scholarly qualifications."

Orin was trying to say something just the right way. At last, he asked, "Would you allow *me* to have a look?"

Met by silence, he added, "I promise there's a reason."

It's too late anyway, she told herself. "All right."

He felt strange entering this room where she spent so much time alone. But then, as he looked more closely at the models, he forgot all of that.

Just as he'd expected, everything was detailed and beautiful. He moved along the streets, first from above, then by crouching down beside them. Small figures stood here and there, like shadows. He imagined himself in their place, seeing what the city was centuries ago.

There were a few things that had survived to the present. There, for instance - "The Musée de Cluny!" he exclaimed, recognizing the old Gothic building and the ruins of the even older Roman baths. Here, in this time, merchants and beggars had set up tents of dingy cloth against the ruined walls and archways.

A long time passed before he stood up.

"I think your dream is entirely reasonable. These *must* go in the museum. On second thought, are you sure you want to give them away?"

"I don't expect that will be a problem. No one would even consider — "

Orin's brow furrowed again as he stepped back into the corridor. "They might. I-You see, I know Jules Cousin, the-"

Claire knew the name. Cousin was the new head of the library at the Hôtel de Ville, and, I found in her thoughts, a colleague of the men organizing the history museum. "How is it possible...?" she murmured, half to herself.

"Joseph knows everyone. He introduced us and we got on quite well. I like to call on him from time to time. We talk about books. I-I've seen some of the objects for the museum that are being stored near his office. Knowing how fascinated you are about the history of Paris, I feel bad that I never mentioned it.

"It's cloudy today," he went on, but differently than before. There was caution in his voice – he didn't know if he should enter this part of her life. "If you're free, I could introduce you to him now. He's in his office, surely."

From her expression, he could tell she wasn't ready to say anything yet. So he tried to think of practical matters. "Would it be possible to bring a small section of a street? Or if it's not, even that single tower might convince him."

"I," Claire cleared her throat. "I could cut away a section. But you're — I'm sure you have better things to do."

"Not really," he confessed. "And your models are extraordinary. If I bring you to see Cousin, I'd be doing a service for the city. Even though I know someone could still decide I'm a spy at any time."

For the first time that morning, she gave an unguarded laugh. "All right. I'm so nervous that I don't know how I'll manage to even get down the stairs, but all right. I-Thank you." She couldn't keep from meeting his eyes.

"Take your time," he said, trying to keep himself steady. "I'll wait here."

Claire turned and went quickly inside, shutting the door behind her. She let herself slide down to the floor and sit. She closed her eyes and breathed.

At last, she opened her eyes and looked at the small streets across from her, critically regarding each building, each bridge until at last she knew which section she'd choose.

It wasn't easy to make a clean cut, but she was so artful that she managed. The ticking of the clock made her remember that Monsieur Rush was waiting. She took a shawl from the hook by her door and covered the section of the model with it. Then, setting it carefully in the crook of her arm, she opened the door.

Orin watched her come out of her apartment with a shawl-covered bundle. He couldn't believe that this was real, that he could help her, and that he'd dared to say so. There she was, her cheeks flushed nearly as pink as the rosebud earrings she wore, her hair the usual tangle he longed to run his fingers through —

"Might I help you with that?"

"Thank you, but I prefer to keep it with me — this way, I'm too concerned with not dropping it to be afraid of anything else."

For a moment, he felt a terrifying doubt. What if Cousin's colleagues didn't want her models, as unbelievable as that would be? No. "Your models are wonderful," he said firmly, as if to reassure them both. "And Cousin is very friendly, and loves talking about books, besides. You'll get on well. Don't be afraid."

She replied with a skeptical look.

"Fine. In your place, I'd be nervous, too. But it's going to be all right."

They moved slowly down the staircases and through the door. Claire was grateful that by some miracle Madame Marcel wasn't there. What would she have told her?

When they found a cab, she placed the model carefully onto the seat and then was obliged to take Orin's hand to climb up.

They both hoped their gloves might stop the reeling, but it happened all the same. All they could do was sit wordlessly and let the world settle as the cab lurched forward.

It occurred to Orin that he'd never ridden alone in a carriage with a woman before. He wasn't even sure this was proper. But then, Mademoiselle Turin didn't seem ashamed or furtive. And anyway, he told himself, who would notice? And if someone did, they were doing nothing wrong. They were the picture of propriety, there in the open cab with a strangely shaped bundle and a perfectly reasonable distance between them.

Claire was too nervous to talk and he was too unnerved, so they rode in silence, watching the streets roll by till they emerged onto the rue de Rivoli. The air was cold but clear, and it felt like one of the loveliest days Orin had ever had in Paris, or perhaps anywhere. *Don't be a fool*, he told himself.

It didn't seem long before they arrived at the Hôtel de Ville. It looked like crowd was forming in the square in front of it, but they had no time to watch – the cab continued to the destination Orin had requested, a nearly unnoticeable entrance on the rue de Lobau.

"Are you ready?" he asked.

Claire nodded and took a deep breath of the cold air.

47

Monsieur Jules Cousin was tall and somewhat stout, with a perfectly groomed, close-clipped beard. His heavy-lidded eyes were surmounted by small, neat eyebrows that gave him an intimidating air, and yet, when he spoke, he welcomed them warmly, asked after Orin's health, told him about a book he'd just finished.

He was also polite enough not to inquire about the unaccompanied lady his friend had brought with him. Rush had never seemed the sort to –

But after his quick introduction, it seemed his intentions might be above board.

Far more importantly, Cousin was pleased to discover that Mademoiselle Turin also enjoyed reading. After discussing their favorite books on Parisian history, the man seemed quite content with this new acquaintance.

"Well," he said heartily, "you're most welcome at this library, mademoiselle, if you'd like to read even more."

She stared in disbelief. Only the wealthy elite could be members of the Hôtel de Ville's library. "I'm most grateful," she hesitated, "but I hope that your offer will stand even if you don't like my model."

Cousin gave a laugh and gestured to where it sat on the desk between them. "Let's see it."

Claire carefully lifted the shawl.

"Ah…" Cousin bent down so that the buildings were at eye level and began his scrutiny. Orin looked on, anxiously trying to spot any flaws, anything that might rule against her.

Claire couldn't bear to watch. She looked around the room instead. First, of course, she stared in wonder at the bookshelves all around them. They rose nearly to the high ceiling, except on the far wall, where they stopped below two tall windows. There may well have been more books here than she'd ever seen in one place, and this wasn't even the library. They must be part of Cousin's own collection.

After a while, she noticed that all sorts of objects were stacked gently against the lower shelves. Some were sculptures hewn in rough wood or worn iron. Others were flat panels. Old signs, she realized, from taverns and inns, shops and boulangeries. She stared in delight, trying to make them out.

The yellow-gold color of a large, rectangular painted panel caught her eye. Set off against its bright background was a dark figure covered in black fur, with a snout that bristled with cruel-looking teeth. Its feet were hooves. Long talons curved from its elongated hands.

She held back a gasp. It was a perfect portrait of Monsieur Rush at night.

He'd told her that he didn't know why he was "ill". Could this sign lead him to an answer?

He was still watching Monsieur Cousin's careful inspection of her model. He had to see the sign – but how?

Just then, Cousin looked up.

"Well, Mademoiselle Turin, I must confess —"

Her breath caught in her throat.

"—this is fine work indeed."

"Monsieur, I…" She couldn't say anything more.

Cousin gave her a gentle smile. "Of course, I must consult with my colleagues. If you both don't mind waiting, I might do so now."

At her nervous nod, Orin said, "Of course we'll wait."

Cousin carefully took the model under one of his arms and left, shutting the door behind him.

"I knew it!" Orin nearly shouted.

Claire laughed with relief, but only for a moment. "Well, Monsieur Cousin likes my model, but what will the others say?"

"They'll be impressed, of course! He said it was fine work!"

"He did say that, but…" She could only think of what flaws they might find. She pictured the streets, with their vivid names, some of them called after taverns –

And then she remembered the sign. She had an idea. She stood up from her chair and started pacing.

Orin broke her deliberately tense silence. "I'm glad for what's happened, but I feel terrible about making you so nervous."

"It's to be expected. This is so important to me. Thank you."

"After all you've done for *me*, I—" He grinned. "Fortunately, your models really are good."

She gave a distracted chuckle. She was making her paces longer, moving closer and closer to the gold-painted sign. And now— "*Aïe!*"

Orin stood up from his chair. "Are you all right?"

"I'm fine. I-I bumped into this sign. This very…strange sign." She was unexpectedly careful with her words, not wanting to offend him. "I've never seen anything like it."

"It's a tavern sign, isn't it? Cousin told me they were collecting them for the museum. He may not be so happy that they stored them in his office, though. He doesn't like disorder."

"I've never seen one like this," she insisted, and then nonchalantly wandered to look at a few others nearby.

"Oh?" At last he came to see.

179

She kept her back to him, but I could watch him. Orin had never looked at himself after the first night he'd changed. But the sight had stayed burned into his mind. *It's like staring into a looking glass.*

"Yes – this one *is* unusual. Very…Intriguing, even. I wonder how he came by it?"

She turned to him. "Is there- some sort of ticket or label on the other side?"

Gingerly, she helped him lean it forward. Yes - there was a square of paper on the back.

Just then, Monsieur Cousin came back into the room. Orin tipped the sign into place.

"I'm so sorry," Cousin told them hastily, setting the model onto his desk and then coming around to search for something in the drawers.

"They…don't like the model?" It was agony for Claire to ask.

"Oh – I think they do, very much I'd say. But it seems some rebels are starting to assemble outside. They've told us to leave as quickly as we can."

Cousin took some dossiers from the drawer. "I'm sorry for this. When things have calmed down, I'll speak to my colleagues again, and send you word of our decision. Will you leave your model with me? I promise I'll take good care of it."

Claire nodded. "Of course. Thank you, Monsieur Cousin."

He gave a curt, almost military nod. "And now, we must go."

I saw Orin square his shoulders. "Just a moment, Cousin– may I ask where that extraordinary sign came from?"

Cousin looked distractedly at where he was pointing. "Ah yes, that fearsome creature —"

The door burst open. A thin gentleman with a red, flustered face and eyes wide with panic was on the other side. "You should have left already! It's certain they'll enter by force! We must go! Now!"

There was no mob at the back entrance, but the air echoed with voices, like distant drumbeats or canon fire. Orin and Claire remembered the growing crowd they'd seen on the way there.

"It won't be long before all hell breaks loose," the flustered man told them.

Cousin, much calmer, simply said, "Then it is best that we disperse."

And so they did, some heading westward, others to the south. Claire and Orin took the nearest small street that led north to the boulevards.

They moved swiftly at first, but soon they realized something strange: All of the tension they'd felt at the Hôtel de Ville hadn't followed them. The world might be changing just a few streets away, and no one here seemed to know.

They walked more slowly now. After a while, Orin's mind returned to what he'd seen. "In all of your study of Paris, did you ever hear of or-or see such a sort of figure as the one on that sign? It was rather unusual, I thought."

Claire felt such pity for him. To ask her about the sign now was so guileless and out of place. But in his place, she'd be desperate, too.

She tried to remember something that might be helpful. "Well....Villon talks a good deal about Paris's signs in his poems, but there's nothing I can think of like that. But then," she added, "not all signs were mentioned in books, of course."

He nodded, hiding his disappointment.

"But," she went on, "I did find out something that might give you an answer." Now it was her turn to feel pleased at giving him a surprise.

"Oh?"

"When we leaned the sign over, I had a moment to look at the label. It said payment for it was made out to Blondin, 16 rue du Pot-de-Fer."

He stared at her. "You're certain?"

"I have a good memory for things like that." It was all the years of keeping the books at the studio.

"Thank you," he told her simply.

Now they were back on the boulevards. Here, too, life was still going on at its usual pace. "I think I should go warn Joseph, in case he had plans to go to the center of town today."

"Of course. And - thank you, Monsieur Rush."

"Now I know someone whose work will be in a museum." He walked away so quickly that she didn't have time to contradict him.

48

There had been plenty to think about since then, including relief that he'd made it to the Grand Hôtel in time to warn Joseph, and the news of what had happened after they'd left the Hôtel de Ville. But from the moment he'd seen the sign, it had been difficult for Orin to keep much else in mind.

There might be a story attached, he mused again and again. There might be a story attached, some name or circumstance – even a name for the type of creature. Maybe that would lead him to something at last, some way to defeat the monster he became, to make it disappear.

Or at least he might find out how dangerous he really was.

After a sleepless night, he'd spent the past few hours in his room, reading to try to pass the time until he reached an acceptable hour to call on Joseph.

"I suppose you've heard the news?" his brother greeted him the moment he walked into the suite. "Of all the days to get it into your head to see Cousin!" He laughed in disbelief.

"There you were, while the Hôtel de Ville was being invaded by radicals, the *current* government held hostage, with their captors standing about and discoursing on tables for hours, reading their lists of names for a *new* government, everyone contradicting everyone else, people coming and going —"

"Cousin and I left long before all of that started." Of course he hadn't mentioned Claire at all.

"And for all their trouble, the rebels have been appeased by promises of a vote." Joseph walked over to a window. "Things look back to normal. Shall we walk a bit and then have some lunch?"

He didn't see his brother tense.

"Actually, I just came by on my way to an errand. There's a book Cousin made me think of. I'm going to see if I might find it."

Joseph yawned. "Be careful, even so."

"I always am."

"True." After a moment, he yawned again. "Maybe I'll go back to bed for a bit."

"The nightlife is hard on a man."

"Not as much as it was before."

"Well...Go have some dreams that will make up for it."

~~

When Orin told the cab driver his destination, the man raised an eyebrow. "You are cert-ain, monsieur?" he asked in broken English.

He could have argued that he understood French perfectly, despite his accent. But he didn't want to waste any time, so he only gave a decisive nod. The driver shrugged and they lurched forward.

They moved fairly quickly, despite the horse's looking underfed (these days, just about all of the horses in Paris were). Soon, they were in the Latin Quarter.

Normally you'd see students here, and eccentrically dressed bohemians and their ladies strolling and laughing together. Today, the couples were huddled against each other out of hunger and cold, not romance. The street vendors, whose unique cries were also a celebrated, quaint part of the neighborhood, gamely plied their wares, but their voices seemed muted.

The cab continued southward, further south than Orin had ever gone. The buildings were shabbier and less formidable. Many were warped with age, their silhouettes curved like a hunchback's spine.

Now and then, a faint, horrid stench came to his lungs. He realized it must be fumes from the filthy Bièvre river, floating and lingering in the damp air.

The streets became narrower. These were the sort Haussmann had eradicated from so many other parts of the city. Never had he been in the midst of such dirt and poverty, even when he'd gone slumming in New York. There, at least, spaces were wider. The narrow passages between crooked, tumbledown structures here seemed designed for the circulation of fetid air.

On the streets around him, children in clothing too thin for autumn played with dirty rags they'd stolen from the chiffoniers on the rue Mouffetard. Refuse was piled in the gutters.

How could he live as comfortably as he did, Orin wondered in horror. How could he not have known about these people, this place?

The horse stopped at the corner of yet another miserable street. "This is as far as I go," the driver told him.

"Thank you," Orin said, discreetly passing him his fare.

The driver put it into his pocket. "After the elections, this will all change. The Commune is for the people. No more being pushed out to places like this because the rents are raised in the better ones. *Vive la Commune!*"

Orin responded with a thoughtful nod that left the driver unsatisfied, and descended. As he walked purposefully towards his destination, his boot grazed an unsavory-looking heap of something. He suppressed a shudder.

The street number was carved into the stone above the building's doorway. "You're here for what?" a cracked voice demanded. It belonged to an old crone who sat on a broken cane chair just inside the entrance.

"*Bonjour, madame,*" Orin greeted her politely, despite her tone. "I'm looking for a Monsieur Blondin. He has something I'm interested in buying."

The lie worked. The crone sized him up for a moment, then said, "Third floor."

Orin passed into a dark, foul-smelling hallway. The old wood creaked as he climbed the stairs.

At the third floor, he hesitated. Which door was the Blondins'? The old woman's voice came to him surprisingly loudly from below: "Second on the left." She must have been listening to his footsteps.

"*Merci*," he called down.

As he approached the door, he could hear voices on the other side of it.

"Well, now Jacques' gone and ruined it! Vauvert named the spot to everyone who was there. If we don't go today—"

"How can we? He can't walk, and he won't be able to lift anything, either."

"Useless imbecile."

"It's not my fault that—"

Orin couldn't stand there all day. The sunlight wasn't going to last forever, and what if this took longer than he hoped? So, he knocked.

The voices ceased immediately. He waited a few moments for someone to answer the door, but there wasn't a sound. He knocked again.

Still no reply.

"Please—" he called out, "My name is…" for some reason, he thought it best to lie. "Monsieur Jones. I saw something you sold to a friend of mine and I wanted to know if I might purchase something like it from you?"

Silence barely had a second to settle when a thin, wrinkled woman with sharp grey eyes opened the door and stared him up and down. Doubtlessly she took in his well-made clothes, but I could feel that she was inspecting him for more than signs of wealth.

"Come in," she finally said.

The room was low-ceilinged and small, and permeated by the smell of a smoky fire and a stew that must have been in the pot over the hearth for a long time (there was a slight, sickly odor beneath the savory ones). Or maybe what was in the pot was fine, and he was only smelling what was left in the dirty bowls that were stacked on a table in the far corner.

He politely tried to look elsewhere. Dusty fabrics were looped through the ceiling beams as decoration. The other furnishings were a table and some chairs of a delicately carved rosewood and a divan with silk cushions. They were surprisingly fine for such a place. As were the lacquered wood jewelry box that sat on the table and the set of candlesticks beside them.

"What was it you wanted?" the woman asked.

"I...I was at the Hôtel de Ville recently and I saw a very unusual sign – perhaps an old tavern sign – that you had sold to Monsieur Cousin."

The woman gazed at him blankly.

Orin persisted. "There was a...sort of monster on it. It was about this size" – he reached his arms wide, and then bent low to show the dimensions, "with a gold background."

The woman glanced at the others in the room: an old man whose mouth had collapsed inward with no teeth to prop it up, a straggly boy who looked to be about fourteen, and a middle-aged man built like a barrel, strong as an ox, with a cut on his ear and a leg propped up on one of the fine chairs.

"Yes, what of it?"

"I was wondering if there might be another one like it. And - how you came by it?"

The woman fixed him as firmly as the mesmerist had those months ago, only with far more authority. "There may be another one...In fact," she stopped and gave a slight smile, "we're going to the town where we acquired it today. We were just leaving."

"Leaving?"

"We have permission to pass through the city walls in the daytime, so that we can return to our home and bring back the possessions we were forced to leave behind when we were evacuated."

Orin knew that some farmers were allowed to work the fields near the city walls, and that foraging for food was encouraged by any who'd share their findings or sell them to the city. He also knew several families who'd fled to Paris from the suburbs, but they never went back to their homes to fetch things. Perhaps they sent their servants?

"We're going today," the woman repeated, her voice firm and persuasive. I thought of the kinds of beings I knew, casting a spell. "But my husband has hurt his leg. A strong gentleman like you could help us lift a few things, and we could show you the very tavern where the sign was. Perhaps there's another one like it there."

Orin felt uneasy. What if they couldn't get back to the city before sunset? "I'm very sorry – I'm not as strong as I look. If you could tell me the name of the town, when the Siege has ended, I'll go pay a call at the tavern."

"Why should I help you," the woman asked coldly, "if you won't help me?"

"I would pay you, of course."

For just a moment, she hesitated. Then, "*Ah bon?* Well then, you'll pay us *and* help citizens in need."

"Go with them, *bourgeois*," the ox-like man's voice boomed. "She'll never give you what you want, otherwise."

"'*Bourgeois*'?" the old gentleman wheezed. "He's a foreigner."

"…who can afford to pay for only words and wants to buy a useless sign. And who doesn't live in this neighborhood," the man retorted. "*Bourgeois*."

The boy spat.

Something menacing hung in the air, like the sourness coming from the stew. But Orin's annoyance at their accusations overcame any fear he might have felt. "I'm nothing like what you think me to be." Now he addressed the old woman. "We must be back by late afternoon."

The woman shrugged. "The gates close at six. We'll have to be!"

"Earlier. Three."

"All right, three-thirty."

The ox-like man laughed. "You see, *bourgeois*? It's always her way. She never gives in."

The woman glared at him. "Oh shut up you useless ——"

"Let's go then," the boy interrupted.

49

It was quickly agreed that Orin couldn't use the ox-like man's papers. His accent and his clothes would give him away if the guards at the city gates started asking questions. And the neighbors might ask questions of their own. Little urchins might follow them, intrigued and hoping for pocket money from a well-dressed stranger. So they told him to hide in the cart instead.

He lay down on his back and slid as deeply inside as he could go. They covered the top with a sheet and propped some empty crates at the open end to conceal him.

Orin shifted away from splinters and tried not to worry. He stared up at the filthy sheet. Someone began to pull the cart forward. He imagined it was the wiry boy at first, but then again, the woman was obviously stronger than all of them put together.

It wasn't easy going. He put his arms beneath his head to keep it from bumping against the bottom of the cart as they rolled over the uneven, slick cobblestones. But there was no way to protect the rest of his body. And there was no point in trying to deduce their direction. Their path twisted and turned so often. Perhaps they were going southward. Or perhaps they were headed south, then following the city wall westward? Or maybe they were heading north.

A long while later, the cart stopped. He could sense a crowd just beyond the sheet. They were waiting at one of the gates in the city wall. For a besieged city, a surprising number of people were coming and going from it.

Orin heard the woman and the old man's muffled voices, then a reply from a voice he didn't recognize. Some laughter, then they rolled through the gate.

He could feel that they'd left the rhythmic ruts of the cobbles for something more unpredictable. At times, the wheels rolled smoothly, and then too quickly, only to end up stuck until the woman and her family pushed and pulled.

It was this way for a while, until suddenly the crates were pulled away and a hand grabbed one of his ankles.

The old woman poked her head inside. "There are no officers here. Come out and help us pull the bloody cart."

Orin's boots met the ground: high, untended grasses. They were in a field a good distance from the city wall. He'd never seen it from the outside. Its dark stonework towered over the grasses like a threat, hiding the beauty that was inside of it.

There were people all around them. Some tilled small vegetable gardens in plots they'd cleared. Others were heading farther out, or moving past them to return to the city.

"Come on," the woman said sharply.

He went to the front of the carriage and took the yoke on his back, and they continued forward.

It wasn't long before he could see houses, a church. "Get back inside," the woman instructed.

They passed a checkpoint and continued on. How far was it? For a moment, Orin was afraid. What if they got lost? What if they couldn't get back in time?

But the fear passed. He was taking an immense risk, but he was going to find some kind of answer at last. He'd see the tavern where the sign had hung. Maybe he'd find out the name of the owner and meet with him.

He felt the hand on his ankle again and slid out of the wagon.

This time, they were on a small, pleasant street lined with large stone houses. Each house had a little front garden full of dull amber leaves and dried stalks, signs of autumn and the absence of their owners.

"Which house is yours?"

Orin really did believe them, I realized. He should have known they had no business in a bourgeois home and wouldn't even have been hired as servants, but he was too caught up in the allure of answers about the enchantment to consider anything else.

The woman looked around and pointed to what appeared to be the largest house.

A slight doubt at last flickered into his mind. But they'd need time to visit the tavern. He couldn't waste it arguing. So he nodded and followed them.

When they reached the door, the woman suddenly stopped. "Oh!" she cried out, in a comically poor performance, "I've forgotten our key!"

The wiry boy walked over to a large front window and roughly pushed and pulled at the shutters, over and over, until they snapped open.

Then, he scanned the ground and found a large rock and began smashing the glass.

That broke something for Orin, too. He finally understood that he'd let himself be fooled. He'd blindly raced towards this light of hope, but he should have waited.

Here he was, far from the city, at the mercy of this family and desperate that the gates wouldn't be shut before they returned. He should have given it more thought, should have discussed it with Joseph.

And why hadn't he? Because he'd been afraid his brother would start asking questions and find out that Mademoiselle Turin had been with him when he'd discovered the sign.

Glass was falling in knifelike shards into the little strip of garden below.

When that was finished, the boy climbed inside the window and the woman climbed up beside him.

"Well," the old man stared at Orin, "you're not good enough to help an elder?"

They walked to the window and Orin lifted the man up towards the boy, who took his hands and pulled him inside.

"And now you," the boy said.

Orin shook his head.

"There are other people coming to this village today. We don't want them to see anyone standing here. And you won't want them to find you here alone."

And so, enraged, Orin climbed through the window and joined them.

The interior was dim; all of the other windows were shuttered. The furniture was covered in sheets that fluttered as they moved from room to room.

At first, they didn't take anything, and Orin felt relieved. Then he realized they were simply deciding *what* to take; after all, space in the cart was limited.

In each bedroom, the boy got down and crawled, carefully stroking the floorboards. In the third one, he gave a triumphant grunt. There, beneath a loose plank, was a box.

"Papers?" the woman asked.

"It's locked." He reached into his pocket and pulled out a small bit of metal.

After some twisting, the box came open. "Jewelry," he reported. "probably paste."

"Take it anyway," the woman said.

"But you knew that, of course," Orin muttered, rolling his eyes.

"What?" the woman turned to him.

"You knew that they were paste, since they're yours."

She gave a cruel laugh.

The real owners of the house had had time to prepare before leaving. There was nothing of immense value left. Still, the group managed to leave with that box, along with china and some paintings ("The frames will fetch a good price," the old man acquiesced).

"Ah," Orin said, as they moved purposefully towards another house, "perhaps your long absence has confused you, and *this* is where you live?"

The boy snorted. "That's right."

More forced shutters and fallen glass followed that. More tours inside of ghostly houses, where Orin imagined families' joys and griefs.

As they approached their fourth house, the woman suddenly stopped and surreptitiously pointed up the street. From far away they could see several figures. They moved with bold confidence, some carrying what looked to be clubs.

"Should we do another?" the boy asked, swaggering a bit.

The woman considered the group. "One more. But let's keep a distance."

"Bring the cart," she ordered Orin and the boy. It was harder to pull with their loot in it, but fortunately, the yoke was wide enough for the two of them to rest on their shoulders. They rolled it behind them until the woman considered it safe.

She signaled them to stop in front of a house that was smaller than the others, though it looked as if it had been well-kept. "All right. Let's be quick."

The shutters were broken, the window was smashed, they climbed inside – Orin had gotten used to the rhythm of it. Soon enough, they were ready to leave. But the woman gave them a persuasive look. "That little table is rather fine."

The old man rolled his eyes. "You never can resist heavy furniture."

"It's real marble," she retorted. "It'll fetch a good price."

"If you can bear to part with it," the boy snickered.

That explained the fine furnishings in their apartment.

"I can for the price someone will pay for this," she said. But it was hard for any of them to believe her. No one was buying furniture now.

Still, the ox-like man was right – the woman always got her way. It took all of them to carry the table out of the window and into the cart. Orin glanced inside nervously, wondering if there would be room for him.

"It's getting late, *bourgeois*," the woman said. "Let's go."

"All right," Orin agreed. "Where is the tavern?"

"Tavern?"

"The tavern where you got the sign."

The boy snickered. "Him and that bloody sign."

"There is no tavern," the woman told him flatly.

The color drained from Orin's face.

"There's probably a tavern here," the old man wheezed. It was almost as if he were trying to console Orin, or to try to defend what they'd told him. Or maybe it was just fatigue in his voice. "But it's not where we got that sign."

The woman nodded. "Where *did* we get that? It got us a pretty profit, but I can't recollect...."

"It wasn't us took it in the first place," the boy cut in. "Remember? You got it from Mariette, who said she got it from that man who used to come around -"

"The one who fell down the stairs two weeks ago," the old man nodded. "She bartered it to us for that stone cross, to bury with him. Poor girl."

"And the man?" Orin's throat was dry.

"Dead, I said," the boy articulated in a mockingly slow drawl, "you stupid *bourgeois*."

Orin glared at him. "You said he's the one who found the sign." He switched to a slow drawl like the boy's. "Where did he get it, you stupid thief?"

The woman and the old man had a good laugh at that.

And then they had another. "How do you think," the woman chuckled, "that we'd know more than that?"

"Mariette, then!" Orin's voice was close to a growl.

"She left after that."

"She threw herself into the Seine," the boy explained.

"Better than the Bièvre," the old man wheezed, and he and the woman laughed again.

"My husband was of no use to us today, but you came along at the perfect time. Surely you understand I couldn't let you go without helping us. Now," the woman's tone became menacing, "you're not going to betray us when we get to the city gates?"

"Why would I?" If he did denounce them, he knew that he'd also be held for questioning.

"He has to get back home, remember?" the boy said, "Probably to dine at some fine place and meet with his mistress."

Now *Orin* laughed, surprising them all. "Do you think that if I had all that, I'd have bothered coming here?"

He went on, raggedly, "You did a fine job taking advantage of me. But if we cross paths again, I won't be such a fool."

"It's a deal," the old man concluded, looking rather satisfied.

Orin pulled the now-heavy cart as far as he could manage, taking turns with everyone. When it was time for him to hide, he lay inside it like a dead man, staring up but unseeing.

He had failed. He had failed and almost lost everything. He *had* lost everything. There was no more hope.

After a while, he drew out his watch. It was just three. The woman had more than kept her word on that, at least…and then he realized, of course, that she didn't have a watch and had simply pretended to negotiate with him. It was only by chance that they were going back to Paris now.

They passed through the city gate, then the National Guardsmen's improvised barracks and found a small side street where no one would see him get out of the cart. He walked away from them without looking back.

~~

As she left the studio that evening, Claire saw Monsieur Rush's coattails disappear into his room. It was one of those days, then.

Worse than she could have imagined.

50

When Claire had first spotted the tavern sign, I was as surprised as she was.

The difference was, I knew its story.

Eighty years ago, when the Revolution had ended, Yselda and I began our long tradition of enjoying the pleasures of Paris. Then, we were among the *Merveilleuses*, women whose audacious fashions shocked the rest of the civilized world. We gallivanted through the city in diaphanous dresses, bright ribbons, enormous wigs.

It made sense to us, for we had never much cared for mortal rules regarding dress. And it made sense to many of the mortals, as well. After the Terror, who wouldn't want excess and eccentricity?

Those were some of the happiest years of my life. But I also began to notice something: Try as I might, dress as I might, cast whatever charms and spells I might, Yselda was always more eye-catching.

We spent quite a lot of time at a particular café, laughing with our fellow *Merveilleuses* and *Incroyables*, our gentlemen counterparts who dressed in outlandish colors and oversized redingotes with enormous lapels and collars. The café was on the Left Bank, not far from the Procope. It wasn't an especially remarkable place – only those of us who graced it with our presence were remarkable (that's how we saw it, anyway). Still, there was one other thing of note: the sign that hung outside.

It was a large, gold-painted panel with an image of a strange, unnamable sort of monster on it. He was somewhat human-shaped, but covered in dark fur. Sharp teeth bristled from his muzzle. He had long talons instead of fingers, and hooves instead of feet. The monster stood on those two hooved feet with his back bent slightly forward, as though he were sneaking off somewhere, or dancing.

The sign wasn't particularly important to me then. It was simply something I often saw. It hung there as I watched the adoring gaze of men always turn to Yselda, despite the new wig I wore or the red ribbons around my alluring legs. It was present at my first heartbreak — a minor incident, fortunately, but one that would be repeated. I'd used all of my charms, but still he'd turned to Yselda…who hadn't turned away.

Years passed and we did and saw so many other things that I forgot the café and its sign. But when I cast my curse, that place of my own first heartbreaks must have still been there, deep within me.

That was how Orin and the sign were connected. And I could never tell him.

51

O rin woke the next morning to the ache of loss. A stiffness, more than the effect of the cart ride, as though his body had been beaten.

He might have gone back to the Hôtel de Ville to inspect the sign more closely. But somehow he knew that there was no other writing, no hidden inscription. There was just that single label, whose address had gotten him nowhere.

It was useless, and he was useless, he thought, as Claire came down the corridor.

"Bonjour, Mademoiselle Turin." He noticed the shadows under her eyes.

Émile emerged from the stairwell. "Sorry I'm late. I had to wait at the butcher's this morning. Marguerite had had enough."

Orin envied him the tenderness he could show.

"What a nasty, cold business!" Émile continued. "Sometimes you do see some interesting things, though, don't you? This morning, a pigeon flew overhead and everyone followed it with their eyes, trying for the life of them to see if it had an important dispatch in its tailfeathers.

"The little fellow landed just beside the queue and stared at us for a while. I think he was waiting for someone to scatter some crumbs, what with the way we were watching him. But we were a waste of a crowd — there wasn't a crumb anywhere."

"Poor pigeon," Claire said.

"Haw haw!" Émile's guffaw brought some life to the cold morning. "He's got it far better than us! If he's a messenger pigeon, he's well-housed and fed, and kept warm with his fellow pigeons, while we slowly freeze and fear everything from Prussians to reds!

"And even if he's just an ordinary pigeon, he's one of the few living things safe in Paris – you know few people would dare risk killing a messenger. Not so for the rats, or even the cats and dogs now – butchers are selling them at Les Halles! Better to be the pigeon!"

Seeing Orin's questioning expression, Émile shrugged. "You might think that's a joke, what with this being a city with so many lapdogs. But then, people aren't themselves when they're hungry." He turned to Claire. "Tell Madame Marcel to keep her cat in sight. I hear cat tastes even better than canine."

"I don't think anyone here would do anything to Hippolyte," Claire laughed.

Émile shook a finger at her. "They will if there's nothing to eat."

"Nothing *good to eat*, don't you mean?" Orin interjected. "After all, there are still dry goods and bread – well, the bread is still somewhat edible, anyway."

"True, monsieur," Émile nodded. "But you forget that this is a city of gourmands. They're starting to give us dried fish or lard at the municipal butcher's. If the people can't have proper meat now and then, they'll find it another way."

He grinned. "You see, it *is* better to be a pigeon."

~~

It was November, and some things had changed, and others stayed the same. The elections set up to appease the revolutionaries ended up stopping the revolution; the majority of Parisians voted to keep the current government in place.

In the towns beyond the city walls, soldiers pushed forward or retreated, fired at each other, destroyed homes and entire streets, shelled old churches, and agonized with bullet or bayonet wounds until death finally took them, or until they were discovered and brought back through the city gates to one of the *ambulances*.

Often, the Parisians tensed with hope. They were constantly certain that with *this* battle, the Siege would end. Many followed the fighting avidly and had their heroes among the soldiers. Their hope and passion might have kept them a bit warmer than those who were less convinced. Still, everyone suffered from the cold, damp days.

~~

An odor of illness and decay emanated from the windows of the Grand Hôtel. Orin and Joseph had come to expect it.

One of the hotel's wings had been converted into an *ambulance*. Unfortunately, regardless of the opulent surroundings, it had a reputation as one of the worst in the city.

The smell didn't reach Joseph's suite, but everything felt different now, sadder, faded.

"Why don't you leave?" Orin asked one day.

His brother shrugged. "Who knows what will happen before this is over? This place you hate so much might become our stronghold. At least the décor is still lovely."

Orin said no more about it. After all, Joseph had been right about so much, including the tins he kept carefully locked in the trunks. Sometimes, they opened one together. Certain contents were better if you heated them, so Joseph bought a frying pan, and they warmed the tinned food over the fireplace, coughing in the acrid sapling smoke. Parisians didn't use coal for their fires, and it was getting harder to find good, dry wood.

Despite the dreary circumstances, cooking this way made them feel like boys, or cowhands sitting around a campfire. "We're out on the frontier after all," Joseph remarked through the smoke.

52

O rin sometimes took a tin back to his room. As he cooked his early supper in his small fireplace, he felt guilty, wondering what Claire had found to eat, wondering if she'd eaten enough.

The memory of the single bad conversation they'd had in the corridor would inevitably come to him.

One day a few weeks before, the newspapers had started to suggest something, honestly but calmly: The city's food supplies were running low.

The next morning, they'd greeted one another as they always did.

"Bonjour, Mademoiselle Turin."

"Bonjour, Monsieur Rush."

They were alone in the corridor. Monsieur Rouline hadn't arrived yet. Orin pushed himself to speak, trying not to think about the mess with the proposal. "I wanted to know if…you might like if I brought you some food every day? I promise it will be the best sort, from Paris's finest restaurants," he added with a joking smile.

Claire hesitated for just a moment. Like almost everyone, she wasn't starving, but a constant hunger gnawed at her, as incessant and insistent as the sound of the canon fire that boomed dully from beyond the city walls.

Real, filling food every day, and no longer having to stand on line…. It was a promise her body ached to agree to.

But she shook her head. "No thank you, Monsieur Rush."

Orin was as surprised as I was. "I-I'm sorry if I misspoke. I didn't mean you would pay for the food – it would be my pleasure to —"

If I say "yes", she told herself, I belong to him.

"I understand," she replied. "And it's very kind of you. But I can't accept."

His silence made her nervous, so she went on, "If I did, people would think – they would think that we had…made an arrangement." Her cheeks were red.

"Oh." He kept his voice cold, but inside he was burning, just like her lovely cheeks. How could he have been so naïve? But then, he reasoned, she wasn't the only person he was planning to help.

He went on coolly, "I didn't mean to make this offer only to you. I thought I might also help Monsieur Rouline and Madame Marcel."

Had Claire not been so embarrassed, or felt so trapped, she would have let them decide. Instead, she simply cut him off. "They'll be fine. We all will be. There's no need. You should give to charity instead."

Does she think I'm that selfish? he wondered. "I already do," he returned, quietly. "You aren't charity, and neither are Monsieur Rouline or Madame Marcel."

The air between them was like ice. Claire found it painful to breathe. "I understand. But I hope you understand me."

When she thought about it afterwards, she knew she wasn't angry at him. She was only tired, tired of fighting her body, tired of these incidents that came, again and again, that made her question her decency, her reason, her heart. Why did he have to be what he was? Why was he the only one who could help her?

The next morning, they were both glad to see Émile on the bench outside the studio. "Well, hello, you two. Have a look at this!" He held up a newspaper cartoon of a cat jumping down the throat of a man seated at the dinner table. "The dangers of eating mice is that your cat might chase after them", the caption read.

Claire and Orin broke into laughter — more than the cartoon merited, but it was what was needed.

That afternoon, Orin came up the stairs just as she was escorting a sitter out of the studio. They exchanged a friendly nod and she mentioned a book he might find interesting.

The next morning, he asked her the author's name.

And so, things returned to the way they usually were. They never spoke about his offer again.

Orin could see they were all hungry, no matter that Mademoiselle Turin said it didn't matter. He wished there were some way to buy food for her and these other meaningful people in his life. He'd even considered sending it to them anonymously, but she'd know where it had come from, and hate him. There was nothing he could do.

When he ate with those thoughts as an accompaniment, all he could taste was cinders.

53

W ork was slow; it always was in the darker months of the year. Claire considered it a time to rest a bit, to work more on her models, to read, to wander her beloved streets and avenues and boulevards.

This morning as she walked, she was thinking about a new process a man named Dagron had invented: capturing vast numbers of letters onto microfilm, which could be inserted into a metal tube that was secured among a carrier pigeon's feathers, in lieu of a single tightly rolled message. When it arrived at its destination, the microfilm could be projected onto a screen and all of the letters transcribed and delivered.

Since the Siege had begun, her correspondence with Paul had been one-sided. There was no way he could have replied to her letters. But now, there was hope. The pigeons didn't always return, especially as the weather had gotten so much colder. Still, the idea that a letter from him just might reach her made her feel a bit like flying.

Suddenly, someone called out her name:

"Claire! Claire Turin!"

She turned around to see a handsome man wearing a National Guard uniform. He was tall and thin, with a fine complexion, dark eyes, neatly combed chestnut hair, and a carefully groomed mustache.

I was alarmed to see Claire's tired expression lift like a veil at the sight of him. "Rossignol?!"

As they exchanged broad smiles and warm words, I sifted through her sudden rush of memories: Claire and her brother as children running happily about the streets of Paris, which then were a scramble of modern buildings and centuries-old, ramshackle ones being demolished (history was being undone in her history).

Other children usually joined them. One was pale with chestnut hair – there he was. The memories were conflated. I saw Rossignol as a child and then as a young man, and even more or less as he looked now, though it must have been a few years earlier.

Walking with him today was an elderly woman in mourning. Like Claire, her careworn face had changed to something much brighter at this reunion.

"Madame Rossignol! How are you?"

"Not well," the woman seemed hesitant to admit. "But getting better. If you have the time, shall we sit together for a while?"

They picked their way carefully along the boulevard's crowded sidewalks, chose the café that seemed the warmest, and spent the next few hours talking mostly of those memories I'd seen.

Sometimes they would mention details of their current circumstances, as well. I learned that the Rossignols had come to Paris from the suburbs and were staying with wealthy relatives on the Île Saint-Louis.

The conversation turned to Rossignol's uniform. "We're fortunate to have you protecting the city, I see." Claire's voice was half teasing, half approving.

Rossignol hung his head a little. "I know you don't care for any kind of involvement in war, but I can't imagine not doing *something*. Though it turns out that's mostly spending long, cold nights on the ramparts."

"I forbade him from joining the *garde mobile*. I told him he could do what he likes, as long as he doesn't join the troops outside the city," Madame Rossignol said, with a firm smile.

Claire nodded. "Well, it's an admirable thing to be watching out for us all. But I agree with your mother – I'm glad you're not going any farther."

Then, she went on, "I'm so happy we ran into each other! I wish you'd told me you were here." She looked radiant.

"I did think of it. But I assumed you'd left, like most of the other Parisians we know." Rossignol shook his head. "I should have known better. I can think of few people who love this city more than you. Of course you'd stay!"

…And then they were back to memories again.

"Do you remember Mengin?" Rossignol asked with a grin.

Claire burst out laughing, and Madame Rossignol echoed the name in askance.

"The fellow who sold pencils," Claire explained. "But he did it in such a strange way, standing outside his caravan dressed as a knight, saying all sorts of bizarre and funny things. And when you bought a packet of pencils, you also received a little coin with his face on it."

"Do you still have yours?" Rossignol asked.

Claire thought for a moment. "I don't know. It must be somewhere…"

"And do you remember…." he went on, and so did she, on and on.

They sat there for so long it began to grow dark. "Oh," Claire gave a start and realized that sunset had come to mean something else for her. She quickly justified her alarm. "I'm afraid I've kept you too long!"

"Not at all," Rossignol told her, "it was a far more pleasant afternoon than we'd anticipated."

"We were thinking of coming back to the Boulevards later this week – perhaps on Sunday," Madame Rossignol put in as they began to say their farewells. "If you're free, we would very much enjoy your company."

To my dismay, Claire agreed. They parted in the vivid grey-blue of twilight.

They would call on each other many more times in the days and weeks that followed. Rossignol was kind and handsome. When I wasn't full of dread, I would listen to Claire's heart when she was with him. She felt safe and as if she'd returned to happier times. Whenever they were outside, they stood closely together. It was as though he could shelter her from the cold.

54

J oseph picked at his plate. He seemed restless — or even angry, Orin thought, looking more closely.

"All right," he said in a low voice, "so we both know it's probably not rabbit. But at least the sauce is good, and we have good imaginations."

Joseph looked up at him. "I have something to tell you – about Mademoiselle Turin."

"What do you mean?"

"I- Yesterday I saw her on the Île Saint-Louis, with a gentleman."

Orin didn't react. He didn't move at all. And then, after a few moments, his lips relaxed into a smile. "Do you think she stays locked up in her studio all day? She does have a social life, Joseph. She was probably out with Monsieur Rouline, or some family friend."

"No- this was...." Joseph pushed the sauce-drowned meat around in his plate again. "This was a young man. Rather handsome. And they were walking together very closely. I think it's over, Orry."

I saw Orin's shoulders subtly square. "Over? Nothing ever began," he laughed. "She even refused my hand in marriage, in case you've forgotten!" Joseph looked away, partly out of regret for the proposal again, and partly because he couldn't bear any of this.

Dear Joseph's romantic heart was breaking. His brother and Mademoiselle Turin seemed truly matched. And now.... He couldn't help but blame Orin's hesitation, his holding back, his refusal to –

"Don't look so sad. I've made many mistakes in this beautiful city, and as soon as the Siege is over, I plan to leave it anyway. I'm better in New York – I'm reasonable there."

"Because there's no one there that you think is worth getting unreasonable over," Joseph muttered under his breath.

"Quite right," Orin retorted, and Joseph cursed himself for forgetting his brother's excellent hearing.

"I'll go back there and live out my life with my books, helping Father with business as much as I can, taking walks along the East River. I'll get to watch the city grow. Maybe I'll make a few investments."

Orin cut and took a bite of whatever was on his plate with a satisfied air, and changed the subject.

Joseph might have believed him. His brother had seemed tired lately. But he was no fool, and even if he had been, he would have noticed that afterwards, as they strolled along the boulevards, Orin suddenly remarked, "I'm very happy for her. She's a wonderful person. I only hope he deserves her."

It was one of those days when the clouds seem to carry darkness instead of rain. They turned at the Porte Saint-Martin and began to retrace their steps. When they arrived at his street, though it was a bit early yet, Orin took his leave, and Joseph continued into the bleak shadows.

55

When he'd first seen that scrap of black paper, the calling card of the Cercle des Thaumaturges, Orin had sensed a strange sort of magic tied to it. When he'd picked it up from the ground in front of the shuttered bookshop, it had pricked at his fingers.

It was probably too simple. They were probably charlatans, just like everyone else. After all, why post an advertisement at a small bookshop?

Still, whenever another attempt to find an answer or a cure failed, he knew there was still the black paper. The magic that exuded from it had to mean something. That was what made it his last resort.

There was, of course, the shopkeeper's cryptic warning: "They are only to be contacted for serious matters, monsieur. They are so curious."

But he ignored it. He lifted the paper from a little box of found things he kept on the mantle and let it prickle in his fingers.

~~

Orin had sometimes considered what he would write to the Cercle. His French would have to be impeccable; he didn't want to give away any information about himself, including any indication that he might be a foreigner. But he *did* want to give them as much information as possible about his condition, without saying too much, even so. That afternoon, as the light faded further, he sat on his bed and leaned on the nightstand and wrote:

Messieurs,

Since the age of 12, I have, each night, transformed from a perfectly healthy man, into a monster. I seem to remain myself in mind; it is only my body that changes, or at least, so far. I was given information that leads me to fear I might one day commit some sort of terrible violence.

I have spent my life ever since in search of a cure, or simply of some knowledge as to what has befallen me and why. I dearly wish that you might help me, as you have helped so many others.

I remain at your disposal regarding a meeting time and place, although I prefer not to travel after my nightly transformation.

I thank you for the care and attention you have no doubt brought to this letter, and eagerly await your reply,

Monsieur X.

Balloon post was the only way to send letters outside the city and there was no way to be certain they'd arrive at their destination. But the post office still operated normally within Paris. The next morning, Orin crossed the Seine and posted the letter far from where he lived.

He'd added instructions to the end of his message. The reply was to be given to the barman at a brasserie not far from that very post office.

Before the war had started, a certain Lord Warwick Hammond, a blustery, fat Englishman, used to go to the brasserie every day. He liked the place so well that he even rented one of the numbered drawers that stood beside the bar as a place to keep his napkin and cutlery in.

Hammond's drawer was number 22, and it had been a long time since he'd opened it. He'd left just before the Siege, but had told his dear new friend Joseph Rush that he would sorely miss the little brasserie and had arranged to keep the drawer for himself until his return. The brothers had sometimes laughed about it being a place where they could receive secret messages, or even keep valuables. Now, Orin would use it for exactly that.

He entered the brasserie and spoke quietly to the barman. "If you receive a letter for me, please wait till the person who's delivered it has gone, and then put it in drawer 22." He ended his request with a few francs, and the barman nodded.

The next day, just after lunchtime, Orin passed by and casually went up to the little drawers. He slid open 22 and found nothing but Lord Hammond's napkin, fork, and knife.

But the following day, there was a small envelope beneath Lord Hammond's napkin.

Orin smoothly tucked the envelope into his breast pocket. Then, he took the napkin and a spoon and sat down at a table, just as any customer would. If someone from the Cercle des Thaumaturges was watching, they wouldn't realize he was Monsieur X.

When his soup arrived, he took a spoonful and surreptitiously swept the place with a look. No one seemed suspicious or out of place, and no one looked very happy about what was in their plate. These days, most restaurants served whatever could be found. There were weak soups of wilted vegetables or weeds floating in a cloudy broth. No one cared to question the meat that was on the menu.

Diners had to bring their own bread. Before the Siege, this might have been an opportunity to show status and taste with a loaf from the finest boulangerie in the city. Now, anything that could be used to make bread had been requisitioned and was close to running out. All of the bread in Paris was grainy, rough, and sour-tasting.

Some of the people at the tables attempted to soften their loaves by leaving them to soak a long while in their soup. But that didn't help much. They still flinched at the texture of the bread against their teeth. Orin tried not to laugh – and it was a sympathetic laugh, anyway; he'd done the same thing at lunch with Joseph.

When it seemed like he'd spent enough time there, he paid at the bar and slipped a few extra francs to the barman. "What did he look like?" he muttered.

The barman shrugged. "Nothing special. Average height, black suit, pale."

He walked aimlessly around the streets for a while, still wary that someone might be watching. When he felt safe, he headed home.

Back in his room, he sat down on the bed and took the note from its envelope.

A spidery script greeted him.

> *Monsieur X,*
>
> *It is our habit to convene at midnight. But in light of your circumstances, and in order for us to witness this transformation that you've spoken of, we invite you to the Ossuaire de Paris, Place d'Enfer, tomorrow, a half hour before sunset. Bring with you the enclosed note to present to the guard at the gate.*
>
> *We are eager to meet you,*
>
> *Le Cercle des Thaumaturges*

56

The good light was gone for the day, so Émile and Claire closed up the studio. They had just stepped into the corridor, chatting and laughing, when Orin's door opened and he hurried out.

Where could he be going with darkness on the way, Claire wondered, and why was he holding a traveling bag?

"Bonsoir, Monsieur Rush," Émile called out.

It seemed Orin had planned to hurry past them, but now he stopped. "Bonsoir."

It was a greeting they heard often, but, Claire thought, whenever he said it, he was returning home.

She was grateful for Émile. "What, have you managed to book passage with a balloon?" he guffawed, pointing to the bag.

I doubt they could see him pale there in the late afternoon shadows. He made his voice light. "Just a quick errand."

Mademoiselle Turin was looking at him with a quizzical expression. He would have liked to make a joke, or even stay and talk for a while. But there was too little time before sundown. "I'm sorry – I must go."

Claire tried to sound cheerful. "We won't keep you. Have a nice evening."

"The same to both of you. Good evening, Mademoiselle Turin," he added for some reason. *If I don't come back.* The thought skittered into his mind like an insect, and he tried to crush it. This was his chance. This was going to work – he would be - He hurried down the stairs, not allowing himself to think of anything more.

"That's strange…" Claire couldn't help murmuring, back on the sixth floor.

Émile shrugged. "All men are mysteries."

"But it's no mystery he falls ill every night—"

"Perhaps he's cured."

That didn't comfort her. In fact, for some reason it only increased her reasonless, rising panic. "I'm going to call on Anne this evening," she said, and moved to continue downstairs with him.

She noticed a glint of surprise in Émile's eyes and cursed herself, but he only asked, "You should take something to keep warm, shouldn't you?"

Claire nodded. Of course he was right.

"Hope you don't mind if I go ahead."

"No! Have a good evening!" She unlocked her door and reached for her mantle on its hook, then raced down the stairs and up the street towards the boulevard.

There, the sidewalks were impossibly dense with people and the street was choked with traffic. How would she ever find Monsieur Rush?

Something strange happened then.

I don't know if it was the same magic that made the flowers bloom on the carpet, or if it was a coincidence, or that mundane magic of seeing someone everywhere when they mean the world to you. Whatever the reason, in the midst of the crowds and traffic, she spotted him in the back of a cab.

Then, another inexplicable thing happened: Despite the traffic, Claire easily found a cab of her own. "Please, you must follow that cab. But don't let them know we're following. It's a matter of life and death."

The driver grinned and coaxed his horse to a fast walk. This reminded him of better days, when finely dressed ladies in a frenzy had the exact same instructions. He'd follow the cab or private carriage in question all the way to the Bois de Boulogne, where Monsieur was inevitably taking a drive with his current mistress.

Maybe, Claire thought, Monsieur Rush was planning to spend the night at the Grand Hôtel with Joseph. Or maybe he really *had* been cured. That caused a strange twinge inside of her. Why wouldn't he have said it?

But why would he think to tell me? she chided herself.

These thoughts were quickly drowned in the waves of dread rolling inside of her.

I felt them, too. I knew from the set of Orin's shoulders that he wouldn't allow himself to reconsider or to be afraid. What weak light there was grew darker. It would be sunset soon.

57

The ride was long, despite the cabs' swift pace. After all, there was most of the city to cross. But at last, we arrived at a strangely open, barren-feeling space. Diagonal lines of Haussmannian boulevards shot away from it in all directions but one, where there was a train station. There was life all around it, but somehow the square felt desolate.

When he'd read the address in the note from Le Cercle des Thaumaturges, Orin had given a low chuckle: La Place d'Enfer – the Square of Hell. It had been called this since anyone could remember, even in the era when I best knew Paris.

For decades now, it was also where you could go to walk among the bones of the dead.

Orin got out of the cab. All around the square, groups of people were furtively picking up branches and debris and cutting down the trees' bare limbs for firewood, but he didn't notice. He only saw the guard standing by the doorway in front of him. He walked swiftly towards the man and handed him the note.

Later, he'd hear that the Catacombs had been walled up so that they wouldn't serve as a hideout for Prussians who might infiltrate the city. But there was no wall here now. Instead, the metal door opened into a bare stone vestibule. A doorway on one side led into darkness. When Orin approached it, he could see a spiral staircase circling deep into the ground.

Lanterns had been placed on some of its steps. Their weak, flickering light only made the steps themselves visible. The darkness remained thick and black.

He started downwards.

After a few turns of the stairway, subterranean dampness crept to his nose and chilled his skin. Down he continued for a long time, a blind, unending descent. Fear began to seep into him like the dampness.

The next time I see the surface, he reminded himself, *it may be as a man entire.*

At last, though it felt impossible by now, the staircase ended in a long, low-ceilinged corridor that had been carved out of the stone beneath the city. Here, not only lanterns, but candles as well, pushed away a little more of the darkness.

Like the staircase before it, the corridor seemed endless. Orin tried to distract himself with thinking of how long it must have taken to set out all of the lights.

Finally, he saw something new: scattered columns painted with black and white bands. He passed through a doorway below a bold-lettered inscription: "Stop! You are entering the kingdom of the dead."

He'd heard of the Ossuary, lined with the remains of millions of Parisians. He passed beneath another archway, with another inscription: *Memento Majori* - To the memory of our ancestors. Now he was surrounded by walls of bones.

They poured out from deep hollows, chaotic in the darkness, but carefully stacked where they were visible to passersby. Skulls and kneecaps were arranged in patterns among rows of arm and leg bones.

Orin hardly looked at them. All that drove him was that thought, ever resurfacing, regular and powerful as a heartbeat: *The next time I see the surface, it may be as a man entire. The next time I see the surface, it may be as a man entire.*

Besides the bones, there was something else he seemed to be ignoring. Or perhaps he couldn't sense it. I could, though. I could feel it in every particle of my being. The air was thick with spells, like tangled weeds in a once-clear sea.

I pushed through the tendrils, drawing great, relieved breaths. I felt strength come back to me. Here, I understood, anyone could perform magic. This wasn't inherent to the Ossuary; the place must have been enchanted by Le Cercle des Thaumaturges.

Immediately, I tried to lift Orin's curse. I fought.

But it held.

I brushed frustrated tears from my eyes. Maybe I could at least *speak* to him here. But the barrier between us remained, like a window of thick, impenetrable glass.

Orin was walking steadily through the curving corridors of bones. He was so eager to meet them, so eager to change everything. But there seemed to be no other living being here.

And then, he reached an alcove where torches were stuck in the walls. A dozen people clad in black emerged from the bone-filled niches all around us.

The men wore their top hats, with the exception of one, who seemed to materialize from a wall of bones itself, not a corner or corridor. And yet, it felt more a parlor trick than real magic. *His* hat was a triangular concoction of black velvet, embroidered with silver symbols. It might have made me laugh, if only his eyes weren't so dark and cold. Maybe they didn't appear this way in the world above, but here, whether he chose it or whether it was the magic revealing some sort of truth, that was what I could see.

I glanced at Orin. He held himself straight, but I could sense that he ached to curve inwards. I don't think it was because the members of the Cercle were gathering closer and closer around him; above ground, the sun was disappearing over the bend of the Seine at Sèvres.

The group's leader (I suppose he was the sort who demands to be called "Master"), the one who wore the pointed hat, broke the silence at last. "Welcome, Monsieur…X. A very secretive man," he said. There was laughter in his voice but it was difficult to tell if it was kind or mocking.

This all seemed a bit like a show. I thought of Cleverman. But there was no beauty here, no oranges sprung from enchanted blossoms.

"Good evening," Orin managed to sound calm. "And I hope that soon I will be saying 'Thank you'."

There came an appreciative "Ah" from the members. Who'd have imagined that a monster could be so charming?

To my surprise, reading their thoughts here was effortless. I wondered at their lack of caution. But I realized that that this was the first real magic they had ever experienced. I had visions of other poor souls begging for relief from broken hearts or imagined curses. I saw the lies and illusions the Cercle used to convince them that they had been healed. The "Master" had been right to want to see Orin immediately – he'd realized that he was different.

"We will do all that we can," The Master was saying. "Now," he made an expansive gesture, "we shall lock you in before the...transformation starts." His hand indicated a niche with a barred door that had been opened for him.

"Lock me in?" Orin balked.

"You said in your letter that you might become violent."

"Yes but...you didn't tell me I would be locked up. And surely," Orin pointed out, "you could all easily overpower me, with magic or otherwise..."

"If we are to help you, you must go into the cage." The Master's voice was firm.

Did Orin have any other choice? If they let him go – which both he and I felt was increasingly unlikely – he'd have to emerge into the world above in his monstrous form.

By now he was starting to suspect that they didn't rely on magic – and so, how could they possibly understand or break any kind of enchantment? He was just a fascination for them, one they could keep locked up and examine as often as they liked. The bookshop owner's words came to him: *They are so curious.*

Again, he found himself at the mercy of liars, and very much in danger.

He looked at the niche. The barred door was far more frightening than the cracked skulls that made up its walls.

Then he shot a look at the corridor he'd come from. As a man, he was a swift runner, and he would run faster still after the transformation. He'd escape and then think of something when he was safe. He tensed, positioned himself to run, and then…. The shadow passed over his hands.

Orin's body went rigid. He staggered from the pain, and the group gathered around him in an unbroken circle, some watching eagerly, others turning away as his body warped and shifted. Hooves burst through his shoes and his face became a maw.

~~

I stood back from the group, trying to think of what to do. Suddenly, I heard footsteps behind me. I could sense that it was Claire.

How had she gotten down here without a note?

The magic of this place was so strong that the answer I sought came to me like a flash of light: she'd simply been lucky. The guard wasn't expecting anyone else and had gone to relieve himself on a wall nearby. She'd slipped inside unnoticed.

I could imagine what she'd felt going down that staircase that led into darkness, a sort of negative of the spiral staircase she climbed every day upwards to the sun, to him.

Some of her memories came to me. She'd visited this place with her family shortly after Nadar had taken the first photographs of interiors in electric light here.

In the long walk she'd just taken, in darkness lit by trembling flames, she'd thought of everyone she'd lost since then.

She'd thought of Orin, as well. I sought out her heart. *He doesn't deserve to suffer. Whatever he is, whatever he is.*

Whatever he is, I don't want him to leave my life.

There was so much all at once – loss and remembrance, grief and hope, there in that flickering battle of light and dark. Tears had fallen from her eyes as she walked.

She'd arrived at the entrance to the bone-filled underworld and continued through its winding corridor.

The bones comforted her. These were the remains of old Parisians, reburied here from the cemeteries that had once existed in the heart of the city. Though no one will ever find them, some once belonged to people she had read about in her books, heroes and villains of the Revolution and the Terror. Others she felt she knew in a different way. She'd read about what the city was like in their time, and how they'd lived. She might even have made models of their homes.

As she'd come further down the corridor, though she couldn't yet see the members of the Cercle des Thaumaturges, she could make out some of their shadows flickering against the still bones. Suddenly sounds echoed to her: gasps and slight screams, and a noise she recognized as someone holding back pain. Monsieur Rush.

Rage rose in her like a conflagration. She had to get them away from him. Heedlessly, she began to run.

I realized she could help me.

I cast a spell.

Now, they would all see her just as I could – not how she appeared, but what was in her soul and heart.

The group had gotten their bearings just as Orin righted himself, fully a monster. The Master pushed him towards the barred enclosure, while others impatiently tore away his clothes, fascinated, coldly curious to see every part of this creature.

And then, a scream rolled towards them.

Every head turned and saw her emerging from the low ceilinged, flame-flickered corridor. To them, she appeared to be a furious spirit, a warrior, some sort of valkyrie — fearsome, pale, shining, dressed for battle, her eyes full of light, her every movement full of fury.

Perhaps the spell was more powerful than I had remembered. There were ghosts around her, and from those walls other ghosts came to join her.

She and they were magnificent and terrible, shining like white-hot flames. I knew that even if all of the other lights were extinguished, there she would be, a fire capable of sending light to every dark corner.

Some members of the Cercle screamed and ran to hide in the niches and shadows. Others only stared, frozen in shock or fear.

Now, things moved very quickly.

Orin broke from the loosened grips of those who had been forcing him towards the enclosure.

I expected him to run - and I hoped that I could stop him somehow, because now I knew how I could save them both.

It had been a long time since I had done a spell like this. First, I concentrated on Claire. I took a breath to begin my incantation.

But another voice spoke.

Orin hadn't run – he'd only moved away from them. Now, he turned, facing down the members of the Cercle. His opened his maw and cried out a spell whose intent was, "You will forget this night." It echoed against the stone.

It must have been something he'd come across in one of his books, but I wondered how he remembered it now? Had he kept it in mind, in case it might ever be of use?

Instantly, the others' expressions changed. I could see through their eyes: All was blurred at first, and then a horrible monster came into focus. Someone screamed.

Now was my chance. I chanted *my* incantation, and the confused Claire, who had stopped running, vanished. The ghosts hurtled back to their bones.

In a few moments, she'd appear in her apartment. At first, she'd be like the flickering flame of a gaslight, then become entirely corporeal, lying on the sofa. I imagined she'd feel as though she'd just awoken from a troubling dream she couldn't remember (thanks to Orin's unexpected spell). She'd rise, get a drink of water, undress, and fall asleep.

Now, on to other things. This next incantation would be more difficult, especially because something had changed. Under the influence of the forgetting spell, the men and women of the Cercle thought that Orin was some sort of demon one of them had unwisely summoned. He'd vanish, they hoped, if the magical permission of this place did. And so, they began casting spells to undo it.

Suddenly, Orin spoke another spell: "You will all forget me."

Then another: "My letters to you and any other traces of me that you possess will turn to dust."

Shaking their addled heads, the members of the Cercle screamed and scrambled to do their part to break down the layers of magic and permissive spells, cruel hands tearing at a beautiful tapestry.

Soon, it would be impossible to escape by any means besides a mortal exit. I raced beside Orin and used the vanishing spell again, but this time on myself.

Please, I prayed, *disappear with me.*

And there he -and, a stroke of luck, his traveling bag - were, floating in the ether at my side. But I knew we wouldn't be safe for long. Outside that magical place, I was powerless within the walls of Paris.

The magic broke within seconds. And so, instead of reappearing in his room, Orin was stuck with me, somewhere in the sky over the city.

We fell earthward.

58

I seized the winds. Down we dipped and descended, so fast that his half-mortal mind barely understood what was happening.

There was a large, darker spot off the mostly dark streets – a park. With the winds' blessing, we fell towards it.

It's fortunate that Orin was in his monstrous form. I don't think a man would have survived the landing.

He lay in the grass, very still, his head turned to the side. For a moment, he thought he was dreaming. Then his mind cleared and he realized that some enchantment had had transported him to another place – perhaps another time? He was staring at a ruined marble colonnade, white in the moonlight, bordering a dark pool of water. No — He recognized it now. He was in the Parc Monceau.

That made him sit up, although unsteadily. If there were a watchman making rounds, he'd probably notice his crumpled form on the grass. He had to hide until sunrise. Still too weak to stand, Orin turned, squinting his eyes, searching until he found an unmistakable silhouette.

It was the little pyramid, his favorite thing about the park. He forced himself to his feet, groaning softly.

His aching body took longer to reach the pyramid than he'd expected. There at last, he stopped to catch his breath and examined its small metal door. He'd always wondered what was inside the pyramid. Tonight, he would find out. The door was locked. He put the tip of one talon into the keyhole and opened it.

There was nothing inside. Orin took a grateful breath, then squeezed himself and the traveling bag that he suddenly realized he was holding, into the small space. Carefully, he drew the metal door shut.

A few hours ago (he marveled), he'd packed an extra set of clothes and a pair of boots. He felt especially glad of his plan now. When the sun rose, he'd be able to put on clothes and exit the pyramid looking like every other gentleman in the park.

Knowing this helped him to close his eyes a little, though neither one of us slept at all, really, in those nighttime hours that remained. A long time later, he heard birdsong. The sky outside was deep blue, then lighter, then overcast gray. Orin changed back to his human form.

This transformation was never painful. It was like something sliding back into place. On the rare occasions he was awake to experience it, I always hoped that the painlessness would make him realize that he truly was a man, not a monster. It hadn't yet.

There would be some time before the park gates were opened, but it would also take some time to get dressed, considering how small the space was – he couldn't even stand. So, he began the difficult work of contorting himself into his clothes.

Then, he waited tensely until he could hear voices and the sound of footsteps on the gravel. Carefully, he pushed open the door until there was a slit just large enough for him to see through. A few people were strolling on the park's dusty white paths. When he was sure they were well past the pyramid, he pushed the door open even farther and crawled out, then quickly drew out the bag and shut the door behind him.

The park wasn't what it had been in the summer and spring, and it wasn't what it would have been any other autumn. The flowers were untended and wilted. Some trees had been cut down, and the grass was dry and bitten by the cold. As he walked along the path towards the entrance, Orin noticed that the pond with its romantic bridge was stagnant and full of leaves. Still, the park's beauty mostly remained. The fabricated ruins were an echo of its new, ruined nature.

He reached the rotunda at the main entrance and passed through the gates, onto the boulevard de Courcelles. Waiting there for a cab to pass by, he tried to ignore how much his body ached.

When he arrived home, it was hard to imagine how he was going to climb the flights of stairs. With a deep breath, he began.

59

W eak sunlight from the unshuttered window woke her. Claire sat
up with a start. She'd missed the breadline.

How had she slept so long, and why was she so tired? When she
concentrated, the only memory she had of the previous evening was
drowsily getting a drink of water from the kitchen.

But the present was the concern now. She got ready as quickly as she could
and hurried up to the sixth floor, where Émile was reading on the bench.

"Sorry I'm late."

"Not to worry." He held up his book. "I've finally decided to take a
crack at *Les Châtiments*."

"How is it?"

He shuddered theatrically.

"Then I'm even sorrier to have kept you waiting. I overslept. Here's the
key – I'll be right back – I have to explain to Madame Marcel."

The concierge was sweeping out the entry hall. When Claire came close,
she saw concern on her face. "Are you feeling better?"

"Better?"

"You don't remember?" the concierge asked. "When you didn't come
down, I knocked on your door this morning. I asked if I could take
your ration card, but you just muttered something and said you'd see
me later. I have to admit…I tried your door, but it was locked."

"How strange….I don't remember anything about last night."

"I'm not surprised. All those mornings waiting outside in the cold must
have caught up to you. I'm just sorry I couldn't take your card and get
you something to eat."

Claire shook her head. "Don't worry. I suppose I needed sleep more than anything else. I have some rice in the cupboard."

"You know, speaking of strange things, I'm not sure it matters to Hippolyte. There are less rats in the building – not that I blame our neighbors – but he doesn't seem particularly hungry, and he hasn't gotten any thinner, has he?"

They both turned to look at the cat, who was contentedly washing his face. His coat glistened. His belly was still quite round.

~~

Despite her inexplicable fatigue, the photographs she'd taken so far hadn't been half bad, Claire thought with relief as she wished another client farewell.

Suddenly, the smile faded from her face.

Monsieur Rush had just come up the stairs. Had he looked this way the first time she'd met him in the corridor all those months ago, she would have been certain he was a gambler coming home after a long, disappointing night.

"Bonjour, Monsieur Rush." She tried to keep her voice from betraying the worry she'd felt since the previous afternoon.

"Bonjour, Mademoiselle Turin," Orin managed, then turned away to wince and continued down the hall.

Claire couldn't help herself. "Monsieur Rush, are you well?"

"Just tired," came his voice faintly from down the hall. He went inside, locked the door behind him, and fell onto his bed, grateful to be there and not in a dark cage far beneath the city. Underneath his clothes, his skin was smeared with purple bruises.

60

He woke hours later, with one thought in his mind: That had been his last chance.

He'd put so much faith into the black card that any other defeat could be erased by it. And in the end, he'd found false promises, just as he had with every other cure he'd ever tried.

He'd tried so many. So many in thirteen years.

He wondered if he should make a new plan. He could reread his books and hope to find something he'd missed, or seek out some miraculous new discovery in a library or in the crates of the few bouquinistes who'd stayed to brave the Siege and the cold. Or maybe he could visit neighborhoods he didn't know and see if there might be some sort of local witch living there, or some esteemed scholar of the occult.

But none of this moved him, really. None of it seemed like anything but a lot of useless work.

Then, why not concentrate on finding a new place that might hold answers? He could go there after the Siege.

But that also seemed like a lot of work for nothing.

A shadow passed over his thoughts. What if he ended his life?

Joseph would be devastated, but his brother had too much life in him for that to last. Their parents would be all right. Some friends would miss him, but certainly be fine. They could all stop worrying about him, and he could stop being disappointed.

The shadow lingered for a while but didn't deepen. Then it passed, and I could breathe again.

61

That afternoon, Claire opened the studio door and took in a stylishly cut fur-trimmed coat, a top hat perched at a slight, intriguing angle, black kid gloves wrapped around the gilded head of an ebony walking stick—

"Bonjour, Monsieur Joseph."

"Bonjour, Mademoiselle Turin. It's been a long time."

They shared an embarrassed silence.

Then, he took up the conversation again: "But you look cheerful as ever."

She laughed. "Do I? I must be a good actress, then!"

"Oh, but you are!"

Claire flashed him a sideways smile. "And what brings you here this afternoon? Have you already run out of cartes de visite?"

He shook his head, and his expression suddenly became serious. "I was wondering if you'd seen my brother. He hasn't been by all day, and he hasn't sent any word."

She nodded quickly. "He's in his room, I think, if you want to speak with him before…"

"…before sundown. Yes. Well, thank you, mademoiselle. It's always a pleasure to see you. We should do it more often."

~~

"Orin?"

He woke up at the sound, somehow sure that this wasn't the first time his name had been spoken. The panicked undercurrent in his brother's voice convinced him of that.

"I-I'm here! I'm fine. I just…"

"Orin, thank God! Where were you? Are you ill? There's smallpox going around, you know - you haven't been slumming around, have you?"

Orin sighed, then struggled up from the bed and opened the door.

"My God," Joseph remarked once they were inside, "you look a fright! What's happened?"

It took him a long time to find the strength to speak. "Do you remember that occult group I told you about?"

"The one you were always planning to call on?"

"I arranged to do just that. The meeting took place in the Catacombs."

"The Catacombs?!"

Orin nodded, even managed a smile. "It was quite the spectacle."

"And…"

The note of hope in Joseph's voice made him want to stop talking. "There's nothing they can do for me. They're just smoke and mirrors."

His brother didn't know just how much hope Orin had truly had in this plan; still, he could feel that it was a grand defeat. He wouldn't say that. Instead, he brought up something practical. "And why do you look so…." A sudden, terrible thought came to him. "Did they hurt you?"

"They tried to lock me up. But…something saved me. Well," Orin stopped. "I saved myself. But —"

"—Why didn't you ask me to go with you? Or at least borrow a pistol? Orry, you could have been—"

"It was no place for you. It was something else, there was something in the air there, I…" He nearly told his brother about the spells he'd cast, but he never spoke about things like that to Joseph. It would make him seem stranger, he thought, more monstrous.

"How did you get out?"

"It was a miracle."

"Well?" Joseph asked impatiently.

"They were leading me to an alcove with a barred door they were planning to lock behind me, and then suddenly a...some sort of furious spirit came racing through the tunnel, with ghosts following behind her. But incredible as it was, I couldn't look closely – I used that time to..."

Again he stopped. No spells. "I used that time to get away from them. Then..." He thought quickly, "The spirit said something and everyone seemed dazed. They stared at me in terror - it was as though they didn't know anything about me, or even what they were doing there.

"A voice told me I was safe, and then – I – something vaulted me into the air and — you know the pyramid in the Parc Monceau? I woke up in there. Well, I didn't know it at first. But when I got out, that's where I was."

Joseph stared for a few moments. Then, "Orin, I almost don't believe you."

"Now are you glad you weren't there?"

"No! I could have helped you!"

"The fall from the sky would have killed you."

"What do you mean, 'fall'? I thought you said you just ended up in the pyramid."

Damn, Orin thought. "No, I thought so, too, but I must have...fallen there or some such thing."

"Did anyone see you?"

"Do you hear anyone talking about a man falling from the sky? They would have been upon me instantly...and dragged me to the nearest Commissariat, thinking I'd plummeted from a Prussian balloon."

"But how could you fall from the sky without being injured? Nothing broken....?"

"This was magic. And anyway, I…wasn't a man at the time, of course. But even so, look." He lifted a corner of his waistcoat and shirt, revealing some of the bruises.

"Orry – maybe you should see a doctor?"

"No need. I feel all right, just sore, and very tired after it all."

"Still, I'd like to fetch someone –"

"There's no time," Orin said tersely. "It's nearly sundown." Then, more gently, "I'm fine. I'll rest and call on you tomorrow morning, and if I still worry you, I promise I'll see a doctor."

"All right," Joseph conceded. Then, he pulled a paper-wrapped parcel from his coat pocket. "Here. I brought you something from the Café de la Paix. It nearly leaked through and ruined my coat."

Orin took the package, which smelled heavenly. "You're a good man, Joseph."

"Like you."

"It's sundown in a few minutes. Have a nice evening and I'll see you tomorrow, early, I promise."

Joseph nodded. "But not too early, all the same."

His brother left and the air felt colder. Orin forced himself to eat, then lay down and slept again.

62

S omeone was banging on his door. He looked up from the book he'd been listlessly reading. "Who is it?"

"It's me!" Joseph's indignation seeped through the wood.

Orin stood and let him in.

"You're dressed?!" The indignation escalated to outrage. "What on earth are you still doing here? You were supposed to call on me! We were supposed to see a doctor or —" He stopped, realizing that his brother had nothing to say for once.

Joseph blamed the book on the bed. "What could be so interesting as to make you forget —"

"It didn't," Orin sighed. "I just...What was the point, I suppose I thought."

"'The point'? The point is that you've had a rather unusual accident. And at the very least, I was waiting for you! I was worried!"

I was relieved to see a faint smile play on Orin's lips. "Is all this fuss because I made you wake up early?"

"It's not funny, Orry! What's the matter with you?!"

That joke was a rarity. In the days that followed, Orin rarely laughed or made any kind of original conversation. He had no life in him.

Joseph sought out diversions. They visited the ramparts, stared in disbelief at the rat, cat, and dog butchers at Les Halles, took a ride on the Petite Ceinture, looked out from the summit of Montmartre. He dragged Orin to afternoon performances and lectures, though these were dull, simply drumming up patriotism that never failed but was tired now, a faded banner.

At night, Orin slept heavily, no need for a lit lamp.

~~

With Claire, he managed to keep his wits about him, managed smiles and insouciance. Sometimes, it didn't even feel as if he were making an effort. Talking to her always left him better than before, as if a bright spot had been burnished into sooty darkness.

Still, Claire sensed something different when they spoke together now. It was like a shadow, or a glimpse into a cavern with a deep, bottomless pool inside.

The city, too, was darkening. November crawled to its end, the cold clinging to it like icicles. The Parisians' hunger grew sharper and the bread got worse.

There was little gas left. Only every third streetlamp was lit each night. The cafes set out oil lamps, the spectators at plays and readings brought blankets to drape over themselves against the chill.

63

C laire decided to ask about the tavern sign.

She'd thought about it often over the past weeks. What could it mean that someone had painted the creature that Monsieur Rush became every night?

But whenever she'd considered mentioning it, she'd worried. What if her words or the look on her face betrayed more interest than anyone should rightly have for what was supposed to be an object of casual curiosity?

But could the sign be the cause of what was bothering him? What if he couldn't find an answer? Or what if the answer he'd found wasn't what he was hoping? That last thought left a surprising dip of fear in her belly.

"Bonjour, Mademoiselle Turin."

"Bonjour, Monsieur Rush. I've been meaning to ask you, did you ever find out anything about that tavern sign we saw in Monsieur Cousin's office?"

Orin thought quickly. If he told her the truth, how could he possibly explain why he'd looted several homes in the suburbs in the hope of learning the provenance of what was supposed to be an object of casual curiosity?

"I did try to call on the Blondin family. It turns out they left when everyone was evacuating the city, just before the Siege. None of their neighbors know where they went. I'm hoping they'll return when it's finished."

So, Claire thought, *maybe that was it.*

"I'm sorry it didn't lead to anything. I know it's not much, but if you like, I can have a look at some of my books. There might be some mention of it somewhere."

A small fissure of light appeared in the blackness. She was trying to help him. But he knew she wouldn't find any answers. "I wouldn't want you to waste your time."

"Oh no, it's interesting to me, too. I really do wonder when it might have been made. And anyway," she gave a small laugh, "the research would be something to keep me busy."

Orin looked at her for a moment with a kind of understanding. "Now it's my turn to say you're kind," he murmured.

"Oh," her cheeks flushed. She recalled how much those words had cut him that day by the Seine. "I-I don't know why I said that. You're always kind."

"Always?" He teased. "I'm sure the reds would tell you otherwise. And anyway," he added, "calling someone 'kind' isn't an insult. Unless it is in Paris?"

Claire grinned. "No, I don't believe it is."

~~

She wandered through the day, thinking of which books to start with.

That afternoon, a sigh from Émile startled her.

"I bet you have no idea what's going on outside."

She looked up distractedly from a page of Villon. "Outside?"

"Outside the walls! We're going to push the Prussians from the plain of Avron, cross the Marne, and try to join the Army of the Loire. If we succeed, we'll be able to communicate with the rest of France."

Claire gasped.

"And then, it may only be a matter of time before we get the Prussians away from here – and maybe even out of France."

"Do you think it will work?"

Émile shrugged. "Ducrot and the others seem pretty determined. But who knows? All we can do is hope."

~~

The whole city held its breath. Everyone waited to hear some word, something more than inscrutable cannon fire.

The line at the butcher's the next morning didn't seem so bad. It seemed like nothing at all, despite the fact that Claire had only slept a few hours. Soon, the Siege might end.

~~

The next day, word got into Paris that there was a temporary armistice. Both sides were using the time to recover their dead.

No one thought – or not enough of them thought – to stop entirely. I will never understand it, mortals choosing to help death.

Crowds lingered at the city gates, watching as the wounded came in. They waited for news that this time they would be free. They continued to hope.

64

Orin was certain now that there was no cure for his condition. But he didn't want to stay in the dark place. He found himself starting to wonder if he could just enjoy the many things there were to enjoy in the world, no matter his fate.

There were others who were able to do so. He thought of the freaks at Barnum's those many years ago, or at the circuses. And then there were those who were afflicted with long illnesses. Why, Ambassador Washburne himself was frequently ill, but he had a family, he had a role that let him help people.

Without trying, Orin always found joy and beauty in life. So why not go on living that way? He thought of what he had: Family, friends, a fortune, and books to read and things to see. Even the things he'd never be able to experience, he could read about or look at in pictures or photographs.

He thought of the scratched sepia images of plots of land he used to examine beside his father in New York. He thought about the photographs Mademoiselle Turin had shown him from the Exposition Universelle.

He thought about Mademoiselle Turin.

Now that there was no hope for him to become a man, she could simply be a friend. He had nothing to worry about any longer. He thought of Joseph's proposal again and winced.

~~

Days passed. Rumors mixed with truths, hope roared over canon fire.

Claire spent the evenings poring over the books that she had already and planning what bookshops she might visit to discreetly page through their wares. She'd only go to the library at the Hôtel de Ville as a last resort. She hadn't heard from Cousin and she suspected her models had been rejected by his colleagues (she tried not to dwell on that now).

She read close to her small fire, shivering as she turned pages, coughing in the smoke, trying to find something, trying to fight her heavy eyelids, until at last she remembered she had to wake the next morning and stand on the breadline. She went to the sofa and rolled herself tight inside a counterpane, turning her back to the weak warmth of the hearth.

~~

The cold was even worse the next day. It crept in through the tiniest fissures in the studio's windowpanes. Émile kept on his greatcoat and Claire kept on her mantle. Despite the sunlight, few sitters ventured out. And maybe that was for the best; her mind was on the book open on the table in front of her.

After a while, she looked over at Émile.

"Do you happen to have Volume Two of Restif de la Bretonne?"

"I-Yes, at home. I'm in the middle of it. Why, do you need it?"

"Sorry, not really – well, perhaps you could just bring it tomorrow and I'll try to look through it quickly."

"Look through Restif de la Bretonne *quickly*? Haw! I'll just give it back to you for now."

"I'm sorry to be a bother. I'm just looking for something. A sign."

"A sign?"

"An old tavern sign, gold-painted, with a very strange-looking sort of monster on it."

Émile didn't reply.

If it were anyone else, she might have gone back to her reading, but this worried her. "Are you all right?"

"I might know what sign you're talking about." He walked over and tore a small corner from a page of the ledger. In a short time, with a few hesitations, he'd drawn a fairly good portrait of Orin in his monstrous form.

"That's it!" Claire shouted in disbelief. "How do you know it?"

Émile stared at her, equally stunned. "How do *you* know it?"

~~

As she tried to come up with a story, to her relief, Émile told his:

"It hung above a tavern near the Théâtre de l'Odéon. Your father and I used to go there. We called it Le Café de la Bête." There was a lovely expression on his face, a calm, blissful smile. He was in the past, those happy years. "We'd joke that the sign was a warning to stay away and not drink and carouse. Of course, we did anyway, like so many others."

Now his usual bemused expression returned. "But the sign's been gone for years. How do you know about it? Did your father mention it to you? Did he make a sketch or take a photograph of it?" Beneath his incredulous tone, there was longing.

For a moment, Claire thought of how time separates the living and the dead. Here was a time in her father's life that she didn't know, just as he would never be alive beside her in the years to come.

She knew that if there *had* been a sketch or a photograph, Émile would have taken it into shaking hands and spent a long while looking at it. So she had to tell him quickly, to keep him from being too disappointed. "I saw the sign. With Monsieur Rush. We were visiting a friend of his, who's acquiring objects for the new Paris history museum."

The secret was out, at least mostly. She went on, as though it were a paltry matter. "I thought I might try to discover where it came from."

"Ah," Émile's laugh had a bitterness to it, like the salt of tears. "History.

"Well, anyway," he went on after a moment, "it's just as well that it will be in that museum."

"You'll be able to visit it."

"True. And I visit *the tavern* all the time. It's changed a bit, but I can still see how it was."

Claire held back another shout. Maybe if they went there — Maybe the owner would know more about the sign and who created it. "Émile," she tried to seem nonchalant, "if it's not sunny tomorrow, could you take me and Monsieur Rush there?"

"If it's not sunny, meet me there instead, so that I don't have to make the cold walk all the way here!"

~~

When she heard Orin's steps on the staircase that afternoon, she hurried to open the door.

"Monsieur Rush!" she called out excitedly. "I have a surprise for you!"

"Oh?" Orin had come in from the streets where, despite the cold, people were lingering, murmuring together as they pored over the newspapers.

"It's the most incredible coincidence! Émile knows about your tavern sign! He knows where the tavern is!"

He forgot everything else. *How is it possible?* "I-I must admit," he managed, "I didn't think you'd find much in your research. But you've done even better than that!"

"You must never underestimate me!" she laughed. "…Even though it really was only luck. If you're free tomorrow, and it's overcast, Émile said we could meet him there. We can ask the owner why he sold the sign, and maybe find out —"

She stopped, realizing that she sounded too eager. "Émile gave me the address, so you can go tomorrow on your own if you like, no need to wait for me and the weather."

It was a tempting offer. Alone, he could ask any questions that might come to mind. But with Mademoiselle Turin and Monsieur Rouline present, he would have to be cautious. Still, he told her, "You're the one who discovered all of this, so you should certainly come if you'd like."

She dared herself to meet his green-gold eyes. "I'd like that very much." The world reeled now without any kind of touch, and they both looked away.

65

T he cold rain made the wait at the butcher's nearly unbearable that morning, but on the other hand, it meant that she would go with Monsieur Rush to the Café de la Bête (a name she'd decided not to share with him).

When they met at noon, Claire felt an excitement that she fought to keep quiet. If Monsieur Rush could learn something about this monster, he might finally find a cure.

Orin didn't feel much of anything. The visit would only be helpful if the tavern's owner knew the person who'd made the sign, or at least what exactly had inspired its creation. Otherwise, it was just another defeat.

But he reminded himself that it didn't matter if there were answers this time or not – he was taking no risk, at least, making no great sacrifice, and he had no expectations.

He helped Mademoiselle Turin into the cab, shivering from more than the cold as her hand rested in his for just a moment. And then their second ride together through the streets of Paris began. He felt as glad as he had on the first, no matter their destination, no matter the chill in the air.

All around them, they noticed crowds gathering. Whenever the cab stopped, they'd hear rumors that finally turned to triumphant shouts: "Victory!" The driver laughed with joy and tried to urge his horse quickly and merrily forward, but the poor creature was having trouble managing the icy cobblestones.

~~

It's never seemed strange to me that I had frequented a tavern that Claire's father and Émile would frequent decades later.

As Émile had explained, it was just a place in the neighborhood, and it was and is a lively neighborhood, full of students and young people. I was young then, and they were young a few decades later, and now, like us, the place seemed to have faded a bit. But maybe that was only because it was so much more vivid in my memories.

Émile was waiting outside the familiar doorway. I could imagine for a moment that I was in my old life, about to go inside for an afternoon drink and merriment. It was strange to remember a time when I didn't have this broken heart.

Claire and Orin hesitated at the doorway.

She thought of how her father must have passed through it so often. The past seemed very distant, and yet so insignificant that she could cross the years and find him again. Why should it be impossible?

She shook her head and returned to the present. Now, her thoughts joined with Orin's: Something could be revealed to them here that could change their lives.

In those suspended moments, as they stood side by side, each of them was also thinking how easy it would be to reach out and take the other's hand. Each of them ached to do it.

Then, Orin let Claire pass before him through the doorway, and followed her inside.

It was smaller than I'd remembered, but that's the way with places that take up so much space in our minds. The true difference was in nearly everything else. The walls had been stripped of their patriotic drawings and decorations. There were modern lamps and smaller tables. Newspapers were folded over long wooden batons.

The window on the far wall caught my eye. I thought of how I'd looked forlornly out of it on certain nights, when everyone was hanging on every word Yselda uttered. I'd tried to find a spell that would make them do the same for me, until I'd realized that there was no spell.

I remembered a young man shyly taking my hand in the shadowy corner there and telling me I was lovely. I wanted his words, his

245

attention, but I didn't want him. I remembered the taste of cheap wine on his lips and I wanted to weep. Outside all the while, the sign had hung. Sometimes when it moved in the wind, I had thought that it was laughing at me.

~~

Émile introduced them to the tavern's current owner, a burly man called Henri who stood behind the bar with a permanent frown on his face.

The place was merrier in my time.

When they asked about the sign, he explained it simply enough: "All I know is that it was ugly. I had it taken down years ago."

"That's a pity." I was surprised at the defensive tone in Claire's voice. "It's going to be in a museum now."

"*Ah bon?*" Henri wasn't impressed.

Now Orin spoke. "Do you know when it was made, or where the tavern's previous owner came from?"

"From the way he talked, I'd say Paris, like me. But we didn't sit down and discuss our lives." The idea seemed almost insulting to him.

Émile grinned in a peacekeeping way. "Any other questions?"

Orin and Claire looked at each other, both lost. There didn't seem to be any other path to follow. "No," Orin finally, slowly said.

"All right then," Émile rubbed his hands together. "I'll buy you both a drink."

This isn't devastating, Orin reminded himself. After all, he hadn't expected any answers. Still, there was an icy feeling inside him. *This* was really the end of it.

And then they sat down and began talking and laughing as usual. Claire's eyes twinkled and soon his did as well, to my happiness.

A long time later, he glanced at the window. "I think I need to be getting back."

"I should, too," Claire said. "The later it gets, the colder it will be. Would you like to share a cab home?" She had no one, but he might be seen by someone.

"My pleasure," Orin agreed, feeling light.

~~

As they walked down the street, they were surrounded by people singing about victory. Paris's troops had crossed the Marne and joined the French army. The Siege would soon be lifted! No more death, no more rats, no more bad bread!

They cheered. And then, they saw a cab and ran towards it, laughing a little. For a breathless moment, Claire braced herself for the reeling that she knew would come when she took his hand.

~~

When the ride ended, she suddenly thought of the loss they'd experienced. Claire's heart ached for him. "I'm sorry we didn't find anything out."

"It's a shame," Orin shrugged, "But at least it was a pleasant afternoon."

That surprised her, but there was no time to ask questions, even if she would have dared to. Sunset was coming fast. They climbed the stairs in companionable silence, pretending not to notice the carpet's flowers curling around their heels.

~~

That night, there was a knock at her door.

"Come out with me!" Anne's eyes sparkled in the meager light. "We won! It's over!"

They joined the crowds on the boulevards. No one cared about the cold or the curfew. Café violinists were threading music through an air humming with happy voices. They danced rounds together and with strangers under any lamppost that was lit. Warm now, they laughed deliriously, almost forgetting why.

For the first time in weeks, Orin sat on his bed with something fixed in his mind, and alive, and…wonderful.

That afternoon, talking, laughing, wondering at her at every moment, and seeing how she, too, seemed to want to be near him, to laugh with him, to share her thoughts, he'd started to think, *What if Mademoiselle Turin cares for me after all?*

And what if I stopped telling myself not to care for her?

He could be with her by day and safely away from her by night. In those dark hours when he wasn't a man, she could work on her models or read – anything she liked. He could give her anything to amuse herself, anything that fascinated her.

In daylight, they could talk as long as they wished and then go out on adventures in Paris – and maybe travel, maybe even go so far as Japan. It had seemed so difficult before, but now —

An excited contentment fell over him.

From time to time, though, it would veer to doubt – *did* she feel the same way? Could she?

And he'd remind himself of the way it felt when their fingers touched, of the way they talked so easily, of her eyes meeting his – and he knew there must be something. There must be something.

He slept the sleep of those in the early days of love – restless, but waking each time with a sense of joy. He forgot his form.

66

I trembled as I watched him dress and prepare himself the next morning. He looked into his little sliver of mirror with a happy expression, occasionally humming some patriotic tune he'd heard the previous afternoon. It might be simplest, he thought, to ask her to join him for a lemonade, and then from there, to suggest they walk along the Seine and browse at the bouquinistes' crates.

He'd forgotten how cold it was. And their last, disastrous encounter there seemed to have slipped his mind as well.

I felt as giddy as he did. What would happen now? Claire wasn't afraid of him anymore, but would she hand him her heart so easily?

He left his room and was surprised by the quiet of the corridor. Then, he shook his head. *Of course*, he thought, *it's cloudy*.

Perhaps he could knock on her door? And, feeling bold and happy and resolute, he set out to do just that.

Descending the staircase, he heard voices. They sounded agitated, then he turned a spiral and there was laughter, then more low talking.

"So it's true, then, Monsieur Rossignol?" he heard Madame Marcel ask as he arrived at the fifth floor. She and Claire and a tall, handsome man with chestnut hair and a National Guard uniform were standing outside Claire's door.

"I'm afraid so," the man nodded gravely.

"Well," he could tell Claire was trying to make her voice sound cheerful, "It's good to see *you*, anyway."

"Ah, that's the spirit!" the man laughed.

Madame Marcel's face sagged with resignation. "I thought it was going to end."

"Oh, madame, it will – it can't last more than a few weeks." The man gently touched her arm. "I'll help you back downstairs, and Claire, I'll wait for you there."

"All right." Her voice was all warmth.

Orin watched wordlessly as this man, this Rossignol, graciously helped Madame Marcel down the staircase, though the concierge normally needed no help at all.

Orin had forgotten Joseph's warning. But now it came back to him, and he knew that this was who his brother had seen her walking with. This man, Rossignol, called her "Claire", not "Mademoiselle Turin". They were close, they had been for a long time. Mademoiselle Turin's eyes were shining.

As unskilled as I was in reading hearts, I could see that her eyes didn't shine nearly as bright as they did when she was with Orin. I was certain now that what she felt for Rossignol was the same sort of love you'd feel for family. I was so relieved.

But Orin still didn't understand. Instead he thought, *I'm a fool.* Her hesitations, her refusal of the proposal, of his offer of food; the day by the bouquinistes' crates – all of it rushed back to him.

Along with it came a memory: the madwoman staring at him in terror, calling him what he really was, a monster.

He had nothing to offer her. He wasn't even a man. How could he have imagined, even for a moment, that she could love him?

He turned to go back upstairs, but it was too late.

"Monsieur Rush! Good morning."

He steeled himself. "Bonjour, Mademoiselle Turin. Is everything all right?"

"It turns out it wasn't true, what everyone was saying yesterday. Ducrot sent the telegram too early. We were defeated."

"No!" For a moment, he forgot about Rossignol. "I'm sorry," was all he could manage.

She nodded. "I'm sorry for all of us. Everyone who died for this folly. And how it's never-ending, the soldiers' suffering and ours. We're all hungry, getting sick, and it's so cold. There's no more good wood left to burn, there's —"

"—horrible bread," He added lightly.

Her chuckle at that helped her swallow tears. "What a disgrace for a tourist to have to eat it!"

"Well I —" He swallowed, felt as though he had given himself a slap. "I'm glad you have a friend to comfort you." And then, he couldn't bear it. "I should go."

To tell Joseph, she thought, and nodded.

It was fast work going down the stairs now. The roses were flat on the carpet today.

He gave a quick, polite nod to Madame Marcel and Rossignol and an old woman with them as he passed through the doorway.

He didn't know where he was headed. He thought only of his footsteps and the cold as he walked.

I, on the other hand, thought, *That damn Rossignol.*

PART 4
FLIGHT

67

The cold traveled everywhere: through the soles of Claire's boots, down her collar and up her sleeves. It pricked her face like needles.

Everyone on line stood huddled within themselves, like pigeons caught in a downpour. Most of the old men had stopped coming altogether.

How easy this had all been to bear just the day before. To think the suffering was coming to an end and then having that hope snatched away, now made it seem endless. *But it won't be endless,* she reminded herself. Rossignol was right: Whatever happened in the coming weeks, the Siege couldn't last forever. Right now, though, surrounded by frost and misery in the damp, cold dark, she doubted that a little.

When she got her rations, it was only cod again.

She couldn't feel her feet as she walked. She stumbled and stared down so that she wouldn't slip on the icy cobbles.

~~

That night, her vaporous breath was with her in the parlor like a specter. Her thoughts wandered to a place I'd never found them, a place I knew she never liked to go.

The death of Claire's parents had been terrible and unexpected.

I saw them as she'd last seen them, more or less as they appeared in their portrait. They were in excellent health and deeply in love, happy and smiling as they said goodbye to Claire and Paul.

They'd taken the train for only an hour or so, to a suburb where a photographer friend had invited them to spend a few days. He'd promised to show them an invention for generating light. "You'll see," he'd written them, "you'll be able to take perfect photographs even on days when the clouds are dark grey!"

Claire and Paul would never know what went wrong during the demonstration he gave on the afternoon of their arrival. The townspeople described a massive explosion, a ball of white-hot fire.

They said that nothing remained of the greenhouse her parents and their friend had been sitting in. Still, Claire had insisted on going to see it.

She still didn't know how she'd managed to board the train. She and Paul rode quietly, then waited for a kind neighbor to collect them and bring them to the site of the disaster.

There was nothing but a few shards of metal frame, burnt black and brittle. The ground was unnaturally dark, a black spot marking disaster. Still, she'd walked and paced and stared, searching for something – the broach her mother always wore, the pince-nez their father always kept on a small gold chain, even just a link from the chain, miraculously glittering against the blackness.

But there was only a lingering smell of burning. That was all that they took away: the proof of how hot and merciless it must have been.

~~

Claire took a breath, then stood and slowly walked to the bedroom.

I understood now why she never slept here. It used to be where her parents slept. When she and Paul had gotten accustomed to their grief and he'd met his future wife, by necessity this was where *they'd* slept.

But when they'd left, it went back to being her parents' room. She knew that her mother and father would have encouraged her to climb into their bed and curl herself into the covers for warmth, but doing that would mean accepting that they would never come back here again.

But it was so cold now. Even the Seine had frozen solid.

She set her candle down on one of the square-shaped bedposts. Then, she turned towards the enormous wardrobe on the opposite wall.

She reached out and turned the tarnished key that rested in one of the wardrobe's doors.

Half of the clothing rack inside was occupied by a row of fur coats and deerskin trousers and shirts – souvenirs from her parents' visit to Lapland, where they, too, had seen the Northern Lights, once upon a time.

Tears sprung to Claire's eyes, and she brushed them away. She carefully took one of the deerskin outfits down and laid it over her arm. She did the same for one of the coats.

Back in the parlor, she undressed until she was only in her drawers and chemise – and then she took those off, as well.

She put on the deerskin shirt and trousers. Her cold flesh felt as though it was rising to meet this other flesh that would warm it. Next, she wrapped herself in the enormous fur coat. What was missing now was a hat. She rummaged inside bureau drawers and found a nightcap I recognized from several of her photographs.

With just that little bit of movement, something like an enchantment occurred. The deerskin warmed and clung to her, like an animal protecting her. The fur covered her comfortingly. Although she'd planned to read for a while, she curled up on the sofa and fell into a deep sleep.

~~

The deerskin and fur smelled like him....

Down the sixth-floor corridor she walked in stockinged feet. She stopped at his door and peered into the keyhole. There was something cold around her neck – a gold chain. She ran her fingers over it, down towards the weight at its bottom.... A golden key lay on her chest.

She lifted it carefully to the lock, and turned.

The door swung open.

There was Monsieur Rush, emerging from what looked like a large black coat. He smiled joyfully at her. Golden light filled his little room.

68

At first, he stayed away from her, like a wounded animal that's retreated to lick its wounds. But soon he reasoned with himself.

There was too little sunlight to stay in late, waiting for her footsteps. And there was no way she could have known what he'd been intending to tell her that day.

I stamped my foot in frustration. If only he *had* said something! This would all be over.

Instead, it had all slid back to what it was before.

He stepped into the corridor. There was Monsieur Rouline, and there she was, at the doorway to the sixth floor. Hippolyte, who had stayed the night with him, curled around his legs as she approached.

"Bonjour, Mademoiselle Turin."

The memory of Rossignol calling her "Claire" mocked him, but her voice drowned it out. "Bonjour, Monsieur Rush. And bonjour, Hippolyte!" She bent down to scratch the cat's chin. "I think he might be the only living soul in Paris who hasn't lost weight!"

Orin's eyes darted away from hers. Then, in a low voice, he admitted, "That's because I feed him."

"You do?"

He nodded. "Your neighbors on the fifth floor – the refugees - have been catching rats, which has obviously diminished poor Hippolyte's food source. I'm just restoring the balance of things."

He tried not to show how nervous he felt. Did Hippolyte count among those she'd told him not to help? To his relief, she laughed, and he found himself laughing a little, too, at his puffed-up speech.

Claire found herself thinking, *His smile is so like what I saw in my dream last night.*

She's not laughing anymore, he noticed nervously. Maybe she was upset, after all. "I hope you don't mind, and I'm sorry – I didn't ask Madame Marcel if I could —"

"Oh," she pulled her thoughts back to the corridor. "No, I know she's grateful! But Hippolyte's staying fat has been our great mystery lately. Do you want to tell her?"

He forgot his discomfort and let a mischievous smile take its place. "Should I? Or is the mystery too much of a diversion to give away?"

~~

Madame Marcel looked at Orin with tears in her eyes. "You are very kind," she managed, and to her surprise, he and Claire laughed.

"Well, you are! I will never be able to thank you, Monsieur Rush."

"I wish I could do more."

"You've done more than enough! And I hope that what you set aside for Hippolyte isn't making you go hungry."

~~

Hippolyte had his extra meals to help him through the frigid days, and now Claire had her deerskin and coat. She wore the first beneath her dress and petticoats, and the latter over everything. Waiting on line at dawn, it was as if the air had become ice, but she barely felt it.

She gave the other coats in the wardrobe to Anne, and to Aunt Honorine and her maid Euphraisine as well. She gave another one to Madame Marcel.

Then, two others for Émile and Marguerite, and another for Marguerite's little children, to be draped over them while they slept, or cut into two smaller coats.

"I wanted to wait until Christmas," she said to each of them, "but it's too cold for that."

257

She told herself that Monsieur Rush probably didn't need a coat. Certainly, he must keep warm enough on his own at night. Still, she had the slightest doubt about this; after all, his room was just beneath the roof.

"Are you bearing the cold all right, Monsieur Rush?" she asked one morning.

It was a strange thing for Orin to be asked. With his wealth, everyone assumed his needs were taken care of. But maybe she was concerned because he never wore any fur. The very idea of it touching his skin in the precious hours he had his human form was revolting.

In the silent seconds before he found a reply, Claire surreptitiously took in his greatcoat. It was a thick, fine wool, and as she glanced at the sleeves, she could see it seemed to be lined with some warm fabric — flannel, perhaps. That was far from luxurious, but then, it dawned on her, maybe he didn't want any fur near his skin. Which might mean that the man she was seeing wasn't an illusion, but the form he really did take on in daylight....

"Mademoiselle Turin?"

She quickly drew her gaze from his sleeves. "I'm sorry," she laughed. "I was lost in thought."

He smiled. "Maybe you were away on some warm island."

"I'm afraid my imagination isn't powerful enough for that."

"I said it's kind of you to enquire, but I'm all right."

"I'm glad to hear it."

"And," he ventured, "are you?"

69

A t night, she wrapped herself in the fur and fell asleep to the smell of him. How strange that he was so close, just at the other end of the staircase, and yet they were both so alone.

In those long nights, Orin would often think the same thing. Back and forth their thoughts moved, down corridors and up and down the staircase like spirits.

The carpets' flowers rose and bloomed in the darkness.

~~

And then one night, a strange noise cracked through the icy quiet.

The strangled wail pulled Claire from her dreams. She bolted up and threw open the door, somehow knowing exactly what it was.

Moonlight was shining in through the window in the corridor. Just enough light for her to see a pair of hands pulling Hippolyte into the doorway across from her.

"Stop!" she yelled. "I see you! Stop!"

~~

Orin's beastly ears were made for hearing at great distances, especially the cries of an animal.

He unlocked and opened his door, thinking of nothing else, running down the corridor.

He heard Claire's voice. He ran faster.

~~

The hands faltered, and Hippolyte turned and bit a finger. That loosened the grip around him - he dropped to his feet and bolted down the stairs.

"What are you doing?" Claire kept yelling. "Do you think you're the only ones who are hungry? How dare you!"

The door shut without a word, and she stood breathless, wanting to scream or sob.

~~

Halfway down the spiral staircase, Orin stopped, suddenly coming to his senses, realizing what she would see –

"Mademoiselle Turin!" He called out. "Are you all right?"

He prayed she was. He prayed she wouldn't look in the stairwell.

~~

She was so shocked at the sound of his voice that for a moment, she forgot herself. She pictured his monstrous form standing somewhere on the spiral staircase.

"I'm fine," she answered at last. "I'm going to check on Hippolyte."

Her footsteps grew distant, then too far for him to hear. He quickly climbed the staircase and closed himself back inside his room.

~~

Claire raced down the stairs, the moon's glow her only light. No sign of Hippolyte at the bottom. She knocked at the door of the lodge.

"Did Hippolyte ask to come in?" she demanded breathlessly.

Madame Marcel's sleep-narrowed eyes widened. "What's wrong?"

"Let's find him first."

In the light of Madame Marcel's candle they made out his silhouette sitting at the statue's feet, licking his fur in an outraged manner.

Claire picked him up carefully, checking that his paws, his ears, everything was there. Hippolyte didn't seem upset so much as annoyed. When she was satisfied, she set him back down, and he ran into the lodge.

"Those horrible people on the fifth floor. They grabbed him – they were going to eat him."

The concierge gasped, then groaned. "I'm not surprised. I—" Her words caught in her throat. "I'm a fool. I should have been more careful. I shouldn't have let him go up there. I only - I know Monsieur Rush has been feeding him, and anyway —"

"— And anyway," Claire put in, "he's always been free to come and go as he pleases here. That shouldn't have to change.

"What monsters," Claire nearly spat.

"They're hungry."

"We all are!"

"But *they* have no reason to care about Hippolyte," the concierge said sensibly.

~ ~

Orin sat on his bed, shaking. She was all right, he kept telling himself, and Hippolyte was well enough at least to have run down the stairs.

It was the first time he'd forgotten himself in such a way. But as time passed, he began to wonder if he'd forgotten himself at all. In that moment, he and the beast he became were allies.

At last, he heard her come back up the stairs, more quietly than he would have thought. Instead of moving towards her apartment, she – he heard her turn towards his staircase. He tensed. She seemed to hesitate at the landing, but continued until she was outside his door.

"Thank you, Monsieur Rush. I just wanted to let you know that Hippolyte is all right."

Then, she turned and went rapidly away.

It was kind of her, Orin thought, it was an honor, for her to come to tell him about Hippolyte. To thank him. But what if the neighbors were waiting to harm her? Hoping it was an irrational fear, he sat hardly breathing until he heard her door close and lock behind her.

70

They met in the corridor the next morning.

"Bonjour, Monsieur Rush."

"Bonjour, Mademoiselle Turin.

So Hippolyte wasn't injured?"

"To our fifth-floor 'neighbors' ' infinite regret. But," Claire added after a moment, "Who knows if they'll try it again? Madame Marcel is keeping him in her lodge."

"He's not used to that. He won't try to escape?"

She sighed. "You've gotten to know him very well. Of course he will. But I'll be watching the fifth floor."

Orin nodded, but I could tell he wasn't reassured. How could she watch if she were busy with sitters, or out on the breadlines, or sleeping? "Can they be evicted?"

Claire shook her head. "They're housed at the government's demand."

"Perhaps there are ways we could convince them to leave…"

"Monsieur Rush!" she couldn't help laughing, "I thought you said you were innocent of plotting against the state! Anyway, who would they put here next? *They* might be able to catch Hippolyte without our noticing."

"True." He decided to listen for trouble at night while she slept – and then, he thought, what would happen if he were the only one who heard something? Would he dare to leave his room and stop it? Or would he be a coward in order to keep his secret? "I…wish I could help," he told her lamely.

"You have! Now those awful people know there are two of us listening, not just me."

"Maybe, but it's not enough. We'll find a real solution."

These words were edged with flame. It was the flame of love — not just for Mademoiselle Turin, but for this life, and for Hippolyte, who had always accepted him, whatever his form.

~~

If you've spent any time in the company of a cat, you know that they have their own sort of magic, something ungoverned by the rules of your world or mine. They can escape from or get into the most unlikely of places. Some can unlock a door merely by looking at it. Despite barely escaping death, that foolish Hippolyte always found ways to slip out of the lodge at night. Orin insisted on giving Madame Marcel some tins of food for him, but it didn't matter; he wanted his freedom.

Normally a light sleeper, Claire barely slept at all now, keeping her ears pricked for the slightest sound in the corridor outside. She already had shadows under her eyes these days. Now, they were marks as dark as storm clouds.

The fifth-floor neighbors came and went, and never seemed to acknowledge that anything was amiss. Madame Marcel didn't exchange the slightest word with them anymore. She couldn't throw them out or ask the building's owner to, and she couldn't make a complaint at the Commissariat; at the rate things were going, they might decide to requisition Hippolyte themselves.

She wished there were mail from the provinces just so that she could hide theirs from them. She was tempted to cut their candlesticks to give them less light.

Claire began to wonder about the other floors. What if they waited to catch Hippolyte when he wandered there? Or what if — though she hated to think it — other neighbors decided the temptation was too great?

Every morning when they saw each other in the corridor, she'd tell Orin that Hippolyte had made it through the night. But the news never put him at ease. He'd also considered the other floors and the other neighbors. Feeling her worry, seeing the shadows under her eyes - for the first time, he wished he could simply, openly, be a monster, and strike terror into them all.

One morning, she didn't give her usual reassuring message, but only asked him, "What do you think we should do?"

"I've been wondering if we might ask Washburne -the American ambassador – if Hippolyte could be transported over enemy lines. But where to?"

"My brother's, in Beauvoir!" she burst out, a light in her eyes for the first time in days.

He nodded. "So that part is settled. But how could we convince him – or anyone – that Hippolyte should be taken out of Paris to safety? I-I thought perhaps he could do something extraordinary...but I don't suppose he does any sort of tricks or anything more useful than what the average cat does?"

"Unfortunately not." Claire sighed. "Thank you for not suggesting we take him to the city gates and let him try his luck in the abandoned towns."

"Someone told you that?" There was a distant expression in his eyes as he thought back to that terrible afternoon a few weeks before. "Did they forget the battles and the marauders? Not to mention the cold?"

"Most people would say none of that matters. He can hunt and he has fur."

Orin shook his head. "The marauders would hunt *him*. Can you imagine – he'd probably go right up to anyone he saw."

He tried to summon some certainty into his voice. "We'll come up with a plan. You're creative and I'm – well, I have a lot of time to think, anyway."

With that, as he sometimes did, he hurried down the corridor, away from her.

71

S he called on Anne. "You can trust me with anything, but I'm not so sure about Aunt Honorine and Euphraisine. I think they're hungry enough to tell me Hippolyte ran away, then serve 'rabbit' for supper. I'm so sorry."

She thought of asking Rossignol, but quickly thought against it. A few days before, she'd received a letter. His mother was ill again. He was at her bedside whenever he wasn't on watch on the city walls.

Émile couldn't help, either. "You know I love our feline friend," he told her. "And Marguerite would be glad for the company – especially such a warm little ball of fur in this cold. But where I live, well, if by any chance he got past our doorway, someone would be there to snatch him up, if not for food, then for the money they'd make selling such a fat prize for someone else's supper." He looked at her with sadness in his eyes. "He's safer here than he would be with us."

~~

Orin wondered if Joseph might be able to help them. But his brother only said, "You hear the creatures like to sleep – why can't he just stay in the concierge's lodge until this whole situation blows over?"

"He's used to roaming. Would *you* like to stay locked up in the same place all night?"

"Perhaps, if I knew I risked being eaten."

"Well, I suppose that settles it – you're smarter than a cat."

Orin removed the sting from his voice, "I know you don't care for him, but do you think you could keep him here?"

"Now I'm not sure that *you're* smarter than a cat. If you say he insists on roaming, he certainly won't stay in the suite. And these days, the staff or my few fellow guests might just be tempted to make a meal of him, themselves."

Orin hung his head, exhausted and defeated.

"Listen," Joseph went on, startled at the sight. "Perhaps I can start making friends with balloonists and see if I might convince one of them to take him away. But he'd add a lot of weight and-"

"I don't think that would work," Orin interrupted. "We need to get him away soon. And he must go to Mademoiselle Turin's brother's. We don't know where a balloon would land, or under what circumstances. For all our trouble, Hippolyte might not even get to safety."

~~

He returned home, his heart so heavy. He was powerless, useless.

The cold and despair had gotten the best of Mademoiselle Turin, as well. They crossed paths quickly, only saying "Good evening."

~~

His spirit ardent as a flame, he wished, as he had wished for days, for a solution. That night, the transformation came as it always did. He shrugged away the lingering pain and continued reading.

But there was something else. I noticed it before he did, and felt as though I were choking.

Orin shrugged again. And more and more often –there was something on top of the thick fur on his back, something like a leather cape. He stood up and, hesitantly, reached behind him.

Yes, there was something — it hung down his back in two sections that came to a point just above each of his hooves. He felt some more, and then shuddered with recognition. The movement inadvertently did what he hadn't wanted to do: the new wings he'd inexplicably grown spread open. He took a breath and imagined a door closing and then they folded back.

This was too much to think about, so he decided to ignore it.

He turned back to his book.

But unsurprisingly, he couldn't pay attention to the words. He was shaking. Not with fear this time, or with sorrow, but with rage. Why had this happened?

Now, he was even more monstrous.

If he lived at Walden Pond, with no neighbors, he would have opened his door and hollered and roared into the air — a man's roar, not a beast's, the roar of a breaking heart that kept breaking, over and over. But here, now, there was no yelling, only little puffs of ineffectual breath, a strange noise that came from his tight chest and escaped through the spaces between his sickle-shaped teeth.

I can't breathe. I can't —

He shut his eyes.

He concentrated on the red darkness, thought of the night of the aurora borealis. He took a breath and let himself imagine Mademoiselle Turin in her apartment just below him, or rather a bit below and down the corridor. Perhaps she was reading a book as well. He breathed again.

~~

I wailed with him that night, and flew through the city with the cold winds. Nothing, nothing, nothing changed, nothing helped. The curse remained, the cold remained, my regretful heart remained.

The curse was supposed to be set upon him and stilled. I didn't even know what would have happened if he'd lost a limb — perhaps it would have been intact when he transformed each night.

It seemed the wings could only come from this outside force, this magic I couldn't understand or control.

But as I grew too tired to fly, I realized it was something else: They also came from Orin's own magic, sprung from that ardent wish.

72

O rin and Joseph went to see the frozen Seine. It was a rare sight. They walked along the quais with the wind biting at their skin, and walked to the middle of a few bridges for different views of the once busy river that was now a solid, unmoving white mass.

Below, some courageous souls ventured onto the ice.

"Good show!" Joseph gamely called out to a fearless fellow who managed to slide across the river's breadth.

Cold and hunger were always present, a low ache inside all of them. Everyone there knew that night would come soon enough and it would be colder still. Still, they could laugh, and marvel at their fast-flowing river, stilled for a while.

Orin's thoughts weren't always on the scene in front of him. The wings were a shadow that never lifted. It was difficult to smile or joke. How much more would he change, he wondered, and at what rate? How much further would he go from being human?

At times, he'd feel a lurching panic and then Joseph's laughter would bring him back, and he could feel the ground beneath his feet —the hard, perpetual stone. He'd take an icy breath, though it hurt, and watch a smoky cloud float from him just as it did from all of the people around him. Then he'd breathe in, more slowly this time, and do it again. Again and again, clouds of his breath over the Seine, until it was time to head homeward.

~~

In the early-fallen night, faraway church bells ring the end of Vespers. Their soft clamor is difficult to make out, lost so often in the thunderclaps of artillery everyone in the city has grown used to.

Orin tries to settle himself with the new wings. It isn't easy to sit with them beneath him. Tentatively, he shifts and lets them sprawl behind him like a cloak.

As he does this, his eyes fall on the bit of sky above the curtain rod. The sky is thick with nighttime clouds. He knows that near the horizon, they shine a dull orange whenever the canons are fired.

Suddenly, an idea flashes to him. I feel it like a bolt of electricity running through the room.

He stands a bit unsteadily and extinguishes the lamp.

Carefully, he moves towards the window. Pulling the curtain away as little as he can, he looks at the sky again, this time scrutinizing it. Then, his gaze wanders down past the chimneys and rooftops, those wonders that sometimes make him forget there's something below – but there is indeed something. Six floors, and hard cobblestones at the bottom.

He closes the curtain and sits down on the floor again for a moment.

Then he stands, willing the wings to open.

And suddenly, utterly ridiculously, he thinks, he's flying around his little room. His hooves dangle below him, like two clumsy shoes.

If he had toes in this form, I'm sure they would be curled. He's only a few inches above the ground, but I can feel that he's terrified. Still, he circles. Over the bed, past the bookshelves. The wings hardly have space to open. Pivot past the fireplace, careful not to knock over the washbasin. And back again.

He flies in circles for a long while.

Then, he closes his eyes and wills the wings to move more slowly. When his hooves softly clack against the floorboards, he wills the wings shut.

He stumbles and falls onto the bed. He stares up at the ceiling. By now he knows its fissures by heart.

At last, he takes a breath, stands up, and flies again.

269

And again.

With each flight, he understands more about how to control the wings. When he lands for the second time, he stumbles slightly, but doesn't fall. The third time, his hooves neatly meet the floor.

He flies circles in the room for so long that I can feel him growing bored. It turns out that this is what he was hoping for. Boredom can give you courage sometimes.

Orin moves towards the window again. This time, he won't look at the sky or the chimneys, and he won't think about the paving stones far below. He considers the slate rooftop just outside. Where could he grip, how could he –

The window seems slightly small for his frame, especially with the new wings. He wills himself smaller and slips outside like a snake. He's not disgusted, but amazed.

He grips the roof tiles tightly with his talons, grateful not to see any faces in windows. Then again, he wonders, would anyone see him in this darkness, clinging closely to the roof, covered by gray wings?

Once he's reached the alcove beside the window, he stops and breathes. He looks at the sky, smells the cold, damp air. Droplets of mist cling to his fur and never come close to the flesh beneath. They run down his leathery face like rain dripping from a gargoyle.

Everyone in Paris is deep in misery now, like a fog. Who would be standing at an upstairs window instead of curled in bed under as many counterpanes as possible, shivering and wishing for morning – and often dreading it at the same time, since it means the breadline? No one is looking for monsters now; cold, darkness, and hunger have taken their place.

Tentatively, he unfolds his wings and makes them beat up and down. Up and down, up and down – he's flying again, this time among the chimneys and rooftops.

He reaches out to them, no longer separated by fear and glass. With a thrill in his belly, he lets himself pivot around one small terracotta tower. Then, he takes a deep breath and crosses back over the gap between that roof and his own. He aims for his window and flies inside, but too fast – he bangs into the bare wall above the mantel and crumples to the ground like a swatted moth.

After a moment, he stands, shaking his head, and closes the window and then the curtains. He's finished his first flying lesson.

~~

Orin rested for a while, and then, to my surprise, he stood up again. I *can't stop there*. He drew back the curtain, looked out into the blackness, climbed through the window as he had before.

This time, he flew upwards, so high that when he looked down, he saw all of Paris below him. It was a dark place now, with the rare street lamp or lit window like a star in the night sky.

In some places, he could make out large, black masses. Narrowing his eyes, he followed their contours. There were the angular forms of the Opera's roof, guarding the onion of its dome. Further south, the Louvre was splayed out like a sleeping animal. The Seine was a trench, its frozen water dully reflecting what moonlight feebly glowed through the clouds. There was Notre Dame, which always seemed to stand proudly, even fiercely, a guardian. Its spire and buttresses were at once beautiful and protective, like a heart's bravery.

He flew towards the church – and crossed the distance far faster than he'd expected.

He was so surprised by everything that he wasn't afraid. He felt embraced by the dark sky, safe above the city he loved.

He glided past rows and rows of unlit buildings and the occasional empty lot that was even now being looted for wood or anything else that might be used for a fire.

He passed the city wall. He could see it unfurling in both directions like protecting arms, wondering why he was leaving them. Past the *terrains vagues*, past the forests cut down months ago, and the deserted houses that the marauders or soldiers might visit again soon.

The sound of the canons grew louder. From time to time, he could see what looked like sparks coming from the gear-like shapes of the forts far below.

He flew higher. Balloons might pass in the cover of night, but he wondered if anyone below would see him.

No one had. Now, he was over enemy territory.

He turned back, wondering how he'd find his window. He brushed the worry aside like vines and strained his strong eyes.

There was the Boulevards' meager light. He used the Opera to guide him slightly eastward. Then, he flew lower, enough to make out the streets, until he found his own – and now, there, that must be his rooftop – yes, there was his window. He landed on the slate tiles and crawled quickly inside.

Always quiet, now he almost cried out in triumph.

He had found a way to save Hippolyte.

~~

It was a strange thing, to watch him sitting joyfully on his haunches, wings half-spread, a smile on his face. His transformation had always meant pain and horror. But now, in the span of only an hour, he saw it differently, or would at least for a while. He was *proud*. And standing there, watching him in my darkness, I was proud of him.

73

B onjour, Monsieur Rush."

Claire was surprised to see his eyes so bright. "I've got a plan."

The light that came into her eyes at this was everything to him.

~~

Downstairs, Madame Marcel was just opening the door to her lodge. Hippolyte darted out and rubbed against Orin's ankles.

"Bonjour," he greeted the cat and the concierge, patting Hippolyte gently.

"Monsieur Rush has an idea!" Claire had followed him down the stairs, a hopeful smile on her face that Madame Marcel reflected back to her, then to him.

"Is it true?"

"Nothing is certain yet." Orin's voice was suddenly grave. "I need to talk to my brother… and meet with a few people. I think it will work, though. I think everything will be all right."

And with that, he nodded his leave, not able to look at Mademoiselle Turin, who was shining so brightly on the staircase, who was more beautiful than he'd ever seen her. He passed through the doorway and headed towards the Grand Hôtel.

~~

"I can help Mademoiselle Turin," he began.

Joseph stared at him in confusion. "With…?"

"With Hippolyte."

"How?"

"Maybe you should sit down."

Joseph refilled his glass and settled into one of the room's many armchairs. "All right then, what are you so serious about? What's going on?"

"I can – I can fly."

Joseph chuckled. "You've been reading too much about the balloons, Orry. Everyone thinks they can fly. It *seems* fairly straightforward, but remember when we saw the balloon launch? A lot's involved. And then, of course, that's without even thinking about how you might acquire a balloon, or passage in one – and then there's the Prussians."

He gave Orin a look, as if to say, "Let's laugh about this together." But his brother didn't look like he was going to laugh.

Orin had never discussed his nightly form with Joseph. Joseph knew that he became some sort of beast, but Orin had never wanted to describe it further. Trying for the first time, he felt terribly embarrassed. He took a breath and reminded himself that he wasn't talking to a scientist or a doctor or stranger, but to his brother, and, really, his dearest friend.

"I have wings," he tried.

"You never told me that."

"I've never told you much of anything about…what happens at night. But this is new. It's only been two nights since I've had them."

"You suddenly grew wings?"

Orin nodded. "I wasn't…happy about it. But maybe, for once, my condition might be useful to someone."

"Useful how?"

He was surprised that Joseph hadn't caught on more quickly, but then, he hadn't in any way been prepared for this sort of conversation.

"I could put Hippolyte into a basket and fly him out of Paris, to somewhere safe. I was thinking, even, to Mademoiselle Turin's brother's studio. She mentioned once that he lives in a small town,

Beauvoir, near Mont-Saint-Michel. I remember it because the name is so obvious. The view of the Mont must be beautiful."

Joseph nodded dismissively at that, and got to what mattered to him: "You're saying you're going to fly all the way there? How – Can you do that? And how long would it take you if you could? What about the Prussians? And-And how would you find your way?"

He sounded more concerned than I had ever heard him.

"You know I've always been cautious. This is no different. I've been researching and practicing. Last night, I tried to fly over Paris and – it was so fast. I'd hardly started before I had to stop myself from flying past one of the forts.

"I did some reading this morning – Mont-Saint-Michel is only 200 miles from Paris. I tried to find the speed of a bird in flight, but then, my wings are much larger than a bird's. I don't believe I would get tired and I do believe I can go quickly. If I orient myself in the right direction, and stay the course, I'd just continue until I reach the coast. Surely I'd see the abbey – it's magnificent."

Joseph rolled his eyes, coming back into his clever self. "It will be *night*, Orry. You won't see anything! And from what I've heard, it's not so magnificent these days."

"Ah, but I can see in the dark!" The triumph of winning an argument with a sibling suddenly replaced Orin's lingering embarrassment.

"Can you?" Joseph took a drink, and suddenly Orin stood and went to the decanter, serving himself.

"Yes. I've always been able to. Not perfectly – not enough to read a book without light," he admitted ruefully, "but enough to see the silhouettes of large objects, like a large rock topped by a church off the coastline, for instance." He walked back to his seat, a smile creeping onto his face. He felt a bit mad – and a good part of it, he realized, was that he'd simply spoken to someone about what he was, about what he experienced every night. What a strange relief.

"So you can fly and you can see in the dark," Joseph mused. "But what about the Prussians? They search the sky for balloons. They've shot many down. How are *you* going to get past them?"

Orin's stomach turned. "That detail does worry me. But then, it seems most of them get past enemy lines safely. That's why they've been leaving at night, as we know."

"-If that's even true. What if it's simply what the government is telling us?"

"*I* believe it's true. How would there be references to letters and *dépêches* and such things?"

"Corruption and lies go deep, Orry. You should know that. We're good liars," Joseph added softly.

"Well, the Prussians are looking for balloons, not for what would look like a large flying animal."

"Is that what you look like?"

"Of course."

"What if you look more like a man with wings, a man with some sort of flying machine? And a basket of who knows what in his arms?"

Orin shook his head. "No."

"It's dangerous, Orry."

"I know."

After a long silence, Joseph spoke again. "What happens when you get there? If it takes you all night and you arrive at dawn, and change back?"

"That would make things easy, if you think of it. I'd wait until a reasonable hour and find Turin's studio and give him Hippolyte. Then I'd find somewhere to hide till nightfall."

"But if you did run into someone, with your accent, and being a stranger in the area, you don't think you'd rouse any suspicions?"

"I could say I come from the American Embassy in Paris – they let me through enemy lines. I was robbed on the way and don't have my papers. I need to try to return as quickly as possible."

"That sounds risky. What if they offer to accompany you back there?"

"Well, at least I *do* know people at the Embassy."

"True…but they'd be terribly curious as to how you found yourself so far away."

Orin thought for a moment, then gave a frustrated sigh. "I could say it was a dare or something like that maybe, brush it off? But anyway," he went on, before Joseph could protest, "I don't think it will come to that. I fly so fast – this will be over in a single night."

"How can you be certain?"

"It's magic, after all."

Joseph downed the rest of his glass. "You've become so daring. I thought I'd approve, but if your plan doesn't work…."

"I'm not a fool. I know this is dangerous. But-" Orin had been prepared to go over an elaborate plan with his brother. He hadn't expected to justify the reason behind it. And he hadn't exactly justified it to himself. He thought carefully. "I've done nothing and now I can."

Joseph's eyes flashed. "Nothing?!"

"Less than a cat, if you think about it." He smiled wryly. "Hippolyte at least catches mice. What have I ever done but wallow? There are ways I could have helped people, maybe even *using* what I am – but I've just let it limit me."

"Don't say things like that!" Joseph's voice was as raised as I'd ever heard it. Orin found himself picturing his brother when he was a little boy, furious at him for teasing him. "Orry – you're my brother. A cat can be replaced, but you're a person! You're a good person."

Orin bowed his head, with a bitter grin. "I'm kind," he intoned. "Merely that." He looked up at his brother. "I want to help her. This is all that I can do. I don't believe there's a cure for my condition. …I believe it's even getting worse."

Joseph was silent for a while. Then: "So what do you need from me?"

"I need you to help me come up with the perfect lie to tell them about how I'm getting Hippolyte out of Paris."

"…Which would be when?"

"As soon as possible."

"Let me think."

After a while, Joseph leaned forward in his chair. "I've got it. It won't be easy," he went on. "But as I said and as you know, we're good liars."

74

T he American Embassy has a balloon scheduled to leave Paris on the 26th. We've talked to our friends there and have arranged for Hippolyte to be on it, if you'll agree. Joseph will bring him, since the launch is at night."

This was what they had decided their story would be: a balloon that didn't exist, departing in four days. Orin would have preferred the "balloon" take off that very night, but Joseph had refused to help if he didn't wait a few days to practice his flying. He knew his brother was also hoping he'd reconsider.

"Hippolyte in a balloon?" Madame Marcel intoned, stunned.

"I know it sounds strange," Orin said gently, "but it has been done. Dogs have been transported in some of the balloons, and of course there are always pigeons."

Mademoiselle Turin nodded in agreement.

"None of the animals were injured or-"

"-captured?" Mademoiselle Turin put in now, as a sudden doubt came to her.

"Well," he conceded, "a few balloons have fallen into enemy hands, as we've heard. But I don't think they'd harm a cat. The Prussians have a sort of honor. I imagine they would keep Hippolyte under close watch, to be sure he isn't carrying some sort of message, but I don't think they'd harm him – and they certainly wouldn't need to eat him. I believe they might even deliver him to Mademoiselle Turin's brother. It's possible, anyway."

"This does seem to be the best solution," Madame Marcel acquiesced.

"At the very least," Orin admitted, voicing their thoughts, "it's the *only* solution."

"And when the balloon lands —" Mademoiselle Turin began

"—The balloonist has our strict instructions. And a handsome fee. He'll see to it that Hippolyte is taken to your brother, regardless of the distance. Otherwise, he's pledged to care for him, himself."

Madame Marcel raised an eyebrow. "You're sure he'll keep his word?"

"A handsome fee," Orin repeated with a grin.

"How can we repay you?" the concierge asked.

"I —" He stopped for a moment, finally showing some uncertainty. "I feel about Hippolyte the way you both do – well, less, since I've known him for a shorter time, I suppose. I have the means; why shouldn't I help?"

"We are in your debt forever." Madame Marcel's voice was mostly grateful, but he could detect the faintest hesitation.

"Don't worry. That won't matter when I'm back in America. But," he added, and here there was something that crept into his own voice in spite of himself, a sort of plaintiveness, "you are both always welcome to visit me there. I hope that one day you shall."

Claire's face had gone pale. "You're leaving, then?"

Orin gave a soft laugh. "Not right now, at any rate."

She laughed gamely in return, but inside she felt as though she were scrambling, trying to climb up a wall.

Of course he'll go, she threw to herself like a rope. *He was never planning to stay here.*

Then there was something else, something she couldn't stop herself from thinking, And it's not as if I gave him any reason to.

But she couldn't, she reminded herself. This thought was a ladder. What kind of future would they have? How could she be with a creature –

— And anyway, she suddenly realized, he'd never shown her anything besides what might be considered friendship. The proposal was Monsieur Joseph's idea. She'd only assumed Monsieur Rush felt the world reel, too, when their hands met. She was fooling herself. He would leave, and it was for the best. It was end of a trip for him, and it would make things easier for her.

But, some part of her softly cried out, *who else will I hear, who else will hear me?*

"Well, we'll have to make the most of the time you're still here," Madame Marcel was saying, her voice full of warmth. "And speaking of that, perhaps you and your brother already have plans, but if not, on Christmas Day, we always have a nice meal here around noon, and I'd be honored if you would be our special guests. Of course," she admitted, "this year's meal will be far from extraordinary, but it's the company that counts, isn't it?"

Orin broke into a sincere smile. "I'd be more than happy to attend – and so would Joseph, I'm sure!"

"It'll be a going-away party, then," Claire said, her voice not at all as cheerful as it should have been. "For Hippolyte, the day before he leaves."

75

That Christmas was one of the coldest, bleakest, most cheerless ever known in Paris. And yet, you must find joy where you can find it, and some Parisians did.

There were the restaurants that thought it a fine joke to print out menus that described their offerings honestly, but in the most elegant of ways ("cat flanked by rats" being my favorite).

Most Parisians celebrated at home, making a meal of what they could. Some exchanged meager gifts, others none at all. The revolutionaries spent another day dreaming of the fall of the current leaders, and that kept their blood warm in the infernal cold.

On the afternoon of Christmas Eve, Orin and Joseph dined at the home of one of their American friends. Everyone gasped when an actual chicken was served. But the brothers' thoughts were mostly on Orin's upcoming flight.

That night, Orin was out practicing again.

He was sad to see so few lights in the windows. There were no sounds of celebrating, either (even though he probably wouldn't have heard them from that height). There was only the rush of the wind and the low, punctual boom of canon fire.

Still, there was some happiness. He was always surprised by how fast he could fly. He wanted to go farther, to make a true trial of it and fly all the way to the coast. But he held himself back and returned to his room to study maps.

It was a good thing he couldn't feel the cold. Far below freezing, it was a cold that normally never came to Paris.

I felt a constant chill – but it was nothing to do with the cold in the air. I didn't know how Orin would be able to do this.

I would have thought he wanted to destroy himself, but I realized that wasn't it at all. It was the foolishness of his heart, which had at last come alive and sent out this desperate, beating message: life, adventure, love, the impossible.

76

It was strange, Claire thought as she woke that morning; this cold, bitter Christmas was the first she had felt happy about since those with her family had ended. It was because she had some lovely gifts to give, she told herself, as she bound ribbons around them.

Orin was busy, as well. On Christmas Day in New York, the Rushes invited friends and distant relatives to come for punch and other treats that were laid out on the long table in the dining room.

Now, he gathered some peach tins and imagined that they shone like the silver service on that table across the ocean.

He descended the staircase with his gifts in a sack, *like a tall, clean-shaven, modern-dressed Saint Nicholas,* he thought, grinning in spite of himself. There was laughter coming from the slightly open door of the lodge. Suddenly, he stopped.

Would Rossignol be there?

Rossignol seemed kind enough, he reasoned. He could bear it. And if not, he could always plead illness and retire.

He squared his shoulders and continued determinedly over to the lodge, knocking as merrily has he could muster.

"Monsieur Rush!" Madame Marcel's cheeks were flushed. "Please, come in!"

The room was long but not very wide, and even when no one but the concierge and Hippolyte occupied it, it had a cluttered air. This was due in part to a large table with far too many chairs (these Madame Marcel and her beloved husband had inherited from his family, and she couldn't bear to part with them).

Pictures lined every inch of the burgundy-papered walls — paintings of no great talent, but pretty. Some daguerreotypes were scattered among them, glittering behind shining glass frames. The concierge's bed took up a shadowy corner against the farthest wall. It was neatly made, and she'd draped what he realized was one of Mademoiselle Turin's fur coats on top of it. Hippolyte was curled contentedly in its center.

There was a weak fire in the hearth, but the number of people were what soon made it warm — and perhaps their happiness helped.

A fashionably dressed young lady with a stunning hat approached him and introduced herself as "Mademoiselle Bertin, Mademoiselle Turin's dear friend."

There was a prim old lady standing not too far from her, with a slightly younger, portly, plainly dressed woman at her side. "It's a pleasure to meet you," Mademoiselle Bertin — Anne, that is - greeted him with poise, even though I could feel her mind bursting with questions. "May I present my aunt, Madame Honorine Bertin, and Euphraisine, her maid, refugees from Sèvres."

I easily read the dour woman's thoughts just then. She hadn't wanted to come to a simple concierge's lodge, but Anne had told her, "Ever since Maman and Papa passed away, I've been invited, and it's the merriest of times, and I will do nothing else. You two may go somewhere else, but without me." And so, with no great connexions in the city, she and Euphraisine had followed.

Orin nodded to them all. "A pleasure to meet you. I hope you are enjoying Paris…as much as one can at the moment, at any rate."

Aunt Honorine shook her head fussily. "It's far too cold. But we make do."

"You will have to return when all of this is over and Paris is pleasant again."

Mademoiselle Bertin shot him a look that said "Keep quiet!" and he nearly laughed, and shot her an apologetic glance in return.

"I am sorry, monsieur," the old lady said. "Who are you? You are foreign. Where do you come from?"

"I'm—"

"- an American prince." Mademoiselle Turin came through the door just then and set down a battered valise.

She gave Anne a kiss on the cheek, and her friend took the opportunity to whisper in her ear "Is that your gentleman?" Claire said nothing, but her cheeks reddened a little.

"An American prince?" Aunt Honorine echoed. "How bizarre!"

Claire thought that if Émile had been there, he would certainly have quoted Baudelaire to her: "The beautiful is always bizarre." She imagined the face the old woman would make at that, and held back a laugh. And yet, it really *was* the perfect way to describe him.

Orin was bizarre, and he was beautiful, pale as a candle and glowing with merriment, his green-gold eyes bright, his dark hair.... She realized she was trying to memorize his features before he left; she would have no photographs.

Just at that moment, there was a commotion outside. With a concierge's instinct, Madame Marcel hurried into the corridor.

"Oh! Bonjour Madame Marcel!" Joseph's voice filled the vaulted entryway. "I've invited the cab driver inside just for a moment, for a drink and to warm up from this frightful cold. I hope you don't mind. He's been a great help to me – well, to all of us!" They heard Madame Marcel gasp, and the curious group now joined her.

Joseph and the driver were trying to unload parcel after parcel from the cab. Wonderful smells wafted over to them.

"You see," he said, "my brother and I are quite embarrassed that we have no cooking skills to speak of. So, we followed our custom and fetched some food from our favorite restaurant. I hope you don't mind."

No one said a word.

But everyone rushed to the cab to help with the wondrous packages.

"This is too much," Madame Marcel protested faintly, when they had placed the food on the table and other parcels on the floor.

"If it is, you're welcome to keep any that's left over," Orin said innocently.

They all laughed and Madame Marcel filled the cab driver's glass again, and then offered spiced wine all around.

"Should we give him something to eat?" the concierge quietly asked Claire as the driver prepared to leave, thanking them all and wishing them a Merry Christmas.

"Don't worry," Joseph surprised them by leaning in to mutter a reply. "He has his own parcel. I'm not cruel."

"You certainly are not!" Madame Marcel exclaimed, and they lifted their glasses in a toast.

"Now that we're all here," the concierge announced, "Hippolyte and I welcome you and thank you for coming, and wish you Merry Christmas! Before we start, I ask that we send a prayer to the soldiers."

For a moment, a draught came into the room, as they imagined how the troops must be suffering beyond the city walls. There weren't enough blankets, and their uniforms weren't made to resist this cold. And there was the cold of fear, of missing family and loved ones. Thinking of this, they felt as gray as the faces in the pictures on the walls, and sent thoughts to the soldiers like little flames, wishing they could warm them.

"We pray they do not suffer and that they return home safely," Aunt Honorine intoned. Everyone gave a low "Amen."

"Let's enjoy this celebration even more for them," Anne said then, and Madame Marcel nodded in agreement.

They unwrapped parcels of meat in a rich sauce, vegetables that were such a rarity that no one noticed they were slightly wilted, and little pastries that had been lovingly made by a baker who had clearly lingered over them, wishing he had more work like that to do.

They also savored the garlic soup and crackers and slices of dried cod that Madame Marcel and Mademoiselle Turin had prepared — they savored everything that filled their bellies and made them feel warm again.

"I don't know what meat this is," Joseph muttered to Claire, with a twinkle in his eye, "but I promise you it's not cat."

He'd said it so softly that there was no way Aunt Honorine could have heard; the look of disapproval she shot them could only have been provoked by Claire's outburst of laughter.

After that good laugh, Claire suddenly felt a bit melancholy. She thought of how much her parents would have liked this very strange Christmas gathering. She wondered what Paul and his wife and child were doing just then.

Orin noticed her sadness. "Monsieur Rossignol couldn't join us?"

She turned to him in surprise. "Oh, I think he's spending Christmas with his cousins. And he may even have to be on the ramparts for some of it, poor man."

"Yes, that must be hard," Orin agreed, sincerely.

He couldn't tell her how he felt — there was no use, since Rossignol had her heart. And he could never comfort her the way that dashing fellow could. But maybe he could make her forget her sadness for a while.

"Shall we exchange presents?" he asked Madame Marcel.

"Of course!"

Anne went first.

Fine handkerchiefs for the gentlemen. For Claire, a forest-green hat with a small brim that dipped towards the forehead like a widow's peak.

It was topped with coral-colored silk roses, and a long ribbon of the same color was threaded through it. "It's the only colorful thing I've made in months."

Another hat for Madame Marcel, simpler but still striking: dark blue with a glossy midnight blue feather curling over one side. "How extraordinary," the concierge beamed.

One for Aunt Honorine and one for Euphraisine, even – though these were far more sober and less remarkable, which suited those ladies perfectly fine.

"Let's all put them on!" Claire said excitedly.

Joseph glanced at his brother. Orin hadn't taken his eyes from Mademoiselle Turin. He watched as she lifted the hat to her head and fastened the vividly-colored ribbon under her pale chin. The ribbon fell just above her birthmark. At that, he looked away.

"May I go next?" he asked, clearing his throat.

There were the bundles of proper, dry firewood for each of them, which everyone held close. If he could take photographs or even sketch well, Orin would have asked them all to pose like this – what a strange world they were in, where sticks were as valuable as bars of gold.

And then, "Mademoiselle Turin, I wanted to give you this, in thanks for all of the help you've given me."

The package was thin and heavy, and so long that their fingers didn't touch when he held it out to her. She opened the wrapping, gasped, then looked at him in disbelief.

"Your own *One Hundred Famous Views of Edo*. This way, you'll no longer need to borrow mine."

"Oh – but this is – this is too generous …." She opened the folder and carefully and lovingly lifted out a few of the prints, passing them around as though she were passing around warm light.

"Thank you," she said, trying to meet his eyes, but he'd already bent down to rummage in his sack again.

"And for everyone – tins of peaches, a gift from Joseph and myself. Open them when you need them most."

A grateful murmur went through the group. I have to say, everyone but Claire was far more impressed with the peaches than the prints.

Madame Marcel had knitted scarves for each of them. It was a good thing that she would have knitted them anyway, as a way to pass many quiet hours, because Aunt Honorine didn't seem particularly impressed, and I'm not sure that Anne would have ever worn such a thing in public. Still, they appreciated the concierge's gesture.

Aunt Honorine gave them all pressed flowers. "From my garden," she said wistfully. "We picked them just before we left."

They all thanked her and hoped she'd be back to see her garden in bloom. Anne wished this even more fervently than the rest of them.

"And now for my presents," Claire said. First, she held out a package to Madame Marcel, who opened it carefully. Though she'd been expecting it, as she'd sat for it just a few days before, her eyes welled with tears. "It's my first photograph in a long while," she said softly, "and Hippolyte's very first."

Claire put a hand on her shoulder. "When he returns from his adventure, I'll take another one of you both together."

Then, she passed out her other gifts: "In honor of Hippolyte."

The carte de visite showed the cat staring upwards at a small hot air balloon, an engraving cut from an old book and suspended by a barely visible thread.

Orin held his copy in his palm, impressed yet again by her talent, her creative mind, and feeling just a bit guilty that Hippolyte wasn't going to ride in a balloon at all. Still, he reasoned, a basket held by a winged monster was also an extraordinary type of transportation.

"And for our heroes, the Messieurs Rush," Claire announced.

"We're glad to help," Joseph said, as humbly as Orin had ever heard him.

"Monsieur Joseph," she continued, "from now on, your cartes de visite are free of charge."

He looked quite happy at this. "That is generous indeed!"

"And for Monsieur Rush." She turned to him and handed him a small packet. "Since you don't want photographs of yourself."

He opened it carefully, stared down, then back at her in surprise.

"Long before you lived there, my father took a photograph from the window in your room. He said it was the best view from our building. I thought you might like to have it. This way, it will always be with you."

Sorrow and gratitude welled inside him. "A perfect present. Thank you, Mademoiselle Turin," he managed.

"Orin, we forgot something!" Joseph comically rolled his eyes at his own absentmindedness.

"Ah…yes." Orin was less playful. He seemed nervous, in fact.

"Mademoiselle Turin," Joseph handed her a large box.

She opened it and gently began to lift out what was inside. Pearlescent pigeon-gray silk trailed from her fingers. Anne gasped and hurried to her side.

Together, they drew it out, the fabric slowly unfolding and revealing itself to be — "A gown!" Anne cried out. "It's stunning!"

Even in the dim light, the gray silk shimmered. The square collar and the ends of the three-quarter length sleeves were trimmed with white lace as delicate as spiderwebs. The same webbed patterns were repeated in the skirt of the dress, starting at its hem and drawing upward at the waist. A soft pile of silk was gathered in the back.

"This must have cost a fortune," Anne whispered.

So far, Claire had said nothing.

The dress was like something she had dreamt of, something a princess would wear in a fairy tale – if fairy tales took place in 1870.

Joseph told her, "We hope you like it. It was supposed to be a thank-you present after that unfortunate matter at the Commissariat, but it took a long time for the seamstresses to make."

The truth of it was, he'd ordered it made when he'd seen how Orin looked at her during his birthday celebration at the Théâtre Robert-Houdin. He'd hoped that he would give it to them as an engagement present, for her to wear at their wedding. But there was nothing that could be done now, no matter how Orin looked at her, no matter how she looked at him, how they laughed together and exchanged thoughtful presents. It was over. His brother wouldn't fight for her.

And that was if he survived tomorrow night – no, Joseph pushed that thought away and said now, "I'm usually pretty good at guessing a lady's measurements." (Aunt Honorine looked as though she might faint.) "But would you care to go upstairs and try it on, to see if I haven't made a mistake?" He gave another furtive glance at Orin.

Claire grinned. "All right."

"What could she possibly have done to merit that dress?" Aunt Honorine asked her maid in a low voice.

"Saved him from prison," Madame Marcel cut in airily, moving past them to offer Hippolyte a plate.

Orin felt strangely apprehensive. Joseph had told him there was a dress. But he hadn't explained that it looked like that. He couldn't wait to see her in it, and he couldn't bear to see her in it.

~~

Upstairs, Claire took off the dress she'd been wearing. Then she gently gathered the skirt of the new gown and slipped it over her head. The fabric fell around her in soft cascades. The silk was like a breath against her skin.

This was a dress for a lady, who would normally have a maid to help her put it on and fasten it. And yet, when Claire tentatively reached behind her, she found only a few silk-covered buttons that were easy to close on her own. It was like some sort of magic. She sighed, and, not daring to look at herself in the glass, hurried back downstairs.

~~

Through the open door, a movement caught Madame Marcel's eye. "It's her!" she called out.

Joseph and Anne rushed beside her, crowding the doorway for a glimpse. Orin stayed back, nearer to Aunt Honorine and Euphraisine (the latter did look rather excited as well), but he could see everything through a gap between them – or perhaps it was magic again.

Claire descended the staircase carefully, looking down at the shining skirt. She wondered how it could shine in the dimness as the daylight began to fade.

Orin saw what he had feared. She was like something from another world, an unforgettable vision. The dress shone in the dimness, the white trim and underskirt like wisps of clouds. It fit her perfectly, hugging her shapely waist, clinging to her bosom, flaring slightly at her hips, gathering in a soft, sinuous pile at the small of her back. But worse still was her neck, free of any collar, the beauty mark mocking him, her brown hair cascading over her shoulder like vines – or nearly. It would always be a bit frizzy, he could tell, and he was so fond of that – and her shining almond eyes, even from here he could see that they shone.

He wanted to look away, he should look away. She wasn't his and she never would be.

But he might die tomorrow, and if not, he'd go back to New York soon, so why not look? Why not?

"It's perfect!" Anne told the brothers approvingly.

"You look stunning!" Madame Marcel called out as Claire approached them, suddenly shy.

"Do you like it?" Joseph asked, and that made her feel at ease.

"You can remain proud of your measuring abilities. It's wonderful. Ever so slightly loose now, but then, once the Siege is over, I'll probably fill it out again," she admitted with a laugh.

"I don't know how to thank you." *And I don't know where I would wear it*, she thought, then decided that she could put it on when she was alone in her apartment at night and pretend to be a princess or a sorceress, moving swiftly down the corridors.

Not long after, Orin could feel the familiar signs of sunset. He quickly excused himself and hurried up the stairs, trying not to imagine Claire coming down them in her gown. Trying not to think that if things were different, he might be attending another party somewhere in the city, with her on his arm.

Instead, he – and now, coming into his room, he stopped. Instead, he would be saving Hippolyte, after all. The change came and he was nearly grateful for it. He waited for a while, hoping that Mademoiselle Bertin and her unpleasant aunt and servant had already left, and there was no risk of them – or anyone - seeing him in the sky. Then, he crept out of the window and took his last practice flight, soaring over frozen Paris on Christmas.

77

W hen he woke the next morning, he could tell it was early. His throat was dry and for a moment he couldn't breathe. Tonight was the night; who knew where he would be this time tomorrow?

He rose as soon as he could manage, and got dressed. The water in his basin was frozen. This had been the case every morning for a long while now. He couldn't help but grin bemusedly as he set his greatcoat on top of it and then sat down on top of that with a book, waiting for it to thaw a bit.

This, at least, calmed him. He tried to find even more solace in the pages of his book. But from time to time, a thought would drift into his mind like a trail of smoke: Would this be the last book he ever read?

He felt afraid again when he was shaving. But after a few fear-sickened moments, he told himself, *Let's be Cartesian.*

He considered the flights he'd made, their speed, how he'd been able to find his way in the near-darkness, how no one in the forts seemed to have noticed him. He thought of the maps, of the compass he'd purchased, he thought of how easy it had become to find his own window and return to it again.

He knew that this was what he had to remember whenever fear came again: weaving and flying easily through the starless night sky and the city below.

The sound of her steps in the corridor made him hurry.

"Bonjour, Mademoiselle Turin."

He savored the smile that spread over her face. "Bonjour, Monsieur Rush. I hope you were able to have a somewhat pleasant night?"

"I was," he replied, realizing it wasn't a lie. "And you?"

"Oh, I stared and stared at the – *my* Hiroshige prints. Thank you so much again."

He laughed, "I told Joseph you'd like those more than the dress!"

"It's a close race. I wore it until I went to sleep. It is the most marvelous gown I've ever seen."

He cleared his throat. He must not forget this – something else he could give her. "I meant to tell you yesterday - if you like, you could write a letter to your brother. We'll have the balloonist deliver it to him with Hippolyte."

He wished he could stay and talk to her all morning. He wished he could tell her what it was like to fly over Paris, how he wished he could do it in daylight to see how it compared to her models. He wished he could ask how she'd made the photograph of Hippolyte and the little hot air balloon, or – But he had to see Joseph, as well. Time was short. And maybe it would be easier to leave her, maybe forever, if he didn't linger now.

"I have to be going, but I'll see you this afternoon when Joseph comes to get Hippolyte."

At this, a shadow passed over her face.

"I promise he'll be all right."

She smiled gamely. "How can you know?"

"I know it because I wish it with all my heart."

"You think that's enough?"

"I do."

"So you *do* believe in magic!"

So she, too, had kept the memory of that conversation from all those months ago. He tried to conceal his surprise. "I confess I've believed in it for a long time."

"Then let's both cast spells that the balloon will make a perfect flight tonight and land safely right outside my brother's door!"

He thought for a moment – really thought, I realized. "All right. Let's close our eyes and imagine it."

"Now," she added, inspired, "turn around twice. Once for the journey there, once for the balloonist's return someday."

They opened their eyes to a world unchanged, but his heart felt a little lighter, as if she'd taken some of the weight away.

~~

When he reached the boulevard, he lingered for a moment. This might be his last day in Paris. He turned up his collar and curled the scarf Madame Marcel had given him closer around his neck. The cold cut like blades; still he determinedly walked down to the Seine.

The ice-choked river wasn't at all like what he'd come to know. But there was a beauty that sang along its banks, that always would, no matter what disaster arose. He stood quietly for a moment, gazing at the facades, familiar friends.

There were no bouquinistes' crates today. No one would stay out in the impossible cold, either to buy books or to sell them. But he thought of the days when they had been there, of browsing through the bindings as the trees shivered in the breeze.

He walked to Notre Dame, who had survived revolutions and catastrophes. He said a prayer there, that he and Hippolyte would survive.

Then he crossed onto the Left Bank and walked a little down the rue Saint-Jacques, turning into the tangle of old medieval streets that separated it from the Boulevard Saint-Michel. Down he followed them until he was standing across from the Hôtel de Cluny and the ruins of the Roman baths.

He imagined himself a small figure in one of Mademoiselle Turin's models, wondered, for a moment, if she might memorialize him as such if he didn't return – no – as she would understand it, if he vanished.

He shook his head. It didn't matter anyway. She might lose a friend, but thankfully, she had Rossignol.

It was funny how life worked out. He was a monster with wings, the only one who could save Hippolyte. Rossignol was his perfect rival, the only sort of man Claire deserved.

Back on the Right Bank, he took in the view along the river once more. *Farewell*, he thought, and headed back to the Grands Boulevards.

Realizing how late it was, he quickened his pace towards the Grand Hôtel, pulling his scarf over his mouth so that the cold air wouldn't make his every breath ache.

Joseph didn't say anything about his late arrival. Instead, he greeted him with a pleading look. "Still haven't changed your mind?"

"No." Orin told him firmly.

His brother gave a heavy sigh. "Shall we go to lunch?"

~~

He couldn't bear to tell Joseph what he'd thought about earlier. There would be no explanation or excuse if he vanished. *So*, he thought, poking at some questionable greens, *let that be one more reason to return.*

He didn't think long on it; he wanted, instead, to savor every moment of this. Here they were, halfway across the world from home, laughing together, eating a strange, horrible meal.

"I'm glad you came to Paris with me."

"Of course you are," Joseph replied, with joking pomposity.

"I mean it."

"Orry," Joseph leaned over his plate, nearly staining his shirt, "there's a balloon leaving tomorrow night. Why don't we tell Mademoiselle Turin

298

and the concierge that the flight's been put off till then, and I'll try to speak with the people involved and —?"

His heart sank at his brother's unchanging expression.

"It would be too late now. You know that. They've already got the weight of what they're bringing figured out. And really," Orin thought of Mademoiselle Turin's questions the other day, "how could we be sure the balloonist would bring Hippolyte to Beauvoir, or even care to try?"

"We'd pay him."

"And he could just as easily lie and say that Hippolyte ran away or died during the flight. The more I think of it, I'm the only one who can do this."

The plates were cleared and dessert came, and they talked of other things. Then, they returned to the Grand Hôtel, ignoring the deathly smell that greeted them in the shifting wind.

In the suite, Joseph offered Orin a drink, but Orin wouldn't take it. "I need to think clearly tonight."

Joseph shrugged and put the glass on top of a nearby buffet, seemingly careless, though he had gone pale. "If I attempted to stop you by knocking you unconscious or administering some ether, I suppose you'd be angry at me?"

Orin kept his voice light, but there was a firmness to it that showed none of this was a joke. "I suppose I would never forgive you."

"It's a good thing I refused that drink," he added a moment later, when the air seemed too heavy.

Joseph smiled gamely. "All right, then I suppose I have no choice but to go through with this."

78

The brothers had never performed on a stage. But now here it was, their perfect dance in tandem.

First, Orin is the center of our attention.

He watches, moved, from the wings, as Claire and Madame Marcel say goodbye to Hippolyte. Tears are running down their faces as they hold him. Madame Marcel buries her face into his fur.

"We should be happy," Claire reasons. "He *is* escaping certain death, after all."

It's not easy to get the cat into his wicker cage. Orin steps in to help them, but Joseph waits to make his entrance. This seems to be out of politeness, but really, I know, it's simply the desire not to be scratched.

At last, Hippolyte is in the cage and Joseph begins his performance: "I think it's time now," he tells them gently as Claire and Madame Marcel pet the cat through the cage door's wicker bars.

Orin realizes he nearly forgot a step. "Do you have the letter?" he asks Claire.

"Oh! Yes – thank you" She draws it from her pocket.

"Of course." As he takes it from her hand, their fingers brush for what might be the last time.

He tries to ignore the world reeling. Instead, he continues the choreography and hands the letter to Joseph, who makes a show of putting it into his breast pocket.

Next, Joseph picks up Hippolyte's basket. "Don't worry," he tells them, "I'll take good care of Hippolyte, and so will our balloonist."

He darts a quick look to Orin, letting his gaze say "Good luck" as well as "If you don't survive this, I'll never forgive you for dying over a cat." With that, he exits the concierge's lodge.

~~

The dance continues.

Orin stays in the lodge, talking to Claire and Madame Marcel. He tries to reassure them and to answer the questions they have. He tries to make them laugh over memories of Hippolyte. They all plan how to celebrate his return.

Meanwhile, Joseph waits outside. After what he hopes is enough time, he creeps back in through the open door and tiptoes past the concierge's lodge. With Orin's key in his pocket, he dashes up the stairs, struggling against the roses. He hopes none of the neighbors will hear Hippolyte's miserable meowing.

At last he's opening Orin's door. He lays the basket and the note carefully on the floor by the foot of the bed and exits.

He hurries down the stairs again, his heels pulling at the tangled stems and rosebuds. Outside the lodge, he hangs Orin's key on its hook.

But now he falters.

His brother is just behind that door. If he spoils the plan now, he might just save his life.

But he remembers their discussion at the restaurant. He knows what love does to someone, and he knows that this is about love. Resigned, he forces himself back outside.

He hurries up the street, pushing himself towards the boulevard and then back home. He'll keep himself busy getting ready and then go out for the evening, though he knows, of course, that his thoughts will keep returning to the sky and to a town in Normandy that he's never visited.

Orin glances at the clock on Madame Marcel's crowded mantle. "I'm so sorry, but I must go."

"Oh, of course," Madame Marcel's eyes grow teary again.

"Be easy tonight," he tells her softly. "It will be all right."

He could finish with a collective farewell, but he knows it might be the last one. "Good evening, Madame Marcel. Good evening, Mademoiselle Turin."

He stops the dance to listen to her voice. "Good evening, Monsieur Rush." He nods and opens the door.

Outside the lodge, his key is on its hook. So, Joseph has managed it. He moves briskly up the stairs, shaking away the thorny vines.

In his room, Orin finds Hippolyte meowing in his basket. The note for Paul is on the floor as well. His feet have finished their steps. He crouches down to touch the soft fur between the bars.

"We're going on an adventure, my friend."

The first pangs of the change come. Hippolyte has seen him in his monstrous form so many nights, but he's never seen the violent transformation. Orin stands and moves away.

79

He waited until the darkness had settled, then longer. Let people finish their suppers and try to sleep, so that there was no chance anyone would see him take flight.

But finally it was time. Orin took up a small pack of necessities, put the compass he'd purchased into his coat pocket, and tied one end of a rope around the handle of Hippolyte's cage and the other around one of his wrists.

Then he squared his shoulders and scooped the cage into his arms. In one sure movement he was through the window. He stared up at the sky, took a breath, and spread his wings.

It was easy to fly over Paris, then past it. After all, it was what he'd practiced. At the city walls, he shifted Hippolyte's cage to the crook of one arm and consulted the compass to be sure of his course. It wasn't necessary yet; he knew he had to fly over Versailles. But why not be as certain as possible?

The air was silent once he'd passed the forts. There was only the rush of wind, the steady beating of his wings, and the occasional plaintive meow from Hippolyte.

"I'm sorry," he murmured.

Now he recognized the shadowy sprawl of the palace of Versailles, lit in places by the Prussians' lamps and fires and candles.

Beyond that, the land was dark. In better times, there might have been a train cutting through the endless-seeming fields, and more light in the towns and villages. He was glad that Beauvoir was almost exactly due west from Paris; he didn't know how he would have navigated a route more complicated than that.

I'll stop and confess something to you, something that I hope Orin will never know, since he was so proud of himself and willing to die. But the truth is, though he did have the strength in his soul and in his wings, I helped him on his flight.

Past the walls of Paris, magic crackled back into my bones, as it had in the Catacombs. It was what I'd hoped for, and I already knew what to do.

I dropped to fly low to the ground, a chill wind among the others, whispering incantations to make the Prussians see nothing in the sky. When there were no more of them, I launched myself upwards again, encircling Orin, conjuring a low light around him that only he could see. Like moonlight, it helped him make out what was below: the soft darkness of forests, the flatness of tilled fields, the shapes of houses and churches and farms.

Still, he was brilliant in his own right, keeping firm hold of Hippolyte's cage, keeping steadily westward (though I kept his path narrow), consulting his compass with the professionalism of a ship's captain — or more aptly, a balloonist charting his course through the air.

Orin was more or less right about the time he needed for the flight. But it felt long, even so. At last, I heard him gasp. The moon's fragmented reflection danced on a moving surface – the waves of the sea. He thought of the maps and engravings he'd pored over, and then sought out Le Mont-Saint-Michel — There. In the distance, to the south, a mountain of stone walls and turrets and arches bloomed like a black rose.

Orin turned towards it, flying slightly lower. I dashed downwards to enchant anyone who might be out at that hour, but saw no one, and flew back up to join him and the mewling Hippolyte. He was there so quickly, and then he executed another turn, veering slightly eastward, following a path of water that led to…yes…he gasped again.

As he'd hoped, a little village was there along the straight slice of river, like a pendant swinging from le Mont-Saint-Michel.

He searched the landscape below him. How could he find – and then, something caught his eye. What looked like a pinpoint of light shone up from a large glass surface. Could it be – he flew down as far as he dared. Yes – yes – it was a lamp, glowing through the glass roof of a photographer's studio.

He gave an incredulous laugh.

The studio sat on the treeless, grassy banks of the river, which made it easy to find. But it wasn't easy to find a hidden place to land. Still, there were some houses on one side - Orin landed carefully in a spot between two windowless walls.

Fear in his belly, he hastily rummaged in his sack and took out an enormous cloak and covered himself, then searched for his gloves and put them on.

Calmer now, he checked his watch and headed to where he hoped the door to the studio (and likely Paul Turin's home) would be.

And then, the exhilaration of his flight left him and a sudden realization made him stop. He lifted Hippolyte's cage so that he could look inside. "Goodbye," he said softly. "When you return to Paris, I won't be there. We'll probably never see each other again. I'm lucky to have known you."

I'd like to tell you that Hippolyte turned to look at him. But he was too distressed and was staring into the back of the basket instead. By now, Orin knew cats well enough not to be hurt by this, and he knew, as well, that this wasn't the most important moment. Those were all of the nights that Hippolyte had come to sit with him, keeping him company in the long, dark hours, at ease with him despite what he what he was. He lowered the cage to his side, untied the rope that connected him to it, and finished the walk to the studio's door.

Paul Turin – or whoever came to the door – would be among the few people to ever see him as a monster, though he hoped his cloak and gloves concealed most of his appearance. He took a breath and knocked.

After a time, there were footsteps on creaky wooden stairs. A key turned in the lock and a man poked his head out, holding a lamp in front of him. In its light, Orin recognized his laughing eyes.

"Monsieur Paul Turin?"

The man nodded, nervously taking in the cloaked figure with the strange, stunted boots.

"I'm a messenger from the American Embassy in Paris. I am to deliver this to you on behalf of your sister."

"My sister? Is she all right?" Paul stepped outside.

Orin felt a fool. He should have started with that. "She's fine," he said, "quite well, even. There's a letter for you."

He gently placed Hippolyte's basket on the ground, and held it out.

Paul took the letter and read it eagerly, his eyes widening.

"You've brought Hippolyte?" he asked, staring up at Orin in astonishment.

Afraid that he might see his teeth inside the cowl, Orin looked away. "Yes."

"This isn't a dream," he heard Paul say under his breath. Then, louder, "I-cannot thank you enough, monsieur. This letter from my sister means more than you can know. And to have brought Hippolyte –"

He shook his head. "Excuse me. You must be terribly cold. Would you like to come inside to warm yourself by the fire and have something to eat?"

"That's very kind of you, but I must go."

"Other cats to deliver?"

Deep inside the cowl, Orin's muzzle twisted into a smile. So, Paul had a sense of humor as well. He understood why Claire missed him so much – and then, suddenly, he had an idea.

"I can give you five minutes, only five – you may write your sister a letter, and I'll see it delivered through our channels."

"You will? Oh – that would be – thank you!"

"Please hurry," Orin urged.

Paul picked up Hippolyte's basket and went quickly inside. He left the door open, and Orin knew it wasn't out of absentmindedness, but a sign that he was welcome there (though he doubted Paul would feel the same way if he removed his cloak).

Paul returned in only four minutes.

Orin hastily put away his watch. "I will see that this gets to her. I imagine that she misses you terribly."

Paul nodded. "She said so in her letter, and in all of the letters I've received from her. I've sent many in reply, but it seems pigeons aren't quite as reliable as postmen."

"I'm afraid not."

"Thank you again. And thank you for helping to save Hippolyte."

"It's my pleasure."

"I can't imagine it's a great pleasure to have journeyed so far in this cold and with enemy troops about."

I felt Orin grow thoughtful. "No….but it's a pleasure to be able to help h- someone."

Suddenly, he remembered the time. Or perhaps he could hear me yelling at him to start back.

"I must go. Take good care of H-the cat."

"Oh, that will be a pleasure for *us*," Paul assured him. And then – "If you can wait just one more moment – thirty seconds –" and he hurried back inside.

"Please," he said, coming out in twenty, "could you give her this as well?" It was a carte de visite of Paul, the woman who must be his wife, and their little daughter.

Orin thought of how much this would mean to Claire. "I shall. Good evening," he managed.

"Good evening, and a safe return to....?" I realized that Paul didn't know Orin had come from Paris – perhaps he was merely part of a chain of strangely dressed men charged with bringing Hippolyte there.

Orin clarified nothing. Instead, he walked swiftly away, hoping Paul wouldn't watch him too closely. Fortunately, Hippolyte gave a loud, pitiful meow at that moment, and Paul went back inside to let him out of his basket.

Back at his hidden spot, Orin hurriedly removed his cape and gloves. Then, he took flight again.

In the air, he consulted his compass and set his course eastward.

The flight to Beauvoir had carried its own sort of fear. The flight back held another. Now that he'd done what he'd hoped, uncertainty started to bite at him. How would he find Paris, for instance, when there was so little light?

Then again, he worried that he'd see dawn rising over the bend in the earth. For all his planning, one thing Orin hadn't considered was being in mid-air at daybreak.

He had a few hours still, but he was moving more slowly now, exhausted. I tried to push him on but he couldn't move any faster. I called on the winds and this time it worked. The air lifted him, as though he were borne on waves.

Now and then I had to dart down again to obscure him from sight. I began to notice that the sky was deep blue. Soon, we could make out the grey silhouettes of clouds. I felt fear like ice inside him and hoped he'd have the sense to land somewhere before long.

308

But what would he find on the ground? He wouldn't let himself risk capture by anyone anymore. So, he flew on.

After a time, he felt something tickling his face. It was a gentle snow, only made driving by his speed. It touched him like playful fingers and kissed his eyelids gracelessly. He looked down to be able to keep them open.

It was becoming easier now to make out the shapes of villages and fields and forests. Our hearts were in our throats.

But there, at last, was the Palace of Versailles. I cast a spell over the occupying army again. We advanced quickly towards fields, now, where we could see military encampments. I thought of the freezing soldiers and for a moment darted down and called upon a warm breeze to visit them. I wished I could keep it there.

Orin forced his wings to push faster against the freezing air. I flew to the forts and made him invisible to the eyes of the soldiers.

Soon, I did the same to the National Guardsmen as Orin flew over Paris's wall.

The city should have been waking, but the cold kept most people inside. All the better; my powers had left me now.

Quickly, quickly, Orin flew, like a falling star. But not falling — desperately flying lower to search for his window. There was Notre Dame, there was the Opera. He tried to keep calm. He veered to the right, had a vision of Joseph falling off the roof of the Sainte-Chapelle, the aurora borealis gone from the sky. He flew slightly upwards – and there, there was his building, and there was his window.

He flew to it fast and hurtled inside and hit the far wall.

He was back. He had done it. He was alive and Hippolyte was alive and safe. He had helped her, he had risked his life, his family's livelihood, everything. He was a fool, he was a hero, he was furious, he was proud. He had done it. He stood up and closed the window, then the curtain. Then he collapsed onto the bed and immediately fell asleep.

80

I watched him sleep for a while. I was overjoyed that we were back here and safe. I was exhausted, too. But I couldn't rest. And so, I drifted away to look in on Claire.

I knew she'd be worried about Hippolyte. But I discovered something much stronger. She slept by the fire, but I could feel her fear in the room.

Her thoughts were easy to read. They were as strong as apparitions.

She'd stayed with Madame Marcel for a long time, until they were both exhausted enough to try to sleep. And then, as she'd started walking upstairs fear had rushed to her like a great wave, nearly toppling her.

But it wasn't for Hippolyte.

Something was going to happen, something to do with Monsieur Rush.

But, she'd reasoned, taking a breath, he hadn't done or said anything unusual before he'd left them that afternoon. He was in his room, as always.

Inside her apartment, she tried to calm herself, undressing quickly in the cold and savoring the relief of the deerskin and fur coat. She took a breath. Then, she unfolded her counterpane and curled up in it near the fire. She closed her eyes and took another breath.

Suddenly, she saw something. It seemed to be one of her favorite Hiroshige prints at first, an eagle turning in mid-flight over a snowy landscape, with a mountain rising in the distance. But now the bird was a monster, the mountain the silhouette of Le Mont-Saint-Michel. She could hear Monsieur Rush breathing, panicking.

She sat up, terrified.

It was just a dream, like all of her other strange dreams. He wasn't in danger, he was just upstairs…. She stood and lit the candle she'd left on the table by the door. Then, she went outside into the corridor.

She moved quietly to the spiral staircase and began to climb, careful not to tread on the fur coat.

When she reached the sixth floor, she strained to make out lamplight coming from under his door or through the keyhole. But there was no light.

She put her eye to the keyhole.

The room was silent and still. The curtains, strangely, were open, and so was the window itself. There was no light but the faint glow of the moon, for a moment uncovered by clouds. She used it to search for him. He wasn't sitting on the floor or sleeping on the bed. What if he was hurt, lying on the other side?

"Monsieur Rush!" she wanted to call out – But then, she realized that she didn't need to. The smell of him, that animal smell, was gone.

He wasn't there.

She stayed, staring in disbelief until at last she forced herself to move away from the keyhole. What would happen if he came up the stairs and found her there, kneeling in front of his door?

She almost hoped that would happen; at least she'd know he was all right.

There was no sound in the stairwell. Slowly, shakily, she made her way down, stumbling once when she slipped on the bottom of the coat.

Back in her room, she paced frantically. What could she do? If she went to find Joseph, he'd know she'd spied on his brother, and that she must know his secret.

If she alerted the police that he was missing, they'd laugh at her. Couldn't a man go out and spend the night elsewhere?

There was nothing to do, no one to help, at least not until daybreak. Claire shivered. She felt a terrible exhaustion. She'd lie down and try to rest. She'd rest, but she wouldn't sleep. She'd listen for his footsteps on the stairs.

Poor girl, she didn't know when he returned, since he hadn't, of course, used the stairs at all.

~~

I returned to Orin's room.

He slept so deeply that it was hard to see him breathing.

Day broke not long after, and he returned to his human form. I watched as it happened, relieved as I always was, and full of bitter sorrow that he wasn't always this way.

I expected he'd sleep for a long time still. But the weak morning light woke him, and, to my surprise, he got dressed and swiftly left his room and hurried down the corridor, then down the spiral staircase.

As he passed Claire's door, I felt an excited relief. Maybe she would hear him and come out. She did, and threw open her door – but by then, he was already on the third flight of stairs, his shoes cushioned by the carpet and its flowers. Had she only dreamt of his footsteps? She went back inside with a heavy sigh.

Orin walked quickly up the street, onto the boulevard. Soon, he was at the Grand Hôtel.

He hurried up the stairs and knocked on Joseph's door.

Joseph could have opened it immediately. He'd been sitting near it the entire night, unable to sleep. But he hesitated. Who was on the other side of the door? Was it Orin or someone already bearing news he couldn't bear?

He took a breath and turned the doorknob.

"Good morning." Orin was pale and tired, but grinning. "Sorry for coming so early."

Joseph didn't make a joke in return. "Orin! My God – you – you did it!" he reached across the threshold and hugged him tightly.

After a long time, he let his brother go. "Come in."

Joseph was so relieved and excited that he didn't even think to offer something to drink or any other courtesy. He sat down in a chair across from the one Orin had sunk into, and leaned forward, and Orin told him everything…nearly. He didn't tell him about the panic at the end, when he'd fought against the dawn.

"I am…" Joseph tried to compose himself. "I'm astonished. I'm glad that cat is safe, since it meant so much to all of you. I'm glad you thought to ask for a letter – and that photograph – from Mademoiselle Turin's brother…we'll have to think of a reasonable way to get them to her. But mostly, I'm glad it's over."

Orin smiled. "I am, too."

"And I still wish you hadn't done it in the first place. Did you realize what a risk it was?"

"I thought of something last night. Do you remember when you and your friends climbed onto the roof of the Sainte-Chapelle?"

Joseph nodded, a bit of pride puffing him up.

"That was *your* risk – and really, for a silly reason."

"Not at all! To be so close to the sky with those lights rolling across it – that's something I'll never forget!"

"All right," Orin conceded, adding facetiously, "though it's not as if you saved a life or anything."

"Pssh, you only saved a cat, which some would argue isn't a creature worth saving at all. What if that entire family starves because they didn't get to eat him?"

Orin laughed in spite of himself. "You're making me forget what I was trying to say! When I asked you about it, you told me that if you want something badly enough, the risk doesn't seem so great. I think that's how I felt. I still knew what I was doing, and I was still afraid. But I was more afraid returning home than I was going there. I only realized when it was nearly over just what I'd done. And I'm glad I'll never do anything like it again."

"I may climb another rooftop if there's an aurora in the sky."

"I wouldn't join you."

They sat for a few moments in happy silence.

Then Joseph asked, "Shall we have some breakfast? I acquired some potatoes last night at the Fête de la Charité."

"How was it?" Orin inquired, with at least some genuine curiosity, but Joseph answered him with a wry grin.

"Not so exciting as flying across France. Although there was a live turkey – and butter. They were the stars, along with Rochefort, who strolled from room to room, paying exorbitant amounts for glasses of champagne and leaving them undrunk. A fine way to give money to the cause. I wish I'd thought of it."

In the end, they opted for the simpler choice of a meal from tins, warmed over the smoky fire.

When they'd finished, they suddenly felt very tired.

"I think I should lie down for a while..." Without waiting for a reply, Orin walked slowly, almost unsteadily, to his old bedroom and shut the door.

Hours later, Joseph awoke with a start. He'd fallen asleep on the sofa, and now most of the afternoon had gone by.

What had woken him was Orin himself. He grinned at his brother and shook his head. "I hope you didn't have anything important planned.

"I'll see you tomorrow morning – but I promise not as early as this. Please save some potatoes for me."

Joseph stood and hugged him tightly again. "Come back as early as you like. I won't consume a single potato till your return. I've never been so happy to see anyone as I was to see you."

81

A soft snow was falling. Claire woke and got dressed, trying to calm her frantic fear, as though putting herself in order might put everything in order.

Still hopeful that such an idea would work, she went up the winding staircase. She might as well sort through the wardrobe in the studio.

She wanted to go to Joseph, to tell him something was wrong. But for all she knew, Orin had spent the night there, though he'd never done that before. She realized, anyway, that she didn't have to take any action at all: If enough time passed without his having seen Orin, surely Joseph would come by to ask her if *she* had.

She tried to amuse herself for a while, trying on different hats, then going through the costume jewelry her family had acquired from theatre friends over the years. Playfully, she placed rings with paste jewels on each finger. She used to do this as a little girl, imagining, then, that she was a powerful fairy queen.

Suddenly, she heard footsteps in the stairwell. It couldn't be Émile; there wasn't enough light today. It couldn't be a customer; with the cold, who would come for a sitting? The footsteps didn't have the jaunty assurance she'd come to recognize as Joseph's. Then –

Claire quickly stood up and tried to take off the rings, forgetting just one as she hurried to the door.

I've often wondered what would have happened if she'd removed it.

She opened the door and saw him, safe and unwounded, crossing the threshold of the stairwell.

"Monsieur Rush! I'm-I'm glad to see you!" She tried to compose herself, settling her face into her usual smile.

But he was smiling radiantly back at her. "I'm glad to see you, too, Mademoiselle Turin. I'm always glad to see you."

He noticed something shining on her left ring finger.

"Why, you're —" So it had happened. Sooner than he'd been expecting, but it was bound to happen, after all. He took a breath, squared his shoulders. "Congratulations. Rossignol is a good man, and very lucky."

He wouldn't meet her eyes; he'd fixed them on her left hand. She gave a start. "Oh! This is paste! I'm not engaged!" She laughed and took it off.

Orin swallowed. "Not engaged? Rossignol must be running late. Or perhaps he's on the ramparts?"

"Rossignol? I don't believe he would - He's a friend I've known from childhood, and…" she took a breath. *After all*, she told herself, *I'm only stating a simple fact.* "…if he did propose, I'd refuse."

Orin stared at her, stunned. "You'd refuse him?"

"I couldn't marry him because I-I love someone else."

She closed her eyes and felt as though she were letting herself fall. It was terrifying, but not more than the sight of his empty room.

He was the only person she'd ever fall in love with. This was the only risk she'd ever have to take. So, she took a breath:

"I love *you*, Monsieur Rush."

As the words left her, a strange thing happened. There was always something tense about Orin. I knew he worried that letting his guard down might let the monster get the better of him. But now, the tension fell from him like a cloak unlaced. He stood there, soft, somehow more real, more human, more beautiful than she'd ever seen him.

"Claire," he tested her name, "I've been in love with you for such a long time."

The flowers stretched from the carpet and surrounded their legs. Vines twirled and grew up the walls, and it was as if they were in the most beautiful enchanted garden. But they didn't see it. They were standing so close, the distance between them so slight, and suddenly, she stood on her toes and kissed him on those lips that had uttered so many funny things, so many kind words, so many thoughts that made her dream and imagine and hope. She kissed him, and he fell into the kiss, the very first kiss he'd ever received or given, and the only one he had ever wanted.

The blooms were everywhere now, covering the doors, circling the studio's enamel sign like a wreath. Could they not smell roses?

When the kiss had finished, their eyes met – hers deep and glowing, his the green-gold of the wildness and wilderness that was inside both of them. They drew together in an embrace — two souls saying to each other, "I've found you."

The flowers twined around them. The sixth floor became a bowery.

~~

When they drew back (slightly), she saw the shadows under his eyes. At her concerned look, Orin thought of the shadows that must be gathering outside.

"It's nearly sunset," he forced himself to say.

It would have been bliss to fall asleep with her in his arms, but it would have been horror for her, he thought. He managed a smile. "Tomorrow morning, we'll tell each other if we've had any interesting dreams."

How strange to say that you love one another and then to part so shortly after. Anyone who didn't understand why would have been disappointed. Still, Claire was surprised to find that she was.

She struggled to smile back at him. "What's a little time apart now? We'll have so many more days to spend together."

He noticed that she hadn't said "and nights". This was going to work – it was going to be all right. His smile now was free and real. Radiant light surrounded them.

"Sleep well, Claire," he said.

"Sleep well, Orin."

Hearing her say his name sent a thrill through him.

The flowers had receded to the carpet, only tangling themselves a little around her bootheels as she walked dreamily towards the spiral staircase.

What a night and day it had been. Orin fell onto his bed and drifted to sleep, so incredibly happy.

~~

What woke him was the cold. He sat up, shivering in the darkness.

It had been a long time since he'd felt cold at night. The temperature must have gotten so low that even his thick fur couldn't keep him warm.

But then – there was no thick fur. He laughed. He must have woken up just as the sun was setting. He remembered dawn earlier that day – had it really been the same day? He'd prayed, then, that the sun would hold off from rising. Now, he was so cold that he ached for it to set.

He stood and fumbled for his greatcoat, then pulled the counterpane around himself for good measure, and waited.

More time passed. He stood and walked to the window, and drew the curtain back slightly. Stars stared down at him between puffs of cloud. He could hear the distant booming of the canons.

It was night.

It was night, and he hadn't changed.

He pulled the curtain shut. This must be something else – first, unexpected wings, and now – He reached for the matches, surprised

318

that he couldn't quite make out the shape of the box in his bedside drawer.

At last, he managed to light the candle. In its flickering glow, he looked himself up and down, ran his hands carefully over every part of himself. Trembling, he stripped off his clothes despite the cold, and examined himself again. No claws, no sharp teeth, no hooves, no fur, no wings. He was just a man.

He sat down unsteadily on the bed.

~~

It was over! I wanted to dance and laugh across all of the rooftops of Paris. For a moment, I regretted that Orin would no longer be able to fly with me. But he was free now, and I was free from my guilt. Everything had ended well, and he and Claire would live happily ever after.

~~

Orin got dressed again and added his greatcoat, then searched for another pair of socks, and wrapped a shirt around his head. Shakily, he lay in bed beneath the counterpane. Now and then, he'd draw out one of his hands and stare at it in the candlelight.

82

I shouldn't have told you to come back so early," Joseph muttered, his hair in all directions, his eyes barely open.

Orin tried to smile.

His brother gently pulled him inside and shut the door. "Are you all right?"

"I think the enchantment is broken."

Joseph's sleepy eyes popped open. "Broken? Orry, Orry!" he whooped, jumping excitedly, "It's over?"

Orin nodded. But he wasn't smiling or cheering or jumping.

Joseph stopped. "What's wrong?"

"We were all fools. The 'human heart' was only someone falling in love with me, apparently. When I came home after seeing you, Cl-Mademoiselle Turin was there, and she confessed that she loved me. She gave me her heart."

Joseph stared at him. "She did? She did!" He did a little sort of delighted dance. "Of course she did! I knew she loved you, Orry!"

His brother wasn't smiling. "But you…don't feel the same?"

"When she told me, I – it was the happiest moment of my life. But I can't be with her."

"I don't understand. Why not?"

"She doesn't know what I am."

Joseph laughed. "What does it matter? That's over now!"

"But what if it comes back?"

"Why would it?"

"If she stops loving me, or loves me less, or…."

"Are you sure it works like that? Maybe you only needed to win someone's heart, and you have! Love does something to you, even when it doesn't last."

Orin took a breath. "If I change back when she's with me, I could hurt her."

"Would you?" There was a note of frustration in Joseph's voice at hearing the same baseless story again and again. "You've never hurt anyone before. You lived with us for all those years without a single casualty. Unless you'd creep out the window and terrorize the citizens of New York without us knowing?"

Orin sighed. As usual, his brother wasn't taking things seriously. "No, I've never hurt anyone, and I've never wanted to. But there's something else: If I change back, even if I'm harmless, she won't want to be with me."

"If you change back – and I don't think you would - you'd be a mysterious creature who can fly wherever he likes again. Surely that has its benefits."

"This isn't a joke."

"No, it's not. Sorry." Joseph sighed. "If I were you, I wouldn't tell her. If you do go back to how you were, worry about it then. Maybe even act shocked, as if it's never happened before."

Orin looked at him skeptically. "You wouldn't do that."

"Honestly, I don't know."

"You don't have to," Orin remarked bitterly.

"Oh, Orry, there's still hope," Joseph's voice was soft now. "She's an extraordinary woman, and she loves you. I don't think she'd run away."

~~

Claire was waiting for him on the bench in the corridor. Seeing her broad smile made the world reel. He moved swiftly to her, and she took

321

his hand, and, laughing, they let the ground lurch. Then he kissed her, and if he hadn't flown before, he would have said that this was flight.

"There was one morning," he confessed a bit breathlessly, "when I thought I might tell you how I felt. And I imagined that I would take you out for a stroll by the Seine. We'd look through the bouquinistes' crates and then have a lemonade somewhere. The thing was," he stopped, "it was nearly as cold as it is today."

Emotions whirled inside her. He really had loved her before. But what had kept him from telling her so? Mostly, she felt so free and so happy. "Well, maybe we could try it."

They got their things and went downstairs, arm in arm, laughing, and it was a good thing the flowers on the carpet rose up; they might have fallen otherwise, since they were so busy looking at one another that they paid no attention to the steps.

On the ground floor, they saw Madame Marcel and said a cheerful hello. She raised her eyebrows but said nothing about the way they stood together now. And while part of this was due to discretion, she'd already had enough surprises that morning.

"It's very strange," she told them, gesturing towards the lady holding her long-extinguished lamp aloft. "The statue's arm was most certainly cracked, and now, there's not even the smallest fissure."

~~

Claire and Orin walked towards the boulevard arm in arm, crossed it, and disappeared down the first street that would bring them to the Seine.

"It *is* cold," Orin admitted after a while, and Claire nodded, teeth chattering. She hadn't worn her fur, though she longed to. Orin always seemed ill at ease seeing it.

"Let's go on for a little while. Let's see if we can make it to the Seine after all," she laughed, with a look of challenge in her eyes. Then, she started to run.

322

Orin followed.

It was the kind of cold that reaches into you and hollows you out. They couldn't run for long. "Let's go on slowly, then," she conceded.

When they got to the Seine, the wind coming off the water bit at them. Blocks of ice floated by. And of course, there were no bouquinistes.

"This is still one of the best walks I've ever had in Paris," Orin told her.

She took his gloved hand in hers.

They turned back and stopped in at the first café they could find. "Maybe we should order *vin chaud* instead of lemonade," she teased.

Afterwards, warmed, they managed to find a cab and headed homeward. Home was more than ever what it felt like. In her apartment, he marveled again at the miniature streets of Paris. "I should have thought of this before we left. It's a far better way to visit the city on such a cold day."

The time passed so quickly. They talked and laughed and looked through books on the high bookshelves. When they realized how hungry they were, Claire managed to put something together, and they sat down at the table she hadn't used in ages, and talked and laughed until – "It's getting dark," she said. Suddenly, he realized what was so often in her voice when she warned him. It was unhappiness.

I waited for him to tell her that now he could stay with her after sunset. I imagined her reaction, overjoyed and puzzled and excited all over again.

Instead, he looked at her sadly and gave her a kiss. "Goodnight," was all he said, and stood up to leave.

"Orin-" she called out when he'd reached the door. Would she ask him to stay anyway? Would she tell him she knew?

But she only said, "Have interesting dreams, and I'll see you in the morning."

He smiled. "I'll see you in the morning."

Then, he opened the door and went down the hall and up the stairs.

~~

Darkness came, and nothing else. He was still a man. He stared in wonder at his murky reflection in the small mirror over the washstand. He rolled up sleeves and pantlegs, took off his socks and examined every toe in the candlelight.

He was truly cured. For a moment, he felt so much possibility. He could stay with Claire. They could travel. He could go to see plays and operas in the evening if he liked, or simply stay out walking with no fear of sunset. He breathed.

But that feeling didn't last all night. Eventually, the expression of worry he often wore came back, and he wrapped himself in greatcoat and coverlets and curled into a restless sleep.

83

The next morning, she was waiting for him on the bench outside the studio, only this time, Émile was there, too. Orin realized that life hadn't stopped now that the enchantment was over and he was living in the paradise of love. There must have been enough light today to open the studio.

"Good morning, Monsieur Rouline." Orin suddenly felt embarrassed.

Émile broke into his usual jack o'lantern grin. "I'm happy for you both, and not at all surprised. And now, I'll leave you alone for a while…" And he stood up, swiped the key from Claire's hand, and shut himself into the studio, whistling a catchy tune.

Claire's cheeks were red, but she smiled. "We'll be back soon," she called out.

"May I invite you to breakfast?" Orin's overstated gallantry made them both laugh.

They chose the closest café they could, to avoid walking in the brutal cold. It didn't matter, it could have been anywhere. All they looked at was each other. There wasn't much of anything to eat, but the coffee warmed them and even if it hadn't, there was simply the wonder of being together.

He had to tell her now. It was such an enormous thing that it would seem strange if he mentioned it later.

He leaned close to her and said quietly, "Something happened. I…think my illness has been cured."

"What? That's – Oh Orin, that's –!" She tried to rein in her galloping heart. *Remember, he thinks you only mean headaches.* "I'm so glad."

Imagine if she knew the truth, Orin thought, and felt ill.

"I can't be certain yet," he warned. "But for the past two nights, I haven't had any headaches."

"I-I'm so happy for you," she tried to measure how quickly she was speaking. This meant everything would be all right. They could live just as any other couple might. "How did it happen?"

"I'm not sure. No one knows why they started, so maybe that's just the way it is."

"Would you like to go out tonight?" Her eyes were sparkling like stars.

~~

There was another challenge that morning: Stay with her in the studio, or make an excuse and go elsewhere. The cameras still made him nervous, but leaving her was even more difficult to bear.

So he stayed, and soon felt at ease in spite of himself, laughing with her and Émile, watching for the first time as Émile showed him how a plate was developed. There were few clients, but those who came were excited to be photographed and glad for a moment of distraction and cheer. He was surprised how quickly the day passed.

Later, as the sun began to set, he didn't leave her parlor. But he did feel uneasy. "I'm a bit nervous to go out," he confessed. "What if I- What if I get a headache after all?"

Without realizing it, he'd given Claire a small way to understand. She thought of what she would do in his place. "Hmm...well, I've heard that headaches may be made worse by light. Do you have a cloak that you could put on if that does happen?"

He was too nervous to think of just how perfect her suggestion was. "I do."

"And-And we won't go far," she added. "After all, there is a curfew, and it's very cold, and — really, you did pick a terrible time to finally be able to go out at night."

When they stepped through the door of their building, he stopped to take in this new way of seeing, dim streets and over them velvet darkness like a blanket.

326

Claire was surprised at what caught his eye. Only every third streetlamp was lit, and whenever they arrived at one, he'd stop and stare up at its flame sputtering against the blackness.

Between lights, they talked.

"When the Siege is over, you'll see – it's so bright, and so lively. We can go to a guinguette, even the Bal Mabille. Oh," she thought aloud, "I've never liked it much, but no one could say it isn't beautiful – you have to see all of those lights among the trees. And," she continued, "we could go to the top of the Montagne Sainte-Geneviève or Montmartre, and look out at rest of the lights below. We could – we could - " She stopped, looked at him excitedly. "I remember you told me you love the Parc Monceau. Imagine if we slipped in one night – what an adventure – and stayed to look up at the stars!"

Orin made a strange sound – a chuckle, she thought at first, maybe a cough.

"I'm sorry – I'm so excited that I've started talking nonsense."

"No. You're talking about dreams. You should. We could sneak into the Parc Monceau, and when we get tired, why not hide away in the little pyramid and sleep there till morning?"

Though he loved seeing her broad smile, he nearly had to look away. *I'll have to tell her the truth long before the weather is warm enough to do such a thing.*

Suddenly, the liveliness of the boulevard began to fade. "I think we have to get back," she said.

At the closed front doors, she nudged him playfully. "You ask."

He shot her a teasing look and gestured theatrically. *"Cordon, s'il vous plaît."*

As they went up the stairs, Claire wondered what would happen now. Would he stay with her? Or perhaps he was too much of a gentleman to suggest such a thing?

Orin ached to stay, to hold her. But at her door, he only said, "Thank you for my first night out in Paris." He kissed her and went up to his room.

84

T here's something I have to ask you," he told her the next morning, feeling emboldened by the shadows under her eyes.

"What is it?"

"Do you remember when I asked if I could get food for you – and Madame Marcel, and Monsieur Rouline and his family – instead of you all queuing for rations?"

Claire tried to find the words to explain herself, but he went on, "At the time, I know you felt insulted. But please, now that we're," he cleared his throat, "now that we're together, no one can say anything they haven't already."

To Orin's surprise, there were tears in her eyes. "I'm sorry about what I said then. It was kind of you to offer, and you were right. For some reason it's so hard to think of stopping, of getting something better when so many others won't. Not that they're all particularly nice," she added wryly.

He nodded. "I've tried to think of things I could do to help people on the breadlines, even just the ones in this neighborhood. I thought of giving blankets or coats – but then, there would never be enough, and it might start fights. And there's no way to replace all of their rations with something better, not anymore, at any rate. What would be enough, or the right thing?

"Joseph and I have given money and supplies to *ambulances*, to the army. When I found out they'd made the soldiers leave their blankets behind before Champigny, I felt even more useless."

He looked at her earnestly. "I want to help everyone in this city – in this world. I never could before when I was - and I can't now, I know. That's too big. But I think- I think maybe that if we *can* help, even in some small way, we should. I *can* help you and Madame Marcel and Monsieur Rouline. I'd be so happy to."

And so, Claire gave up her place on the breadline. *At least*, she thought, *it will make the wait that much shorter for the others.* And of course, her ration would go to someone else. She hoped it would be a *Mère Michel.*

~~

Every morning, Orin and Claire would meet on the sixth floor and decide if the day was bright enough for the studio to open. If it was, he stayed with her there, talking, laughing, reading, and watching Émile develop plates, as enchanted as I felt at the sight.

On overcast days, they'd set out for the Boulevards and take a meager breakfast at a café. Then, they would roam the city for as long as they could stand the cold. Back at home, they'd sit in her parlor and read, often looking up from a page to share their thoughts.

Then they'd go back out again for lunch and often supper. Although even the finest restaurants served only passable food these days, Claire didn't mind. "I'm always glad not to cook," she laughed.

They'd walk again until they couldn't bear it, and then it was back home, laughing and talking, reading the evening journal and laughing a bit less.

"It's strange to sit with you when it's dark outside," she said to him one evening.

"I can say the same."

Whenever she saw his eyelids grow heavy, she'd wish he'd fall asleep there beside her. She'd try to will it to happen. Instead, he'd yawn and stand up, stopping only to kiss her goodnight.

One night, he remarked, "It's been such a part of me, I didn't realize I would feel lost without it." She knew that she could only wait.

If only she could have told him she knew his secret, and not to be ashamed. There is no shame, she thought. He couldn't help what he was, no more than anyone could.

85

One morning, she was paler than she had been in a long time. "They killed Pollux and – now Castor."

Like anyone in love, Orin cherished every exchange he and Claire had had. He'd kept those conversations close, and sometimes he would revisit them, as he used to secretly creep down to the larder at night and steal a treat of some sort when he was a boy, before my enchantment had come.

He recalled it vividly now, how her sparkling eyes had softened, a smile on her face, as she'd told him about the day she and Paul had ridden Castor and Pollux, two gentle elephants at the Jardin d'Acclimatation who were beloved by all Parisian children. The memory was a relic of her life before she'd lost her family, before some of her favorite parts of the city had disappeared. She'd shared it with him that day because she'd found out the elephants had been moved to the Jardin des Plantes for safety during the Siege.

As things got harder and the animals there started to be sold off as food, Orin sometimes felt a twinge of worry. He couldn't imagine they'd ever sell Castor and Pollux – not with how popular they were. But then, other elephants had been slaughtered and sold (even though everyone agreed that elephant meat wasn't very good). And the Siege had lasted too long. No matter how beloved they were, how could you feed two elephants, when there was so little food left?

It wasn't a surprise to Claire, just a dreadful conclusion. Another loss in a string of losses, some greater, but all amounting to something she'd never have again: her parents, her brother close by, her city unscarred by the shells; the old streets, the shade of the old trees. Once-happy Parisians who now were dying on the battlefields. They were no more, and the elephants were no more.

She began to sob the way she only ever sobbed when she was alone. Orin understood. He held her close.

86

There was a way he might help her, a little.

The next morning, as they'd planned, Joseph knocked on Orin's door.

When he opened it, Orin saw an embarrassed look flash across his brother's face. "What's the matter?"

"I'm terribly s- Oh - She's not here? I thought—"

Orin shook his head. "We sleep in our own quarters."

Joseph stepped inside and shut the door.

"Really? I -That is, you've already said you belong to one another."

Orin was silent.

"If it's – well, if you want to be *careful*, I can easily get you some 'French letters', you know."

"I'll keep that in mind."

"If this is Mademoiselle Turin's preference, I'm sorry, Orry. I meant no offense to—"

"- It's my decision," he said curtly.

"So you're a gentleman through and through." Joseph nodded approvingly, though I could tell he couldn't quite understand it.

"I want to do right by her. She still doesn't know —"

"— Oh, Orry, is it *that*? It's been so many nights now – it's over, I keep telling you —"

"— and when I tell her, I'm going to lose her."

A silence settled around them, a silence of misery for Orin and of sad surprise for Joseph. What had happened to his brother had left scars.

Still, Joseph tried to help. "You know I think you're wrong about that."

"Would you stay with someone who told you something like that? At best, you'd think they were mad. At worst, you'd be afraid, wouldn't you?"

"Not necessarily."

"Then you're an extraordinary person."

"Of course I am. But you do Mademoiselle Turin a disservice. You don't think she's extraordinary as well?"

Orin took a breath. "I know she is. Let's get this letter to her. It will do her good."

They stepped into the corridor. "It was brilliant of you to think of asking her brother for all of this," he remarked. "You must have been exhausted after flying all those hours to save that cat, and on top of that, you couldn't have been at ease."

Orin shrugged. "You say I always underestimate people. Is it possible *you* underestimate *me*?"

Joseph gave a loud laugh at that, which happened to mask the sound of footsteps hurrying down the spiral staircase.

They'd expected to find Claire in the studio with Monsieur Rouline, but the cold was so strong that she'd gone downstairs for her mantle. On the way up, she'd heard their voices and had stopped to listen. Maybe she'd find out why Orin didn't stay with her at night. What she'd heard instead made her nearly stumble off one of the iron steps.

She caught herself and struggled to stay perfectly still. At the burst of laughter, she made her escape, dashing down the few steps to the fifth floor. She waited there a few minutes, then slowly climbed the staircase again, as if she'd been in her apartment the whole time.

She skillfully feigned surprise at the sight of the brothers waiting for her on the bench. "Monsieur Joseph!"

"Mademoiselle Turin." He rose and made his usual bow. But I could feel a deep gratitude in it, and even of a sort of congratulations on her triumph. She'd broken the spell.

"I've had a visit from a messenger this morning. The Embassy received its mail bag and in it was this."

That part of their conversation she hadn't heard. She took the folded paper from him, opened it, and gasped. "It's-It's from Paul — my brother." She read quickly. "Hippolyte is there — safe! And my brother and his family are well."

Claire read the letter again, slowly this time. Her eyes were shining, and there was a happy, nearly disbelieving smile on her face. Now she turned her attention to the carte de visite that had been folded inside the paper. She spent a long time gazing at the portrait, the image of her little niece already on her way to growing up. She'd missed so much, but it wasn't entirely due to the Siege, she had to admit. When it was over, she'd go visit them at Beauvoir.

How strange to think of her family in the future, rather than the past.

~~

The new year came nearly without them realizing it. There was little sense of celebration in the cold city.

"Here's to a better year," Madame Marcel said, raising her glass.

Here's to love, Orin thought, *even if she won't love me once she knows.*

87

By late December, the Prussians had grown impatient. They began to bombard the city. It grew worse as the days went by, until the shells were like an unrelenting torrent of rain falling steadily onto the Left Bank.

From the moment it had started, Claire had told Émile that he and Marguerite and the children should stay with her. Or, if they wanted space of their own, Orin offered to put them up at the Grand Hôtel. "It's not as grand as usual, but it's still quite pleasant."

Émile had brushed the offer away. "We'll be fine."

"Aren't you afraid?" Claire demanded a few mornings later.

There were stories every day of homes, shops, churches, even something unheard of in war – hospitals – being hit with shells. But most of the people in the Latin Quarter didn't seem very bothered by it all. Many of them slept in the basements of their buildings, even set up their living quarters there for the time being. Little street children sold fragments of fallen bombs to souvenir-seeking visitors from other neighborhoods.

"Basements are interesting places," Émile chuckled. "Did you see this?" He drew a folded paper from his pocket, a newspaper cartoon that showed a group of people living underground, their clothes spotted with mushrooms.

~~

The bombs fell onto a boarding school on the rue de Vaugirard, killing four children who were sleeping in their beds.

The thought of those children so far from their families stayed with her. Somehow, Orin knew the night would be hard. And so, he didn't leave her.

As the hours passed, the cold invaded the room. They tried to laugh and to make each other laugh. This was all they could do. They talked until they fell asleep sitting on the sofa, Orin in his greatcoat, Claire in her mantle, both covered in counterpanes.

88

Often, when sad thoughts weren't with them, they would kiss and grow so warm, their hands traveling everywhere. He'd run his fingers through the wild hair that had mostly escaped her chignon, and lean down to kiss the birthmark on her neck. She liked to take his remarkable hands in hers and lift each palm to her lips. It would always end with him drawing back, frustration and apologies in his eyes.

It wasn't just that he was a gentleman. Claire was certain there was something else.

Sometimes she wondered if he regretted being tied to her. Now that he was free of the curse, he could easily marry the most beautiful woman in Paris if he liked. Or perhaps he wished she were more fit for the high society he came from.

No, that couldn't be. She'd try to think of walking on the streets of Paris, holding hands so tightly, of the occasional kiss when neither one could bear it, and simply, and most of all, the love she saw in his eyes every time he looked at her.

~~

She did allow herself to ask one thing.

"What will happen when the Siege is over?"

Orin set his book aside and looked at her in confusion. Was she expecting him to tell her there was still hope for the French? She couldn't believe that. She read the newspapers.

"Well, the French will have to pay reparations, and —"

"— you're going back to New York."

His breath escaped him. He'd forgotten that.

"You'll come with me," he said lightly, but there was plaintiveness there, questioning.

"What if I don't want to live in New York?"

It was easy to answer her, since it was what he felt in his heart. "I want to live wherever you are, so I'll follow you there." He stopped and a teasing glimmer came into his eyes. "It is Paris, right?"

89

The second-best letter Claire received during the Siege was delivered one morning in mid-January.

Fearing bad news, she opened it quickly and sought out the signature. The color drained from her face.

"Excuse me," she said to Orin.

"Is everything all right?"

"I…There's no great calamity. I just need to read this alone."

She went up the stairs with heavy footfalls. The moment her door was shut behind her, she began to read:

> *My dear Mademoiselle Turin,*
>
> *Please accept my excuses for the lateness of this letter. As I am sure you can understand, these have been strange and tumultuous months. But I am pleased to inform you that my colleagues were finally able to consider your model. They are in agreement with me that your work would be a perfect addition to the forthcoming Museum of the History of Paris.*
>
> *If you are still interested in offering us this gift, I will await your instructions regarding the transportation of your models to our offices, where they'll wait until the museum is opened to the public.*
>
> *Yours faithfully,*
>
> *Jules Cousin*
>
> *PS It would be a great pleasure to see you and M. Rush again one of these days. Please feel free to call on me at your leisure. My office door and, please remember, the doors of the library are always open to you.*

She looked up from the letter in disbelief, then re-read it to be sure she wasn't mistaken. And then, strange girl, she lay down on the floor beside those rows of plaster streets and cried.

But it didn't last long. She knew that Orin and Madame Marcel, who'd given her the letter, must be worried.

She washed her face and went downstairs, still not certain her good fortune was real. But slowly, she began to accept it. A smile spread across her face. By the time she arrived at the ground floor, she was radiant.

~~

This was something to celebrate. And besides, why not bring some joy into the cold, grey days?

One night after Orin left, Claire opened the locked cabinet of a small dresser and checked something inside. Then, smiling, she sat down and began writing invitations.

~~

A few days later, accompanied by the dull noise of the incessantly firing cannons, they made their way to Madame Marcel's lodge.

Joseph looked impeccable as ever in his perfectly tailored greatcoat. His top hat sat at its usual jaunty tilt (though it must be confessed his ears were a bit red from the cold).

Anne came from the same direction, wearing a fashionable dress of jet black, its layered skirt trimmed with beads shaped like water droplets. She slowed for Aunt Honorine and Euphraisine. It was nearly impossible to find a cab now. They walked wrapped in their furs and huddled against the cold.

The group coming from across the Seine was a more pleasant party: Émile, his arm linked with his Marguerite's, and a boy and girl, perhaps eight and ten years old.

"All right," Émile guffawed, "is everyone cold enough?"

They nodded, teeth chattering. "Then, let's run for a while!"

And they did, until they felt warmer, and then stopped and walked until it was time to run again.

Madame Marcel was already in her lodge and Orin was with her, helping her move her many chairs to just the right places, as Claire tinkered with a tall metal box with a pipe sticking from the top and a lens emerging from its middle like a curious animal craning its neck. A large white bedsheet was pinned to the wall opposite the lens.

By the time everyone arrived, the lodge was dark but for a single candle that sat on the table. They found seats using the light from the open door.

"What's that?" Marguerite's little girl asked, pointing to the strangely shaped box.

Claire answered. "It's a magic lantern."

She lit another candle that was inside of it, and closed the lantern's small door. Then, she gently slid a long, glass pane into a slot behind the lens. Suddenly a painted image of a little girl in a red hooded cape appeared on the cloth-covered wall.

Le petit chaperon rouge.

She asked the children to tell the story, and slid the pane when the scene changed, so that a new image appeared. By the time they came to what the wolf said as he pretended to be Red Riding Hood's grandmother, everyone was playing the part and laughing riotously.

Still, each time Claire drew the pane of glass further and revealed a new image, they went quiet for a few moments, admiring the rich colors and the simple magic that light and painted glass could conjure upon the wall.

They had another fairy tale, and another. *La belle au bois dormant. Le chat botté.* And then, the candle had burned too low, and it was time to say their farewells.

Aunt Honorine and Euphraisine were polite and stiff, though maybe a bit warmer than before. "I remember magic lantern shows from when I was a girl," Aunt Honorine told her. "I didn't realize they would be so amusing to me now."

Anne followed them, rolling her eyes. "When will the Siege be over?"

The friends laughed.

"You look lovely," Claire said.

"*You* are in love and look even lovelier. I'm so happy for you."

When she'd told her about Orin, Anne wasn't surprised. "I've seen you together," she'd said simply. "But what could possibly have kept you two from saying anything for so long?"

~~

Émile and Marguerite had gathered up the children.

"How are you?" Orin asked them.

"We're doing all right," Marguerite replied.

Claire spoke frankly. "I ask Émile every day for you all to come and stay with me, or to accept Monsieur Rush's offer of your own room at the Grand Hôtel."

"And miss out on all the excitement?" Émile burst out, and Marguerite laughed. Claire and Orin couldn't quite understand it, but I read it in their thoughts. It wasn't madness, but a sense of belonging to somewhere and needing to stay there.

"Wasn't the magic lantern the most extraordinary thing you've ever seen?" the little girl asked Joseph.

Far from it, he thought, glancing at his brother and Claire. "It was beautiful," he answered diplomatically.

When he took his leave, he and Orin shared a handshake and a grin.

"Congratulations," he told Claire. He was referring to her models' acceptance into the museum. But there was more and there always would be. *Congratulations on breaking an unbreakable spell. Congratulations on freeing my brother.*

90

I t was time. Orin couldn't say why. Maybe it was because he was so happy. The longer he and Claire felt this way, the worse it would be for both of them when it ended.

These days, the roses on the carpets were only wild in occasional moments when Orin and Claire couldn't help it – fingers brushing, a kiss, a long, happy gaze, a shared laugh – well, the roses were quite often wild, but right now they were calm.

"There's something I must tell you," he said softly as they carried the magic lantern upstairs.

There was dread in his voice. Claire felt her hands nearly give way.

By now they'd arrived at the fifth floor. He held the magic lantern as she opened the door to her apartment. Then they walked to the little dresser in and slid the box carefully inside.

Claire forced herself to stand and turn to him.

Orin looked as though he were ill. "I…hope you'll forgive me. I should have told you this from the start. I-I wish I could have."

He walked nervously to the sofa and sat there, and she came to join him, but on the other end.

"I…" He gave a frustrated sigh. "You're going to find this difficult to believe – even someone as extraordinary as you. But I promise it's the truth. And anyway, why would I lie?

"When I met you…for most of my life, in fact, I wasn't ill. It wasn't headaches. I….Every day at sunset, I would become a monster.

"Not – I don't mean this as a metaphor, and it's not a joke. And I'm not mad. I would become a terrible monster and then change back to a man at daybreak."

He stopped and stared at the sofa cushions, bracing himself.

Claire tried to meet his eyes. "Orin. I know."

He looked up in disbelief. "You…"

"I know. I found out months ago." She told him about seeing him through the keyhole.

"*I'm* sorry that I - that I watched you. I couldn't understand what I was seeing, and I had to know if…"

"And you…" he was puzzled now, "…you weren't worried that I might hurt you?"

"At first. And then I came to my senses. Every time I saw you, you did nothing but read or sleep or maybe pace a little. There was nothing violent about you." She stopped and gave him a pointed look. "You *are* kind.'"

"Oh!"

"That was shortly after I'd seen you through the keyhole. I…realized that I was being a fool."

"You weren't! How could anyone have seen that and not been afraid?"

"They would only have to know you. And think reasonably. And I," she sighed and went on, realizing something as she spoke, "I abandoned you. I knew you weren't dangerous – and I loved you, but I let you go."

"There's nothing reasonable about what happened to me. Who wouldn't have been afraid? Of course you couldn't think of loving something like that!"

She shook her head. "You weren't a 'something'. But I was a fool."

"You had a perfectly normal reaction to—."

"—I almost drove you back to New York."

"Maybe I wouldn't have gone, after all. Or maybe I would have come back."

They were quiet for a moment, and then he took a breath. "I know what made me better, but I can't promise it will never happen again."

"What made you better?"

"You gave me your heart."

"What? That's all?"

He laughed. "That's everything. Even if it hadn't cured me."

No one had ever spoken to her that way. The words moved her deeply. Still, she relied on her usual teasing smile. "How do you know that's what cured you?"

"When I was younger, a madwoman came to my family's home and said she had a message for me. She said there was a way to break the enchantment I'd been under for years: a human heart. If only she could have explained it...."

Now his gaze grew distant. "But then...if I'd understood, would I have spent every moment trying to find someone to love or marry me?" And here was a thought that had occurred to him often, accompanied by something like vertigo: "I probably would never have come to Paris and found you."

He met her eyes again. "But the thing is, I know nothing about this enchantment. What if you stop loving me? I'm terrified of the power you have over me."

Claire gave a laugh, though tears were in it. "I'm terrified that one day *you* might not love *me*. My heart would break. Maybe anyone who loves someone else is a bit frightened of them."

"Maybe so.... But even if you still love me, if this is only a temporary cure for some reason, or there was something more to be done, some spell or incantation I could never know – or maybe it has to do with what my mother is - there's a chance I could become a monster again. I want you to know this so that you can make a choice now and be free of me."

"Free of you?" She took his hand.

These days, the world didn't reel when they did this, or at least, the reeling was very brief, more a pleasurable little thrill that quickly dissolved into a feeling that this was where their hands belonged, joined with one another.

"I don't want to be free of you."

He looked at her skeptically. "What if I become a monster again and I —" She had to understand. "What if I hurt you?"

"Did you ever feel that you wanted to hurt anyone when you were a monster before? Or a man, for that matter? From what I understand," she went on, feeling daring, "you somehow thought to use your monstrous strength to get Hippolyte to safety."

"How did you-"

"I heard you and Joseph talking one morning in the corridor."

"That was careless of us."

She nodded. "So, it was true?"

"Yes. But it's a long story."

"I hope you'll tell it to me one day. But even without knowing the details, it's more proof that the only things you ever did when you were…in that other form…were either very dull, or quite heroic."

Still, she and I could tell he wasn't convinced he'd never be a danger to her. Something more was needed.

Suddenly, a light came into her eyes.

Somehow, she remembered.

I was more certain about this than anything: This was Yselda's doing. I searched for her in the air around us.

Claire spoke, as if recalling a dream. "That night, in the Catacombs…You could have hurt all of those horrible people."

Orin gave a start.

"You could have killed them, even, to get away. But you didn't."

He turned away from her and that night came back to him, the cold fear, the black-clad figures reaching for him – but nothing then, and nothing now, made him think of violence.

Claire saw his shoulders shaking for a time, and then he turned back to her suddenly, and it was like that moment in the corridor when she'd said she loved him. Another heaviness had parted from him, and he was light, and so beautiful.

"The Catacombs," he managed, "how do you know about that night?"

"I was there. I-I ran towards you. I tried to pull you away with me, but— "

He was looking at her strangely. "The valkyrie?"

"What?"

"I saw a sort of…warrior…a spirit – did you – was it some sort of illusion?"

"I didn't do anything."

"I don't know how you became what you were then, but thank you."

"But why didn't I remember what happened till now? Or" she grasped at the fragmented memories, "what happened just after?"

"I cast a forgetting spell. I suppose it must have affected you, too."

"You cast a spell? I thought you could only do card tricks, and you refuse to show me even those!"

"I might know a little more magic than that."

"Better than card tricks," she murmured, and then laughed. "How could I give you up? I'll never meet anyone more interesting!"

"How could I be more interesting than a woman who once became a valkyrie?"

He cleared his throat. "I suppose this means we'll have to consider staying together."

Claire grinned. "For the rest of our lives."

"Whatever I am."

"Whatever you *look like*. I know what you are."

"A beast."

"A prince."

He reached for her hand.

91

There was one other thing Yselda did before vanishing back to where she had been all this time. She put a message in my mind. I imagine she knew that if she'd stopped to speak to me, we would have argued.

She'd felt what I'd done from the moment I'd cast the curse. But even she couldn't break it. And so, she'd decided to use it. But in order for her plan to work, she needed to leave.

She probably would have had to leave anyway, she conceded. What I'd done had made her realize what danger Orin might be in if any of her enemies knew she had a son. *They're far better spellcasters than you,* I could hear her taunt, but not entirely unkindly.

Her plan was to use my curse to help Orin find his true love. She sought out that other soul and found it across the ocean. Over the years, she helped things along a little, by putting certain books into Orin's hands from time to time and by letting Charles remember her connection to Paris.

Once Orin arrived here, she knew, the two souls would find each other.

92

S unlight filtered through the shutters, dappling their faces gold and gently waking them.

Orin thought back to the previous night. Pleasure, then the peace of falling asleep with her in his arms, and waking to a new day, a new adventure even… He felt a boundless, wild joy.

Claire turned to him and smiled. "There's something I think I should show you."

~~

Preparing a plate on her own always brought a flood of memories. She was a little girl again, and her mother and father and Paul were waiting just outside the door of the darkroom. For a moment, tears swam in her eyes.

When she opened the door, Orin was sitting stiffly in front of the camera.

Claire had told him, "You don't seem completely convinced that the enchantment's ended. Maybe you'd like some scientific proof, as well?"

What would the lens reveal? He was so afraid that it was easy to keep still as the interminable seconds passed by.

She slid the protected plate into its slot and then, in that soft way he loved, she ordered, "*Ne bougez plus.*"

Together in the darkroom, they watched as an image appeared on the glass. Though everything was its opposite, they knew that one thing wouldn't alter when the image was set to paper: His hands, his skin, his form — everything looked like nothing but what belongs to a man.

93

I 'd like to show you a few more magic lantern slides, fleeting and bright and very strange images, for the time of the Siege was strange, as you now know.

Here's a scene of a crowd. The Parisians mourn quietly and laugh loudly, and those on the Left Bank don't run away from the bombs, only burrow deeper into their homes and cellars. They are remarkable.

The next image: Grey bread, nearly blue. This is not an error by the colorist.

Another: Soldiers are desperately rushing forward. It's the Battle of Buzenval, the final push, and when it ends, most Parisians will know that there's no hope for victory.

Now let's look at a happier slide. Orin and Claire are dressed in Japanese kimonos. Orin's lips are parted; we see his words in small writing at the top of the slide:

"I wager we'd look even better in these if we were in Japan. Why don't we go when the Siege ends? After Beauvoir and New York? But" (It's all written on one line, but imagine a pause now) "it'll be difficult to travel unchaperoned. Do you think you'd like to marry me?"

Orin is holding a ring. In its center is a ruby, red as heart's blood.

Roses twine around the borders of the frame and around Claire's reply: "I would."

The Siege has ended. Here are trains returning to the city, bringing food, here are people standing outside the city walls, looking euphoric. Here are homeward-bound refugees (among them we see Aunt Honorine and Euphraisine waving goodbye).

I can't help but be angry at Rossignol, though I know he's entirely blameless. But *you* might be concerned about him. So I'll include a slide that shows him and his mother, both happy and in good health, returning to Levallois.

On to the next slide. Here are the restless in Belleville and the rest of eastern Paris, ready for another change. But that won't happen for a few weeks.

Now the show is finished. Let's go outside.

~~

Orin and Claire climbed nearly to the top of Montmartre. They didn't continue to the other side to observe the old battle sites and the ruined villages beyond the city wall; instead, they looked at Paris, below them and stretching to the horizon.

"I had an idea," Orin said to her. "When we return from our travels, I thought I might try to find and help people like me...if there are any."

"I think that's a fine idea." Claire gave him a little kiss, and then added, a smile playing on her lips, "Very kind."

They laughed and he pulled her close. Inside them was a sense of happiness and imminent adventure. I was the joyful wind running through their hair and then over the city below.

With time, Orin had come to wonder something. Perhaps the curse hadn't been entirely broken when she'd given him her heart. Maybe to fully end it, he'd had to stop thinking of his own heart as something unworthy. He'd had to let himself fully love her.

He stood and gazed out over the blue-gray rooftops, a man, holding her hand.

349

Dear reader,

I hope you enjoyed *Hearts at Dawn*.

If you can, I would be endlessly grateful if you'd share your honest opinion of it by writing a review on sites like Amazon and Goodreads, and by posting about the novel on any social media platforms you might frequent.

If you're not really an "online person", talking about it in real life with fellow book lovers would also be much appreciated!

Reviews and discussion are especially important for self-published books like this one, since they help spread the word and give the work a sense of legitimacy.

Even a short review or comment of just a sentence or two is helpful.

Most importantly, thank you for taking this reading journey with me. I hope it transported you away from from your worldly worries for a while.

Warmly,

Alysa Salzberg

Author's Note

Hearts at Dawn was born in the Bibliothèque Drouot, a small, low-ceilinged library that occupies one floor of an ugly building in the Grands Boulevards neighborhood of Paris.

At the time, I taught English to adults in French businesses in the area, and that was where I'd head during my lunch hour.

There are many books in the Bibliothèque Drouot, despite its small size. I usually kept to the fiction section, but one day I was browsing my favorite nonfiction one, History, and a spine in one of my favorite shades of blue caught my eye. I drew the book from the shelf and looked at the title: *La Vie à Paris pendant le siège 1870-1871* by Victor Debuchy.

I vaguely knew Paris had been under siege during a portion of the Franco-Prussian War. Like many Parisians — natives and transplants - I'd heard that the besieged city's inhabitants had ended up eating rats (which turned out to be true) and stormed the zoo to eat the animals there, as well (which turned out not to be).

But that was all I knew, so, I figured, why not learn more?

Debuchy's book is a compendium of information about everything related to the Siege, from politics to street cleaning to food to popular songs. I learned so much from it, but what stayed with me most strongly was what a weird time that four months was if you were living in Paris.

And then, somehow that thought twined itself around a story that's always floating through my head, my favorite story: Beauty and the Beast.

I imagined the scene where Beauty returns to the Beast's castle, desperately searching for him, and discovers him dying in his garden. Only, in this version, the garden was the zoo in the Jardin des Plantes, and all around Beauty and her Beast was chaos as the hungry people of Paris killed or stole the zoo's animals for food.

It stuck with me, and finally I decided that I'd write about it.

This resulted in a surprising casualty. After some research, I learned that the people of Paris didn't loot the zoo; instead, the animals were progressively, legally purchased, most notably by the upscale Boucherie Anglaise, where they were usually sold as canned delicacies. And so, the scene that had inspired my story wouldn't work.

Still, there were so many other dramatic moments that did happen during the Siege. It was a strange and extraordinary time, and one that's not very well-known, since it's nestled between all of the changes and innovations and beauty of the Second Empire and the revolution and violence of the Paris Commune, which started about two months after the Siege ended.

Maybe my story was also a way to put this brief period of history into the spotlight. I'd be joining the ranks of a few other fiction writers – mostly French – who've explored this moment in time.

I hope you enjoyed Hearts at Dawn. I hope it let you escape from anything you wanted to escape from for a while. I'm glad we were together in my beloved city of Paris, and I hope you'll come back again, in these pages, in others, and in real life if it's a trip you dream of taking.

On historical accuracy

It's taken me a long time to write Hearts at Dawn. That's meant a long immersion in primary and secondary sources, as well as many years of strolling in the Parisian neighborhoods I describe in the book. Most of them look roughly the same as they did in 1870.

But the more I live, the more I realize that there's no single, "true" way to capture a place or time.

I hope I was able to do the era justice. I wanted above all to capture the bravery and humor of the Parisians stuck inside their city walls (...or totally being allowed to go outside them most days). I wanted to show my respect to the soldiers, the sick and bereaved inside the city, those who died in the bombardments, and the animal victims of the Siege, as well.

I've done my best to capture the Siege of Paris through the eyes and hearts of my characters. I hope that nothing has jarred you out of this little bit of fantasy time travel. If it does, feel free to chalk it up to the narrator, who only experienced this time as a brief flash in her very long existence, and might have gotten certain details confused with previous or later eras.

If you'd like to learn more about the history in Hearts at Dawn, feel free to visit www.alysasalzbergauthor.com.

Historical Figures and Other Real People

In addition to people who are mentioned in passing, including the names of generals, politicians, photographers, and notorious figures like P.T. Barnum, there are a few historical figures and other real people who appear in the pages of Hearts at Dawn or who have an important influence on its characters.

I did my best to portray them and I hope they'd be happy with the results.

They include:

~ Cleverman (1797 or 1798-1878)– François Eugène Lahire (stage name: Cleverman) was a magician who owned and was performing at the Théâtre Robert-Houdin in 1870. The theater's founder, Jean-Eugène Robert-Houdin, is one of history's most famous magicians (Houdini's stage name is an homage to him), and Cleverman kept many of his illusions and automatons in his show, while adding his own touches as well.

~ Juliette Lamber (1836-1936) – A writer and feminist, Juliette Lamber went by a few different names, including Juliette Adam and Juliette Lambert. During the Siege of Paris, she was the wife of Edmond Adam, the head of Paris's police force. She used her wealth and power for a number of good causes, including running an ambulance. Although she's mostly known for her fiction works, *Le siège de Paris : journal d'une Parisienne*, a collection of her letters and journal entries written during the Siege, was an immensely helpful resource to me when researching Hearts at Dawn.

She was an excellent witness of history, giving incredibly detailed eyewitness accounts of events like the storming of the Assemblée Nationale and the night that the Parisians learned of Napoleon III's capitulation. I wanted to feature Juliette in a scene in Hearts at Dawn out of gratitude for this, and also because she inspired Joseph's climb to the top of the Sainte-Chapelle to see the aurora borealis. Her account of that night makes some strange sort of reference to wishing she'd done just that. In real life, as in my novel, she was busy tending to the sick in her ambulance while those wondrous lights were in the sky.

~ Elihu Washburne (1816-1887)– Elihu Washburne played many important roles in US politics. Among them, he was the US Ambassador to France from 1869-1877, which means that despite enduring the hardships of the Siege and the Commune, he still loved Paris and his job enough to stay! I wanted to mention Washburne because judging from his letters and journal entries (of which you can read many in the book Elihu Washburne: The Diary and Letters of America's Minister to France During the Siege and Commune of Paris by Michael Hill (pub. Simon & Schuster, 2012)), as well as the opinions of his contemporaries, he seems like a very nice person. Dealing with chronic ill health, he was also an inspiration to Orin – although their problems were of course very different.

~ Léon Gambetta (1838-1882) – A bombastic and bold statesman, Léon Gambetta proclaimed the Third Republic to a massive crowd in front of the Hôtel de Ville in Paris. About a month later, he left the city by hot air balloon, to rally other French troops to come to the aid of the City of Light. And those are only two of the many interesting – even bizarre – events in his short life story.

~ Jules Cousin (1830-1899)– Jules Cousin was the head of the Bibliothèque de l'Hôtel de Ville and closely involved in the founding and growth of one of my favorite museums in the world, Le Musée Carnavalet, which is dedicated to Paris's history. The collections being acquired in Hearts at Dawn are things you can see there today, from old shop and tavern signs, to detailed scale models of Parisian neighborhoods at different points in history. There are lots of other neat things to discover, too!

I haven't been able to learn much about Cousin as a person. But he seems like a good egg, so that's how I chose to portray him.

~ Mengin – Sometimes spelled "Mangin", this pencil-seller became famous for the dramatic displays he put on when peddling his wares on the streets of Paris. Dressed as a knight, he stood outside his caravan and gave humorous speeches alongside displays showing the strength of his pencils. It was apparently quite a show. The Guide de Paris Mystérieux by François Carradec and Jean-Robert Masson (pub. Tchou, 2019) recounts that he became a bit of a celebrity – and quite rich selling his reasonably priced pencils! As Rossignol says in Hearts at Dawn, you could get a little coin with his face on it if you bought several pencils.

Unfortunately, not much has been written about Mengin. I first learned about him from a small entry in La vie parisienne sous le second empire by Henri d'Alméras. But there is someone else who wrote a bit about Mengin: none other than P.T. Barnum! I was putting the final edits on Hearts at Dawn when I learned that Barnum admired him and made him the subject of the third chapter of his book The Humbugs of the World. You can read this chapter – and the entire book - for free online.

~ The elephants Castor and Pollux - Castor and Pollux really did exist. They were beloved animals at the zoo of the Jardin d'Acclimatation and they met the tragic end I describe in the book. They're just two of the numerous animal victims of the Siege.

~ Émile Rouline is based on James Mark Emmerling, a dear blogger friend and amazingly talented writer. Like Émile, he was smart, philosophy-obsessed, kind, funny, a lover of a good political cartoon, and a unique soul. Émile's beloved adopted family, dental issues, and wrongful arrest are based on stories from James's life. Bipolar disorder is another part of the real and fictional James's stories. This condition is what took the real James's life.

The loss is staggering, from the grief of those he left behind, to the loss of what he could have written. James's work was brilliant and challenging, sometimes silly, sometimes serious, always memorable.

He once told me that he hoped to visit me in Paris someday. I believe his spirit travels the world, laughing and discovering and marveling, but this book was another way to make that happen.

James was a prolific blogger, but unfortunately most of what he wrote has been lost due to blogging site shutdowns and his choice to delete some of his work. You can read what remains, as well as learn a little more about him and his life, on the website dedicated to him, https://rememberingjamesem.wixsite.com/hijim.

For Further Reading

These are the sources that were most helpful to me when I was writing Hearts at Dawn.

Rather than following a standard academic bibliography format, I've decided to list them in a way that facilitates online searches. Whenever possible, I've credited the author and, for recent books, the publisher.

You can find a longer list of resources (including images), as well as additional information and links to free online versions, at www.alysasalzbergauthor.com.

~ La vie à Paris pendant le siège 1870-1871 by Victor Debuchy (pub. Editions L'Harmattan, 2000). The book that inspired my story.

~ Le siège de Paris : journal d'une Parisienne by Juliette Adam (also called Juliette Lamber or Juliette Lambert) (available for free online)

~ Tableaux de Siège by Théophile Gautier (available for free online)

~ Camp, Court, and Siege: A Narrative of Personal Adventure and Observation During Two Wars: 1861-1865, 1870-1871 by Wickham Hoffman (available for free online)

~ Elihu Washburne: The Diary and Letters of America's Minister to France During the Siege and Commune of Paris by Michael Hill (pub. Simon & Schuster, 2012)

~ En ballon ! : pendant le siège de Paris, souvenirs d'un aéronaute by Gaston Tissandier (available for free online)

~ Paris 1870-1871 : L'Année Terrible (Mémoire en Images) by Jérôme Baconin (pub. Editions Sutton, 2007)

~ Diary of the besieged resident in Paris by Henry Labouchère (available for free online)-

~ Lights and Shadows of New York Life by James D. McCabe (available for free online)

~ Journal du Siège 1870-1871 par un bourgeois de Paris by Jacques-Henry Paradis (available for free online)

~ La Cuisinière Assiégée ou L'Art de Vivre en Temps de Siège (available for free online)

- Les Douze Heures Noires : La nuit à Paris au XIXe Siècle by Simone Delattre (pub. Albin Michel, 2004)

~ La vie parisienne sous le Second Empire by Henri d'Alméras

~Memoirs of Robert-Houdin, ambassador, author and conjurer by Jean-Eugène Robert-Houdin (available for free online)

~"Chronologie du siège de Paris (1870-1871)" (https://fr.wikipedia.org/wiki/Chronologie_du_si%C3%A8ge_de_Paris_(1870-1871)). This Wikipedia article is only available in French, although the English Wikipedia entry on the Siege of Paris is also worth a read.

~ Un atelier en maquette (Model photography studio). Exhibited online and on-site at the Musée Suisse de l'Appareil Photographique Vevy, this model of a 19th century photography studio shows the step-by-step process involved in making wet collodion photographs. (https://www.cameramuseum.ch/decouvrir/exposition-permanente/un-atelier-en-maquette/)

~ Lumière de l'Oeil is a shop selling antique lamps. It doubles as a wonderful museum, le Musée des Éclairages Anciens (the Museum of Old Lighting Methods), where you can ask owner Monsieur Ara questions and see demonstrations (by appointment) of different types of gas lighting. The museum and shop are in Paris at: 4, rue Flatters - 75005 PARIS – FRANCE. You can contact Monsieur Ara via his website (http://www.lumieredeloeil.com/lumiara/en/index.html) to set up an appointment for a demonstration.

~ Lumière de l'Oeil
website (http://www.lumieredeloeil.com/lumiara/en/index.html), also run by Monsieur Ara, is an amazing resource for information about lighting techniques from the 18th to the 20th century. It includes a multi-

lingual lighting glossary, lots of helpful images, and links to additional information and resources. (In French, English, and German.)

~Le Grand Hôtel, 110 ans d'hôtellerie parisienne, 1862-1972 by Alexandre Tessier - An impressive thesis paper on the history of the Grand Hôtel. Pages 177-178 specifically cover the role of the Hôtel during the Siege.
(http://theses.scd.univ-tours.fr/2009/alexandre.tessier_3307.pdf)
(available for free online)

~ Victorian Paris (https://victorianparis.wordpress.com/) is a website run by author Iva Polanski. Polanski blogs and shares information about life in Paris during the Victorian era, including details like how people bathed when living on high floors in apartment buildings with no running water. Her site is delightful and diligent, and an incredible resource.

You can find additional resources on the Siege of Paris, New York in the 1850's and '60's, magic tricks, and more, on my website, www.alysasalzbergauthor.com.

ACKNOWLEDGEMENTS

I'd like to thank my beta readers, Jennifer Hanks and Eirene Allen.

Jennifer, you have always been a good fairy in my life. Thank you endlessly for that, and thank you for reading my book and sharing your thoughts. Warm thanks, too, to book cover reviewers Gilbert and Harrison Hanks.

Eirene, thank you for your help and insights, and thanks for always making me think and laugh, whether on your site WhyHomer.com, or in our emails and conversations.

To Natasja Hellenthal of www.beyondbookcovers.com I'm forever grateful for her beautiful cover design, not to mention her patience with my questions, requests, and generally nervous air. You're as kind as you are creative.

Thank you, Meagan Salzberg, for transforming my website logo from an amateur sketch to something that looks professional and polished, and for bearing with my very long messages! You are my hero!

Erika Salzberg, thanks for always being there to give your opinion on things like author photos and back material, at very short notice!

A new "Thank you" to friend and passionate typesetter Rip Coleman, who motivated me to proofread again and who so incredibly kindly offered to fix typesetting errors in the print version of this book. Rip, you are truly a "Nicevillian"!

Thank you to Monique Grell for always making me feel like a star.

Mom, this isn't exactly a werewolf story, and that makes me wonder even more what you'd think of it.

Thank you to my family for letting me sleep in on the weekends so that I could stay up late writing (and maybe also watching a few cat videos). D., thank you for saving me from a technology-induced meltdown.

Thank you to my beloved Ali, who loved me when I was beautiful and when I was ugly, in the light and in the dark. I wrote so much of this book while you sat on my lap. I miss you every day. I will love you forever.

And thank you, dear reader, for coming on this journey with me. I hope you enjoyed it.

Biography

Alysa Salzberg was born in the United States, where she grew up. But her heart was always in Paris, which has become her adopted home. She lives there today with her husband and son.

Besides them, she loves books, cats, history, movies, art, antiquing, celebrity gossip, and cookies.

You can find out more about her and Hearts at Dawn on her website, www.alysasalzbergauthor.com.

Made in the USA
Middletown, DE
12 September 2024

60795175R00217